sourcebooks
landmark

Title:	The Woman and Her Stars
Author:	Penny Haw
Agent:	Jill Marsal
	Marsal Lyon Literary Agency
Publication date:	March 3, 2026
Category:	Fiction
Format:	Trade Paperback Original
ISBN:	978-1-7282-9548-0
Price:	$17.99 U.S.
Pages:	336 pages

Praise for

THE WOMAN AND HER STARS

TK

TK

TK

TK

ALSO BY PENNY HAW

The Invincible Miss Cust
The Woman at the Wheel
Follow Me to Africa

THE
WOMAN
AND HER
STARS

a novel

PENNY HAW

sourcebooks
landmark

Copyright © 2026 by Penny Haw
Cover and internal design © 2026 by Sourcebooks
Cover design by James Iacobelli
Cover images © Crow's Eye Productions/Arcangel, Flow 37/
Shutterstock, Margarita Balashova/Getty Images

Published by Sourcebooks Landmark, an imprint of Sourcebooks
1935 Brookdale RD, Naperville, IL 60563-2773
(630) 961-3900
sourcebooks.com

Cataloging-in-Publication Data is on file with the Library of Congress.

Printed and bound in [Country of Origin—confirm when printer is selected].
XX 10 9 8 7 6 5 4 3 2 1

For Laurence and Glen,
because this is a story about stars, a sister, and her brothers

GLOSSARY

APERTURE: The opening in a telescope through which light travels. The larger the aperture, the more light the telescope can gather, improving the clarity and detail of the observed objects.

ARQUEBUSADE: A lotion, typically containing alcohol, used to clean wounds during the eighteenth century.

CHESTERFIELD: A style of sofa invented by the Earl of Chesterfield in the mid-1750s with a low seat and high back to allow men wearing suits to sit comfortably.

COMET: A celestial object consisting of a nucleus of ice and dust. When near the sun, it heats up and releases gas, forming a glowing head and often a tail. Comets were significant in eighteenth-century astronomy for expanding the understanding of celestial bodies.

FORTY-FOOTER: A giant telescope with a forty-foot focal length for deep-sky observations. William Herschel's forty-footer was considered "a wonder of the world."

GEORGIUM SIDUS: Means "George's Star" and is the name William Herschel originally gave the planet Uranus in honor of King George III when he discovered it in 1781.

HANOVER: The Kingdom of Hanover is a former state of northwestern Germany. It was administered by the House of Hanover, which ruled Great Britain and Hanover as part of a personal union from 1714 to 1837.

LAUDANUM: A tincture of opium mixed with alcohol, widely used in the eighteenth century as a painkiller and sedative but also highly addictive.

NEBULAE: Fuzzy, cloud-like regions observed in the night sky, made of gas, dust, and sometimes star clusters. In the eighteenth century, nebulae were important in the study of astronomy.

NEWTONIAN REFLECTOR: A type of reflecting telescope invented by Sir Isaac Newton, which uses a concave primary mirror and a flat diagonal secondary mirror to reflect light to an eyepiece, improving magnification and image clarity.

REFLECTOR TELESCOPE: A telescope that uses mirrors instead of lenses to gather and focus light. Reflector telescopes became more widespread in the eighteenth century due to improvements in design and materials, with the Herschel family leading the way.

REFLECTORS: The mirrors used to gather and focus light in reflectors. Also referred to as specula.

ROYAL SOCIETY OF LONDON: A learned society founded in 1660, dedicated to promoting scientific knowledge. It played a key role in the scientific advancements of the Enlightenment Period, including astronomy and physics.

SMALLPOX: A deadly infectious disease caused by the variola virus. Devastating outbreaks occurred during the eighteenth century.

SPECULA: Mirrors or reflectors used in telescopes, particularly reflecting telescopes.

SPECULUM: A mixture of copper and tin, which, once cast, can be polished to make reflective surfaces. It was used for telescope reflectors or mirrors, which were referred to as "specula."

TURNSPIT DOGS: Dogs specifically bred to run in a wheel, known as a turnspit, which rotated a spit for roasting meat. Turnspit dogs were commonly found in kitchens in eighteenth-century households in England.

TYPHUS: A group of infectious diseases caused by Rickettsia bacteria, often spread by lice or fleas. Typhus was a common and deadly disease in the eighteenth century.

TWENTY-FOOTER: A telescope with a twenty-foot focal length, like the "forty-footer" but smaller in size. Such telescopes were used for detailed astronomical observations.

URANUS: The seventh planet from the sun, discovered by William Herschel in 1781. Initially referred to as "Georgium Sidus," it was later renamed Uranus.

CHAPTER 1

July 1782
Bath, England

IT WASN'T THE FIRST TIME I'D FACED CHANGE WITHOUT THE PROSPECT OF opposing or escaping it. If it was my brother's will, it was my destiny, wasn't it? Still, when Dr. Watson confirmed William would give up music because he had been appointed King's Astronomer, I sank onto a chair like someone much older than my thirty-two years.

Neither the doctor nor Alex noticed. Their conversation continued as I stared outside with little regard for the trio of housemaids waiting for a cart drawn by a gray pony to pass. I didn't marvel at the morning light bathing the houses opposite in honey-colored tones. Nor did I admire the burgeoning of the lime tree saplings lining the street like leafy sentries. On any other day, I'd have cherished the sights of Bath's lively lanes, the proliferation of trees, and the way the sun lit the buildings. Today, my thoughts were otherwise occupied.

With my brother's new occupation came the obligation of living close to court. King George III would demand William always be available on short notice. Should His Majesty, Her Majesty Queen Charlotte, or their guests wish to sweep the skies for celestial objects or discuss astronomy on a whim or otherwise, my brother would have to immediately pack his telescope and hurry to Windsor Castle to indulge their curiosities. Bath was almost a hundred miles away. William would have to move, and because I took care of household matters for him, and sang only with his orchestra, I'd have to go too. Besides, William was a man of his word. He'd honor his promise to our mother, which meant I must stay with him.

I stood, took my bonnet from where it hung against the wall, and made for the door. Alex squinted at me from beneath his brows as if surprised to find me in the room. Had he forgotten I lived there and he was visiting?

"I'll be back shortly," I said, avoiding his eye.

Outside, the sticky air sent me hurrying down the cobblestone streets to the shaded footpath following the River Avon to the edge of town. I lowered my head and, with the brim of my hat encircling my face, realized I was panting like a dog on a hot day. Clenching and unclenching my fists, I slowed and breathed the way William had taught me to do before launching into song. I exhaled, inhaled for four counts, held still for four, exhaled for another four beats, and repeated the exercise.

Calm breathing begets clear thinking, I told myself once, twice, thrice.

Ten years had passed since I, fearful, artless, and without a word of English upon my tongue, had arrived in Bath from Hanover. At twenty-two, I'd been unschooled in everything but scrubbing floors, sweeping ash, and knitting socks and ruffles. For weeks, I'd hidden my face in my bonnet and stood, pinned to the sidewalk, gawking at the processions of ornate carriages drawn by the grandest horses I'd ever seen. I was dazzled by how their glossy coats provided earthbound backdrops to the frothy headdresses, flimsy gowns, and extravagant overcoats paraded by the townsfolk. I'd been as spellbound as I was shocked.

The daily routines of Bathonians had seemed to involve little more than showing up and showing off on the streets before disappearing into places with peculiar names, like the Pump Room, Upper Assembly, and King's Circus. Eventually, I learned that, while indeed most were in Bath to see and be seen, others came to take the waters, immersing themselves and drinking the naturally warm water, which promised to heal all and every ailment. Whatever their reasons for visiting the town, they came with light hearts and heavy purses.

After the drab, earnest garrison town and laborious confinement of my childhood, the opulence and frivolousness first struck me as affected and excessive. Hanover might've been on another planet. However, as life would have it, the novelty waned. Although I didn't participate and never removed my bonnet, I came to admire the fanfare and reckless gaiety that swelled and spilled onto the streets. I'd settled in and learned the ways of the locals, and one day, as I gazed out onto the street, I realized I belonged. Bath was home.

It was no coincidence I'd experienced the warmth of fitting in shortly after I'd sung for an audience with William's orchestra for the first time. When I'd arrived in England, astronomy was little more than a pastime to my brother. Then, he was a musician, conductor, teacher, and the esteemed musical director of Bath's public concerts. Music was everything. Indeed, William fetched me from Hanover with the single-minded intention of teaching me to become a useful singer for his concerts.

The Herschels were a musical family, with my brothers following our father's profession as a military bandsman. However, during my childhood, though I'd dreamed of learning how to sing, my mother's rules prohibited me from doing more than chanting quietly to myself as I scrubbed her flagstone floors. With William's instruction in Bath, I discovered a new world and became a different person.

Whether rehearsing or performing, I never felt more alive than when my voice lifted to meet the musical notes and vibrations of my brother's music. My skin tingled, my heart swelled, and my blood seemed to flow faster. Sometimes, I imagined I'd taken flight and soared above the band and audience. When I sang, diminutive, scar-faced Caroline transformed into someone powerful and commanding, a soprano whose voice and passion took her and everyone within earshot to an unexpected and marvelous place.

Indeed, my brother's lessons and concerts, and Bath's hunger for entertainment, parties, and socializing brought me music. Singing gave the shy girl from Hanover a life she'd never imagined. But it wasn't only Bath's musical ways I'd miss. The town's fashionable streets, pretty gardens and paths, and the vigor of its inhabitants typically energized me. Now, though, as I thought of moving, my legs felt heavy. I paused to watch the Avon flow deep and slow, breathed in its silty scent, and admired the leafy branches arching across it. A pair of swans glided by, silent and graceful. I envied their serenity.

I don't want to be anywhere else, I thought.

It was only when I felt a tiny, tell-tale splinter of rain on my arm that I noticed the dense, charcoal-bottomed clouds billowing in my direction. I turned, homeward bound, but it was too late. Within a few steps, heavy raindrops pelted my bonnet and skirt.

Confident the shower wouldn't last long, I ran to an alder tree and pressed my back against its lichen-coated trunk. The canopy offered little shelter, and with the rain coming thicker and faster, my arms were soon damp.

That's when I saw the little dog huddled against the door of a garden wall several yards above me. Although shallow, the alcove offered better shelter than the tree. I lifted my skirts and scrambled up the bank. As I approached, the animal shrank from me. When I ducked into the doorway alongside him, he tucked his scraggy tail between his legs and bolted beneath a nearby bush.

"It's all right," I called after him as I settled in the dry recess. "Come back. There's enough space for the two of us."

He stood, head and tail hanging. The spindly plant he'd chosen provided scant cover. Water soon dripped from his wiry brown coat, rivulets trickling between his ribs. I shook my skirt. The dog started and stared at me in alarm. I shuffled to the far side of the alcove, crouched and leaned against the door. He blinked, alarm replaced by resentment.

"I'm sorry. I didn't mean to chase you away," I said, patting the ground alongside me. "Come. There's ample place."

The dog looked down. He had the long body, pointy snout, and short, bowed legs typical of the many strays that skulked around the streets and alleyways of Bath. His elongated, oval shape made me think of a comet, the first of which I'd seen when my father led me and my brothers out one icy, clear Hanoverian night and pointed out what I briefly had imagined to be a distant, dirty snowball with an odd glow and a tail. It was my introduction to the stars and their heavenly companions.

"They're the out-of-work progeny of turnspit dogs," William had explained when I'd commented on Bath's proliferation of homeless hounds, most of whom were small and misshapen, like me. "They're bred to work in kitchens where they're placed in wheels and forced to run to turn meat as it roasts over the fire."

I'd stared at him. "Caged in a wheel and made to run?"

"Yes," he'd replied.

I'd pictured the small pack of dogs I'd seen tearing across a meadow near our village in Hanover. Their energy and eagerness were exhilarating. I'd imagined leaping over the grass and charging into the woods with them. The idea of dogs trapped and working in hot kitchens troubled me.

"Are they treated kindly when they're not turning the Sunday roast?" I'd asked William.

"I don't know. I've heard they're sometimes taken to church where they're made to lie on their owners' feet to warm them," he'd replied.

Having until then always been a servant and never waited upon, I'd been uneasy when we'd moved to 19 New King Street a few years ago and William employed a cook. For weeks, I'd looked away when she served us, sitting on my hands to prevent myself taking plates from her. However, learning to accept help in the kitchen was one thing. I couldn't imagine putting a dog to work there, particularly one as pitiful as the creature cowering beneath the bush.

I tapped the space alongside me again. "Come, Comet. Come," I called.

He ignored me, and I was ashamed. All I'd wanted was to get out of the house and calmly acquaint myself with the idea of leaving Bath. It seemed wrong to have caused the animal discomfort. I stood, stepped into the rain, made my way down the slippery bank, and once more leaned against the tree. It didn't take long for the dog to slink back into the alcove, where he shook his coat, sat, and looked at me, his dark eyes reproachful.

CHAPTER 2

July 1782
Bath, England

As I'd anticipated, the downpour didn't last long. However, it was enough to soak me. I took off my bonnet, squeezed it, and tied it back on. The bodice of my dress, already close-fitting, clung to my skin. My skirts were heavy, and my toes squelched in my shoes. There was nothing to do but head home.

"Goodbye, Comet," I said, glancing at the dog.

He looked the other way.

Despite my soggy feet, I was side-stepping the puddles along Chapel Row when, alerted by the urgent rapping of knuckles against glass, I saw the statuesque form of Miss Lydia Hudson at a window. Even at home, her hair was piled high, a perfect, powdered mound held aloft by a ribbon matching her lilac gown. I raised a hand to greet her, but she motioned I should meet her at the door. Itchy and eager to get out of my wet attire, I groaned quietly but nodded my compliance. It would be rude to refuse her.

Miss Hudson was a confidant of Miss Anne Fleming, the dance teacher William had engaged to teach me the ways of English gentlewomen when I arrived in Bath. For reasons unclear to me, Miss Hudson also attended my lessons, adding an unremitting flood of commands to the teacher's instructions.

"Your curtsy should be lower, Miss Herschel. You want it to be explicit."

"Head up, Miss Herschel. Lengthen your neck. You're tiny enough—like a sprite—without allowing your head to disappear into your chest."

"It's 'weather,' Miss Herschel 'Weather.' Not 'wezza.' Remember, we practiced last week."

When my lessons with Miss Fleming had ended, Miss Hudson surprised me by regularly calling on me at home. Later, she was often in the audience when William and I performed. Moreover, and even though I rarely had occasion to accept, she frequently invited me to concerts, recitals, and card parties.

Now, she opened the door. "Miss Herschel! You're wet!" she said as if I might be oblivious to my sodden state. "Come in. I'll call for a towel for you."

I stayed on the doorstep. "No. Please don't trouble yourself, Miss Hudson. I'm on my way home and—"

"Nonsense!" She stood back and ushered me into the hallway. "I can't let you go on like that."

She turned her head and called into the house. "Abigail! Bring Miss Herschel some towels. Quickly. And then we'll have tea."

So it was that I, damp and uncomfortable despite Abigail's vigorous toweling, came to perch on the edge of a chair in Miss Hudson's drawing room.

She handed me a cup of tea. "You must be so proud of Mr. Herschel. The King's Astronomer! What an honor. Will he give up some of his musical responsibilities? Even someone with his extraordinary energy surely cannot do it all."

It didn't surprise me she already knew about William's appointment. News traveled fast in Bath, and that people were talking about how His Majesty had appointed the town's musical director a court astronomer was gossip-worthy, shocking even. For many, William's interest in astronomy had only come to light the year before when he'd discovered a planet and delighted King George by proposing it be called "George's Star," or Georgium Sidus. Until then, Bathonians had admired only my brother's musical prowess. Unlike me, they hadn't regularly found him slumped over his notes at the table in the morning after he'd spent the entire night stargazing. Only those close to William knew how his curiosity about celestial objects had evolved into an obsession, which eventually outweighed his interest in music.

"He'll be back from London tonight. I don't know his plans, although I understand they'll include leaving Bath to live closer to court," I replied.

She stared at me over the rim of her teacup, her narrow eyebrows curving sharply upward. "Leave Bath? Out of season, you mean?"

I shook my head.

"What? For good? He'd leave permanently? Surely not. What about the music?" she asked.

"My brother must be closer to Windsor Castle. His Majesty requires him to work full-time as an astronomer. He's to give up music. We will have to move."

"*We?* But surely your place is here, Miss Herschel?"

"Not without my brother," I replied, glancing away.

Aside from William and Alex, no one in England knew the life I'd fled in Hanover.

Miss Hudson put down her cup. "But if he dedicates himself to astronomy, what will you do? If you moved anywhere else, you'd have to live in London to experience performing opportunities similar to those offered by Bath. Even then, they'd be lacking."

I smiled, hoping to make light of it. "I've only ever sung with my brother."

She stood and walked to the window. I marveled that someone so powerfully built moved with such grace.

"But you've worked so hard and become so accomplished despite, um, despite everything," she said, turning to me without lifting her eyes to my face. "Why, even the Marchioness of Lothian declared that you pronounced your words like an Englishwoman when she heard you singing the Messiah at Easter. And let's not forget how Mr. Palmer proclaimed you 'an ornament of the stage' after your performance at the Bath Theatre." Finally, she looked up. "You could sing with another orchestra."

She made it sound so simple, and yet I shuddered at the thought. "I couldn't. I've never—"

Miss Hudson ignored me. "There's no place better for you than Bath. Could you not move in with Mr. Alex Herschel?"

That she imagined I could swap one brother for another wasn't unreasonable. William and Alex were equally good men who might've seemed alike to those who didn't know them well. After all, they shared a history. Both had moved to England from Hanover and were musicians, and—though not one to observe the skies—Alex was fascinated by the instruments required by astronomy. When William had grown frustrated with the expense and limitations of the telescopes available and decided to build instruments, Alex's interest was piqued. He was a patient, meticulous tinkerer. Together, my brothers began designing reflecting telescopes, incorporating curved mirrors rather than the glass lenses used in refracting telescopes. I was roped in to help cast and polish the reflectors, and although I'd rather be singing, the three of us worked well together. However, while William had the energy and optimism of a hare in springtime, Alex was dour and pessimistic in all seasons. Even if I wasn't beholden to William, the prospect of living with Alex held no appeal.

"No, I must go. I help him with his astronomy and take care of household matters," I said.

"My dear Miss Herschel, you said it yourself; your brother will be a member of the royal house. He'll employ others. Your service will be unnecessary," she said.

I wondered what Miss Hudson would think if she knew how miserable I'd been in Hanover, how I'd come to leave and how terrified I was I'd be made to return. Even after surviving life-threatening episodes of smallpox and typhus—the former would forever be publicized by the deep pits on my face, and the latter had inhibited my growth so I'd never be taller than an average ten-year-old—I had suffered. I recalled how, shortly after my father's funeral, I'd overheard my mother and oldest brother, Jacob discussing my future.

I was accustomed to the sneer in Jacob's voice, but still it stung. "She says she wants to go to school like Sophia Elizabeth, William, Alex, and I did. Wants to be a governess. Insists she should at least learn music."

My mother had groaned. "It would be an absolute waste," she said. "She must stay away from others. Remain here in the house. There's no hope for her with her ugly scars and puny body. No man will ever want her."

Jacob sighed dramatically, as if my very existence weighed heavily upon him. "She should be grateful for the roof over her head and that we feed her. It's not unreasonable to expect her to repay us by keeping house."

"She should be grateful," my mother had echoed.

My tears had flowed hot and fast, and I'd wanted to burst through the door and tell them I didn't care no man would want me. Matrimony held no appeal for me. My parents had never seemed content with one another, and I'd seen what marriage had done to my sister.

Sophia Elizabeth—the oldest of my siblings and seventeen years my senior—was a sprightly, hopeful young woman before she married Mr. Griesbach. She radiated warmth in an otherwise cold, dark home and had taken care of me with patience and affection I'd not received from our mother. It was Sophie Elizabeth who'd gently washed and dabbed the swollen cysts strewn across my face and body while I recovered from smallpox and who'd chastised my brothers when they mocked my tiny form. I was shocked when she'd told me about her pending nuptials.

"Don't worry, Little One," she'd said, stroking my hair. "I'll visit often and ensure Mother doesn't work you too hard. Even she can't expect you to take on my chores and keep up yours. You'll see, Caroline; it'll be fine."

I'd stood quietly alongside my brothers as our sister laughed and waved us goodbye after her wedding. I prayed for her quick return. However, Sophia Elizabeth didn't visit for more than a year. Marriage and her new home consumed her. When eventually she came, it was fleetingly and I didn't recognize the exhausted, irritable wife and mother my sister had become. Her smile had disappeared into a low-slung chin I'd never seen before. Sophia Elizabeth's husband and child demanded all of her. I'd held up my hands to her. They were rough and raw from the endless washing and scrubbing I undertook at Mother's behest. My sister had promised to defend me.

"There's nothing I can do," she said, turning away. "I have my own difficulties."

Sophia Elizabeth no longer had any time, energy, or affection for her sister. I'd been abandoned.

"It's the lot of a wife," said my mother, when I cried about how haggard, cold, and frustrated by everything and everyone my sister had grown.

I didn't want a husband. All I wanted was to be educated so that I might find purpose beyond cleaning. I was as curious about the world as my brothers were. I listened to their conversations about bold adventurers who crossed the oceans, explored faraway shores, charted the stars, looked deep into matter, and philosophized about music, poetry, mathematics, and the human psyche.

I don't want to be locked away in Hanover. I want to know more about the mysteries of the world, I'd imagined yelling at them.

Instead, I'd turned, knelt at the hearth, and scrubbed the floor, afraid that if Jacob and my mother saw my tears they'd throw me out. They believed I was worthless, and I had no evidence to the contrary.

What would Miss Hudson say if I told her how lonely and despondent I'd been until William returned from England and rescued me? I imagined her horror if I explained how our mother and Jacob had only agreed to my leaving with William when he reimbursed them for the cost of a servant to replace me. What would she say if she knew he'd promised to send me back to Hanover if I wasn't useful to him? That even after all these years, Jacob regularly wrote to William to ask if I might be dispatched back? I pictured her shock, but sipping my tea, I said nothing.

She persevered. "You're settled here, happy."

"My brother brought me to England to help him. He has a new profession. I'll have to adapt," I said.

"So you'll learn astronomy?" asked Miss Hudson.

I smiled. "Yes. If that's what he requires."

Already, I helped William by writing up his observations, copying catalogs, and working on the telescopes. I knew a little about astronomy. However, he'd trained me to be a singer, and for the first time in my life I felt I'd achieved something significant. I'd mastered my voice. I saw how my singing moved audiences as they gazed at me, their eyes shining and mouths ajar. I loved it and, as William's interest shifted, couldn't ignore the pinch of resentment I felt about his abandoning music for astronomy. Yet, if I was to remain useful to my brother and stay in England, I'd have to attend him wherever he went and whatever he did.

Miss Hudson patted her coiffure as if it might've shifted. "I see why you want to stay with him. He's admirable. Talented. Interesting. A very fine gentleman." She sighed. "But if you stayed in Bath, he'd surely visit?"

"I wouldn't be much use to him here." I stood. "Thank you for the tea. I must go."

She followed me to the door and, as I turned to say goodbye, took my hands in hers. "If you do reconsider and stay, you can count on me to include you in as many social events as I can, Miss Herschel. If you go, I shall write to you and visit you in your new home. It would upset me greatly to lose our friendship, to have you and Mr. Herschel gone from my life."

"Thank you," I repeated, feeling myself redden at her intensity.

I drew my hands from hers and stepped onto the sidewalk. She sighed once more before closing the door.

The clouds had cleared, and the only evidence of the storm was my heavy skirt, clammy feet, and a few puddles lingering in the shade. I noticed a small, dark form on the other side of the street opposite Miss Hudson's door. It was the dog.

I approached, stopping about two yards from him. "Hello, Comet," I said.

He stared at me, motionless. I turned and walked away. When I got to the corner, I glanced back. He was following.

CHAPTER 3

July 1782
Bath, England

ALEX RENTED A ROOM ELSEWHERE BUT WORKED ON THE TELESCOPES IN THE house William and I shared when he wasn't practicing or performing with his band. So, it was no surprise to find him still there after I'd changed into dry clothes.

"There's soup on the table," I said from the doorway of the room where my brothers had installed a turning machine.

"You might stay in Bath," said Alex as he followed me to the dining room. "We could find a house together, perhaps even take over the rent here."

It was one thing for Miss Hudson to imagine it possible, but that Alex might propose we share a home was surprising. He and William were five and twelve years older than me, respectively. Even so, I didn't think of Alex as a protective older brother. That was William's role. But that wasn't the only reason Alex's suggestion was strange. He was engaged to be married.

"I doubt Miss Cohlman wants to set up home with her sister-in-law," I said.

He sat at the table. "It's unlikely the betrothal will proceed."

I stared at him, expecting more. He ignored me and buttered a slice of bread. Alex had always been the most reticent of my five siblings, slow to smile and as wary of change as he was of strangers. Only William could tenderly lure him from his recurring, gloomy moods, which could appear as suddenly as a cloud covering the moon. Alex's brooding had diminished since he'd met Miss Cohlman. Now the fog was back. I didn't ask what had happened. If he was to confide in anyone, it would be William.

"I'm sorry," I said. "Even so, I'll go."

"You'll stop singing? You're unlikely to find opportunities to perform in Windsor, particularly without William's involvement."

"Ha! It amuses me that you, who had so little hope for my singing, should be concerned. Have you forgotten you repeatedly told William it would be impossible for him to teach me music?" I teased.

Alex gave me a blank look. "You're right. I didn't imagine you'd be good. There was no evidence you were musical when you were a girl."

"Because no one cared enough to contemplate I might be capable of anything more than cleaning and serving them," I said.

He bobbed his head. "Ja, ja, I know. But William did, and he was right. Why not enjoy what you've learned? Your voice is good and improving all the time. You could make a living from continuing to sing in Bath. Why give it up to follow William? There are very few ready audiences around Windsor. You're admired in Bath. You'll receive offers from other directors."

"But I only sing for William. You know I cannot, will not perform with anyone else," I replied.

Alex's knife clattered lightly as he laid it on his plate. "But you're not a circus animal," he said. "You don't have to sing or dance for a master. You might get over your fear if you tried. Then you could perform with any conductor, any orchestra."

I stared at him. Had he forgotten the other reason? The one that worried me even more than the idea of singing without William?

"What about the terms our brother agreed to so I could leave our mother's home?" I asked quietly.

Alex frowned. "That was years ago. Surely she and Jacob wouldn't insist you…"

He didn't finish the sentence. It had come back to him. He recalled that, with our mother's health failing in recent years, Jacob and his wife were more eager than ever for me to return to Hanover. They wanted me to care for our matriarch.

I sighed. "I'll help William mind the heavens."

Alex shook his head. "It's a pity. You love singing. Do you even care about the night sky?"

That Alex doubted my interest in astronomy was understandable. Although I was curious about the night sky and enjoyed helping William outdoors when the weather was good, I was dedicated to music. I'd complained to Alex repeatedly over the years about how studying the stars distracted William from our musical endeavors. It had seemed unreasonable given how much time and effort he'd dedicated to turning me into a singer.

My lessons had begun on my arrival in Bath. In addition to teaching me music and the country's language and customs, William taught me mathematics.

"You can't have one without the other," he'd said. "Music is not only an art. It's also a science. Music is mathematics. It features time signatures, beats per minute, and formula-based progressions. Sound, pitch, frequency, and resonance are based on scientific principles. To learn music, you must learn mathematics."

Eventually, his dogged instruction and my diligence paid off. I understood mathematics, assimilated enough Englishness to blend into Bath society, and mastered my voice. I also rallied the courage to present my tiny, blemished form to audiences.

"She could be a fairy," I'd heard someone whisper minutes before my first performance.

"More like a scaly elf or pixie," came the reply.

I'd felt my face redden. The words had stung, echoing in my thoughts until the orchestra struck up and I began singing, when I'd held the gaze of my detractors and recognized their discomfort.

Even fairies, scaly elves, and pixies can sing, I'd imagined telling them.

After the performance, William's satisfaction lit so fierce a fire in me I was certain others could feel its heat. I'd never been happier or felt as secure and fulfilled. I'd learned to do something that made me proud. Although I dreaded ever seeing my mother and Jacob again, I wished there was a way they could hear me sing so that I might savor their astonishment. I fantasized they might even have been ashamed of themselves.

However, as my confidence as a vocalist grew, so too did William's fascination with the stars. The more time he spent at his telescope, the less he had for the talent he'd nurtured in me, the thing that bound us together: music.

"I don't understand it," I'd complained to Alex one morning, when I'd found sheets of music on the floor, cast off the table to make space for telescope parts. "Just when it seems I've become the singer he wanted, he's more interested in the heavens."

During the intermission of a concert one evening, William slipped out through a side door. When he hadn't returned moments before we were due to commence performing, my pulse quickened. Why hadn't he come back? I raced across the room, but as I reached the door, it opened, and he reappeared.

"Where've you been?" I asked.

"The moon," he said, smiling. "Its mountains have never been clearer. I can't wait to get home. Come; let's get this over with."

As soon as we arrived home, he took the seven-foot telescope he and Alex had built into the street. Alex stopped by shortly afterward, and I told him how anxious I'd been about William's disappearance.

"He wouldn't tolerate that from anyone else in the orchestra," I complained. "Imagine his fury if we dared sneak out to look at the moon during a concert."

"Well, he was back in time, wasn't he?" said Alex.

"Yes, but I wish he wasn't so distracted by the heavens when we're busy with music," I'd replied.

When I'd gone outside to William a little later, I saw a tall, lean stranger with oversize silver buckles on his shoes and a long-tailed riding coat approaching from the other direction. He was on his way home from a dinner party and stopped to ask William what he hoped to see through the telescope.

"Tonight, I'm trying to measure how high the mountains on the moon are," said my brother. "In general, I want to understand the structure of everything up there, how big the heavens are, how old its objects are, and who might live there."

"Oh? You're not interested in measuring the stars for navigational purposes?" asked the man.

"No," said William. "That's taken care of by the learned men in Greenwich. I'm interested in understanding much, much more. Would you like to look?"

Thus began my brother's friendship with Dr. William Watson. He visited again the next day and urged William to write up his celestial findings and submit them to the Bath Philosophical Society. A few weeks later, he introduced my brother to the Royal Society of London. Dr. Watson was also among the first of a long line of stargazers to ask William to build him a telescope. Nothing was the same after that.

Our home, which previously reflected our musical undertakings, was turned into a series of cluttered workrooms. A cabinetmaker occupied the drawing room, shoving aside furniture to make way for half-built tubes and stands. Alex found a large turning machine in Bristol, brought it to Bath, and set it up in a spare bedchamber to grind glass and turn eyepieces.

The kitchen was used to melt and cast speculum to make reflectors. Although speculum—a little arsenic was added to make the melted copper and tin more polishable once it set—was practical for the large mirrors William's telescopes required, it wasn't easy to work with and required hours and hours of polishing to turn it into effective reflectors. Once, William polished continuously for sixteen hours, during which time I fed and watered him like a mother bird feeding a chick.

Sifting great mounds of horse dung for molds for the speculum was among my tasks. "I don't think many other sopranos spend their days sieving manure before scrubbing themselves so that they can perform at the Bath Theatre," I'd muttered to Alex as he lugged another bucketful of muck into the kitchen.

One afternoon, I was at my brother's writing table in the parlor copying a catalog Dr. Watson had lent William. There was some urgency because the doctor wanted the directory back and William and I were to perform that night. Distracted by the melodies and harmonies playing silently through my mind as the concert drew closer, I struggled to focus on the detail of the astronomical objects on the pages before me.

If only William gave me the catalog earlier in the week, I thought.

I heard my brothers' murmured voices in the kitchen, where they were pouring speculum into a pounded horse dung mold I'd prepared earlier. I stopped working and sat back. I'd ask William if Dr. Watson might leave the catalog with us for another day, I decided.

As I rose from my chair, an almighty blast rocketed through the house, rattling the windows and furniture. Clutching the chair as if I might be swept away, I heard my brothers' cries of alarm, interspersed with indistinct crashing sounds from the kitchen.

"William! Alex! What's going on?" I shouted when the air stilled.

"Well," came Alex's grim response eventually. "That's not good."

I went to the kitchen door and peered in. "Are you all right? Is it safe?"

"Yes," replied William, sighing loudly. "The damage is done."

The melted metal had seeped through the compost and onto the floor as my brothers poured it. The cold stone floor had fractured and exploded, sending jagged pieces of shingle hurtling in all directions. Some had even smashed against the ceiling. That none of the bits had hit William and Alex was miraculous.

"We'll clean up," said William, glancing at me. "You get on with the catalog."

"But what about the concert?" I said. "Shouldn't we be preparing for it?"

"We are prepared, Lina," he replied calmly. "Go back to work. The catalog is important. I'll let you know when we need to hurry."

Alex caught my eye and shrugged. He understood my frustration.

Thereafter, although William did what he was committed to as a musician, his fascination with astronomy amplified rapidly. My resentment was tempered with resignation as I grew accustomed to his shift in focus, and although music remained my priority, I helped him with his astronomy whenever he asked, which he did more and more often. Even when he didn't need me at his side, my brother never missed an opportunity to place his eye to his telescope and scrutinize the sky.

One night in March 1781, he was examining the small stars near the constellation Geminorum when a visibly larger star caught his attention. William examined it for a few more nights and, believing it to be a comet, reported it to the Royal Society. He hadn't received a response yet when he called me to his desk one afternoon.

"I'm beginning to doubt it's a comet," he said, pointing to his notes. "Will you check these calculations for me."

It didn't take me long. William's mathematics lessons and the note-taking I'd done for him meant I was familiar with such numbers. His calculations were right. The result was astonishing. The distance between William's "comet" and the sun was nineteen times the distance of the sun to Earth. The object probably wasn't a comet but a planet.

"That's extraordinary!" I said, surprised by how excited I was by the discovery. I was also delighted my brother had asked me to check the numbers and even more so that I could do so. Mathematics wasn't helpful only for music.

"Ah, you see! The skies are full of surprises. That's what excites me," he'd said, as if the moment explained any questions I might have about astronomy.

Weeks later, members of the Royal Society and astronomers from other countries agreed, and the planet Georgian Sidus sent my brother's name to the top of the list of the world's notable astronomers. When William was awarded the Royal Society Copley Medal for the discovery, Alex and I suspected stargazing would take over our brother's life.

Now, at the table with Alex, I sighed as I tipped my bowl forward to fill my spoon with soup.

"It's not true that I don't care about astronomy. It's just that I've spent a decade learning to sing. I understand music much better," I said, ashamed to admit how uneasy I was about the idea of giving up the only thing I'd achieved in life. What if it was the *only* thing I was good at?

Alex leaned back and regarded me grim-faced. "If you're determined to go with William and be useful, you'll have to learn astronomy. He'll have neither the time nor the inclination for anything else," he said.

I swallowed and pushed my spoon around the almost empty bowl.

"Do you ever decide upon anything without first being certain that it'll serve William?" he asked.

Still, I didn't respond.

"Does it ever occur to you that you fled Hanover to escape being our mother's servant, and yet you've embraced the role for William?" he asked.

The room suddenly seemed small and hot. I wished I were outside again, away from Alex and his infuriating questions.

"It is not the same," I said through gritted teeth. "You know that. William has given me an education. I am not his servant. But I must remain useful to him if I'm to stay in England. I don't want to go back to Hanover."

Alex exhaled loudly. "It's just that I wonder what you'd do if the time came that our brother didn't need or want your service."

I glared at him. "I'm sorry you're miserable, but I resent you trying to drag me into whatever wretched place you find yourself."

We sat in silence for a moment until he stood, muttered his thanks for the meal, and left the room. I waited a while longer, trying to compose my thoughts. I shouldn't have allowed Alex to provoke me. If William had been there, he would've known what to say to lift our brother's spirits. My worries made me vulnerable to Alex's moods. I hadn't felt as uncertain about my future since I'd arrived in England. I had to remain useful to William, but giving up singing would be a high price to pay.

I got up and went to the window to look for the dog. He'd followed me home from a distance earlier. When I'd arrived at the door, I'd peered across the street to where he'd stopped, sniffing at a wall as if oblivious to my existence. He was sitting there now. I took a piece of bread, went to the front door, and opened it. The dog looked at me, his ears raised.

"Come, Comet," I called.

He stood but didn't approach. I lifted my hand to show him the bread.

"I'll leave it here," I said, placing it on the doorstep.

He watched but didn't move. I went inside, closed the door quietly, and returned to the window. It didn't take long before Comet stood, slunk quickly across the street, snatched the bread, and vanished.

CHAPTER 4

July 1782
Bath, England

I was cleaning an eyepiece when I heard the front door open and close. Slinging the cloth over my shoulder, I went to the hallway and watched as William shrugged off his coat. My neck and shoulders, tense from the contemplations of the day and polishing efforts, relaxed, and for a moment I felt foolish for worrying.

William is home, and all will be well, I thought.

Although he wasn't as broad as Alex, William was slightly taller. However, his height and demeanor made him seem much bigger. At forty-four, he had the energy and ambition of a twenty-year-old. With his wide, high forehead, angular nose, and lively eyes, he was the most handsome of my brothers. Although Jacob was undeniably our mother's favorite child, she believed William's cleft chin was a sure sign he was marked for greatness. But it was his curiosity and warmth that drew people to him. Regardless of who they were, where or why they were introduced, William never forgot a name once he heard it. And no one forgot William when their paths crossed.

He saw me and smiled. "There you are, Lina."

"Congratulations," I said.

"Ah, you heard. Dr. Watson, I presume?"

"Of course. He was here first thing this morning. Welcome home. Though it won't be for much longer, I believe," I said, gesturing to the walls.

William frowned. I took his coat and turned away, regretting my petulant tone.

"There was a dog on the front step. Ran away when I approached. Do you know anything about it?" he asked.

"He followed me home earlier. From the river."

"River?"

"Yes," I replied. "I fed him and thought we might take care of him."

When William didn't respond, I looked up. He was staring at me, eyebrows raised.

"Miss Hudson says dogs make good companions," I said, trying to sound casual.

William chuckled. "Yes. Dogs that are accustomed to people make fine pets, but the animal at the door looks feral, like he's never seen the inside of a building."

"Perhaps, but I'll lure him in. Train him." I spoke as if I'd given the matter a great deal of thought. In truth, it hadn't occurred to me until then. Despite having given the dog bread and even a name, I'd been trying to make up for stealing his shelter and hadn't imagined bringing him inside until William mentioned him. Now, though, I saw the advantages. A dog would be a loyal and consistent companion. His affections and interests wouldn't alter, would they? He'd be dependable and stay at my side wherever I had to go.

"I didn't know you wanted a dog. What'll you do with him?" he asked.

"Feed him. Keep him safe and warm. Walk him. Miss Hudson insists promenading is not only socially advantageous but that the exercise and fresh air are also beneficial to one's health. Having a dog will induce me to walk more," I replied.

"I see. Of course. I hope you succeed in training him." He was smiling now. "Did Dr. Watson tell you the appointment means I'll have to move close to court?"

I nodded, noting he said "I." Did that mean he imagined I might not move with him? Surely not?

"I found a house in Datchet," he said.

"Datchet?" I echoed.

"Near Windsor. It's not far from the castle and abuts a large grass plot where I'll erect the twenty-foot telescope," said William.

Again, he spoke as if I wouldn't be there. What was he thinking? I was about to ask when Alex appeared in the doorway.

"So, the twenty-footer. You'll need my help then," he said.

Encouraged by the success of the seven-foot reflector and eager to see deeper into the night sky, William had drawn up plans for a much larger instrument. He and Alex intended to make a nineteen-inch-diameter reflector, which they'd place in a twenty-foot-long tube mounted with an eyepiece. The telescope would be supported by a wooden frame with a platform on top, from which William would observe. One of the obstacles my brothers had faced when they'd imagined building the machine in Bath was that it would require a sizable, open piece of land, which wasn't easy to come by. The move to Datchet would solve this problem.

William turned to Alex. "Yes. I'll need all the help I can get from both of you," he said, going on to say the Datchet house was not only large enough to accommodate the twenty-footer but also suited his plans to construct other telescopes.

"Of course, I'll be at court a great deal. My role is something of a personal astronomer to His Majesty and quite distinct from that of the Astronomer Royal occupied by Dr. Maskelyne. He's located at Greenwich and is principally involved with matters of navigation. I'll attend to His Majesty at Windsor, and he might visit when the large telescope is ready. He says I'm to educate, entertain, and update him and whoever is in court on astronomical matters. It's his hope my discoveries will entrench the court as the world leader in understanding the heavens," said William.

He named other astronomers he'd met during his visit to the Royal Observatory, conceding there'd been "plenty of sitting around and making idle chatter when we could've been working." I was unable to hide a smile. Few people were as dedicated to their work and as irked by time-wasting as William.

"You'll have to get used to it," said Alex dryly. "You're at the whim of His Majesty—and cheap at the price."

"What? Why do you say that?" asked William.

Alex shrugged. "Dr. Watson said of your annual salary of two hundred pounds, 'Never bought a monarch honor so cheap.' He's unimpressed."

William chortled. "He urged me to follow astronomy, but Dr. Watson isn't happy about my leaving Bath. I don't think any amount would please my friend. I've tried to assure him our friendship will endure, but he's unsure about the move."

"He's not the only one," said Alex, looking at me.

I glared at him, giving my head a small shake.

William narrowed his eyes. "Would you stay, Lina?"

"Of course not," I said, my heart beating fast. "How will I help you in Datchet if I am in Bath?"

Alex smirked. "Is that why you fled the house when Dr. Watson gave us the news even though there was a storm brewing?"

"I went for a walk to ponder matters. To think about the move. The storm was unexpected," I said, looking down to avoid my brother's scrutiny.

"I assumed you'd come with me, Lina," said William "You're helpful and I hoped—"

"Of course I'll help you." I looked at Alex. "Our brother is melancholy due to matters of the heart and has misinterpreted my mood accordingly."

"Is that so?" William asked Alex.

Alex blew out his cheeks. "I saw Miss Cohlman walking with a gentleman two evenings ago. They were talking familiarly. When I visited her the next day, I asked about him. She acknowledged he was a former suitor. I inquired whether the man was pursuing her afresh. She didn't deny it."

"I'm sorry. What will you do?" asked William.

Alex hung his head and sighed.

"Would you like me to ask Miss Cohlman to return your ring?" continued William.

"If you would," said Alex quietly, "when you have time. Now, though, I want to show you the progress I've made on the reflector."

They left the room as if it was settled I'd leave Bath.

Later that evening, I took the stool and small table Alex had made me for note-taking into the garden where William was already at his telescope. The moon was not yet visible, but a sprinkling of silvery stars was strewn across the vast, dark canvas like granules of salt spilled on a black worktop. Even though I didn't understand the night sky like William and couldn't imagine it intriguing or satisfying me the way music did, I loved gazing at the heavens quietly for a few minutes before getting to work. In those moments, the stars were mine. I silently greeted them one by one, imagining they flickered their response. *How splendid the heavens are,* I thought, *and how lucky my siblings and I are that our father awoke our interest in their infinite mystery when he took us to watch the comet decades ago.*

If Sophia Elizabeth hadn't already left home by then it might've been different, but Mother had objected to my inclusion in the expedition. "Girls shouldn't go out in the dark—especially one as sickly as her!" she'd called out as we trailed one another outside.

"She's no longer ill," replied my father in the contemptuous tone that characterized my parents' interaction. Had they ever even liked one another? Or was that what marriage did? Turn beloveds into adversaries?

"Pah! Do you believe that? Look at her," snapped my mother. "It'll be on your head if she falls ill again."

"As if I'd expect you to take care of her," he said. "Come, Caroline. The air outside isn't fetid like it is in here."

My father's rare defiance had made me want to squeal with delight. I was thrilled to be with him and my brothers and to make out the comet with its bright, coin-shaped head and long, fuzzy tail. But it was William, by far the most curious and brightest of his six children, with whom Father had lingered at the fireside, talking about science and philosophy. Their conversations continued whenever occasion allowed until Father died. *How proud he would've been of William's appointment,* I thought, glancing at my brother as I placed a small lantern on the table with my quill, ink, and paper and sat down.

William didn't take his eye from the instrument. "Ah, there you are. Do you have everything?" he asked.

"I do."

"I've been trying to identify a new double star in Orion. Take down the following."

"I'm ready," I replied, quill poised.

"Following ten Orionii, I saw very distinctly double at least a dozen times pass through the whole field of view with both eyes, but was obliged to darken everything."

He spoke slowly and precisely, allowing me to inscribe his exact words without interruption. I'd done it so often that even though I didn't always understand everything, I recognized the words and phrases and knew their spelling.

"I suspected my right eye to be tired, and know it to see objects darker. Therefore tried the left first, and saw it immediately pass through the field double several times. Saw the same afterward with the other eye. No star twinkled except Syrius and those as low. The evening exceptionally fine for telescopes."

He paused. I looked up. "That's it," he said.

I was surprised. Typically, when the sky was clear, William kept me taking notes for hours. Even when it was bitterly cold, we usually kept working.

"Really?" I asked.

"Alas, yes, but I have some urgent correspondence to attend to," he replied.

"All right. I'll add this to the index," I said, referring to the list of William's remarks on practical observation, which I'd created to support his annotations on how other pairs of eyes and even one person's left and right eyes might judge things differently. We hoped to use the information to improve the magnification used on the telescopes.

"You're looking forward to having more space in Datchet," I said as I stood and glanced around the tiny garden.

William turned to me. "Yes. At last, we can begin work on the big telescope. It's the only way we'll ever know just how vast the skies are and the extent of the changing nature of the stars. No one else will do it. My audience with His Majesty, Dr. Maskelyne, and their learned friends these past weeks confirmed it'll be up to me to build more capable instruments."

"And to man them," I added.

William tipped his head back, his eyes on the stars again. Where others might see bright objects against the darkness, some twinkling more vibrantly than others, William saw distant island universes. Where others admired the quiet beauty of the heavens and were in awe of God's handiwork, my brother sought to structurally organize the sky. I was more curious about each object's purpose. For surely God had reason to hang everything exactly where he had, didn't he? How might we explore the possibilities and learn his reasons? I might not understand astronomy the way I did music, but I recognized its fascination.

My brother sighed, but when he spoke, I heard the smile in his voice. "We live in an extraordinary age. A marvelous era. We're going to create instruments that will show us what lies beyond the world we know. We'll use them to see and understand things our parents and grandparents never even imagined. We're fortunate to exist at this time. To be a part of the great exploration of the heavens."

A horse neighed from somewhere nearby, lonely and uncertain. Another answered it, a quiet reassurance, and I imagined a groom bringing the two together in a stable.

"Yes, an extraordinary age. That, it surely is," I said, struck again by how William appeared to have forgotten music entirely.

He gave no indication he'd heard me. "It'll help a great deal if Alex comes to Datchet whenever he can. I've come to rely on him."

"He said he's willing to be there for a few months," I replied.

"Yes." He ran his hand over his head. "I'm sorry about his disappointment with Miss Cohlman, but it works in my favor."

"He'll languish for a while but won't give up. There'll be other women to woo. Our brother is determined to marry," I said, wondering again why Alex was so eager to find a wife. Like me, he'd witnessed not only how miserable marriage had made our sister but also how cold and argumentative our parents were with one another. On many occasions, our mother had left the room without greeting Father when he came home in the evening. She'd storm back in shortly afterward and berate him for some misdeed, such as not having paid the dairyman, forgetting to convey some news, or muddying his boots, which I'd be dispatched to clean. I couldn't recall their exchanging a kind word.

William rubbed his chin. "Perhaps he'll meet someone in Datchet. It might encourage him to visit more frequently. Or even stay."

I took a deep breath, no longer able to ignore the anxiety that had gnawed at my stomach like a hungry rat all day. "Will I be able to sing in Datchet or thereabouts?" I asked, aware of the quiver in my voice.

He stared at me, blinking fast. "Sing? In Datchet? No, of course not. I thought you understood that. I've given up music for the appointment. We're to dedicate ourselves to astronomy."

"But if I—"

"No. There'll be no concerts in Datchet. There's court, of course, but His Majesty has his own musicians. Even if you could perform there, I thought you'd help me. We discussed it earlier, didn't we?"

My heart raced. "Yes, we did. I know. I simply wondered if there might be a chance I could continue performing, a little at least."

William didn't respond immediately. I shifted my feet. The night was so still, if I hadn't known better I might've imagined the stars were holding their breath, listening to our conversation.

"Do you want to stay in Bath?" he asked eventually.

I closed my eyes and shook my head.

He spoke quietly. "You might learn to sing for other directors if you were willing to try."

I shook my head faster.

William sighed. "I received a letter from Jacob just before I left for London," he said.

"Urging you to send me back to Hanover, I guess?" I swallowed with difficulty. It felt as if a pebble were lodged at the back of my throat.

"Mother does very little for herself these days," he replied.

"So if I don't assist you with astronomy, you'll send me back?"

"That's not what I'm saying. But if you stay in Bath—"

"I won't stay! I can't. I'll come with you. It's settled. I'll come to Datchet and work alongside you," I said, breathless now.

If I stayed in Bath and found, as I feared, my singing talent depended on my performing with William and no other musical director, I'd be useless to everyone in England and my brothers would insist I return to Hanover. While others might believe it possible, my doubts that I could sing with anyone but William ran deep. He was my guide and shepherded my voice. I understood and trusted his direction. Even if I'd had the confidence to try, there was no time to experiment with other orchestras and conductors. The instant I floundered, Jacob would demand I go back. Regardless of how frail my mother might be, I shuddered at the thought of returning to her and my life as her servant. I couldn't risk squandering the opportunity of learning more about astronomy and remaining useful to William. Besides, I'd lived with my brother for a decade and couldn't imagine a safer, more comfortable arrangement.

William scowled. "But if you don't want to come, I'm sure—"

I grasped his forearm. "I *want* to come. There's nothing more to say. I am coming with you. I only wondered if it might be possible to perform again. I understand now. You wouldn't have time for music even if it was possible. And neither would I."

He stared at me without speaking for a moment, his eyes searching mine. I didn't flinch.

"Are you sure? You'll come to Datchet and give up music for astronomy?"

"I am," I said, giving his arm a firm squeeze. "There's nothing more to discuss."

William held my gaze once more. Finally, he nodded and smiled. "All right. Good. I'm pleased. Now I must get to my letters."

As he went to the house, I looked at the stars. "Well, that's it then," I said. "I guess we're going to get very well acquainted."

CHAPTER 5

July 1782
Bath, England

WITHIN DAYS AND WITH ALEX'S HELP, WILLIAM AND I BEGAN PACKING MY brother's precious instruments and our furniture, household items, and clothing in preparation to leave Bath. We were to be in Datchet at the beginning of August.

It took several days to lure Comet into the house by offering him food every few hours. Initially, he'd snatch the item, bolt outside, and disappear. However, as the days passed, he slowed his sprint to a trot, and eventually he'd eat within a few feet of me.

Making friends with the dog helped distract me from my concerns about leaving Bath. I'd accepted that I'd stop singing and move, but I knew I'd miss the familiarity and beauty of the town. Comet's accompanying me to Datchet was something of a consolation. It would be like taking a tiny piece of Bath with me.

One day, the dog chewed and swallowed the bacon I'd given him and came to me, his tail slowly moving left and right. I was surprised by the dark intensity of his eyes and, when I reached out and stroked his head, the softness of his fur. From there on, he stayed around longer, seeking not only food but also my attention. Eventually, he stopped vanishing at night. A few days later, although he shrank from my brothers' attempts to pat him, the dog remained close at my heels and pressed into my hand when I patted him.

"Lie there for a while, Comet," I said one morning as William and I arrived in the dining room to resume swathing instruments and tools in cloth.

My brother chuckled. "It's a good name," he said. "He's certainly the right shape. But I suspect he's going to prove less transient than a comet. He seems resolved to stay with you. I guess he's coming to Datchet."

"Of course," I replied, pleased with my success with the dog and William's response. "He'll let us know when guests arrive."

"Ah, that reminds me. The men at the Royal Observatory insisted that once the townsfolk are aware I'm a member of the court, they'll let us be. The villagers are apparently respectful of the king's men."

I murmured my appreciation, thinking of the countless heads that regularly popped above our garden wall in Bath. Alex said they were like "daisies in a meadow in springtime." They belonged to strangers eager to catch glimpses of the telescope when it was in the yard. Cook said our neighbors gave onlookers a variety of explanations for the instrument. Some insisted it was a newfangled cannon William and Alex had designed for the military.

"Others laugh at them and say it's designed to trap the sun's rays and channel the warmth indoors," she'd said.

Another theory was that William had built it to examine the clouds, estimate their density, and foretell how much rain the town might expect. A more fanciful rumor claimed the telescope was a fairy spotter. Even when William took the time to explain its actual use, the telescope and the many night hours my brother spent with it provoked a steady stream of gawping and whispering.

"Perhaps we should hang a sign on our gate at Datchet saying 'Residence of the King's Astronomer' so there's no mistaking your intentions," I said.

We were interrupted by knocking. I went to the door, expecting to see Dr. Watson, who'd spent even more time than usual with us since William's return. However, it was Miss Hudson.

"I wanted to ensure I had your new address," she said, glancing at the boxes as she swept into the room. "You do know, don't you, Mr. Herschel, how sad Bath is to see you and your sister go? Naturally, we're very proud of you, but at the same time, we mourn your loss."

William smiled. "Thank you. That's most kind of you. But the town is so full of musical talent you'll soon be distracted. By next season, we'll be forgotten."

"Never, sir!" she said. "Did your sister tell you I plan to visit you in your new home? I have no intention of letting our friendship wane despite the miles between us."

My brother glanced at me. I hadn't mentioned it. The awkward moment was diffused by Alex's arrival with another box.

"You're not leaving too, are you?" she asked him after they'd exchanged greetings.

"I'll go for about two months and return once they're settled," replied Alex.

"That *is* good news. Perhaps, later in the year, we might share a carriage and visit your brother and sister together?" she said. "We've agreed we'll not allow distance to get in the way of our friendship."

Alex frowned, his eyes on William, who smiled benignly once more and took the box from him.

While she declined my offer of tea, Miss Hudson dallied for almost an hour. Untroubled by our silence as we continued to pack, she prattled on about various concerts and recitals she'd attended recently and the emptiness of Bath now that the season had ended. Finally, slipping into her reticule the card upon which I'd written our address in Datchet, Miss Hudson bade my brothers a "sad farewell," and I escorted her to the door.

On my return, I heard Alex say to William, "She'll not wait until later in the year to visit you. I wouldn't be surprised if she arrives in Datchet shortly after we do."

"With so many of her friends having left for the country or London, she fears she'll be lonely. I suspect she was counting on Lina being in Bath when the season came to an end," said William.

"Lina?" said Alex. "It's not Caroline she wants to visit in Datchet."

William looked up, ready to speak, but when he saw me in the doorway, he laughed instead. "Alex's heart is muddling his thoughts again," he said.

I looked at Alex, aware of a strange prickling in my arms. "You believe Miss Hudson wants to visit us in Datchet to see William?"

"It's possible she wants to visit you both. No doubt she values your friendship. But it's clear to me that she's enthralled by our brother."

William laughed again. "Of course she's not. He's teasing. Pay him no heed."

His laugh was the most natural sound I knew. Typically, a chortle from William warmed and comforted me. It signified everything was fine. However, Alex *didn't* tease. He rarely joked about anything. When he spoke, it was in earnest. If Alex recognized something in Miss Hudson, he wouldn't comment about it because he was jesting but because he believed it to be the truth.

That women admired William wasn't news. I'd seen how they watched him and tittered when he gave them his attention. However, he didn't favor any of them. Unlike Alex, William wasn't interested in getting married or starting a family. I'd always assumed our sister's and parents' marriages affected him the way they did me. Or perhaps it was just that he'd always been too busy for dalliances. Either way, his disregard for matrimony reassured me. I hadn't had to worry that he'd marry someone who might want me gone from their home. Without William's munificence, no money of my own, and no prospects or the tiniest inclination to be married myself, I'd be without a place to live and at the mercy of my other brothers if he was to marry. Why, a wife might so deeply resent my bond with William that she'd side with Jacob and insist I return to Hanover.

Indeed, I was grateful I didn't have to worry about William's nuptials. However, I felt a stab of betrayal at the thought of Miss Hudson's being intrigued by our brother rather than simply being my friend. Was that why she'd pursued a relationship with me? I recalled our interactions over the years and saw that, aside from my lessons with Miss Fleming and a few chance encounters, Miss Hudson had *always* sought me out when William was present. *How foolish I was*, I thought as I walked across the room to Comet and patted his head. But it would be all right. I had a new friend.

CHAPTER 6

August 1782
Datchet, England

My initial reaction to seeing the house at Datchet was relief. Unfortunately, the feeling evaporated as quickly as steam from a kettle.

On the first of August, William, Alex, Comet, and I took the coach from Bath to Slough, where we spent the night at the inn. The next morning, we set off on foot for the little village we were to call home. It was a warm day, and we hugged the shade of the dense hedges and avenues of trees wherever we could. The two-and-a-half-mile route passed farmyards, fields, and woodlands before bringing us to the slow-moving Thames, which we followed to the outskirts of Datchet. When William finally pointed out the house, I was so soothed both by the idea of having arrived *and* the sight of the wagon full of William's instruments and furniture that I didn't immediately notice anything else.

It was Alex who drew my attention to the state of the house when he addressed William. "Well, Brother, you didn't exaggerate its proportions. But you might've mentioned its condition."

The large, redbrick building with its steep roof and tall, narrow windows and doors appeared to have been built by someone with means, ambition, and a sizable family or hopes thereof. However, many seasons had passed since then, and it was now in disrepair.

"Look at the warped doors and windows. And those walls. They're all but crumbling," continued Alex.

He placed his bag on the ground and looked to where Comet was nosing about beneath a mass of scraggly rose vines. "If this was once a garden, it shows little evidence of ever being tame, let alone ordered."

Alex was right. The garden was bedraggled and overgrown, but it was the house that held my attention. The window frames, once white, were discolored and peeling. Several panes were broken and others missing. At least three shutters hung askew and banged freely against the walls, threatening to detach at any moment. Portions of the low stairway leading to the front door had disintegrated.

"It needs a little attention, I concede," said William. "But wait until you see the rooms and stables. The space it allows for our instruments and work more than makes up for the inconvenience of having to take a hand to a few matters."

"Will we have help?" asked Alex as we walked toward the wagon.

"Yes. The landlord said he'd send a young man from the village. He's probably inside," replied William.

However, aside from the wagon driver—an old man whose vital years had long since passed and who lugged a few light boxes for us—we had no help that day. We found a letter in the hallway informing us that the man promised to William had been jailed the previous day for crimes unknown.

"We'll get someone," said William when he found me surveying the blackened kitchen later.

A half-burned log lay in the hearth like a corpse on a bed of white ash. Shards of shattered glass had been brushed into a pile against a wall, and a hodgepodge of broken pots, pans, and utensils sat abandoned on the table. The floor hadn't been swept and, where it wasn't sticky, crunched underfoot. The room's single window had been barricaded with old wooden planks. There was a damp, oiliness to the air. I averted my eyes as Comet trotted from the room with something long, dark, and oval in his mouth. I hoped he'd bury it outside, uneaten.

William touched my elbow. "Come and look at the stables. You'll be pleased by how we'll be able to set up the workbenches and grind the mirrors there. I want to get a horse. I'll need one. There's plenty of space for the animal and our work. Did you see the laundry room?"

I nodded.

"I'm going to use it as a library," he said. "The doors open onto the backyard, where we'll erect the twenty-footer. That way, I'll be able to dictate notes to you from the telescope while you stay warm indoors. It'll work well." He clapped his hands. "Yes, indeed, I'm well pleased."

Left alone with my thoughts, I pondered how excited my brother was by the many spacious rooms, stables, and ample grounds. On the other hand, I couldn't help but worry about the ruinous condition of the house and the cleaning it required. Even if we could repair it and get rid of the current clutter and grime, it would be an ongoing task. We'd need several people to maintain the house and garden, staff I wasn't certain we could afford. If not, would William expect me to render the services of housekeeper, cleaner, and cook? Would I work like a servant as I had in Hanover? Was this what I'd given up Bath for?

Alex intercepted me as I made my way across the yard toward the stables. "We'll take it on, room by room," he said. "I'll be here for two months. Much can be done in that time."

For once, he was encouraging, but it didn't help my mood. "Yes, but still, it's so big and such a mess."

He frowned. "We'll find servants. I'll inquire in the village tomorrow."

I met his gaze. Alex's eyes were steady with concern.

"We'll need all the help we can get if we're to piece this place together before you go back." I meant to smile as I spoke, but I fear it might've resembled a grimace.

True to his word, Alex rose early the next day, went to the village, and returned in the company of a gardener willing to begin work immediately.

"I told Mr. Harris we also require a cook and maidservant. He couldn't think of anyone but has asked his wife to give you a tour of the village and shops later this week," said Alex as we watched the gardener duck his gray head to enter a shed near the stables and reappear quickly, a spade and a hoe balanced on his shoulder. Mr. Harris's step was spritely, belying the deep lines etched upon his face.

The gardener's wife arrived a few days later. "I only have an hour," she said, her scowl and thin-lipped countenance leaving me no doubt about her disinclination for the task.

"Of course. I'm grateful for your guidance and won't dally," I said as I took a basket and followed her from the house with Comet at my heels.

We walked without conversation for a while, with Mrs. Harris setting the pace. Her wheezing made me want to suggest we slow down. Instead, I eventually said, "It seems the people of Datchet are an extremely busy lot."

She turned to me. "What do you mean?"

"Well, aside from your husband, we've not managed to employ anyone—despite my brother's having told the landlord we'd require servants when they met last month," I replied.

Mrs. Harris scoffed. "Ha. Mr. Harris likes to work close to home. That's why he's available."

"And the other villagers? Are they all tradesmen and farmers?"

"Not all. Those who aren't in the service of His Majesty at Windsor or the Duke of Montagu at Datchet Manor have found work in London that pays better. It won't be easy to find help here—unless you up the wages," she said.

Comet trotted ahead, sniffing the watery ditch running parallel to the road. Gradually, the buildings huddled closer together in a mishmash of timber, stone, and slate. Although they varied in size and height, and some structures portended status and wealth, I couldn't discern a distinctive style. It was nothing like Bath.

At a point at which the road intersected several smaller streets and the buildings were most concentrated, Mrs. Harris pointed left and right and, speaking quickly, said, "Butcher. Not large. Be there early in the week for the best cuts. There are two bakeries. That one on the corner is best. That's the dairy shop. Vegetables are best bought at the marketplace on Wednesday and Friday. You'll find fish there too. The apothecary is that way, not far from the seed shop and ironmonger. Ask at the ironmonger for directions to the cobbler."

Finally, she stopped, breathless. I took a moment to look around and run through the list. I might've missed something, but Datchet was small, and the shops were close to one another. It was unlikely I'd get lost. A wagon drawn by two weary-looking ponies clattered by, and a few villagers went about their business.

Mrs. Harris, having recovered her breath, cleared her throat and adjusted the wide apron over her skirt. "I'll say goodbye to you here, Miss Herschel. My sister is waiting," she said.

"Oh. Indeed. I'll see myself home when I've made my purchases. Thank you, Mrs. Harris."

As she bustled down a narrow alley, I walked a short distance toward the river, where an unruly row of trees grew along the muddy slope separating the water from the buildings. There were no cobblestone walkways or smooth, dry footpaths to promenade upon in Datchet. No shiny carriages, pretty gardens, or colorful gowns to admire. The few villagers who hurried about were dressed for function, not display. They chose hardy materials in subdued colors. Few petticoats bloomed, and the women wore broad aprons akin to that of Mrs. Harris. Men favored simple shirts and breeches, and I spotted only one in a waistcoat. The shops might be adequate, but Mrs. Harris had made no mention of a stationer, dress shop, milliner, physician, or even a chandler. There was no evidence in Datchet of novelty, fashion, luxury, or refinement. No place for music, theater, recitals, or card games.

I thought about the money William had spent on Miss Fleming, the many months I'd applied myself to learning the ways of an English gentlewoman, and the years I'd dedicated to training to sing.

All that, for this?

Everything had changed for me—again. How certain I'd been when William brought me to England from Hanover. Now, though, having left Bath for Datchet, I couldn't quell the doubts. Despite how I resolved to stay with William and help him in any way I could, a tiny voice nudged my consciousness.

Who will you become in Datchet? You abandoned the best of yourself in Bath.

I watched the Thames flow wide and slow and breathed in its briny scent. When we'd seen it on our way to the house, William had said its name meant "the dark one." It made sense. The river, as dense as molasses, moved so quietly and leisurely that it gave little inkling of its power and proportion. It was almost beguiling, and for a fanciful instant, I imagined it was stealing a part of me, that part who'd imagined, when my singing made eyes glisten and hands clap, that I could be more than William Herschel's sister. Would I have the chance to re-create myself as his assistant in astronomy and experience that sense of achievement again?

"You thieving beast! Get out!" came a loud shout from behind me.

I turned to see Comet hurtling toward me, pursued by a man whose long, dark curls bounced as he sped across the road with the agility of one accustomed to moving quickly. It took me a moment to realize he was brandishing a cleaver.

Comet dashed beneath a hedge a few feet away from me, and when I took a step to position myself between the dog and his pursuer, the man skidded to a halt.

"Out of my way, girl!" he hollered.

I took a deep breath and stretched to my full height. It wasn't unusual for people to mistake me for a child when they saw me from a distance. Usually, I'd pretend not to have noticed. Their awkward apologies were worse than their blunders. I recognized the surprise in his eyes when he took a second glance at my face.

"Is it your animal?" he asked, his voice lower now but no less annoyed.

The man—the village butcher, I deduced, given the blade in his hand— was around my age, of average size, and clean-shaven beneath the tousled head of black curls. His face was narrow and fine-featured, and his brown shirt and breeches were strangely clean for a man whose trade was meat.

"What happened?" I asked.

"He snuck into my shop and stole a cut."

I went to the bush and peered in. Comet stared back, eyes bulging. "But he carries nothing," I said.

"That's because he dropped it when I chased him down the stairs. He's a thief, I'm telling you, and now I have a spoiled cut to show for it."

There was a pause. I wondered how damaged the meat could be if Comet had carried it only briefly.

"Is he with you?" the butcher asked.

"He is."

"Then you'll need to pay for his thievery, miss."

"Show me the meat," I replied.

Following the man to his shop, I glanced behind to see Comet slink out from under the bush, his eyes on me. The dog's time on the streets of Bath had taught him to stay in the shadows until it was safe.

A slice of pork—a little larger than my hand—lay on the stairs just as the butcher had said. He picked it up and carried it into the shop, which was, as Mrs. Harris indicated, small. It was surprisingly ordered and clean. I followed him to a counter across a floor covered with wood chips. Cuts of meat were neatly arranged on the countertop, while a hook suspended from a rafter held a whole carcass against the wall. What was unexpected was, in the far corner, a chair and a small writing desk, upon which lay a notebook, writing quill, and inkwell.

The butcher cleared his throat and, with my attention now, laid down his cleaver and flipped the meat onto a cutting board. I leaned forward to examine it. A thin layer of dirt and a few puncture marks identified it as Comet's loot.

"A wipe with water will surely restore it," I said.

"To your satisfaction, then, miss," he replied with a glimpse of a smile.

"How much is it?"

"Tuppence."

"You jest," I said.

He didn't respond.

"That's twice what I would've paid in Bath," I added.

The butcher shrugged. "I doubt it. And anyway, it was not in Bath that your dog ran into my shop and pilfered my wares."

"Well, we're in the country now, Lina," chuckled William when I told him and Alex how I'd come to purchase the pork as we ate it that night. "We can live off eggs and bacon, which surely cost nothing to speak of."

"Bacon? From the butcher who charges a tuppence for this?" I said, annoyed that he should make light of it.

"Are you sure he didn't raise the price to make up for having to chase your dog from his establishment?" asked Alex in a serious tone.

I glared at him.

William laughed again. "You've made a fine meal out of it. The day ended well. We have enough space to build and erect telescopes without having to fall over the instruments in the house and garden. The kitchen isn't full of loam, and you don't have to move tubes and eyepieces every time you want to sit down. Once the twenty-footer is erected, I'll be able to observe without having to explain what I'm doing to an endless stream of passersby. This place is ideal for my work. That's all that matters, isn't it?" he asked.

I didn't reply, but he was right. Cleaned and cooked, the meat was good, and it was pleasant not to have to move telescopes and parts of telescopes whenever you wanted to do anything. However, I wished William occasionally paid even a little attention to matters other than building telescopes and observing the skies. Alex and I had worked tirelessly in the house while our brother, intent on getting his workshop set up, spent all his time in the stables. William came into the house for meals and the few hours of sleep he surrendered to each night. He didn't seem to notice the rooms we'd cleaned and arranged, the repairs Alex had undertaken, or even the fact Mr. Harris had cleared the path from the house to the stables. The only time he'd commented on the work in the house was when Alex threw open the doors of the old laundry.

"Well done, Brother!" said William, looking in from outside as he carried a mallet to the stables. "We need to ensure that they're easily opened and bolted. You should lower the area outside and lay some cobblestones. It'll be easier to keep clean."

For a moment, Alex had watched William walk away before he turned to me. "The King's Astronomer knows what he wants and has no doubt he'll get it."

"That's why we're here," I'd replied.

Now, as Alex and I cleared the table and William returned to his workshop, I silently chastised myself for hoping for something different from my brother. He *had* to focus on astronomy. Alex would return to Bath for the season in a few weeks, and it would be up to me to keep house. However, once we were settled, I would surely also be able to apply myself to interesting, purposeful work. William would teach me astronomy the way he'd taught me music. My days and nights would once more be occupied by matters more fascinating and important than mending curtains, cleaning rooms, and cooking food. I just needed to be patient.

CHAPTER 7

September 1782
Datchet, England

WITH SO MUCH TO DO TO REPAIR THE HOUSE AND MAKE IT COMFORTABLE, THE weeks passed quickly. After a fortnight, we'd employed a young stableman called Thomas and Hannah, who doubled as a maid and cook. By September, most of the rooms were clean and livable, and Comet relocated his rat hunting to the stables and shed. Alex and Mr. Harris had restored many of the damaged windows, doors, and walls, and the garden was tidier with the grass cut and some of the beds turned.

A month of sharing a house with Alex revealed to me how greatly I'd underestimated him. Whereas William's intellect, energy, and ambition had always impressed me, Alex's constancy, pragmatism, and diligence drew new appreciation from me. Not only did he make the house habitable, but he also ensured my life was easier.

The day after Comet's run-in with the butcher, Alex had offered to go to the village to buy provisions on my behalf until we appointed a maid. I knew I should've insisted on doing it myself. Shopping was my responsibility. However, I was so grateful to be able to avoid the cheerless center and brazen butcher that I'd accepted. A few times a week, Alex took the list of supplies

I wrote and returned with items. He did so without comment or complaint, except for once when, on his return, he pointed to a package.

"There are some extra slices of bacon in there, courtesy of Mr. Corden," he said.

"Who is Mr. Corden? Why did he give us bacon?" I asked.

My brother raised his shoulders. "He's the butcher. Said he'd not had the opportunity to properly welcome us to the area."

I stared at his retreating form, uncertain who of the two men was the more mysterious: my brother or the butcher with the bouncy, black curls.

I was not the only one who benefited from Alex's selflessness and efforts. When he wasn't helping me or working with Mr. Harris, our brother assisted William and Thomas assemble workbenches, hang tools, and turn the stables into something of a telescope factory.

Whereas previously I'd judged Alex for being shy, cheerless, and solemn, I now saw that he was also thoughtful and wise. His earnestness and prudence encouraged the calm clarity we required to face some of the uncertainty and challenges presented by being in Datchet. Alex was reticent. He said little, but when he spoke, he was worth listening to. He didn't squander his energy on trivial matters. When Alex applied himself to a task, he did so with creativity, vigor, and resolve until the job was done. While in Bath he had seemed indecisive, I now realized that Alex was simply averse to rash decision-making. He was often better at solving problems than William and I were.

We'd always known that Alex would be in Datchet for only two months. He was to return to Bath in October to resume work as a musician. Even so, William and I tried to persuade him to stay.

"I'm certain we'll be able to make up your income and more if you remain and help build telescopes," said William. "The orders will come as more astronomers see our instruments. His Majesty has already indicated he would like to improve those at Greenwich."

"But you don't have orders yet," said Alex. "We cannot all live off your salary. I must return to Bath. Besides, I want to make music."

I tried another tack. Unlike me, Alex was accustomed to working with different bands and music directors. "Perhaps you could find work as a musician in London. You could continue to live here and travel there for work. We have so much space, Alex. It seems silly for you to rent rooms elsewhere."

He was unmoved. "My interests are in Bath."

I wondered if his interests still included Miss Cohlman. It would be like Alex to hope he might rekindle the romance.

Regardless of what we said or how often, Alex's resolve to return to Bath remained firm, and as William was frequently summoned to Windsor and spent more and more time there, I began counting the days until October. Little over a month before, I'd scoffed at the idea of living with Alex, and yet here I was, dreading his departure.

It wasn't just that he was helpful, but also that, with William increasingly absent, I'd miss his company. Also, despite the fact the house was more comfortable than it was when we'd arrived, it remained excessively large and drafty. It was an eerie place, particularly when William and the servants were gone and Alex, Comet, and I were left to try to breathe life into the big rooms.

It was in this mood of gloomy anticipation, as I arranged William's notes in the library early one September afternoon, that I heard hooves and wheels on the gravel driveway. William was at court, and Alex was in the stables. I assumed it was someone delivering material for my brothers, until Hannah tapped on the doorpost.

"There's a lady come to see you, Miss Herschel," she said. "Miss Hudson from Bath."

As if about to attend a lesson with Miss Fleming and her friend, I straightened my skirts and patted my hair as I hurried to the door. No letters had passed between me and Miss Hudson since we'd said our goodbyes. Despite her insisting she'd visit, I hadn't given the possibility any thought once we'd moved. Was Alex right about her interest in William? He'd warned us she'd visit soon. Indeed, there she was, her voluminous hair patted and powdered, and her matching gown, gloves, and feather headpiece filling the hallway like a frothy, pale blue vision. We spoke over each other.

"Miss Hudson! What a surprise!"

"Miss Herschel! I'm sorry I didn't let you know—"

With the excitement over and both of us seated in the drawing room, Miss Hudson explained that her aunt, who lived in Kensington in London, had sent a carriage to Bath to bring her niece to visit her for a few weeks. Once on the road, Miss Hudson had—on something of a whim, she insisted—told the carriage driver they'd stop at Datchet.

"I shouldn't have come unannounced, I know. You've barely settled," she said. "But it seemed a pity to pass by without, at the very least, having a cup of tea with you."

"But you should stay the night," I said.

"Really? Since you insist, of course I will," she replied.

When Hannah brought us tea, I told her to ask Thomas to help Miss Hudson's carriage driver stable and feed her horses.

"What a change this is," said Miss Hudson as Hannah left the room. "Servants, stables, and such a large house."

I followed her gaze as she looked around. The drawing room was the finest of the rooms downstairs, and that day, with the afternoon sun angling through the windows and William's best furniture in place, I could see why she might believe our circumstances had improved. However, I suspected that when she ascended the creaking stairway with its misaligned banister and saw how sparingly furnished the rest of the house was—including the guest room—she'd realize that size, servants, and stables didn't account for everything.

"It helps that my brother can build his telescopes in the stables. He's converted a large part of it to workshops. You must recall how cluttered our Bath home was with instruments and the construction thereof," I said.

"How you managed, I do not know." She turned her head to survey the room again. "Yes, this is a great improvement. It's just a pity you're so far away from Bath."

"But we're close to Windsor and that's why we're here," I replied.

"Yes, indeed." She took a sip of tea. "Does your brother spend much time at court?"

"Every week, he's there longer. He's away three nights this week."

She stiffened. "He's away? Now?"

"Yes, since Monday. He'll return on Thursday—unless His Majesty decides otherwise."

"Oh. I shall have to be gone by then." She paused for a moment and then said, "Actually, Miss Herschel, I was too hasty in accepting your kind offer to stay. I *must* leave this afternoon, or my aunt will worry."

"Oh! Are you certain? That's—"

She ignored me. "Is Windsor Castle not close enough for Mr. Herschel to return each night? To sleep in his bed? Isn't that why you moved here?"

"Most of his work happens at night, and if His Majesty or anyone else at the castle wants to observe the heavens with him, he has to be there," I said, not bothering to explain how William's travels back and forth also required transporting his seven-foot telescope, which, given its size and fragility, was no mean feat.

"Of course," replied Miss Hudson.

"What's more, he relies on a court carriage. He can't simply up and go whenever it suits him," I added.

"He hasn't a horse? A carriage?" she asked.

"Not yet, no. He's hoping to get a horse soon. He's impatient for one even. Not only because it'll make his travels to court and back easier but also because he loves the animals and riding," I said.

Miss Hudson's eyes lit up. "Yes. Miss Fleming's brother entertained us with stories about how Mr. Herschel rode across the kingdom teaching music before he settled in Bath. The distances he covered were immense. Mr. Fleming said your brother traveled so far and worked so hard he often slept on his horse."

"He did, but not often," I interjected.

"He said Mr. Herschel was taken in by dukes and duchesses who were so impressed by his dedication and music that they invited him to stay and entertain their dinner parties," she continued.

"There was one occasion—"

She wasn't to be interrupted. "Mr. Fleming said that no man has ridden farther or touched as many with his music as your brother." She sighed as she leaned back in the chair. "And to think he is lost to us. To music. To Bath. Oh, I am sorry to miss him."

Miss Hudson didn't linger much longer. Without the chance of seeing William, she was soon on her way. As I waved her goodbye, I realized she'd barely inquired after my well-being.

CHAPTER 8

October 1782
Datchet, England

ALEX'S RETURN TO BATH ECLIPSED THE SIGNIFICANCE OF MISS HUDSON'S BRIEF visit, and it was my brother I was thinking of as I stood in the library a week after his departure. Although William and I had repeatedly asked him when he might visit again, Alex had refused to say. He didn't like dealing with possibilities.

"I'll write when I'm certain," he'd said.

Being in Datchet without Alex was as lonely as I'd feared. It didn't help that William was away when he'd left and still hadn't returned. Outside, Hannah was chatting to Mr. Harris as he raked a rusty carpet of leaves from the path. She threw back her head and laughed at something he said. I felt the same nick of resentment and loneliness I'd experienced the evening before when Hannah mentioned, when she was about to leave, that she'd planned a surprise meal to celebrate her husband's birthday.

After she'd gone, I'd sat and stared into the fire, Comet curled up at my feet. I'd imagined the swell of music as the orchestra played, and I'd sung the "Hallelujah Chorus" from Handel's *Messiah* until the dog lifted his muzzle and gave a long, pleading yowl.

I'd stopped and patted him. "You're right, Comet. It doesn't sound the same without the orchestra."

Although I'd recognized the comedy in Comet's response to my singing, I was miserable. The house was large and cold, but it was habitable and the servants took care of most matters. I was restless and eager to learn more about astronomy so I could work alongside William. However, the demands of His Majesty meant my brother was at court a great deal, leaving no time to teach or include me in his work.

Now, as I watched Hannah leave Mr. Harris to his raking and walk toward the house, I looked around the library. I'd arranged William's books and notes on the shelves Alex had built. The furniture had been carefully positioned so that when William finally had time to observe the heavens in the yard, I could sit inside and make notes as he called them to me. The ink was ready for mixing, there was a quill waiting, and the room was clean. There was nothing more for me to do. I paged through the copy of Christian Mayer's *Double Star Catalog,* which I'd made for William months earlier. Perhaps, if I was lucky, William would come home with another catalog that required copying. It was a good way of studying the stars. I wanted to learn, work, and occupy my days productively. The weather was turning, and soon, even my daily walks with Comet would be checked.

When I lifted the catalog to place it on the shelf, I discovered a letter lying beneath it. The single page was neatly folded, but the seal was broken. It was addressed to William in Jacob's hand. I opened and read it.

In his typically abrupt manner, Jacob spared a little ink thanking William for his recent letter before getting to what was clearly the purpose of the correspondence.

Given that you have settled in Datchet where our sister cannot sing and have even employed servants, I do not understand what use Caroline is to you. You say she helps with your stargazing, but in the next sentence, you write how frequently you are at court. It angers me to think you are disregarding your agreement with Mother. If Caroline is not useful to you in England, she must return to Hanover and take care of our ailing mother. My wife is increasingly bitter about how much time she must

*spend attending Mother, who is not only old and sick but also evermore
ill-tempered, and I cannot ask more from her. I insist you honor your word
to me and Mother and send Caroline home.*

I wasn't surprised by Jacob's words. I knew he wanted me back in his and
our mother's command. However, the letter stressed the urgency of my learning more about astronomy and becoming more useful to William. It wasn't just
that I was curious, keen to understand the heavens, and eager to be engaged. I
also worried William might concede that I might, after all, be more useful in
Hanover than I was in Datchet and yield to Jacob's demands. I had to prove I
was indispensable to William soon.

A knock at the door interrupted my thoughts. It was Hannah.

"Thomas says there's a man arrived at the stables with a horse for Mr.
Herschel," she said.

A horse? That was unforeseen. It was unlike William not to tell me to
expect something as important as the delivery of a horse. Of course, he'd been
eager to get one ever since we arrived in Datchet, but he'd said he'd have to
wait until after winter. The repairs to the house had been expensive. Something
must've changed and he'd forgotten to mention it. I pulled on my cloak and
went outside, where I found Thomas talking to a man who'd dismounted and
held the reins of a saddled horse in one hand and the halter rope of another in
the other. The unsaddled animal was a tall bay with a strip of white down his
nose. His eyes darted from left to right as if he too was uncertain about why
he'd been led to Datchet.

Thomas saw me. "Good day, Miss Herschel. I'm sorry to have disturbed
you. It's just I didn't know anything about a horse arriving today," he said.

"Neither did I," I replied, looking at the man.

He tipped his hat. "I beg your pardon, miss, but I've ridden from London.
Your man says this *is* the home of Mr. Herschel, King's Astronomer, which is
where I was instructed to deliver him," he said.

"But where is he from? Did Mr. Herschel tell you to bring him?" I asked.

"No, Miss Herschel. He comes from the stables of Lady Charlotte Sutton,"
he replied.

There was something familiar about the name. *Was Lady Sutton one of the many people William had met since his appointment?* I wondered. Even if she was, it didn't explain why William hadn't warned me about the animal's arrival.

"Were you to deliver him with a note, perhaps?" I asked.

He shook his head. "Lady Sutton's niece gave me no reason to think you weren't expecting him, miss."

"Lady Sutton's niece?"

"Yes," he replied. "Miss Hudson."

Startling both the men and horses, I emitted what Miss Fleming and Miss Hudson would've condemned as "a most unladylike splutter" had they heard it.

"Miss Hudson?" I repeated. "Do you mean Miss Lydia Hudson of Bath?" The man nodded. "Aye, that's her."

"Hmm. I don't suppose you know why Miss Hudson sent him?" I asked.

"I don't, miss," he said. "I'm sorry, but it wasn't my place to ask."

"No, of course not," I said.

I could only guess that the horse was a gift from Miss Hudson to William, which was absurd and inappropriate. Polite society would be aghast. Not only was the idea of an unmarried woman giving any gift—let alone one as expensive and extravagant as a horse—to an unmarried man with whom she had no familial connection or contract improper, but it was also shocking she imagined William would accept it. When I'd told him about her visit to Datchet weeks earlier, he'd responded as I'd expected, with polite indifference. There was no reason to imagine my brother was keeping anything from me. The interest was one-sided, all hers.

The horse shifted his weight and snorted impatiently. Shiny, lean, and alert, he was a splendid animal. But even if she'd sent a donkey, Miss Hudson's notion that my brother would accept her gift was ludicrous. How others could interpret her imprudence might be scandalous. Her folly and indiscretion shouldn't be exposed. The horse would have to be returned but in a manner that protected everyone involved.

As I stepped closer, the animal arched his neck and rolled his eyes toward me. "Of course! I'd forgotten Miss Hudson's kind offer to lend *me* a horse," I said, stroking his shoulder before turning to the man. "Thank you for bringing him."

He blinked. "He's for you, miss? Well, he's very young and spirited. I hope—"

I cut him off, not wanting to add to the fib. "Thomas, take the horse to the stables and ask Hannah to prepare some refreshments for this kind man before he returns to London."

Thomas scratched his head. He had a question or two for me.

"The stables, Thomas," I said, evoking my firmest tone.

William found me reading in the drawing room when he returned early the following afternoon. His smile was wider than usual, and his eyes glistened as they did when he was especially amused.

"Thomas tells me you're set on learning to ride," he said. "I had no idea it was something you wanted to do." He glanced at Comet, who stood near my chair, his tail wagging slowly. "First a dog and now a horse."

I closed my book and set it aside. "He's not for me."

"But there's a beautiful young gelding in the stable. Lent to you by Miss Hudson, says Thomas."

It was a relief to hear William hadn't anticipated the horse's arrival. Although I'd told myself it was nonsensical, I'd briefly worried the previous night that my brother and Miss Hudson might've shared an understanding they'd kept from me.

"The horse is, as I understand it, a gift to you from Miss Hudson," I said.

"A gift? For me? Of course not! You must be mistaken. Your wanting to learn to ride is unexpected, but Miss Hudson's presenting me with a gift, a horse, is preposterous," said William, his smile replaced by narrow-eyed incredulity.

"Yes," I replied.

He stared at me. "But that makes no sense. I mean to get a horse, of course, but that she… Did you mention I wanted one when she was here last month? What did you say? What would induce her to do such a thing?"

"I did. I told her you planned to get a horse. She responded with a detailed account of what Mr. Fleming had told her and his sister about what an eager and accomplished horseman you are. There was no mention of her sending you a horse," I said.

"Are you certain he was delivered to the correct house?" he asked.

I explained my exchange with the stableman and how I'd pretended the animal was on loan to me to avoid gossip.

"You haven't written to Miss Hudson then? No note sent back with the man?" he asked, sitting on the chaise lounge opposite me.

"No. I thought it better to wait for your return."

William rubbed his head. I felt a nip of anger at Miss Hudson. It was inconceivable that someone as refined as I'd believed her to be was so impetuous. Was her infatuation with my brother so compelling it ruled out all common sense? It annoyed me that she hadn't considered how upsetting her behavior might be. She risked both her and William's reputations.

"I'm at a loss as to how to fix this," said William.

"Send the horse back. There's nothing else to do," I replied.

"Yes. Of course. But without explanation? She's your friend, Lina. Even if she weren't, I wouldn't want to insult her."

I clenched my teeth. "Miss Hudson isn't—well, she's an unusual friend. I fear she might've overstated her regard for me because she's fascinated by you. I think Alex was right. Her interest in the Herschel family has less to do with me than with you."

William frowned but didn't argue.

"I believe she wanted me to stay in Bath because she hoped it would encourage you to visit. When that didn't work, she concocted a reason to come to Datchet. Having not found you here, she induced her aunt to give her a horse to send to you," I continued.

"Her aunt? The horse isn't hers?" he asked.

"I suspect not. The man who brought the horse said he came from the stables of Lady Sutton. That's the aunt she's visiting in London," I said.

"Good gracious! It gets worse. What, I wonder, did she tell her aunt? What would've persuaded Her Ladyship to give her niece a horse to offer as a gift to a man she barely knows?" said William, scratching his head again.

We were quiet for a moment. Then it came to me.

"Maybe Miss Hudson kept the truth from her aunt. She's elderly and in poor health. Lady Sutton might've given her the horse without knowing her intentions, and since the man who delivered the animal received such vague instructions as to the purpose of the animal, we can return him with similar vagueness," I said.

He looked at me. "How so?"

"I'll write to Miss Hudson, thanking her for her gift but insisting I cannot accept it. My letter will indicate we believed the horse was for me. I might even write how I briefly entertained the idea of keeping him and learning to ride but that *you* insisted we could not accept such generosity. We'll send the letter with the horse. There'll be no mistaking the gesture," I said.

William exhaled. "Hmm. A little devious, isn't it?"

"It'll save us all from embarrassment," I replied.

The room was quiet until Comet, asleep on the carpet, whimpered and twitched as if dreaming of rabbits.

My brother laced his fingers together and stretched his arms above his head. "All right. I can't see an alternative. I trust you to be explicit but kind. There's no need to humiliate her. It's misguided, but, well, I'm not sure what she hoped to achieve by it." He rubbed his forehead. "But we must do it soon. Write the letter, send it with the horse, and say nothing about it to anyone."

I wondered whom he thought I might have occasion to talk to. I knew no one in Datchet, and Miss Hudson was the only visitor I'd entertained.

"He's a beautiful horse, bursting with energy. I'm tempted to take him for a ride, but my conscience won't allow it," he added as if thinking aloud.

"If the horse would benefit from the exercise, you might—"

"No!" He chuckled and stood up. "Remember, we believe the horse was for you, not me. And anyway, I have something for you, a gift, which I trust you'll accept with great pleasure and no misgivings. Wait while I fetch it."

A gift? For me? These two days had certainly produced some unexpected turns. The only other gift my brother had given me was money to buy a gown for my first performance in Bath. I'd been overwhelmed by nerves and hadn't truly appreciated the gesture or the gown.

William returned moments later carrying what I recognized as a telescope wrapped in cloth. He laid it on the chaise lounge and unwound the fabric. I wasn't wrong, but this telescope had a much larger aperture than usual. It was also significantly shorter and fatter.

"It's yours," he said. "A two-foot Newtonian reflector. It's unique. I designed it especially for you to sweep the heavens and hunt for comets."

I stood, staring at him. I was speechless. My own telescope? Despite having watched my brothers make instruments for years, I'd never imagined owning one. When had William found the time to build it? How had he done it without my knowledge? While I'd been worrying that he had no time to train me to work with him, he'd been making me a telescope. I felt light headed with a mix of emotions. Excitement. Gratitude. Joy.

Before I could assemble my thoughts to speak, Thomas appeared in the doorway. He was carrying what might've been a boxy, three-legged wooden stool.

"Put it here, Thomas. Thank you," said William.

The young man placed the contraption before us and left.

My brother rubbed his hands together. "First things first," he said, lifting the telescope. "See how powerful it is with the big aperture and its wide-angle vision? It has a four-inch reflector that provides an observational field over two degrees."

I peered at the instrument. "But when? How?" I was babbling like a child. "I mean, four inches?"

"I know! It allows you to see faint objects brightly while simultaneously providing a view of the surrounding stars," he said.

"And this?" I asked, pointing at the wooden apparatus. "This is its frame, is it?"

It was. William had designed the telescope holder so that I could comfortably carry it and the telescope wherever I wanted and set it up to observe, even when I was home alone. A series of pulleys and a winding handle would allow me to easily and accurately adjust the height and angle of the viewing lens.

"I don't know what to say. I thought—" I said when he paused for a breath while demonstrating the apparatus.

His eyes met mine. "Alex said I should tell you, but I wanted to surprise you."

I returned his smile. "You succeeded," I said, glad he hadn't given me a chance to tell him how my idle, recent days in Datchet had given way to worrying he wouldn't have time to help me learn more about astronomy. "It's a wonderful surprise. Will you show me how to use it tonight?"

William chuckled. "I told our brother you'd be excited and that once you begin observing the heavens, they'll fascinate you like they do me."

"I hoped you'd have time to teach me but never imagined having my own instrument," I said.

"Once we've erected the twenty-footer here, you can take notes while I observe. But if you can also mind the heavens alone when I am gone, it will help me comprehensively record the stars and nebulae. You can sweep for comets and record everything you see. We'll discuss your observations and, once I've checked them, add them to the catalogs," he said.

I carefully lifted the telescope and balanced it across my arms. It was cold and solid against my skin and, despite my surprise at its existence, significant in a way I hadn't expected. I hadn't yet placed an eye to it, but already the instrument had clarified my thoughts.

William wanted me to help him, but I wanted more. I wanted to understand everything, to watch the stars, hunt for comets, and try to understand more about the heavens. I wanted to learn as much as William, to feed my curiosity and find answers to questions no one thought to ask. The telescope was the key to a new world for me, a world in which I'd learn to love the stars as much as I loved music.

I looked at the instrument, slowly gazing from the eyepiece to the aperture and back again. It dawned on me that the heavens could be the chance for me to become someone more than the tiny, scarred woman who cared for and served others. I'd once proved myself useful to William as a singer. Perhaps, by making discoveries valuable to the world, I could finally show my mother and Jacob I could be useful beyond our family.

CHAPTER 9

October 1782
Datchet, England

THE MOMENT THE INKY POINT OF MY QUILL TOUCHED THE WRITING PAPER, I realized I'd been thinking about what I'd like to say to Miss Hudson for hours, perhaps ever since I'd discovered she was behind the arrival of the horse.

I wrote quickly, editing the sharp edges of my thoughts as I expressed my surprise, thanked her for her charity, and explained why *I* couldn't accept her gift. She had to understand William sanctioned what I wrote. It was also crucial the letter didn't invite discussion. It wouldn't do for Miss Hudson to consider sending the horse back and explaining my mistake, saying he was meant for William. I concluded as emphatically as I could without being impolite.

> *We are, as my brothers assert, a modest family determined to maintain*
> *a reputation of propriety. Out of respect for you and society and to avoid*
> *any possible misunderstandings or breaches of decorum, we cannot accept*
> *your kind offer under any circumstances.*

"Take a look," I said, handing the letter to William. "I hope I have the tone right and that my words leave no room for misunderstanding."

He nodded as he read. "It's well done. You've spared her injury and given her no reason to question your sincerity. Why, it even makes me wonder if it's not possible she *did* mean you to have the horse."

"Ha! As if I've ever given anyone the slightest idea I might wish to learn to ride," I said, laughing.

"You've surprised us before." He gestured at Comet, who was curled up on the rug. "I have no doubt Miss Hudson will visit you on her way back to Bath and you'll have a pleasant time. You've given her no cause to feel slighted. I'll tell Thomas to deliver the letter to her when he returns the horse tomorrow."

I folded the page, addressed and sealed it, and placed it on the table before walking to the window. It was dark outside and, I suspected, cold, but the skies were clear. When I turned to William, he was already on his feet.

"I'll get the telescope. You bring the frame," I said, going to the chaise lounge, where—reminding me of an artist's model—the instrument reclined upon its cloth wrapping.

We went into the garden, setting up the telescope in a dark corner far from the flickering light of the indoor lanterns. The air was still but even icier than I'd feared. However, as I rubbed my hands together and gazed at the gently twinkling tapestry of stars and the faint glow of the Milky Way, the anticipation of using my own telescope alleviated the cold.

Hello again, I said silently as I looked up at the stars.

"It's all yours," said William, pulling his collar around his ears after having peered through the eyepiece and making a few adjustments. "Take a look and I'll show you how to fine-tune it."

He'd pointed the aperture at Saturn, and although I'd observed the planet's rings through William's telescopes before, they had never seemed more ethereal. I lingered, fascinated by the mystery of the spheres. Would we ever know why they existed or what they were made of?

Little by little, I moved the instrument horizontally, searching for objects against the dark backdrop the way William had taught me. What I'd seen as a hazy smudge of light with the naked eye turned into a dazzling ball of stars, alive and shimmering like dancing shards of glass. I swept again until the aperture settled on Messier 42. Without the advantage of William's teaching, I probably would've mistaken the nebula for a simple cloud lit by moonlight, causing an unusual greenish hue. However, I knew otherwise and spent several minutes admiring how the stars banded around the swirl of dust and gas, as if drawn to its beauty. It was no surprise some believed that the gates of heaven were located behind Messier 42.

"You're pleased, I take it," said William, who'd stood, unusually quietly, alongside me as I observed.

"I am," I said, continuing to look. "But what gives you that impression?"

He laughed. "It's one of the coldest nights of the year and you haven't complained. And it's not as if you've never looked through a telescope before."

I didn't respond. It *was* different. I'd never had my own telescope or imagined observing alone previously. Although he'd invited me to look through his instruments for instructional purposes, William had always been the primary observer while I'd taken notes. Until now, magnified stargazing had been limited to snatched moments for me. With my own telescope, I could observe whenever I wanted to and for as long as I liked.

William insisted astronomy involved as much calculating, writing, and drawing as it did observing. It was about examining the heavens, recording everything, comparing what you saw with the atlas and what others had recorded in catalogs, calculating orbits, analyzing your records to reveal potential new findings, and reporting them. That hadn't changed. What was different was that I had a telescope, which meant William had faith in me to undertake it all—and alone whenever I wanted.

That night—although I went indoors at some point, pulled on another woolen petticoat, and returned with an additional overcoat for William—we spent several hours observing. With every minute, I grew more excited. The telescope was the perfect size and weight for me, easy to use, and comfortable against my eye. I'd never felt more immersed in the swirls of cloud and color, pathways of stars, and deep, dark depths of the night sky. But it was more than what the instrument could do that excited me; it was what it meant I might do.

William's gift sparked new ambition in me. He wanted me to be his assistant. I would oblige. However, having my own telescope meant that when he went away or didn't need my assistance, I could be more. I could learn to practice astronomy independently, to be an astronomer like him. The realization made me sigh.

"What is it?" asked William. "Are you tired?"

I shook my head but said nothing. I wasn't ready to reveal my dream. If I did, he'd almost certainly remind me there were no women astronomers or, indeed, any women members of the Royal Society. Women weren't philosophers or scientists. William would probably say it was impossible for me to become an astronomer, and I might believe him. What's more, to avoid being sent back to Hanover, I had to continually prove my usefulness to William. I couldn't risk him questioning it. So, I'd say nothing. There was much to learn, but I was thrilled by the prospect of working toward something that could give me even more joy than I'd found singing. Not only was I fascinated by the heavens, but also much of the work was undertaken alone and quietly. It pleased me that, in my new role, I wouldn't have to once again find the courage to present my tiny, scarred self to an audience.

From there on, whenever William was away and the skies were clear and the night air not too painfully cold, I went into the garden with my telescope. My priority was to learn what William called "the real heavens." The identities and positions of the fixed stars, constellations, clusters, and nebulae were not secure in my mind. Unlike my brother, I couldn't point out an object and find it again without consulting the atlas. If I was to learn, I'd have to approach the heavens the way I'd tackled singing: with practice, practice, and practice. By repeatedly sweeping the heavens with my telescope, noting my observations, and checking them, I'd memorize the primary structure of the sky. This, I hoped, would eventually allow me to find anomalies and make discoveries.

It wasn't always possible to observe. When winter drew her curtains across the skies and sprinkled the earth with ice, I sat close to the fire with Comet, studying the atlas, William's catalogs, and my notes. I was determined to fasten the objects to my mind.

Finally, after several studious wintery months, William happened to be away on a clear, calm night. The temperature was so mild and the air so still, I persuaded the dog to accompany me and my telescope into the garden.

"You're sure to find a mouse over there to entertain you," I told him, pointing to a clump of long grass several yards away.

Comet ignored my suggestion and curled up alongside my stool. His quiet company in the large, eerie yard wasn't all that pleased me. From the moment I began scanning the heavens, I recognized objects and patterns. In fact, before I moved from one celestial body to the next, I could anticipate the sequence. "It's working," I whispered, as if Comet were invested in my efforts. "I'm getting to know them."

With every body I recognized—open star clusters, nebulae, galaxies, and globular clusters—I experienced a flicker of excitement. I didn't yet know them all. A few I distinguished but couldn't name. However, I recognized the feeling. It was the same soothing familiarity I'd experienced in Bath when I sang for an audience. I was at home, not in front of an audience this time but beneath the night sky with my stars.

I closed my eyes for a moment and let the feeling linger. Then I resumed scanning. Everything was in place until I spotted a faint, diffused patch of light in the Andromeda Galaxy. What was it? Why hadn't I noticed it previously? Or had I forgotten it?

Holding still, I saw that the hazy area contained several blue stars. It had the fuzzy, starry speckled features of a nebula. Could it be? Thinking I might've confused its location, I slowly scanned the expanse around it. Even then, it was unfamiliar. Was it possible I'd discovered an unrecorded body?

"Imagine that!" I said. "If it is what I think it is, it could be my first significant step toward becoming a true astronomer."

Comet raised his head.

"I know." I got to my feet. "I'm getting ahead of myself. It's possible I've overlooked it. Let's go inside and check."

The dog followed me and settled on a rug on the library floor while I pored over the atlas and catalogs. He didn't move when I returned outside to continue observing. It didn't matter. By then, I was too excited to fear the darkness of Datchet. The nebula wasn't recorded in Messier's catalog. I couldn't be absolutely certain until William saw it, but the thrill of imagining I might've discovered my first celestial object made me feel as if I were floating through the night air.

Finally, exhausted and certain I'd seen enough, I left the telescope and went to the low stone wall running along the front of the property. Ignoring the moss and fallen leaves cloaking the boulders, I clambered up and lay down on the wall's flat top, my eyes to the skies. The rocky surface was surprisingly comfortable. Or perhaps I was simply distracted by the stars, which had never seemed livelier or more bounteous. Were they shining for me? Encouraging me? I breathed in rhythm to their flickering, imagining their light warming and filling me. If William confirmed I was right about the nebula, it might be the ideal time to tell him about my ambitions to learn as much about astronomy as him. Would I be brave enough to do so when the sun lit the sky and the stars disappeared?

The following afternoon, I thrust my notes at William the moment he arrived home.

"Slow down! Slow down!" he said, once he'd deciphered enough of my babble to understand why I was excited. "Let me take my coat off, and we'll go to the library and discuss it calmly."

Moments later, he examined my sketches and notes while I repeated my announcement in more measured tones. His silence didn't surprise me. He was thinking, comparing and checking. However, when he finally spoke, I was disappointed by his apparent indifference.

"Everything you've noted indicates it's a new discovery, but I'll have to observe it myself to be sure," he said.

"Of course," I replied. "If the weather holds tonight, we—"

"I won't be here tonight. I came to fetch an eyepiece and must return to the castle immediately," he said.

"But—"

"I'll look for it tonight from Windsor. If it is what you propose, it will be there when I return. In fact, it's the perfect object to examine with the twenty-footer."

I stared at him. "But the weather might change. And the twenty-footer? But that won't be possible for ages yet."

The metalwork for the tube for the twenty-footer was almost complete, and planks for the frame and platform had been cut and were ready to assemble, but the reflector was still to be cast and polished.

William stood and went to the door. "Well, Lina, you keep an eye on your alleged nebula until then. You've done well. Keep hunting and you'll find more. Perhaps even a comet."

That night, with my telescope strained on the nebula, I lamented William's muted response to my news. I knew he'd be cautious about it. He had to check my claims, but I'd expected him to be more excited, not only about what I believed to be an unrecorded nebula but also by the idea of my having learned enough to spot it. Did he doubt me or think my discovery was simply good luck? I was glad I hadn't revealed my ambitions to him.

CHAPTER 10

June 1783
Datchet, England

T<small>RY AS</small> I <small>MIGHT TO FOCUS ON ITS MERITS—THE COUNTRYSIDE WAS PRETTY, THE</small>
stables provided ample space for work rooms, and the garden was big enough
for the twenty-footer and ideal for observing through my telescope—Datchet
failed to charm me. It didn't help that, despite the efforts of both Alex and Mr.
Harris, the house continued to deteriorate. The building was old, the materials
were decomposing, and the repairs were makeshift.

Although Mr. Harris had long since lost the agility of youth, he depend-
ably climbed ladders, perched on the steep roof, and patched every leak
Hannah and I reported. Unfortunately, two or three more seepages inevitably
revealed themselves with the next rains, and the damp settled into the floors
and ceilings in furry smears of mold. At times, the wind swept inside through
the warped doors and window frames with such velocity, Comet's ears fluttered
when he crossed its path.

Alex might've offered solutions had he visited. However, when he wrote
to say he was once more betrothed, William and I knew he'd be even less
inclined to leave Bath when the season ended. We were consoled by the fact
his intended wasn't Miss Cohlman. This time, he'd settled on the widow Mrs.

Margaret Smith. We were yet to meet her, when we received a letter from Alex telling us they'd exchanged vows at Walcot Church in Bath.

"Don't be disappointed," said William as he handed me the letter. "We knew Alex wouldn't rest until he was married."

He was right, but I was aggrieved, nonetheless. Marriage would probably keep Alex from us. Besides, I couldn't understand why he'd wanted it. He'd seen how getting married had strangled the joy from Sophia Elizabeth. Surely he'd also noticed how little our parents seemed to care for each other? All evidence indicated matrimony bred unhappiness.

If only Alex were as wise in that regard as William, I thought.

At forty-five years old and seven years Alex's senior, William had proved, contrary to what society expected, it wasn't necessary to take a wife. Although we'd never spoken about it, I was sure William believed as I did that, despite what others felt, marriage was unnecessary and disruptive. Why hadn't Alex followed his lead?

It wasn't just Alex's happiness I was concerned about. We'd hoped his being with us in Datchet would ease our mounting financial woes. William wanted him to help build telescopes. The more quickly commissions were completed, the sooner we'd be paid. I'd wanted Alex to continue patching up the house. We couldn't afford anyone else to do it. Our expenses rose every month. Paying for materials for the telescopes, particularly the twenty-footer, and William's trips from Datchet to Windsor, Greenwich, and London and back, and transporting his instruments and other components added up. We were forever short of money.

Among my daytime tasks—I never missed an opportunity to observe at night if William didn't need me—was keeping a close eye on work on the twenty-footer when William was at court and, at all times, managing the accounts for the house and all the machines under construction.

With a focal length of twenty feet, a clear aperture of eighteen and a half inches, and a sweeping power of one hundred and fifty-seven, the twenty-footer was, of course, the most ambitious, expensive, and time-consuming project we'd undertaken. It also involved the complex design and assembly of a frame and platform to house the tube.

Despite the unfinished and unsteady nature of the frame, once the instrument was more or less operational and installed, my brother insisted on clambering about on the platform in the dark and sweeping whenever the skies were clear.

"I know it's not ready, but I must test it," said William when I expressed concern about his safety.

One night, he finally used the twenty-footer to observe and verify the nebula I'd seen with my telescope.

"Here, Lina," he said later, pointing to his notes on the cloud of dust and gas. "Your discovery, your name. It's a moment of great pride. I shall notify Greenwich right away."

William had written, "This nebula was discovered by my sister Caroline Herschel, with an excellent small Newtonian sweeper of twenty-seven inches focal length and a power of thirty. I have therefore marked it with the initial letters, C.H. of her name."

Feeling churlish about wishing he'd shown more enthusiasm when I'd first seen the nebula, I returned his smile. It *was* "a moment of great pride," and it felt good to eventually receive my brother's acknowledgment for the discovery.

"Does having one's initials alongside a nebula make one an astronomer?" I asked, only half joking.

My brother laughed. "It makes one an able assistant with an excellent sweeper," he replied, confirming my doubts were justified. William was unlikely to have taken me seriously if I'd revealed my ambitions.

In addition to trying to complete the twenty-footer, William was occupied by demands for other instruments. In this regard, Dr. Maskelyne visited from Greenwich to discuss four telescopes His Majesty wished to present to royal courts elsewhere.

William was in the workshop, so it fell to me to show Dr. Maskelyne to the library while Hannah went to call him. I'd met Dr. Maskelyne in Bath when my brother discovered Georgium Sidus, but our exchange had been limited to an introduction. Now, in Datchet, I hoped my nerves weren't evident as I invited him to sit.

He glanced around. "Does your brother have a preferred seat?"

I was surprised. Dr. Maskelyne was an imposing man. His broad torso was snugly enclosed in a double-breasted black dress coat and his expansive forehead sloped backward, disappearing beneath a powdered wig with several neat rows of horizontal curls. With a title like Astronomer Royal, Dr. Maskelyne, I presumed, might sit wherever he wished. However, as he looked at me, apparently awaiting my answer, he blinked and smiled self-consciously, and I recognized his reticence.

Great men, I thought, *are also earthly beings.*

"He likes to sit near the window, but this is the most comfortable chair in the room," I replied, gesturing to the wide horsebone chair in which I usually sat.

"You've adjusted comfortably to your changed circumstances I hope, Miss Herschel?" he asked once seated.

"We have," I replied, hoping he hadn't noticed just how ramshackle the house was.

"I believe you're assisting your brother with his work."

I nodded, wondering how he knew.

He smiled and answered the question as if I had voiced it. "I heard your brother made you a telescope. Splendid. I have several assistants and cannot imagine achieving much without them."

I wanted to say how it pleased me to hear him so liberally appreciate his assistants, but I hesitated because I wasn't sure how to express it without embarrassing him. William appeared, and the moment was gone.

"Thank you, Lina," said my brother, dismissing me after he'd greeted his colleague.

How I wished I could stay, listen to their conversation, participate even. I wanted to get to know Dr. Maskelyne better, to ask him what his assistants did, how their work helped him, and whether any of them were women. However, assistants were not included in meetings with royal astronomers. Dr. Maskelyne and I said our goodbyes, and I took my leave.

CHAPTER 11

December 1783
Datchet, England

Eager to deliver the four telescopes ordered by His Majesty and be reimbursed for them before Christmas, William asked me to help him, Thomas, and Mr. Harris polish the reflectors. We were working quietly side by side when the double door leading into the workshop eased open, giving access to an icy blast. I looked up to see Hannah. Behind her, the sky, previously strewn with a smattering of clouds, was now blanketed in dense gray.

"A visitor, Miss Herschel. It's your friend Miss Hudson," said Hannah, closing the door and leaning against it to keep it from blowing open.

William glanced at me from across the room, his eyes twinkling as if to say, "I told you so."

It was unexpected. Thomas had come back from London after returning the gift horse without a word from Miss Hudson. When he'd arrived at her aunt's house, he was told the giver of the gift was out for the day and that he should leave the letter, take the horse to the stables, and return to Datchet.

We heard nothing from her. For a while, William had remained sure she'd visit on her way back to Bath and offer an explanation. I was doubtful, and since we had no idea when she might undertake the journey and were both busy, we stopped wondering what her silence meant. As the months went by, I'd stopped thinking about Miss Hudson until this moment. I straightened, took off my gloves, and wiped my hands on my apron. "Did she ask for me or Mr. Herschel?" I said, looking at my brother. His eyes crinkled in amusement.

Hannah frowned. "Most certainly you, miss."

I followed Hannah across the yard and, recognizing the horse and carriage near the door, felt my heart speed up. Its acceleration reminded me of how I'd felt after I was sent from the room when William had asked Mother if he could take me to England. I'd anticipated the worst, that she'd insist I stay. *This is nothing like that, Caroline,* I told myself now.

Still, I felt a little lightheaded as I entered the house and went to the drawing room, where Miss Hudson stood, her back to the fire. She was wrapped in a full-length, long-sleeved bottle-green pelisse, which fastened in the front with large buttons and a belt that buckled beneath her bosom. I'd forgotten how high she wore her hair. She'd never looked more regal.

"My dear Miss Herschel! It's been too long," she said, swooping across the room and taking my hands in hers. "My goodness. No gloves in these bitter conditions."

"I was wearing an old pair for work and only now removed them," I replied, immediately regretting how defensive I sounded. This wasn't a lesson with Miss Fleming. There was no need for me to explain myself. "This is a surprise. Are you on your way to visit your aunt again?"

"My aunt? Oh no, you didn't hear. She succumbed to illness last year when I was visiting her. So unexpected. So sad. But, well, she was in poor health and at an advanced age. We shouldn't have been surprised."

I stared at her, uncertain how to express my condolences. She didn't let the moment linger.

"Yes, she died. I've since moved to London—into what was her home—to keep house for my cousin. He's *so* grateful to have a lady to take care of household matters. Never married, you see. Yes, I live in Kensington now. I haven't been to Bath since I moved. However, I do hope to visit next year. I miss my friends there. Particularly Miss Fleming."

Has she always talked so quickly and without pause? I wondered. It was almost as if she didn't want me to speak.

"Oh, your little dog!" she exclaimed as Comet settled near the fire. "You still have him. What a comfort he must be to you in this large house. Are you still alone here?"

"My brother William is here," I replied. "He's in the workshop."

She twisted to look out of the window as if she might see William. I noticed the clouds had gathered even closer.

"So, you're not passing through on your way to or from London," I said. "Did you—"

"I wanted to see you. It was another of my whims. I've meant to write but haven't found the time. My life changed quickly when my aunt died and I moved to London. Last night, on impulse, I decided if the weather looked like it would hold, I'd come and visit you. And here I am."

Hannah arrived with the tea tray.

"Did Mr. Harris say anything to you about whether we'd have rain today, Hannah?" I asked.

The gardener was uncannily accurate when it came to foretelling the weather. Hannah and Thomas teased him about his mystic ways. Mr. Harris laughed and insisted that anyone who'd worked outdoors in Datchet for as long as he had understood the weather "as well as they knew the hairs on their hands."

"He said it'll snow before nightfall," said Hannah.

Miss Hudson's eyes widened. "Snow! I noticed the clouds when we crossed the Thames near the village, but snow? Surely not?"

I caught Hannah's eye as she added wood to the fire and had no doubt she was thinking the same as I was: *If Mr. Harris says it'll snow, it'll do just that.*

"We'd better get your horse and man under shelter, Miss Hudson. It'll be wise to stay over," I said.

She raised a gloved hand to her mouth and sat down heavily. "I had no idea. No, Miss Herschel, I cannot impose on you. We'll return immediately. If it gets too bad, I'll find an inn and stay there." She settled into the chair with a sigh. "I'll have a cup of tea and leave right away."

"Hannah," I said, catching her attention as she walked toward the door.

"Tell Thomas to show Miss Hudson's man to the stables." I turned to Miss Hudson. "There's no reason for them to be cold while they wait."

Our guest had accepted a third cup of tea—all the while keeping up an unflagging stream of conversation about fashionable life in London—when I heard a familiar clumping outside. It was William stomping his boots against the stairs to dislodge the dirt. I looked out to see a light swirl of snowflakes dance across the window. Miss Hudson followed my gaze but continued her story about a recent visit to "the delightful Twinings tea shop." However, she did stop talking when William appeared.

As they exchanged greetings, I saw none of the agitations I'd experienced in Miss Hudson earlier. In fact, with my brother's arrival, her prattling slowed as if his presence soothed her.

"I've told Mr. Harris and Thomas to go home," said William, addressing me now. "You should tell Hannah the same." He turned to Miss Hudson. "Your man and horse are safe, warm, and fed for the night."

"Thank you, Mr. Herschel. I'm so grateful to you. If anyone in London had warned me about the weather, I wouldn't have set out. By all accounts, it seemed the ideal day to visit for tea and be home by dark," she said.

William's smile didn't falter, but it seemed to me he was avoiding my eye. Did he believe her? Even if the weather hadn't turned, she'd arrived too late to return to London before nightfall. Moreover, why had she insisted earlier she *wouldn't* stay overnight when it was clearly her intention to do just that?

I left them together and went to tell Hannah she should head home. As I came out of the kitchen, William was about to go upstairs, presumably to change.

"Did she say anything to you?" I asked after checking that the door to the drawing room was closed.

He stopped two stairs up and narrowed his eyes at me. "About what?"

"The horse, of course."

"No. I assume you haven't discussed it either, then?" he said.

"She hasn't given me the chance to say much at all," I replied, keeping my voice low.

William shrugged. "Then we shouldn't ask."

"What?"

"It was ages ago. Her aunt died. She moved to another city. Her life has changed. She didn't write to you when we returned the horse and hasn't since. We haven't seen her. If she chooses not to mention it, we should respect that. It's possible she was ashamed and embarrassed. She might've even forgotten about it," he said.

I stared at him. "Forgotten? How could she have forgotten something as significant as sending you a horse? How can you imagine that's even possible?"

He took another step. "I don't know what she was thinking, what she *is* thinking. But I don't believe it prudent or polite to ask. If Miss Hudson wishes to enlighten us, she will."

Prudent? Polite? Weren't those courtesies *she* owed us? I wanted to argue and ask my brother what he was thinking. It was one thing to be baffled by Miss Hudson's behavior, but I seldom doubted William. However, he ascended the stairs before I could arrange my thoughts.

Miss Hudson was standing at the fireplace again when I returned to the drawing room. She'd removed her pelisse to reveal a delicate, cream-colored dress that mimicked the shape of the green outer garment but for the dress's neckline, which was low and lacey. I was once more struck by her stylishness. She'd always been fashionable, but there was something more sumptuous and moneyed about the London version of Miss Hudson. Her glow of good fortune and health prevailed even against the room's modest lighting and furniture and the rattle of the snow-filled wind at the windows.

As if someone had opened a faucet, she began talking about London again the moment she saw me. It was as if I'd never left. Comet groaned from his spot near the fire, heaved himself to his feet, and slunk away grumpily. He was probably too warm, but he might also have been distancing himself from Miss Hudson's nattering.

Finally, her description of another popular shop came to an end. It was immediately followed by an account of how she and her cousin went to the park on weekends, where they promenaded in esteemed company, and how they were occasionally entertained by showmen with squirrels. There, they also admired carriages and coaches.

I murmured my validations as Miss Hudson spoke of "phaetons," "broughams," "gigs," "barouche-landaus," and various other modes of transport, which I'd neither heard of nor cared to. It was only when William reappeared that she hesitated long enough for me to suggest we go to the dining room.

Once again, everything changed in my brother's company. He and our guest quietly took their places at the table. Savory steam wafted off the stew Hannah had left for us as I spooned it onto our plates. For a while, we ate without talking, the gentle clinking of cutlery against crockery punctuated by the whoosh and wail of the wind as it swirled around the house. Finally, Miss Hudson made noises of appreciation, set down her knife and fork, and looked at William.

"Tell me about your work, Mr. Herschel. Have you made any more exciting discoveries? What's it like being at court?" she asked.

William swallowed, dabbed his mouth, and sat back. It came as no surprise that he responded politely to her questions, but I hadn't anticipated the extent of his answer. He detailed the many hours he spent explaining the heavens to His Majesty at Windsor Castle and how, at home, he observed, cataloged, and wrote about what he saw.

"I know it's not possible in my lifetime, but I want to know everything there is to know about the universe. With every observation, I see how little we understand, but I won't give up," he said.

Miss Hudson listened, occasionally interrupting to ask for clarity on various points. Her tone and volume were much altered. From prattling, voluble, and self-absorbed in the drawing room, she'd become measured, muted, and attentive in the dining room. The incessant chatterbox became an inquiring scholar. She could've been a different woman.

"You haven't mentioned how much time you spend constructing telescopes," I said, addressing my brother.

The corners of his mouth lifted, and he glanced at Miss Hudson. "Of course. I sometimes forget the instruments take up as much time as everything else put together. I've been trying to find mathematical workmen, opticians, and other artisans who might be able to help me the way our brother did in

Bath. Alas, such skills aren't easy to come by. That's why you found Lina working alongside me and our gardener and stable hand today," he said.

William explained how we'd spent months building the twenty-footer and described the many advantages of such a large machine. He chuckled as he told her about the endless hours of grinding and polishing necessary to perfect the reflectors and how easily they cracked during construction or when the weather turned.

Unobserved, I cleared the table. In the kitchen, I saw a bottle of port William had received as a gift from someone at court. Hannah had left it out with three goblets, imagining we might enjoy it after supper. Strangely reluctant to prolong the evening, I put it away.

There was nothing unusual about William's affability. He was always friendly and had quickly learned the ways of the English when he'd arrived in the country as a penniless musician. He knew if he was to be invited into the homes of the wealthy and educated—whether to entertain or teach music—he'd need to understand their customs. William had told me when he'd brought me to Bath how fortuitous the timing was. By then, it was not only acceptable for some paid performers to mix in society, but they were also increasingly admired. However, it was important to fit in as seamlessly as possible. It helped that my brother was naturally charming and generous with his knowledge. Nowhere was this more evident than in his friendships, most notably in the one he enjoyed with Dr. Watson. He and William exchanged regular letters, and Dr. Watson visited when he traveled between Bath and London. However, I couldn't remember ever seeing my brother respond as warmly to a woman as he did to Miss Hudson that wintery night in Datchet.

I stood in the kitchen, where, although their words weren't discernible, it was clear the conversation didn't flounder. It was unlike William to linger at the table after he'd eaten. On most other stormy nights, he would've eaten quickly and hurried to the library to work on his papers, make notes, or decipher mine. Was he beguiled by Miss Hudson? What had happened to the brother who, until now, had seemed impervious to romance? Had her attempt at giving him a horse moved him in a way I hadn't perceived?

He and Miss Hudson looked at me when I returned to the dining room, murmuring their appreciation for the meal. I didn't respond. Instead, I stood behind my chair, my arms folded, a pose I hoped would signal the end of the evening.

"Did Lina tell you about her work?" asked my brother.

Miss Hudson shook her head, her eyes on me.

"She's a great help to me, running back and forth, carrying or testing instruments for me, watching the clock, making notes, copying catalogs, and keeping the accounts in order," he said.

"Really? I had no idea!" she said, blinking theatrically. "From singer to assistant to the King's Astronomer. Your talents are many, Miss Herschel."

It wasn't just her overreaction and insincerity but also her condescending manner that annoyed me. I was also angered by William's description of my tasks. Had he forgotten my telescope and my ability to scan the skies independently? What about the nebula? Why didn't he mention it and explain how significant my discovery was to our understanding of the heavens? He seemed to value only my contributions to his own work. I took hold of the back of the chair. My knuckles were white against my skin, but my skull prickled hot with rage.

"It's nothing," I said quietly, barely disguising my contempt. "All I am, all I know, I owe to my brother. I am only the tool which he shapes to his use—a well-trained puppy would do as much."

For a moment, even the wind was suspended. Miss Hudson's cheeks colored, and she touched her hair, glancing at William from beneath her eyelashes.

"Ah, Lina," he said, his voice low. "That's not—"

"It is," I said through clenched teeth. "And it won't change."

Miss Hudson's eyes flashed in my direction.

"Nothing will change it." My mouth was dry. "No boundless feminine fascination or unexpected visits in fancy carriages or equine gifts from London will change it. You will not seduce my brother and upend my life."

"Caroline!" said William, smacking his palm lightly against the table. "You forget yourself. Miss Hudson, my sister didn't..."

He looked at me, blinking rapidly. For once, my brother was at a loss for words. He wanted me to apologize. But it was too late. For the first time in my life, I'd given in to my frustration and expressed it. I was angry at her coquetry and at his responding to it. Above all, I was upset by how unimportant I felt.

"You'll find a bed made up for you in the bedchamber two doors left of the landing, Miss Hudson," I said, and I left the room.

CHAPTER 12

December 1783
Datchet, England

Despite my agitation, I fell asleep soon after I pulled up the covers that night and slept solidly. It wasn't the first time my body had sought relief from distress through slumber. To everyone's amazement eleven years earlier, I'd slept deeply several times during the arduous six-day journey from Hanover to England with William. He and our fellow travelers had remained vigilantly awake in fear for their lives as we hurtled toward the coast in a mail wagon and were later tossed about on stormy seas in an open boat. I'd escaped the terrors by sleeping for hours at a time.

"I envy your brain's response to angst," William had said during the trip when he awoke and dragged me onto the carriage roof to show me the stars.

It was probably, I'd thought sleepily, *possible only because I had him to watch over me.*

Now, however, as I awakened to the light softly framing the curtains in Datchet, all calm forsook me. As if my resting mind had created and compared a list of rights and wrongs and found an imbalance against me, I realized how foolish I'd been the night before. It didn't matter how I felt. If I upset William, he could send me back to Hanover, where I'd be destined to slave for Jacob and nurse my mother, whose repugnance for me would no doubt have multiplied in my absence.

The wooden floor was icy beneath my bare feet as I rushed to open the curtains. It had stopped snowing. Though the sun shone weakly between scattered clouds, its rays reflected so brightly against the white garden I narrowed my eyes. Even so, I saw the tell-tale dark prints of hooves and wheels leading from the yard. I hurriedly dressed and ran downstairs, where I found Hannah clearing two breakfast settings. Comet trotted to me from the kitchen, his tail wagging.

"Where is he?" I asked Hannah as I patted the dog.

"Good morning, Miss Herschel," she replied. "In the workshop, I believe. Shall I serve your porridge?"

"No. I'll be back shortly."

Comet skipped ahead across the yard. The snow was lighter than I'd anticipated, but with the trees solid and bare, the white blanket gave the impression the world had been stripped of color overnight. Alerted by the dog's arrival, William met me at the open doors of the stable. He pulled on his coat.

"Let's walk a little," he said, glancing behind to where Mr. Harris and Thomas were working.

My stomach churned. It wasn't just that I hadn't had breakfast. For William to leave the workbench to talk to me, even for a few minutes, was unprecedented.

"I'm not dressed for it," I said.

He didn't look at me. "It won't take long."

We retraced my steps in silence until we arrived at the dirty, sludgy tracks of the carriage, which we followed toward the gate. "She wanted to leave last night," said my brother, breathing fast. "It was all I could do to stop her from going out in the storm."

"William, I didn't—"

"I have *never* been so ashamed." He stopped and turned to me. I couldn't look at him.

"What were you thinking? She was our guest. We'd agreed we'd not mention the horse. And then…then you behaved like a spoiled child, threatened that someone else was getting more attention than them. It was shocking, absolutely shocking!"

I felt dizzy and looked around for something to hold on to. At any other time, I would've reached for my brother's arm. He was alongside me, but the distance between us had never felt greater.

Ahead, Comet stood in the tracks, looking back, waiting for us to walk on. I took a step forward, my legs trembling.

"I'm sorry," I said.

William sighed as we walked again. "I didn't know you last night. The sister I know wouldn't have spoken to *anyone* like that, let alone a friend."

"But is she a friend?" I asked.

"What do you mean?"

"Alex knew in Bath. Remember? He mentioned it. And the horse? It's obvious. Miss Hudson isn't fond of me. She's not interested in *my* friendship. She's interested in you. She's wily."

My brother's silence told me I might be right.

"I shouldn't have been rude to her last night," I continued. "But her deviousness made me angry. She's manipulative. I didn't want her to—"

William clasped my arm. "Stop it. There's no excuse for your behavior. Even if Miss Hudson *is* interested in me and my work, that doesn't mean she isn't your friend. Has she shown you anything but friendship since you've known her?"

"But she isn't—"

He ignored me. "No, she has not. I agree that her giving me a horse was inappropriate, but it was nothing more than that. Inappropriate. And forgotten. Last night, we were having a perfectly enjoyable conversation until you became jealous and threatened."

"I didn't. It wasn't that. I—"

"You practically said as much. 'Nothing will change.' Those were your words. What did you mean?" he demanded.

I looked at my feet. My shoes were wet and grubby. I couldn't tell him how his words and manner had hurt me. "I was thinking of Alex and Sophia Elizabeth," I said.

"Alex? Sophia Elizabeth?"

"And how marriage stole them from us," I mumbled. "If you...if Miss Hudson..."

My brother turned to me and opened his mouth as if to speak, but he sighed instead. Surely he understood how my life would change if he took a wife? He knew I dreaded returning to Hanover. I wished he'd reassure me it wouldn't happen, but he was silent.

"I'll write to Miss Hudson. Apologize, explain," I said.

"Is it possible to explain? I don't think so," he replied. "But yes, you should apologize. I doubt it will change anything, but you should do it. Immediately."

"Yes," I said.

William ran his fingers through his hair. "I know it was difficult for you to give up music, but I thought you'd settled here. If you're unhappy, perhaps—"

"I'm not!" My ears were ringing. "I'm not unhappy. I just—"

He held up his hand. "You know how desperately Jacob and Mother want you to return."

"No! Please, William. I'm sorry. Don't send me back. I'll do anything!" I snatched his hand and held it between mine. "Please."

He blinked and took a breath. "All right. All right."

I stared at him, pleading.

His eyes softened and he took his hand from mine. "It's all right. I must get back to work."

My head spun as I watched William walk toward the workshop. He hadn't exactly threatened to send me back to Hanover, but he'd reminded me it was possible. Surely he wouldn't be so cruel? He'd said it because he was angry, hadn't he? Even so, I'd have to tread carefully to keep him from thinking about it again.

I stood for a while, practicing my breathing exercises to calm my thoughts. Finally, the echo of William's words, "You know how desperately Jacob and Mother want you to return," faded. However, I couldn't stop thinking about how hurt I was by how he'd described to Miss Hudson my role as his assistant. I'd responded by lashing out with sarcasm, but it didn't deter my ambition to learn to be an astronomer. Perhaps, if I proved my skills and gained recognition thereof within William's circle, I might one day experience a taste of independence.

The week that followed was as cool in my brother's company as it was outdoors. It didn't snow again, which allowed William to put Thomas to work stabilizing the frame for the twenty-footer. However, this ceased when, with Saint Nicholas Day over and Christmas approaching, William insisted the servants stay home with their families. As such, my brother and I worked side by side, exchanging a few perfunctory words. It was only on Christmas Eve, as we ate a modest supper of roast fowl and vegetables, that I ventured to ease the tension between us.

"I wrote to Miss Hudson the very day I said I would. Hannah posted the letter that evening," I said.

William didn't look at me. "Hmm."

"I spared no words expressing my regret at my unfair treatment of her and asked her forgiveness," I continued.

He leaned back, his eyes on me now. "Yes, she wrote to me, saying your letter had arrived."

"She wrote to you? But why didn't she reply to me?" I asked.

"Perhaps she will, in time. Her letter to me was a short note, thanking me for my cordiality and acknowledging your apology," he said, folding his napkin.

"But you said nothing to me," I said.

"I just did," said William, pushing back his chair and getting to his feet. "And there's nothing more to be said on the matter."

I went to bed hoping my brother's mood would thaw in the morning, but alas, Christmas Day had never been more subdued. Even in Hanover, when I'd spent much of the holy day in the kitchen, I'd been less alone. After we'd been to church, William went into the library. I almost followed, hoping he'd ask me to do something for him. But when he closed the door, I understood he didn't want me there.

I buttoned up my cloak again and called Comet. As he trailed me outside, wagging his tail in anticipation of adventure, I recalled our dubious introduction at the riverside in Bath. Who would've thought the surly, wet dog I'd unintentionally chased from his shelter would become my only friend?

Comet and I had established a few favorite walking routes in recent months, all of which took us away from the village. With everyone else doing whatever the people of Datchet did on Christmas Day, the road and footpath we followed were empty. I looked across the wintery fields, trying not to think about William and Miss Hudson. I was unsuccessful. Had he already replied to her letter, or was he writing to her now? Had my outburst achieved exactly what I'd dreaded: brought them together with me cast aside? If it had, there was nothing I could do to change things. Miss Hudson had chosen not to respond to my apology directly despite the humility of my letter. It could only mean she'd seen it as an opportunity to extend her contact with my brother.

Although it was a clear day, the air was so cold it burned. As such, I chose the sunny path that took us along the banks of a small river rather than the one through the trees. Comet shoved his nose deep into the long grass near the water, occasionally pouncing when something moved.

I was watching the dog, amused and pleased to be distracted from my thoughts, when I heard the crunch of footsteps on the path behind me. Comet raised his head and gave a low growl. I turned to see a man walking toward us. His outfit—dark coat, waistcoat and breeches, and white linen shirt with frilled front—gave the impression of a gentleman. He might also be a farmer still dressed for church. As he drew closer, I saw he was neither. It was the butcher, Mr. Corden. Comet, apparently also recognizing him, barked loudly as he darted between us.

Mr. Corden stopped, looked at the dog, and then at me, his jaw clenched.

"Comet! It's all right," I shouted. "Stop it!"

The animal glanced at me, uncertain, but he quietened.

"You startled him," I said.

The butcher frowned and then, with a tiny smile, said, "Merry Christmas, Miss Herschel."

"Merry Christmas, Mr. Corden."

We were silent for a moment, Comet stock-still between us.

"Do you think he'll allow me to walk by?" asked Mr. Corden eventually. "Or shall I turn back?"

As if in response, Comet gave a low growl. I covered my mouth with my hand, trying to disguise my amusement. Our eyes met and Mr. Corden chortled, which set me giggling freely. He stepped back, laughing unreservedly. Comet added to the noise by barking again, which, in turn, troubled a covey of partridges. The birds burst from the grassy riverbank and flew away, adding to the cacophony with their rapid *kut, kut, kut* cries. Comet spun around and took off after them.

Our laughter died with the dog's departure. Abandoned by our canine chaperone, we were uncertain how to behave. Mr. Corden looked across the field where Comet continued to charge after the birds.

"Will he come back?" he asked.

"Yes," I replied. "I might have to wait a bit, but he'll return."

"Would you like me to stay? Until then? To be sure," he asked.

He looked younger than I recalled. Perhaps it was because when we'd met, he'd been annoyed and serious. I hadn't noticed the unusual light gray color of his eyes then either, but I remembered his hair, how curly and shiny it was.

Did I want him to stay? Yes, I did. Laughing on the footpath with the butcher was the happiest I'd been since Miss Hudson's visit. It was Christmas, a time to be merry and gay. If Alex had been with us and I hadn't maddened William, we would've exchanged small gifts, enjoyed a special meal together, and perhaps even made some music.

"No," I said. "There's no need to stay. He'll be back shortly."

"Well, if you're sure," he said.

"Yes, I'm sure."

Mr. Corden bobbed his head. "In that case, I'll be on my way. Merry Christmas, Miss Herschel."

"Good day, Mr. Corden."

He'd taken a few steps when I called after him.

"Oh, Mr. Corden." He turned to me. "Thank you for the bacon."

He narrowed his eyes, confused.

"You sent extra slices of bacon with my brother. To welcome us to Datchet last year," I said.

The butcher smiled. "My pleasure, Miss Herschel."

CHAPTER 13

December 1783
Datchet, England

THINGS WERE UNEXPECTEDLY EASIER AFTER MY ENCOUNTER WITH MR. Corden, but not because William gave any indication of having pardoned me. He was up before me every morning and still busy when I went to bed. There were nights he didn't sleep. However, I'd long since stopped voicing my concerns about how little rest he got and went on as if I didn't notice. He remained distant as I worked alongside him. However, I was no longer unnerved by his coolness. Something had changed for me.

After being largely isolated in Datchet for more than a year, I'd forgotten it was possible to be invigorated by the company of anyone other than my brother. Meeting Mr. Corden again reminded me of something my father had told me years earlier.

"Laughter is the best beginning for a friendship," he'd said, which had left me wondering when he imagined I might have occasion to meet anyone who might become a friend, whether through laughter or otherwise. I'd rarely left the house in Hanover.

Although the timing of Comet's growl might've been comical, it didn't warrant the amusement the butcher and I had awarded it. My outburst was a roundabout response to how unsettled I'd been since Miss Hudson's visit. I couldn't explain Mr. Corden's mirth, but it didn't matter. As Comet and I had made our way home that day, I'd realized that laughing had dispelled the tension, and I felt calmer than I had for weeks.

Thank you, Mr. Corden, I'd thought.

The nights since Christmas had been cloudy and bitterly cold, which meant William and I stayed indoors, writing up the catalog of nebulae and comets. The advantage was it prevented William climbing the rickety frame to use the twenty-footer telescope. Despite Thomas's best efforts, the frame remained clumsily incomplete. The platform—more than fifteen feet from the ground—was yet to be fully assembled, and the temporary crossbeam shook and wobbled under William's weight. Moreover, the ladders weren't braced. Scaling the shaky frame in the dark was dangerous enough but riskier still when the wood was damp.

On the last night of December, I was beginning to think I might go to bed when William stood and went to the window.

"Exactly as Mr. Harris predicted! The clouds have parted slightly," he said. "Quickly, Lina, let's go."

"The twenty-footer?" I asked, hoping against all odds he might choose to use one of the smaller telescopes.

"Of course," he replied.

I hurried to the hallway, returning with William's coat and my cloak. As I followed my brother to the door, Comet raised his head and regarded me briefly through half-open eyes before tucking his nose between his paws.

The night air was piercing, but William seemed impervious to it. His teeth glinted as he handed me the lantern, and I resolved to share his enthusiasm and remind him of my usefulness. Treading carefully over several half-frozen puddles, I balanced the lamp on the ground and held the ladder as he ascended.

"The clouds are moving fast," he called. "I can see two large patches with stars, but that could change soon. I need you to go around and use the winch to adjust the lateral position."

"All right," I replied, still supporting the ladder.

Although I hadn't done it myself, I'd seen William and Thomas wind the large handle to move the tube. However, I'd only move from the ladder when my brother was safe. I watched, my head tipped back as far as possible, as he stepped onto the crossbeam.

"Is it slippery?" I asked.

"It's barely damp. Go quickly, or we'll miss our chance," he said.

I left the ladder and lantern and hurried to the other side of the structure. It was dark and uneven underfoot. As I approached the winch, I took my eyes off the barely lit, slushy ground to locate the handle. In that instant, something hard, cold, and sharp ripped through my skirts and into the flesh of my right leg, bringing me to an excruciating halt.

The pain took my breath away. My head swam, and for a moment, it seemed I'd faint. I closed my eyes and groaned as I fumbled about to ascertain what I'd smashed into. It was the pointy end of one of the large iron hooks supporting the winch.

A sudden, clear memory flashed through my mind. Alex was talking to William: "At the butcher's today, I realized the hooks onto which he hangs joints of beef will be perfect for our design. He said the smith in the village made them for him," he'd said.

Now, with my leg impaled by one such hook, I might've been a joint of beef. Although the piercing was just above my knee, the pain spread until my whole leg burned and throbbed. I wanted to sit, but, firmly attached to the hook, I couldn't move.

"Breathe, Caroline, breathe," I whispered. "It'll be all right."

I pulled off my gloves and slowly leaned forward to move my skirt. Blood flowed over my fingers, warm and sticky. I tried to raise myself onto the toes of my left foot, but rather than disengaging me from the hook, the movement sent another wave of agony up my leg and into my back. I gasped, dizzy once more.

"Lina! You need to wind the lever toward me," shouted my brother from his dark station above me.

I swallowed and opened my mouth, meaning to call for help, but all I could manage was a moan.

William didn't hear me. "Lina! Make haste! We're going to miss it. The clouds are moving fast. What are you doing?"

"Nothing," I whimpered. "I'm hooked."

As it was, William was unable to tear me free without sacrificing about two ounces of my flesh to his machine. I don't remember his detaching me or our returning to the house. He told me later, as he'd carried me inside, that I'd pointed out that the sky was once again fully enclosed and apologized he'd missed the stars.

I awoke to the vaguely familiar, gravelly voice of a woman. "Aye, I helped the midwife deliver my grandchild, but I'm not a physician. I can't help. I'm sorry," she said, although her tone suggested annoyance rather than regret.

William spoke from somewhere else in the room. "But the wound needs cleaning. Can't you do something?"

"No. No. Wouldn't want to touch it. What if I make it worse? No. I don't know what my husband was thinking getting me up in the middle of the night. I can't do anything, can't help," she reiterated.

I opened my eyes and recognized the disgruntled face of Mrs. Harris hovering above where I lay on the sofa. Although my knee throbbed and my thoughts were muddled, the gentle crackle of the fire and Comet's questioning look from across the room were soothing.

"Go home," I said, my voice stronger than I felt.

William stepped into view and peered at me, his eyes narrow with worry. "You're conscious. Good. No, Lina, you need help. We'll—"

"I can take care of it. It'll be all right," I said, slowly pushing myself into a position from which I could bundle up my skirts and examine the bloody mess above my knee. William blanched and turned away. The wound was raw and oozing, but the bleeding had slowed. There was a dark stain on the towel folded beneath me. I carefully covered the lesion again.

Mrs. Harris caught my eye as she shuffled toward the door.

"Good night," I called.

She'd no sooner left the room than there was a tap at the door. It was Mr. Harris, who'd been waiting outside.

"I have the remains of a bottle of arquebusade the physician gave me when I put a spade through my toe some time ago," he said, his eyes on William. "It's for cleaning wounds. I'll go and get it."

"Tomorrow will do, Mr. Harris," I said, lying back again.

"No, not at all, Miss Herschel. I'll return immediately."

"Thank you," said William.

Later, when Mr. Harris had walked his wife home, returned with the potion, and left again, I asked William to bring me some warm water, a clean cloth, and a kerchief. He placed everything on a small table alongside me.

"I wish I knew what to do," he said, rubbing his head and averting his eyes.

It was unusual for William to be unsure and unhelpful, but his antipathy to this situation was typical. Our mother had said how he'd often collapsed when presented with blood when he was a boy. Even discussions about injuries made him woozy.

"I'll take care of it," I said. "Once it's clean and bound, I'll call you, and you can help me upstairs."

He bowed his head. "I'm sorry, Lina."

"For what?" I asked, trying to smile. "You didn't hang me on the hook. I should've been more careful."

"I was rushing you in the dark. You hadn't worked the lever before," he said.

"It's not difficult if you stay away from the hooks," I said.

William grimaced as he inadvertently glanced at my knee. He stood and half turned away from me. "I've been demanding recently," he continued, pulling at his collar as if he was suddenly hot. "There's so much to do. And I overplayed the incident with Miss Hudson. You wrote to her and apologized. I shouldn't have continued punishing you."

"It's all right. You—"

"No, it's not all right, Lina. You are indispensable to me. You never complain when we work through the night. You're always willing to do anything to help. You and Alex turned this place into a home without any labor from me. You gave up a comfortable, lively life in Bath to live in this cold, secluded place because of me. And then, when you do something that displeases me, I treat you like a disobedient child and ignore your penance. It was unreasonable."

I was dizzy again and wanted him to stop. "Truly, Brother, I'm—"

His hands were in his hair again. "When I saw you impaled on the hook because I'd told you to hurry, it made me realize how difficult I can be. I'd barely spoken two words to you for weeks, but when I needed help tonight, you didn't hesitate."

If my leg weren't aching and my head were clearer, I might've taken the opportunity to tell William how I'd felt when he described my work to Miss Hudson, that I wanted to be more than an assistant, and how I dreaded being sent back to Hanover. Instead, I reached for my skirts.

"I'm going to attend to my leg now. Give me a few minutes," I said.

With it nearly impossible to bend my knee, the next few days were exhausting. Initially, I hobbled, stiff-legged, to the workshop, hoping to be of use to William. However, it was soon obvious that, with the men having to constantly hand me tools and move materials for me, I was an encumbrance. As such, I confined myself to the library, seated at the writing desk with my right leg propped up alongside me. It was an uncomfortable position in which to write. My back and shoulders grew stiff, forcing me to move frequently. Within hours, my entire body ached. My sleep was also interrupted when the injury throbbed, and I had to lift the blankets and slowly shift into another position.

It didn't help that the wound continued to gape. Despite my removing the covering, clenching my teeth against the sting of the arquebusade as I swabbed the spot, and binding it with a clean kerchief every day, the gash remained fleshy and swollen, with little sign of scabbing.

For the first few days after the accident, Comet watched me closely. Every time I'd heave myself upright, he'd scramble to his feet, his eyes bright with hope.

"No, Comet, we're not going out. It's unfair, I know, but it'll heal even more slowly if we're impatient," I explained.

After a while, resignation replaced anticipation. It didn't stop him sighing loudly as he lay about on the library floor. Exactly when Comet began taking himself out, I cannot say. I'd notice his absence, and then, a while later, he'd reappear, trotting to me as if proudly announcing his return. Assuming he'd been hunting rats in the yard or stables, I wasn't concerned. My confinement shouldn't be his. It was only when Hannah went to the market one morning that I discovered the extent of the dog's adventures.

Mistaking the loud knocking at an outside door as that of Mr. Harris or Thomas—William sometimes sent them to collect an item or ask me something—I called that he should come in.

"In the library," I shouted.

The door opened, but the footsteps were uncertain, which made me suspect it was someone who didn't know the lay of the house.

"In here!" I called again.

The footfalls drew closer, and a curly-haired form filled the doorway. It was Mr. Corden. Even more unexpected was that he had, tucked under his arm, a sheepish-looking Comet. I stared at the pair, dumbstruck. Comet looked down. Mr. Corden held my gaze. Guessing the dog was once again guilty of pilfering, I braced myself for another scolding. That Mr. Corden had come all the way from the village with him indicated the scope of Comet's crime.

I took a deep breath and, finding my voice, gestured to my propped-up leg. "My apologies, but I can't stand up to take him from you. I've hurt my leg," I said.

The butcher placed Comet on the floor. The dog shook himself, gave his captor a sullen glance, and skulked across the floor to me.

"Ah, so that's why he was out alone," said Mr. Corden, his tone surprisingly mild. "I'm sorry to see you're incapacitated."

I stared at him. "Where did you, erm, find him?"

"On the ring road, beyond where our paths crossed at Christmas," he replied.

The ring road? Comet hadn't been anywhere near the butchery.

"That's almost a mile away," I said.

"I was on my gig and saw him trotting along the footpath near the road. I looked about for you, but he was alone. Thought I'd bring him home, since I'd be passing by," he said.

Comet sighed loudly as he lay beside my chair. "I'm surprised you caught him." My face grew warm. "I mean, after you'd chased him from your shop."

Mr. Corden chuckled. The sound took me back to our meeting on Christmas Day. "I was surprised myself," he said. "I suspect he was distracted by the enticing scent of my vehicle. Or perhaps he knows I'm a forgiving sort."

"Thank you. I had no idea he strayed so far. I mean, he's been restless without our walks, but I imagined he confined himself to the yard," I said.

"Perhaps your brother can take him out until you're able?" he suggested.

"I'll see what I can do," I said, knowing I wouldn't ask William. It wasn't that he disliked the dog, but my brother was far too busy. The only person who might agree to take him out for a short walk was Hannah. I'd speak to her.

Mr. Corden glanced around the room. He seemed reluctant to leave. Did he expect something? Refreshments? If Hannah had been there, I could've offered.

"Will you be incapacitated for long, Miss Herschel? What does the physician say?" he asked.

"I don't know. I haven't seen a physician. I'll be fine in a few days." He raised his brows. I rattled on. "I ran into a hook on my brother's machine when we were out observing the stars about a week ago. I left the lantern in my haste and didn't see it. You'd recognize the part. My brothers were inspired by the meat hooks in your shop. They use them to support the winch. Anyway, it was unfortunate. I was hooked, like a joint of beef, for a brief time."

"What? A meat hook?" He came closer. "Miss Herschel, you must have it attended by a physician. I don't know how severe the wound is, but you wouldn't want it to fester. You should see Dr. Lind. He's a gentleman and a very thorough physician."

"Of course. Yes, I'll consult him if it doesn't heal. I'm cleaning it. I'm quite sure it'll be fine," I replied.

He wasn't convinced. "But you don't want to leave it too long. The hook might not be used to hang meat, but it might still have been soiled. My father, he was also a butcher, once sliced off his—"

Whatever Mr. Corden's father sliced off remained a mystery to me. Our conversation was interrupted by Hannah. It was no surprise she knew the butcher. Datchet was a small village. However, I hadn't guessed they might be friends or that she knew his history with Comet.

"Oh, Miss Herschel! You must've feared the worst when Gabriel appeared with the dog," she giggled after I'd explained how the butcher had brought Comet home.

After once more urging me to call for the physician, Gabriel Corden declined my offer of something to eat or drink and left. However, he lingered in my thoughts all afternoon.

There was nothing extraordinary about his having brought Comet home.

That was something any considerate person would do. However, the way he'd delayed in the library and his urging me to see the physician seemed more heartfelt than the average attention of a well-mannered acquaintance. Were we friends? The notion both pleased and unsettled me. The idea of having a friend in Datchet was agreeable, but it also attested to how lonely I was. On the other hand, what did it matter? Even if the glimmer of a potential friendship existed, it couldn't amount to anything. Gabriel Corden was a tradesman, the village butcher. I was the sister of the King's Astronomer, William Herschel. I didn't know *exactly* where that placed us on the social ladder, but I was certain Mr. Corden and I did not occupy the same rung.

Back in the library the next day, I was determined to continue working on William's catalog. I wanted to alleviate my brother's concern that my injury might interrupt the project. Unfortunately, with my damaged leg propped up, I couldn't stay in one position for long. It was as I once more shifted about that Hannah—recently back from exercising Comet—appeared at the door.

"Dr. Lind is here to see you," she said.

"Dr. Lind?" I echoed.

"The physician."

"I know, but how—"

"He says Gabriel, erm, Mr. Corden said he should see you."

So it was that Dr. Lind investigated and treated my wound.

"I might've sewn it closed had you called me earlier," he said. "The skin and flesh are too shrunken to do so now."

"But it *will* heal, won't it?" I asked.

He took a small container and a brown paper bag from his case. "Oh, yes. But it will take longer than it would have, and the scar will forever be more distinct."

Thoughts of scarring didn't bother me. I'd been scarred for as long as I remembered, and this one wouldn't be visible to everyone. On the other hand, I regretted the wound could've healed faster if Dr. Lind had come sooner. I watched as he gently swabbed it, applied ointment, and covered it with lint before binding it with a light bandage.

"I'll leave the ointment, lint, and this extra bandage. You should keep dressing it regularly as I have today," he said. "And stay as still as possible."

"How long before I can resume life as normal?" I asked.

He straightened, put his hands on his hips, and stared at me. "Well, Miss Herschel, if you were a soldier with such an injury, you would be entitled to six weeks of nursing in hospital."

CHAPTER 14

April 1784
Datchet, England

With the arrival of spring came clearer skies, and since I'd recovered from my injury, our nights were as busy as our days. William observed whenever he could, calling his findings from the twenty-footer to me while I sat at my desk near the open doors of the library. Happily, the frame was complete, and I no longer held my breath as he ascended the ladder. Nor was I alarmed by every rattle while my brother was on the platform. I even confidently adjusted the winch as he required when neither Thomas nor Mr. Harris was around, and I wished Alex could see what he'd helped design in action. When William was away, I'd use my instrument to observe alone, pleased by how well acquainted I was with the heavens and ever more eager to discover new objects.

While we'd finished and delivered several new ten- and seven-foot telescopes to His Majesty and other customers by the end of winter, the demand for my brother's instruments didn't slow. We needed the money, so William accepted every order, and we worked harder.

I began rising earlier and having breakfast with my brother at dawn. Sometimes, he hadn't been to bed. Thereafter, while he went to the workshop or court, I'd take Comet for a half-hour ramble. Every morning, exhilarated by the fresh traces of the wild creatures that had roamed the paths and fields over-night, the dog scampered ahead, nose down and tail wagging. Occasionally, he'd sniff out a rabbit and pursue it until it disappeared down its burrow or into the dense bush. I enjoyed watching his endeavors and was also entertained by the dog's unshakable optimism that he might one day catch a bird before it took flight. His energy was unflagging.

It was during one of these outings I spotted Mr. Corden walking down the lane. I hadn't seen him since he'd brought Comet home. He didn't notice me, but his presence—so far from the village that early—piqued my curiosity. I'd assumed he lived above the butchery and imagined when I'd encountered him at Christmas he'd also been taking advantage of the dry weather. Now, though, seeing him in the vicinity again, I wondered if he lived elsewhere.

"Aye, he lives above the shop," said Hannah when I asked. "But, since his father died, his old mother has been up the road with her sister on Big Tree Farm. He might visit her and spend the night at times."

I wanted to thank the butcher for sending Dr. Lind, and I looked for him every morning from then on. A week or so later, as Comet and I left the yard, I recognized his lengthy stride as he came toward us.

He tipped his hat as we grew closer. I returned his greeting, and we stopped.

"As you see, Mr. Corden, my leg has recovered, and I'm once again ensur-ing the dog has adventures enough to prevent him from straying," I said, gesturing to Comet.

"And I'm pleased by it," he said with a small smile.

"It was kind of you… Um, I wanted to thank you for asking the physician to call on me," I said, wondering why I felt nervous expressing something so prosaic.

He rubbed his neck. "I happened upon Dr. Lind as soon as I got to the village after returning the dog. So, I mentioned it to him, hoping it wouldn't be forward. I mean, it was none of my business, but it seemed it might help. A physician attending you," he replied, speaking fast.

"It did, and I'm grateful," I said.

We stood for a moment. There was nothing else to say or to delay us. I wished we could simply chat. I'd tell him how, after exercising the dog, my daylight hours were spent in the workshop, where I was once again grinding and polishing reflectors alongside the men. I might've said how, with summer approaching, His Majesty was demanding more and more of William's attention at court and that we'd found it necessary to employ two more men. But I said nothing.

Mr. Corden swallowed. "It's good to see you about, Miss Herschel. I'm sure he's pleased too," he said, tilting his head in Comet's direction.

"Yes. Indeed. Well, good day, Mr. Corden."

"Good day, then," he said, tipping his hat once more and walking on.

I didn't notice the dewdrops on the grass on the way home that morning. Neither did I stop to admire the carpets of bluebells beneath the trees. Whether Comet came across any rabbits or chased any birds also escaped me. I'd awoken in good spirits but was now melancholy, disheartened by the unsatisfying encounter with Mr. Corden.

Despite having told myself previously that we couldn't be friends, I'd hoped it might be possible. He'd been as cordial as ever, and there was no reason to think he was unhappy to see me. However, I now saw we had nothing in common. When I was hoping to bump into him, I'd imagined telling him about my work. I'd wanted to say how I'd grown to love the solitude and silence of the garden on the darkest nights. I'd describe how it never ceased to amaze me how focusing on one star inevitably revealed galaxies beyond, layered constellations that glittered like splintered diamonds in the dust. I'd imagined describing the moon with its shadowy valleys and tall mountains, and telling Mr. Corden my brother believed it might be inhabited and how, when I trained my telescope upon it, I searched for fields, houses, and other signs of life. I'd explain how I'd learned to use catalogs, numerical tables, and the astronomical clock Alex had built for us to make calculations, and how I prepared records for publication. I'd imagined telling him how little anyone on Earth knew about the night sky but how I thought about it all day and couldn't wait to learn more.

I'd wanted to tell him this and more, but I realized it would be meaningless to him. Did he know or care to know anything about the heavens and astronomy? Why would he? Mr. Corden was a tradesman who owned a butchery. There was nothing beyond Comet's antics that might connect us.

CHAPTER 15

April 1784
Datchet, England

Despite our employing more men and accepting every commission that came our way, it remained difficult to balance output and income. William's salary from His Majesty, which was eked out quarterly, had not covered the expenses for the twenty-footer, and it was essential to make and sell more and more other instruments to have enough money to pay our debts and salaries and to eat. For the most part, William was tireless and optimistic. However, the number of hours he spent observing at night, assembling and delivering telescopes during the day, and attending to His Majesty's demands both day and night increased every week. The extent and pace at which he worked were unsustainable. I wasn't the only one who worried about his health.

We were anticipating a visit by Dr. Watson, when my brother received a note demanding his immediate presence at Windsor Castle.

"The carriage will be here to fetch me within an hour," said William, folding the note.

I tried to object. "But Dr. Watson—"

"Yes, I know. He'll be here by nightfall. Please explain and apologize on my behalf. I'll return as soon as I can tomorrow," he said.

That evening at dinner, Dr. Watson asked about our work. I described a typical day, noting the predawn starts after stargazing through the night. He raised his brows at the number of telescopes we were building and scowled when I told him how often William had to drop everything to go to Windsor. My brother wouldn't want me to complain on his behalf. However, it was impossible to attenuate his workload or ignore how he struggled to satisfy the role of King's Astronomer on his current salary.

"I always thought it was too little," said Dr. Watson, placing his cutlery on his plate. "Of course, one might argue that if your brother did *only* what His Majesty expected of him, he'd be comfortable. Other men in his position would live at court, eat, drink, listen to music, and talk about the heavens when anyone asked. But not William. He wants to make the best telescopes, see and understand everything, to enlighten not only His Majesty and everyone at court but the whole world. He won't rest until he does. He does too much. He's his own worst enemy."

He was right. Suggesting William do less and sleep more was futile. His industry was compulsive. Another man might've found a smaller, less expensive, and more comfortable home than the ramshackle place we occupied. But a tinier house wouldn't come with a garden large enough for the twenty-footer. Or stables with space to construct instruments. Or rooms to convert into libraries and studies. Our work was our life—as it had been when we were musicians. The difference was that music had sustained us, while astronomy threatened to sink us.

"What can I do?" asked Dr. Watson, as if reading my mind.

"I don't know," I said. "If only there was a way to petition His Majesty for an increase in salary."

He pursed his lips.

I held up my hands. "No. I know it's not possible. King's Astronomer was a new role created for William, and he says he's yet to prove his worth. So, what might you do? Hmm. The same as usual: Give him your friendship and support. Encourage him to rest and eat more." I chuckled. "Of course, he'll take his meals with us while you're here and assure you that he'll get more sleep. But as soon as you leave, he'll ignore everything you said and continue as before."

He shook his head. "What does he need aside from more money and rest?"

"One thing William has owned to wanting since we've been here is a horse," I said.

Dr. Watson took a sip of water and swallowed. "He's never mentioned it to me, but I can see how it would make his life easier."

"Yes, it would save time, as he wouldn't have to rely on carriages from court. William's wanted one ever since we got here, but every month the money we try to set aside for a horse is needed for materials for instruments. It's impossible to save," I replied, pushing the memory of Miss Hudson's gift from my thoughts.

"Hmm," said Dr. Watson, his tone pensive. "And he's a very able horseman." He lifted his goblet. "Do you think your brother might accept a horse on loan from me?"

"You have a suitable animal? One that you wouldn't miss?" I asked.

He bobbed his head, took a sip of water, and put down the goblet. "A mare who belonged to my father. He's no longer able to ride. I took her in, hoping Mrs. Watson might occasionally go out with me. She rode once. It rained, and she hasn't expressed any desire to do it again. The mare is getting fat and bored. Your brother would do me a favor by exercising her."

"Why don't you sell her?" I asked.

"She's young, and I might use her myself in a few years," he replied.

William returned the following afternoon. I wasn't privy to their discussions, however, three days later, when Dr. Watson's groom rode the mare into the yard, William called me.

"Isn't she pretty?" he said, taking the reins from the groom and patting the mare's sweaty neck.

Chestnut, with four white socks and a thin white strip running down the center of her face, she *was* pretty.

"Hello, Juno. It's good to meet you. You and I are going to have a splendid time," continued my brother.

Dr. Watson caught my eye. He smiled, raised his shoulders and rubbed his hands together. Despite being several years younger than William, he could've been a proud father. How lucky my brother was to have a friend like him.

The day before he was due to return to Bath, Dr. Watson accomplished an even more astonishing feat. He somehow persuaded William to set down his work for a few hours of leisure. We three, said my brother's friend, should follow the servants to the village and join in the festivities of the annual spring fair. Dreading the stares of strangers when they noted my stunted stature and scarred face, I felt the instinct to resist.

"I'll finish this," I said, pointing to my polishing. "With the men already gone, we'll be behind."

"Three hours and no more," said the doctor, assuming a stern tone. "If your brother can pry himself away from work, so can you, Miss Herschel. I insist."

William shrugged and smiled. "Come, Lina. He'll be gone tomorrow, and we can once more work all we want."

It was a warm, windless morning, and after changing into a green summer gown and matching bonnet that I hadn't worn since leaving Bath, I accompanied the men and Comet out of the yard. The dog, assuming we'd follow our usual route, immediately turned left at the gate. When I called him the other way, he ran frenzied circles around us. I hoped since we were walking toward the village, he wasn't thinking about visiting the butchery.

Datchet was transformed, not only by the sunshine, trees trimmed with fresh foliage, and flowers blooming wherever they'd taken hold but also by colorful bunting strung from gables, fences, and poles. It was nothing like the place Mrs. Harris had shown me. Gone were the dull tones and shabbiness of the buildings and the furtive glances of those who inhabited them. Doors and windows had been thrown open. A row of carriages lined the square. The vehicles were harnessed to a glossy cavalcade of horses, who stood sleepily in the sunshine. Even the cobblestones seemed to shine, lifted by a cheery melody emanating from somewhere alongside the river.

We made our way toward the cluster of small stalls near the water, where throngs of people wearing their Sunday best milled about. Children of all sizes darted through the crowds, laughing and calling out to one another. As three small boys sped between us, Comet took up an unusual position close behind my heels.

Dr. Watson turned to William. "Is this the same sleepy little country place you described in your letters?" he teased.

"The very same," replied my brother, shaking his head.

We stopped to watch a juggler expertly toss and catch a startling selection of fruit at a mesmerizing pace. A sizable audience crowded around a booth watching a puppet show. It drew loud jeers and roars of laughter. On the far side of the lawn, a trio of musicians played lively tunes with a flute and two fiddles, eliciting dancing among a growing group of villagers. I stood alongside William as he watched and listened, his head nodding in time.

"Do you miss it?" I asked.

"No," he replied without hesitation. "It's wonderfully cheerful. Music is lovely. But no, I don't miss it. What about you?"

"No," I echoed quickly.

Although stargazing happily dominated my thoughts now, I wasn't yet brave enough to reminisce about music. I'd given it up and had no time for regret. Still, I couldn't help wondering how I would've responded if William had said he *did* miss it. Would I have conceded the same? It didn't matter. My brother had chosen a different path for us.

Dr. Watson, who'd wandered off to examine the wares of some nearby stalls, returned. "There's some interesting-looking fare on offer," he said. "I'm going to try some. What about you?"

As we followed him, I breathed in the yeasty aroma of ale. It was quickly replaced by the honeyed scent of mead, which was, in turn, drowned by the dense, smoky smell of meat roasting. Dr. Watson went toward the smoke, stopping at a stall where cuts of meat sizzled over a layer of coals.

"Hmm, smells good," he said. "What have you, my good man?"

I recognized Mr. Corden before he looked up, but not soon enough to move away. He lifted his head to answer Dr. Watson but saw me first. It made no sense for us to be tongue-tied. We had no reason to be shy. However, as our eyes locked and held, I felt the blood rush to my face. The gaze lasted long enough for William to intercept it. He looked at me, his brow furrowed.

Mr. Corden broke the spell. "Good day, Miss Herschel, Mr. Herschel, sir," he said, straightening. "The lamb's feet are particularly good. I also have some rabbit and fowl."

William and Dr. Watson stepped forward to examine the meat. Mr. Corden looked at me again. "Fine day for a fair, isn't it?" he said before glancing pointedly at Comet. "And I see his ban has been lifted. Allowed back in the village again, is he?"

"He's no trouble today. We're both a little overawed by the crowd," I said.

"Yes, the sunshine has that effect on the people of Datchet. Do you—"

Dr. Watson interrupted him with a question about the meat. I stood for a moment, wanting to stay but uncertain why. William glanced at me again, his eyes betraying his curiosity.

"I'm going to get some strawberries. Perhaps we can meet in the shade over there?" I said to my brother, pointing to a tree on the edge of the lawn.

The men continued talking to Mr. Corden for some time after making their purchases. I watched from a distance, wondering how it was possible to converse at such length about meat.

Dr. Watson carried a leather folder bound with twine beneath his arm when he came to say goodbye to me in the library the following day.

"Farewell, Miss Herschel. Wish me luck," he said, lifting the case.

"Luck? For what?" I asked.

He raised his brows and smiled widely. "Your brother has entrusted me with the plans for a most ambitious project. We sat up all night plotting. Ask him for the details. I must be on my way," he said, before striding from the room.

It was only that evening when the men had left and William and I were alone in the workshop that I had a chance to inquire.

"Dr. Watson left, wielding a dossier of papers this morning, saying you'd been up all night plotting. What was he talking about?" I asked.

He chuckled. "I showed him the plans Alex and I drew up ages ago for constructing a giant instrument, one of such proportions and power double the size of the twenty-footer—it would answer all the questions we have about the heavens," he said. "They were rough, incomplete sketches. But Dr. Watson was so excited by them, he insisted I clean them up and add more detail. We even estimated the expense of producing and running the machine and added the numbers to the notes."

I'd seen enough drawings and calculations for proposed instruments over the years to picture the papers. "And now? What will he do with the documents?" I asked.

"My friend believes they'll strengthen my case in applying for more money." He sounded amused.

"But shouldn't you make the application yourself?" I asked.

He sighed. "Possibly, but I don't have the time, and I fear it's premature. Dr. Watson insisted otherwise and I was persuaded. If nothing else, it will give me an idea whether there is any appetite among members of the Royal Society and His Majesty to build bigger instruments."

Although William and Alex had often discussed constructing bigger instruments, it seemed fanciful to me. The twenty-footer was an extraordinary machine and had taken years to build and perfect. Building and operating one twice the size was improbable. William's tone of resignation suggested he felt the same. We were quiet for a moment.

"The butcher at the fair yesterday, erm, Mr. Corden, was he the man who hounded Comet from his shop when we first arrived in Datchet?" asked William eventually.

"What? Oh, yes. That was him," I replied, trying to ignore the violent thumping in my chest.

"Have you seen him since?"

"Yes, of course. I must've told you he returned Comet after finding him wandering on the ring road shortly after I ran into the hook," I said, pretending indifference.

William looked up. "Oh? No, I don't believe you told me *who* it was. As I recall, you said someone from the village returned the dog. How curious the very man who chased the dog away brought him home to you. I think I would've remembered that."

"Perhaps you're right. I might not have mentioned it was him. It didn't seem important," I said.

"But then it follows he was also the man who asked the physician to call on you, doesn't it?" he asked, squinting at me now.

I nodded.

He exhaled. "If I'd known, I would've thanked him."

I shrugged, my eyes down.

"It makes sense now," he said.

"What?" I asked, my heart beating even faster.

"He asked about the telescope and was curious about how it works. I assumed Thomas, Mr. Harris, or one of the other men had told him about it, but it's possible he noticed it when he was here. He said he'd read about the Georgium Sidus."

Mr. Corden knew about the planet William had discovered? He'd *read* about it? I was surprised but didn't look up or utter a sound.

"He's the first butcher I've ever met with an interest in astronomy. Seems like an educated, decent man," William added.

"Oh? Yes, I suppose so," I managed.

"You're not certain?" he asked.

My ears were hot and ringing. I wanted William to stop talking about Mr. Corden.

"Well," I said with a nervous snort. "He's a butcher. That's all I know."

I felt my brother's eyes on me. I kept my head down and continued polishing, hoping he hadn't noticed how I'd colored.

"Yes, indeed," he said after a lengthy pause. "Anyway, I invited him to come and have a look at the twenty-footer. He said he'd like that very much."

CHAPTER 16

June 1784
Datchet, England

Juno didn't disappoint us. William no longer scowled when he was summoned to Windsor. Instead, he cantered away on the mare smiling and, whether hours or days later, returned still beaming.

The horse, he said, wasn't a joy only to ride but also to know. She was fast, responsive, and sweet-natured. Even when it was necessary to transport instruments and a carriage was sent, my brother chose to ride Juno cross-country and meet the carriage rather than be driven to and from court. There was color in his cheeks, his eyes were brighter, and his steps were lighter. I saw glimpses of the brother I'd known when we'd walked home after particularly rousing music performances in Bath years earlier. I saw the hints of the William I'd seen when he'd identified the planet and fellow astronomers had shared his excitement. Juno brought him something he'd missed since we'd moved to Datchet. Unfortunately, it wasn't enough.

As we'd hoped, having the horse meant he was home more. Rather than spending nights at court, he'd ride back and forth. However, Juno's influence didn't extend to reducing the demands on William's time. If anything, with the days longer and the skies clearer, he rested less than ever, and eventually, for the first time, my brother conceded to his dissatisfaction.

"His Majesty wants another ten-foot telescope," he said when, on his return from the castle late one afternoon, he patted Juno, handed her reins to Thomas, and walked to the house with me. "He also wants me to spend more time with him and Dr. Maskelyne in Greenwich this month."

"You've been with him so much of late," I muttered.

William groaned. "Yes. I wish there were a way of being in three places at once, but honestly, all I want to do is observe from here and write up my findings. How am I ever going to discover more about the heavens if so much of my time must be spent making telescopes? I left music to be an astronomer, not an instrument maker for others."

And I want to be an astronomer, not an assistant, I thought, feeling a nudge of shame for my self-interest.

Although the initial euphoria of owning a telescope had waned, the satisfaction of being able to scan the skies alone when William was away continued to burn warm within me as one month blurred into another. I'd continued to study the skies and check what I saw against the records with near obsessive energy. I was determined to learn all there was to know and—oh, how the thought made my heart hop!—to discover more about the unknown. At the same time, I could not let William down. He counted on my note-taking and clock-watching when he was observing, and he needed me to write up his findings and work on the catalogs. He also relied on my keen eye to manage the books, order materials, and monitor progress on the telescopes under construction. No matter how far-reaching my dream of being an astronomer was, I had to keep my feet firmly on the ground in my role as William's assistant.

I watched as he sat on the stairs in the hallway and began unfastening his riding boots. Fleeting insensitivity aside, I was troubled by William's discontent. It was one thing for me to know he was doing too much but another to hear him acknowledge it. Not for the first time, I wondered how I could supplement William's income. I could be his assistant and dream about becoming an independent astronomer, but it would all come to naught if we fell prey to bankruptcy. Most worrying was that insolvency would almost certainly mean returning to Hanover for me. I had to do something, but what? The only way I knew how to earn an income was by singing, which I'd given up by leaving Bath and being afraid to perform with anyone other than William. I'd have to think of something else.

"Is there any way, as Dr. Watson suggested, that we could raise the price of our telescopes?" I asked.

He looked up, ran his hands through his hair, and shook his head. "It would be disingenuous to increase the price of the instruments simply because we want to make fewer."

I persevered. "What about the fact that the instruments are in such demand? They're valuable. Doesn't that warrant an increase?"

"If only it were that simple. The problem is we *must* make instruments for others. We need the money. If we make them too expensive, someone else will start making them for less, and we'll lose the business. Without the income from the instruments, we'd have to give up this place, which would make things even more difficult for us," he replied, stretching his legs out in front of him.

I looked at the wide, wooden staircase that rose behind him. The banisters were faded and rough in places. Alex and Mr. Harris had reinforced them here and there, but the wood required oiling and polishing. Although the house wasn't as uncomfortable in summer as it was in winter, the roof still leaked, and the ceilings sagged like the bellies of pregnant cows in several rooms.

"Of course, we need the outdoor space and the stables, but don't you think it might be worth looking for somewhere else to live?" I asked. "We don't need such a large house that requires so much attention. It's possible we could find somewhere less expensive, which has space for the telescopes and workrooms."

"I've wondered the same," said William. "The smith in the village told me about a place called Clay Hall in Old Windsor that might be suitable for us."

"Oh? Will you have a look at it?"

"Yes, but I must see to some other matters first." He sighed. "Also, it would be a tiresome thing, moving. Particularly the twenty-footer, which we've taken such care to set up here. We'd have to give it considerable thought."

"But it would surely be best to do it before the end of summer," I said, enthused by the idea of living in a less derelict house and saving money.

We were interrupted by Hannah with news that a visitor had arrived for William. My brother scowled. "I wasn't expecting anyone," he said.

"He said only to bother you if you have a moment, Mr. Herschel. It's Gabriel Corden, the butcher," she said.

William got his stockinged feet. "Of course," he said, handing his boots to Hannah. "I'll be with him shortly. Lina, will you take Mr. Corden to the telescope? I'll meet you there when I have my shoes."

If Mr. Corden was surprised to see me instead of my brother, he didn't show it. Instead, he greeted me warmly, asked after my health, and acknowledged Comet with a pat, which—to my surprise—the dog not only allowed but also lingered, hoping for more.

I led the way to the telescope. Mr. Corden stared up at it without speaking. Typically, people expressed disbelief at its size when they first laid eyes on the long tube and tall, lattice-like frame. It was possible, I remembered, that he'd seen it when he brought Comet home. Leaning forward with his hands behind his back, he circled the machine as if he were inspecting a horse. I watched, wondering what he might be thinking. Did he know anything about astronomy aside from the fact that William had discovered a planet?

"Ah, the offending hooks," he said when he arrived at the winch. "I'm pleased to see the sharp ends have been capped."

I went to him. "We have Mr. Harris to thank for that. If it had been left to my brother, a simple warning about what happened to me would've sufficed."

"Surely not?" he said.

"I jest, but the truth is, my brother is so busy he must often rely on others to take care of these kinds of details. Mr. Harris and Thomas are godsent," I replied.

"From what I've heard, Mr. Herschel is a fine employer and teacher. Thomas and Mr. Harris are considered experts on all matters concerning the night skies by the rest of us," said Mr. Corden.

It pleased me to hear that others saw what I knew to be true. William cared about the men in his employ. He took for granted they shared his interests and aspirations and believed them to be as dedicated to their work as he was. Mr. Harris and Thomas were called upon to work uncommonly long hours. It didn't occur to William that they might consider work no more than a means of earning an income. He explained to them the workings of the instruments and their purpose and described his observations as if the workers understood as much about the heavens as I did. As such, they knew a great deal and had skills few others possessed. I hadn't imagined Thomas and Mr. Harris might share their knowledge with others. But why wouldn't they? William, his astronomer colleagues and I weren't the only ones who wanted to know and understand the heavens.

"My brother told me that you've read about the Georgium Sidus," I said. "I didn't know you were interested in astronomy."

Mr. Corden looked at me. "You didn't ask."

"No. I didn't. It didn't occur to me. I, well, I—"

"You couldn't imagine a butcher might be interested in anything other than animal carcasses," he said.

I looked down. "No, no. Of course not. It's not that. But I—"

"It's all right, Miss Herschel. I'm jesting now. I understand. You wouldn't expect me to know anything about the skies. You might be surprised to discover I can read and write."

He spoke without bitterness. Even so, I felt my cheeks bloom.

"I was fortunate," he continued. "My father—he was also a butcher—was determined I should be educated. For a reason he never explained, he didn't want me to also become a tradesman, a butcher. I was sent to live with his brother in Ashe, where the vicar's wife ran a small school. My uncle insisted my father wanted me to become a clergyman, but he never said as much to me. He died suddenly—my father—and I had to hurry back to Datchet to work in the butchery. It's the only means of income my family has."

"You have no brothers or sisters to help you?" I asked.

"I have two younger sisters. Both are married now with their own families. My mother is poorly. She lives with her sister, but I must provide for her."

He must've perceived pity in my expression.

"I don't mean to complain. It's a good business, the butchery. I'm grateful to my father. He might've hoped I would do something else, became something more, but he left us an honest means of earning our keep. And, with the learning I received, I can, if not understand, at least appreciate other things, including machines like this," he said, smiling as he motioned to the telescope.

"Ah, Mr. Corden," said William, walking toward us. "Let me try to increase your appreciation of it."

I left the men, returned to the workshop, picked up my cloth, and resumed polishing. With Thomas grooming Juno and Mr. Harris busy with some carpentry outside, the quiet, methodical nature of my work allowed me to continue thinking about Mr. Corden. That he was educated shouldn't have surprised me. The writing desk in his shop was a clue. Also, he was eloquent and measured. If not for my reserve—and, I conceded, prejudice—I might've learned more about him earlier. But even if I had known, what then? What was it I hoped for? All I understood was that there was something about Mr. Corden that set him apart from other men. Thinking about him and seeing him both pleased and unsettled me.

CHAPTER 17

September 1784
Datchet, England

No fortune is finer than an unexpected one, but it rarely comes without conditions. That was my sentiment after William flung open the door of the library one overcast afternoon and strode across the room with such vigor that Comet crept from where he lay at my feet and hid behind the couch.

"We are saved!" said my brother, waving a letter at me. "We won't have to move after all."

Although he'd not finalized the rental, William had been to see the place in the nearby village of Old Windsor. Clay Hall would, he'd told me, do. While the house was smaller, the grounds were large, and there were several other buildings on the property suitable for workrooms. Crucially, it would cost less to rent and maintain. However, I'd sensed something made him uncertain. It was probably the practical difficulty of moving while we were so busy. I felt torn by the idea of leaving Datchet too. On the one hand, the thought of living somewhere less rundown and easier to warm—particularly with the change of seasons upon us—appealed to me. However, the efforts required would be immense. Also, it would put a few more miles between me and Mr. Corden.

"How so? What's happened?" I asked.

He flapped the letter again before laying it down in front of me. "It's from Dr. Watson. He presented my plans for the giant instrument—the ones I thought premature—and listen to this, Lina," he said, taking a deep breath. "My friend has raised the promise of two thousand pounds for us. I must repeat it to believe it myself. Two thousand! Read it. Tell me I'm not deluded."

I read it. He was not.

Determined to improve things for my brother, Dr. Watson had met with several members of the Royal Society, expressing his concern about William's situation. He wrote in his letter:

I began by telling them it would not do for the King's Astronomer to struggle. You gave up a prosperous profession in Bath to dedicate yourself to leading the kingdom, indeed the world, in astronomy. How will you continue to discover anything worthwhile when you can barely find time to eat and sleep? I insisted it would not do and said that if His Majesty wants to make the best possible use of the brilliant mind of Mr. William Herschel, it should not be so abused. Then, when I saw how they nodded their heads, I produced your sketches and calculations for the forty-foot telescope and explained how advantageous the machine would be to your work. It was the clincher. While a few were aghast at the costs you forecast, most understand great inventions and discovery do not come cheap.

To our great advantage, Sir Joseph Banks, the president of the Royal Society and adviser to His Majesty, agreed with Dr. Watson most heartily. In fact, Sir Banks declared that, if the world's inhabitants were to learn about its wonders under King George's reign, then His Majesty must grant his explorers more generous funding. As such, he'd urged the king to pay William two thousand pounds so my brother could get to work on the giant instrument forthwith.

"But William," I said, my voice tight with concern. "You're to build a forty-foot telescope! Is that even possible? It wasn't easy to create the twenty-footer." I thought in particular about how difficult it would be to build the enormous reflectors. Working with the melted metal and perfecting the grinding and polishing of the disk once it was cast and set remained a challenge for us, even with small mirrors. "And how will that improve our situation? Is the demand for building telescopes not the very thing that keeps you from your other work?"

"The designs are preliminary, but it can be done. A forty-footer will take me farther into the universe than anyone else believes possible. It will be extraordinary. And you haven't read the second page," he said, smiling at me from where he'd thrown himself on the couch opposite. "The money will be paid in tranches, with the first arriving before we begin work." He leaned forward, elbows on his knees and hands clasped together. "Think of what it will allow us to observe, Lina."

I turned the page and read on. My hand trembled slightly. It was exciting, but there were conditions and I felt a familiar combination of anticipation and anxiety.

"Sir Banks stipulates that His Majesty will require regular accounts of proceedings and you should expect frequent visits from his men, perhaps even His Majesty himself." I said, aware of a gnawing in my stomach as I scanned Dr. Watson's words. "And, did you see this? 'The instrument must be ready by 1789.' Is that feasible? Did you estimate how long it might take to construct?"

William waved his hand. "Not yet, but the money will allow us to establish our own forge. I'll employ more men, artisans, and experts. We'll be able to focus on it, and once things are up and going, I will have time to devote to observing, and we'll write up my discoveries. We'll be more industrious and productive than ever," he said.

"Until we're interrupted by important people—His Majesty even—who want to investigate your work," I said.

"Yes, but even then, everything will be different. It's exciting, Lina. It's what we need to revolutionize astronomy. I must write to Alex tonight. Perhaps he'll come if I assure him he'll be paid."

It seemed unlikely, I thought. Alex had yet to visit with his wife. When I'd written to ask him if they might come, Alex had replied that "it didn't suit Mrs. Herschel as yet." I couldn't see how news of William's fortune would change her mind, but I knew Alex would be pleased to read of it.

"Yes, everything will be different. Congratulations, William," I said, trying to ignore the image of the royal entourage traipsing into the yard. What would they make of the shabby house? What would the king and his men think of William Herschel's sister?

My brother grinned at me, slapped his thighs, and jumped to his feet.

"Where are you going?" I asked.

"To tell the men. We need to finish the instruments we're busy with without delay and get the word out that we need an ingenious smith," he said before practically running from the room.

It had been threatening to rain all day but was still dry, and with William's news having interrupted my work, I decided it was a good time to take Comet out. In truth, I hoped I might encounter Mr. Corden whenever I left the property. However, I hadn't seen him since his visit to see the twenty-footer. As it was, I was deep in thought about Dr. Watson's letter, and it was only when I noticed Comet looking behind me, his ears pricked, that I registered my name.

"Miss Herschel!"

I turned to see the butcher loping toward me.

"I'm sorry," he said, puffing as he stopped. "I shouldn't have shouted, but you didn't hear me, and, er, well, I thought I'd say good day."

He glanced at his boots. It made things easier for me, knowing that he was also bashful.

"Good afternoon, Mr. Corden," I laughed. "I was preoccupied. Are you going to visit your mother?"

His eyes rounded. Of course, he hadn't told me she lived hereabouts; Hannah had.

"Yes. I seem to be going the same way as you. Would you mind if I walked with you? I'll go left at Twin Oaks. But if you'd rather be alone with your thoughts, I'll hurry ahead and not bother you."

"I won't tell Miss Fleming if you don't," I said as we walked on.

"Miss Fleming?"

"She was tasked with teaching me the proper ways of an English lady when I arrived in the country."

"What? You're not *really* an English lady?" he teased.

I laughed, certain that Miss Fleming and Miss Hudson would've chastised me, not only for my association with Mr. Corden but also for my unlady-like lack of verbal restraint. It had been a long time since I'd thought about the women. I'd even stopped wondering whether Miss Hudson still wrote to William. Her name hadn't been mentioned since his remorse after my accident.

"Oh, indeed, I *am* an English lady. But perhaps the kind of English lady polite society approves of in Bath is different from the one walking her dog down the lane near Datchet," I said, feeling quite lightheaded by my daring.

Mr. Corden chuckled, and we walked without talking for a while. It didn't feel wrong. Even the weather was obliging. The clouds were densely packed in a manner that made them appear grumpy but innocuous. There was a light breeze, which, as it rustled dry leaves on the roadside, seemed to whisper that autumn was upon us. Comet trotted confidently ahead as if born to the country rather than on the streets of Bath.

"How is Mr. Herschel?" asked Mr. Corden eventually.

"Very, very well, I'm happy to report," I replied. "He received some particularly good news today that promises to make things easier for us."

"I'm pleased to hear it," he said.

I wanted to tell him more. Everything, in fact. However, it seemed that the details should come from my brother if they were to be announced.

"It seems we'll be expanding our work," I said instead. "Perhaps, in a few months, William will be able to show you what he's doing and explain."

"I'd like that," he said. "And what about your work, Miss Herschel? What are you working on?"

That he didn't press for more information about William's news pleased me. However, I was uncertain about his interest in my efforts. Women weren't meant to strive to do more than support men. What would he think if he knew my ambitions? Would he be appalled by how unladylike they were? Or amused by what many might believe was fantasy?

"My undertakings involve helping my brother," I replied, rearranging my shawl across my arms and shoulders. "I do what I can to support him."

"Oh? That's not the way Mr. Herschel described it to me," he said. "He told me you having learned to sweep the skies with your own telescope is like having another astronomer in the house. That your understanding of the heavens, what to look for, and how to observe is excellent. He said if I wanted to learn about the stars, planets, and all other heavenly objects, I could learn from you."

I was stunned. What a contrast this was to how William had described my efforts to Miss Hudson. Also, he occasionally thanked me for assisting him, but he never praised me or commented on how much I'd learned. He seemed unmoved by my enthusiasm for astronomy, which was one of the reasons I still hadn't told him how I dreamed of being his professional equal. William had never given me reason to believe he might think it possible. Indeed, it surprised me he'd commended my abilities to the butcher.

"He said that?" I asked.

Mr. Corden held up his palms. "He did."

A tiny voice in my head urged me to be proud. It was true that I understood a great deal about the heavens. My brother had guided me and given me a telescope, but I'd also taught myself by diligently observing, studying the atlas and catalogs. William's instructions and scrawled notes made me familiar with names, terms, times, and numbers. However, if I wasn't independently intrigued by the heavens, curious to know more and determined to be an astronomer, I'd know only what William had time to teach me. So, he'd told Mr. Corden having me there was *like* having another astronomer in the house. What would he say if he knew I wanted to be an astronomer unequivocally? I wished I could, but it wasn't something I'd admit to. William wanted an assistant, not a colleague.

We reached the top of a short hill, and as we descended the narrow road closely bound by impenetrable hawthorn hedgerows on either side, I made out the distinct shape of the two large trees on the edge of the road. We were almost at Twin Oaks.

"Will you, Miss Herschel?" said Mr. Corden.

"Will I what?" I asked.

"Teach me what you know about heaven?"

I stopped. So did he. We stared at each other. I wanted to say yes. The idea of sharing what I'd learned with him pleased me. I also wanted to tell him how I wished to be an astronomer and how what William had said to him encouraged me. But still, I was uncertain. What if I was giving William's comment too much importance? What if both men believed it unlikely that a woman would ever be taken seriously in astronomy? I had to protect my dream.

I began to explain. "I don't think it—"

There was a low rumbling and rattling, which, as it drew closer, made the Earth tremble. I looked around. What was it?

"Coach!" shouted Mr. Corden.

Drawn by four horses, a large carriage hurtled into view around the corner. It was coming at us at great speed. Ahead, Comet disappeared under the hedge.

Good idea, I thought, but I didn't move.

Occupying the full width of the road, the horses didn't slow. As I raised my eyes, I saw the coachman pale at the sight of us. He shouted something unintelligible and fumbled for the reins as if he'd just woken up. It was too late. The horses were upon us, and with the spiky hedges on either side, there was nowhere to go. I opened my mouth to scream, but my voice was gone. I stood, frozen.

Just as I closed my eyes and imagined that I felt the steamy breaths of the horses on my skin, fingers wrapped around the top of my arm, and I was flung backward into the hawthorn. Mr. Corden threw himself, face forward, against me. The coach thundered by in a pulsating dust storm.

For a moment, we remained still, stamped into the hedge, bodies pressed together. I opened my eyes to see the carriage disappear over the hill and then looked up to find Mr. Corden's eyes on mine. Our chests lifted and fell in unison as if we shared a breath. I saw how, despite the cool temperature, tiny beads of moisture collected above his top lip. I'd never been as close to anyone.

He moved back, slowly releasing my arms. I hadn't realized until then that he was still holding me. I extracted myself from the bush.

"Are you all right?" he asked.

I nodded, although the sensation of being impaled by thorns and branches lingered. "Do you see Comet?"

We walked to where I'd seen him disappear and found him wedged between the lower stems of the hedge. With some coaxing, he finally emerged, quivering. I crouched to pat and stroke him.

"It's all right, Comet," I said. "We're all fine. Let's go home."

"I'll accompany you," said Mr. Corden.

"No, of course not. We're almost at Twin Oaks. You go on."

He lowered his eyes. "I'd like to. See you home safely, I mean."

"Truly, Mr. Corden, it's not necessary. It was just a scare, and I'm completely recovered." I looked at Comet. "And he'll be fine soon too."

He sighed. "Well, if you're certain."

"I am."

Our eyes met again, and we smiled.

"It's unlikely we'll come across another coach," I said. I was stalling, reluctant to bid him farewell.

He might've felt the same. "No. It was unusual. I don't think I've ever seen such a large carriage on this road before."

"It was fortunate you were with us," I said.

He looked at his feet and took a step toward me. "Miss Herschel, there's something—" I held my breath as he lifted his hand. "There's a sprig of hedge in your hair."

I stood motionless as he untangled the twigs and leaves. Then, with a small bow, he handed it to me.

"A memento," he said. "Good day, Miss Herschel."

It was only as I walked home that I realized even when he was within inches from me, Mr. Corden never seemed to notice my scars.

CHAPTER 18

February 1785
Datchet, England

THE MONTHS FOLLOWING NEWS OF THE TWO-THOUSAND-POUND GRANT WERE busier than any we'd known. The property vibrated and hummed with industry. Everything was also much easier.

We could afford the salaries of skilled people, which unchained William from the workbench and allowed him to devote his time to the roles of overseer and designer. Although he conceded they "might still evolve, and particularly when Alex had time to apply his mind to them," William refined the plans for the forty-footer and, at my request, showed them to me.

With an octagon-shaped tube of forty feet long and five feet in diameter, the Newtonian-type telescope would require at least two, but perhaps three, reflectors each of which would measure up to fifty inches in diameter.

"Fifty inches!" I repeated. I'd understood the giant telescope would require reflectors of grand proportions, but I hadn't anticipated just how large they'd have to be. "How—"

"Yes, they'll weigh about half a ton each and cost us between two hundred and five hundred pounds each to manufacture," said my brother.

"But—"

"Don't worry. We won't attempt to make them ourselves. It wouldn't be possible. Working with such volumes of speculum and creating such large reflectors will need expertise and a dedicated work force we don't possess. They'll require at least twenty men to cast, grind, and polish. I'll find a foundry in London and they can be shipped up the Thames to us," he said.

"Do such experts and expertise exist? After all, no such reflectors have ever been constructed," I said.

I wanted to be hopeful, but even as I reminded myself that just because something *hadn't* been done didn't mean it *couldn't* be, the extent of the project worried me.

However, William was fueled by optimism. "We'll be the first, but I'm confident I'll find someone. The twenty-footer didn't exist until we built it. Now, take a look at what I plan for the gantry," he said, pointing to his drawings.

The telescope, he said, would be supported by a wooden frame built on a platform, allowing it to be turned on its axis by two men. The angle and position could be minutely adjusted by William, who'd climb a series of ladders to the viewing platform at the mouth of the telescope.

"And this," he said, placing his finger on an enclosed, wooden booth at the bottom of the gantry, "is where you will sit with your desk, clocks, atlas, and notebooks. It'll be warmer than sitting inside with the doors open."

"Warmer, yes. But will I hear you?" I asked, picturing myself closed up in the box-like room with no view of the stars.

"Hopefully," he replied. "I am accustomed to having to speak loudly to you."

"Perhaps a long metal pipe running from the top into the booth would allow us to communicate without shouting," I said.

"Hmm," said William, examining my face as if he hadn't seen me for a while. "That's an excellent idea. I'll add a note immediately."

Work on the forty-footer didn't exempt William from continuing to attend to His Majesty's demands and observing the night sky with me taking notes and adding our findings to our catalogs.

As ever, on clear nights when William was away, I swept the skies alone, eager not only to continue learning but also to make discoveries that might demonstrate my abilities to others. Although I kept my dream of being a fully fledged astronomer to myself, I was absorbed, diligent, and motivated; perhaps as much so as my brother. But our challenges weren't behind us.

The increase in employees and activities—not to mention the unprecedented size of the telescope under construction—meant operations quickly outgrew the stables. That didn't slow matters. Just as my brothers had transformed the bedchambers in our house in Bath into workrooms, so rooms in the house at Datchet filled with materials, tools, apparatuses, and workers.

Excited by the size of the fireplace, Mr. Campion—who was, said William, "the region's most able and inventive blacksmith"—wasted no time in erecting a forge in the large upstairs bedchamber Alex had occupied. William's specialists also included a cabinetmaker; a joiner, accompanied by several journeymen; and an expert in brass, who quickly became known as the "Brass Man."

"The only man who has better skills with brass is Alex," said William. "I hope he and the Brass Man can work side by side one day. They'll excel."

"I hope the floors withstand the weight of your endeavors," I replied, watching a procession of men lugging blocks, hammers, tongs, chisels, and equipment I didn't recognize up the rickety stairway.

William's small nod suggested he hoped the same, but he said nothing. He might, I thought, have noticed how I'd ignored his mentioning Alex. I'd given up wishing our brother would visit us.

"I also hope the hearth will endure the relentless heat of Mr. Campion's fires," I added.

What I discovered the next day, when they appeared before me in the library, was that Alex and his wife were *already* en route from Bath when William had casually dropped Alex's name into our conversation. Once more, William had wanted to surprise me, and again, he had succeeded.

For a moment, I stared at Alex in disbelief. I'd imagined marriage would harm him, as it had our sister, but he looked as robust as ever.

"Good day, Caroline," he said with an uncertain, lopsided smile.

I was across the room, standing in front of him with his hands in mine before I could gather my thoughts. Comet scrambled to his feet and followed me, wagging his tail.

"Alex!" I swallowed as I felt my eyes well up. I looked at William. He was beaming. "Why didn't you tell me?" I asked.

He raised his shoulders. "And ruin the chance of *this*?"

"Margaret," said Alex, turning to the slight woman at his side. "This is my sister, Caroline. Caroline, my wife, Margaret."

She was as narrow as me but taller, of course. Her pale, thin face was framed by soft, fair curls, and she wore a broad, white neckerchief so high it covered her chin. With so much of her hidden, her eyes seemed unduly large. She reminded me of a dormouse I'd once observed peering out from between two blades of grass as I'd walked with Comet.

"At last," she said, though she looked terrified. Was she? Of me?

"Yes, at last. I—"

Before I could complete my greeting, Alex's wife turned sideways, lifted a gloved hand to her mouth, and began coughing. He gently patted her back, looking at me. "She began feeling unwell an hour or so ago." He glanced at Comet. "Animals seem to make it worse."

She was gasping and coughing now, hand to her chest and bent double. I moved away, calling Comet.

"Did Hannah prepare a bedchamber?" I asked William, having to raise my voice to be heard.

"Take mine. I'll be fine on the sofa," said William. "You know where it is, Alex."

So, Mrs. Alex Herschel was led to William's bed, where she stayed and was waited upon by her husband and Hannah. Comet was confined to the kitchen, where he lay at the door waiting for me to take him out.

"Perhaps you should call the physician?" suggested William when Mrs. Herschel was no better after a few days.

"It's a bad spell," said Alex. "Typically, it passes within a week."

I held my tongue but couldn't quash my disappointment. Alex could only spare us seven days and he spent most of it tending his wife. By the time they returned to Bath, she and I hadn't exchanged more than an incomplete greeting and a goodbye. While I acknowledged my brother's health hadn't been harmed by marriage and he didn't seem unhappy, the visit did nothing to assuage my misgivings about it. I still couldn't see any advantages to being married. However, William insisted he was pleased with their stay.

"Our brother has lost none of his skills. He was so helpful. Such a worker," he said. "Oh, that he could be here all the time!"

"Pity he had to spend so much time nursing Mrs. Herschel," I said.

William scowled. "I'm sorry she was ill. She seems like a kind woman. It would've been good to get to know her better. I told her they should return as soon as possible."

I'd grown so accustomed to the noises, I stopped hearing the stomping of boots, pounding and grinding of metal, and incessant opening and slamming of doors within days of the workers' annexing all available rooms in the house. My nose no longer twitched when it sensed smoke, hot metal, or sizzling water. The library was something of a sanctuary, and there, with the door closed and my head bent over my work, I ignored the reverberations of industry all around me. Who needed peace when our hopes of seeing farther into the night sky were being melted, molded, and beaten into shape?

One especially cold February morning, following a night of heavy snowfall, Mr. Campion went up the stairs as I came down. I'd already noted that his dedication was surpassed only by William's. It was unlikely any of the other men would fight their way through the snow to work that day.

"Good morning, Miss Herschel," he said.

"You're a devoted man, Mr. Campion," I replied.

He smiled. "I struggled to fall asleep last night thinking about a piece of metal that resisted me yesterday. When I awoke this morning, I had the solution. No snowstorm was going to keep me away."

Comet followed me to the library, where William was already at his desk, having had a fire burning in the closed room for long enough to have created a cozy haven. I sat and applied myself to checking the calculations of the nebulae I was to add to the catalog.

We worked in companionable silence for about an hour until, without warning, a deafening explosion from directly overhead almost rocketed us from our seats. I pushed my hands against my chest, where my heart thundered violently, and stared at William. His eyes bulged.

"What on earth!" he exclaimed. "Could it—"

His words were drowned by what sounded like the low rumble of wheels over cobblestones directly above our heads. William leaped to his feet, his chair tumbling backward.

"Come! Get under!" he shouted, falling to his knees and scrambling beneath a small table in the center of the room.

The sound grew louder, and as I crawled alongside my brother, it turned into a thunderous cacophony of splintering wood and crashing debris. I grabbed William's arm and pressed my face against the fabric of his jacket.

We hunkered on the library floor until the sounds faded and finally disappeared. I raised my head to see Comet cowering below my writing desk some feet away.

"Come, Comet. Come," I whispered.

The dog looked at me with the same dubious expression he'd worn when I'd appropriated his shelter alongside the Avon. He trembled but didn't approach. I looked at the table's spindly legs and saw that those of my writing desk were sturdier.

Clever dog, I thought.

William shifted as if to go. I pulled him toward me just as the sound started again. This time, it was a mournful groan, followed by creaking and more crashing.

"It's the floor! We must get out before it comes through the ceiling and crushes us," I said when it was quiet enough to be heard.

He held up his hands. The sudden silence was eerie.

"What are we to do?" I whispered.

"Wait a while."

Comet panted. I called him again. "Come here."

This time, the dog did move. But, instead of coming to me, he skulked away and stood at the closed door that led into the hallway. He understood the urgency of leaving the house.

William slowly eased himself away from me and turned to look up. "I don't think it's the floor," he said. "At least, not the one above us. Stay here. I'll investigate."

It occurred to me to object. It wasn't safe. However, what else was there to do but find out what had happened? He and the dog left the library. When I heard William on the stairs, I stood and followed. Comet was at the front door. I opened it and watched him bound over the snow to the stables, where I imagined he'd bury himself in the hay in Juno's stall.

I gingerly made my way upstairs and headed toward the sound of William's voice in Alex's former bedchamber. The room was unrecognizable. Miraculously, the floor *had* held. However, the roof and ceiling above Mr. Campion's forge had collapsed into a messy heap of broken planks, shattered slates, and piles of dirty snow. The blacksmith had narrowly escaped being buried beneath the rubble by diving into the large, metal half tube lying against a wall. Now, he leaned against the doorpost, staring at the mess. On the other side of the room, the fire spat as if indignant at the snow melting around it.

"It was always a risk, operating a forge in a bedchamber," said Mr. Campion, rubbing his jaw.

I looked up at the gaping hole exposing us to the gray sky. More snow looked imminent.

"It might not have had anything to do with your work, Mr. Campion," I said. "This house, this roof, everything here has been crumbling for years. Look at that." I motioned to the clutter of planks. It was obvious from how and where they'd broken that water had permeated the wood, causing it to swell and weaken. "The rotting started well before we arrived. And then, the weight of the snow, one final snowflake, perhaps a chilly gust, and it all came down."

Mr. Campion glanced at William.

"We're lucky you weren't injured," said my brother.

"I can't remember ever moving so fast," replied the blacksmith.

William shook his head. "We must leave this place as soon as possible."

That night, William wrote to Mr. James Kent, who was the land agent responsible for the house my brother had seen in Old Windsor shortly before we were told about the grant. The rental agreement arrived a few days later.

"You'll like it," said William when I quizzed him about Clay Hall. "It's smaller and homelier than this monstrosity. It'll be easier to warm. The grounds are ample, and the outbuildings are linked to the house by a short, covered walkway. It'll be convenient. I've already decided how I'll arrange the work areas."

"What about the roof? Did you examine it?" I teased. "And the windows and doors?"

"The place seems in good order. I took my time inspecting it when Mr. Kent showed me around," he said.

"You haven't met the owner?" I asked.

William shook his head. "He lives in London. The family hasn't used the place in years."

Although Clay Hall was only about two miles from Datchet, and Hannah, Thomas, and Mr. Harris had agreed to remain in our employ, moving was a substantial undertaking. We'd accumulated vast quantities of tools, instruments, furniture, and other materials since arriving in Datchet, which required sorting, packing, and transporting in several wagons.

Once the move was underway, William went to the new house to oversee the unpacking while Comet and I stayed in Datchet to finalize the dispatch of each load.

When the last wagon rolled out of the yard, leaving Comet and me waiting for the carriage that would take us, I sat on the stairs in the hallway of the empty house with the dog at my feet. Spent and unsettled, I put my elbows on my knees and rested my head in my hands. The moment had arrived, but I wasn't sure I was ready. Of course, I was eager to leave the unsound house, which I feared might collapse entirely during the next storm. However, I'd miss the lanes, fields, and woodlands Comet and I knew so well. Places we might encounter Mr. Corden. Clay Hall wasn't far away, but our paths were unlikely to cross in Old Windsor. I'd probably never see him again.

In fact, with so much happening when work began on the new telescope and then preparing to leave Datchet, the frequency and duration of my walks with Comet had diminished. I hadn't seen Mr. Corden again after the incident with the stagecoach until Christmas, when William had pointed him out to me at church. He was with others—his mother, sisters, and their husbands, I'd guessed—and although he'd greeted us from across several pews with a nod, there was no opportunity for conversation.

Now, as I sat alone in the empty house, there was a light tap at the front door. Comet scrambled to his paws, barking.

"Come, Comet. It's time to go," I said, standing.

I opened the door, expecting to see the carriage William had sent. Instead, it was Mr. Corden. He stood about a yard from the door, the breeze ruffling his dark curls. I stared at him. Had I conjured his presence simply by thinking about him?

"Thomas told me you'd be leaving today. I thought I might've missed you until I heard the barking," he said.

"Yes, we're still here, waiting to go."

I saw the hint of a smile, the one I'd first noticed in the butchery. "I wanted to bid you farewell, Miss Herschel."

"Thank you, Mr. Corden," I replied.

There was an uneasy silence. What was there to say aside from goodbye? I looked across the yard to the stables. Empty, they looked dark and cold. The garden, though much tidier than it was when we arrived, had remained largely bare. Although he was a gardener, Mr. Harris hadn't had much time to plant or tend to it over the years. I watched Comet approach and sniff Mr. Corden's boots.

"It'll be odd not looking out for you when I pass by," said the butcher, bending to pat the dog.

I wondered what he'd think if I said I'd miss him. I couldn't admit to it. Was there nothing I could say? Miss Fleming had tried to teach me the art of conversation. She'd said not to be afraid of opening discussions with well-worn topics. I ran through the other points I recalled from her lessons: Ask questions. Encourage others to talk about themselves. Don't feel that you must impress them with your wit or opinions. Never raise subjects about which you know nothing. Don't discuss scandals.

"The weather doesn't seem sure what to do, does it?" I mumbled.

Mr. Corden glanced at the sky. "No, it doesn't. And you'll no doubt be pleased to see the last of this place after the snow came through the roof."

Hannah and Thomas had kept him well informed.

"Yes, I'm eager to go," I said.

He glanced down. I saw how he'd interpreted it.

"No," I said, feeling breathless. "I mean, I'm eager to leave this house. But Datchet… Well, I've grown to enjoy the countryside. Comet will miss the, erm, rabbits."

Our eyes met for a moment. The clatter of hooves announced the arrival of the carriage as it turned into the yard. Mr. Corden exhaled.

"Would it be acceptable, Miss Herschel, if I write to you at Old Windsor?" he asked.

I took a breath. "What would you write about?"

He chuckled and glanced at the carriage as it drew closer. "I'd asked after your health and Mr. Herschel's, of course. And perhaps about the stars."

"The stars?"

"I know you didn't agree to teach me when I asked, but I've been trying to learn as much as I can alone. I correspond with my old teacher. She's very kind. Maybe you could fill in what she doesn't know," he said, talking fast.

"Old Windsor isn't that far away. Perhaps, in a while, you could come and see the progress on the new telescope," I said.

"I'd like that if Mr. Herschel agrees," he replied.

William didn't have time to entertain general curiosity about his work. However, he'd enjoyed showing Mr. Corden the twenty-footer, and I knew he would make an exception for him. Perhaps it mattered to William that the butcher was the only friend I'd made in Datchet.

"You might also come to see Comet," I said.

"Of course," he replied, smiling. "And I'll visit the butcher in Old Windsor and warn him about the dog's wily ways."

CHAPTER 19

June 1785
Clay Hall, Old Windsor, England

WILLIAM WAS RIGHT ABOUT THE HOUSE AT OLD WINDSOR. THE WINDOWS AND doors didn't rattle or gape, the brickwork was solid, and the rooms, stables, and yard were large enough to accommodate the many workmen and implements under construction. Within days of moving, the hammering, grinding, pounding, and stomping sounds I'd known in Datchet settled into my ears again.

With the twenty-footer reassembled in the yard, work underway on the other telescopes, and summer upon us, William and I commenced sweeping every clear night until daylight. Despite Clay Hall's slight distance from Windsor Castle, the ride, said William, was prettier. The expression I'd come to think of as his "Juno smile" was back. Comet was soon at home too, having discovered new rodent hunting grounds in a patch of long grass in the garden. Until one hot June morning, I believed we'd found the ideal place to live and work.

Unfamiliar carriages and wagons carrying people and material regularly arrived at Clay Hall. I was so accustomed to their coming and going I'd stopped looking out of the window at the sound of hooves and wheels. As such, I was taken aback by the sudden appearance of Miss Hudson alongside William in the library doorway one morning.

Poised, high-haired, and ornate in a cream-colored gown with all the trimmings, she stared at me, cool and composed, as if she might be on her way to a summer luncheon and I, delaying her passage. My brother, on the other hand, looked flustered. He stooped and didn't meet my eye. A chill charged through me. We'd studiously stopped talking about Miss Hudson. I'd been certain she and William were no longer communicating. Now, with her at Clay Hall and his sheepish demeanor, it seemed I might be wrong.

I got to my feet. "What a surprise, Miss Hudson," I said, mustering a smile and avoiding looking at my brother. "You found us. I mean, here, at our new residence. Are you well? Shall I call for tea?"

She glanced at William as if requiring his consent. He cleared his throat. "Of course," he said. "Tea."

Miss Hudson's mouth lifted at the corners, but her eyes were steady, and she said nothing.

William took a deep breath. "Lina, Miss Hudson is here to, erm, she's here for a specific purpose."

A specific purpose?

My thoughts scattered in several directions, but one theory came to the fore: Miss Hudson had come to Clay Hall to see William. They'd been in touch ever since her fateful visit to Datchet. They'd continued to exchange letters. William had visited her when he was in London. He'd written *and* visited. The relationship had evolved into something of significance, something they were about to announce. She'd insist I go. He'd send me back to Hanover. All this and within an instant my mind conjured.

"She doesn't know, Mr. Herschel?" asked Miss Hudson.

I tried to swallow, but I was parched. I looked from one face to the other, feeling dizzy.

My brother exhaled. "Miss Hudson's cousin owns Clay Hall."

"Cousin?" I repeated.

"Yes. He's our landlord," he replied.

Again, I looked at her, at him. "Is that it?" I asked eventually.

Miss Hudson raised her brows. William nodded.

That was it? *That* was their announcement? Lord Sutton, the bachelor cousin whose affairs Miss Hudson helped take care of in London, was our landlord. Relief flooded through me like rain upon desiccated earth.

I hadn't asked, and William hadn't told me the name of the owner of Clay Hall. That it was Miss Hudson's cousin explained his uneasiness. He thought I'd believe he'd deliberately hidden the information from me. Why would I? It had probably slipped his mind. The connection was a coincidence and, compared to what I'd imagined, not important. I wanted to embrace him and reassure him that there was no reason for him to feel uneasy.

I shrugged, unable to hide a smile. "Well, I—"

Miss Hudson spoke over me. "The reason I'm here is to inspect the property. My cousin is unwell. It's unlikely he'll be able to travel for some months. He's asked me to take care of several matters, including issues of tenancy."

William looked at his shoes. There was something more going on. The room buzzed with tension. Was she still angry with me? Was that what this was about?

"I hope that doesn't mean you won't have time to stop and visit for a moment," I said, determined to ease matters. "As I wrote to you after I behaved so badly at Datchet, I deeply regret that evening. My outburst was unwarranted. I am sincerely sorry for my disrespect and for the damage it did to our friendship, Miss Hudson. I hope that you will give me a chance to prove my remorse and mend our relationship."

I felt William's eyes on me but was uncertain whether he approved or was unhappy I'd brought up the incident.

For a moment, no one said anything. The only sound was the skin-chilling rasp of rough metal on smooth metal from Mr. Campion's quarters. The grating noise seemed fitting, given Miss Hudson's hostility.

Finally, she spoke, "Perhaps you could call for tea while Mr. Herschel shows me around our property."

As they left, I pondered her words, "*our* property." What did that mean? Were she and her cousin so attached she considered Clay Hall hers? Or was she simply reminding me that *she* was in control here?

Half an hour later, my brother and Miss Hudson reappeared in the dining room. Neither said a word as she sat, but I sensed William was even twitchier. She rested her elbows on the table and placed her hands together.

"As I said, Mr. Herschel, we knew you'd use the house to manufacture your instruments. That was understood. However, the extent of your industry far exceeds what was expected and what is acceptable. What I saw at Datchet was that you used the stables for your workshop." She sighed, and I wondered what she would've thought had she seen the state of the Datchet house in our latter days there. "Now, however, you've brought some of the work into the house. You must understand how worrying this is. The place was not built to be a factory. Moreover, I'm greatly disturbed to see that you've cut down three trees."

William, seated at the table too now, ran his fingers through his hair. "I explained exactly what I planned to do here to Mr. Kent before I signed the lease. I even sketched it out for him, Miss Hudson. As your cousin's agent, he must've explained it to Lord Sutton. Perhaps we should send for him, for Mr. Kent, so that you can ask him yourself," he said.

"It makes no difference what you and Mr. Kent discussed," she argued, looking at me as if I might back her. "I repeat, it's the extent of what you're *actually* doing, what I've seen today, that worries me. The house will not withstand the conditions, and the garden will be ruined."

I handed Miss Hudson her tea and, wanting to somehow demonstrate to my brother that he had my support, glanced at him as I slid his cup across the table. He looked away.

"So, what do you want us to do? Do you want us out?" I asked, my eyes on Miss Hudson now.

She shook her head. "No, Miss Herschel, no. As I explained to your brother, I simply want certain activities, the damaging ones, stopped. You should find a foundry, workshops, and whatever you require elsewhere in the village to grind, cast, and pound metal. You can live here, but you cannot continue to use Clay Hall like this. And you certainly cannot fell more trees to get better views."

William placed his cup in its saucer with a light clatter. "You worry about damage, Miss Hudson, but did you see any? We've been working here for several months. We haven't dented or scratched anything beyond what can be expected of normal wear. Yes, perhaps the use of the rooms is unusual, but we work carefully. There's no reason to do otherwise. As for the trees, I specifically asked Mr. Kent's permission to remove them before I signed the rental agreement. He confirmed he had your cousin's agreement. I don't understand your objections. We are legitimate, cautious tenants. Clay Hall is ideal for us. It's perfectly located, we're settled, and we have employed and trained workmen who live in the area. It will be costly and disruptive to move our work elsewhere again." He paused, leaned toward Miss Hudson, and added quietly, "Also, it's unnecessary, Miss Hudson. I assure you we will not harm the property. You have my word."

For a moment, as their eyes locked across the table, the room was quiet. Even the rasp was still.

We were interrupted by a tap at the door. It was Hannah. "I'm sorry to intrude," she said. "Mr. Corden is here, Miss Herschel. He says you're expecting him."

CHAPTER 20

June 1785
Clay Hall, England

THE TIMING OF MR. CORDEN'S VISIT COULDN'T HAVE BEEN WORSE. HANNAH was right. I was expecting him. Not necessarily that day, but sometime in June or July. There'd been letters. Not many, but enough to sustain our friendship and keep me informed about his ongoing interest in astronomy. I'd replied to them all, describing how we'd settled at Clay Hall and how work was progressing. Mr. Corden had said he'd pass this way in June or July and asked if he might stop by. I'd mentioned it to William, and he'd agreed, saying that if he was home, he'd be happy to show the butcher around. I'd looked forward to seeing him and had even imagined telling him how I was quietly working to become an astronomer. For the first time, it seemed I might trust someone with my secret. I'd even thought about mentioning how I dreamed of one day reporting my findings to the Royal Society myself and writing papers under my own name. I'd wondered what Mr. Corden might say if I asked him if he thought a woman might ever be welcomed by the Royal Society. But now, as we sat in the dining room with Miss Hudson, I wished he hadn't come.

I stood. "Excuse me. I won't be long."

William frowned. "Where are you going?"

"I thought—"

"Hannah, please show Mr. Corden in. And bring us a fresh pot of tea," he said.

I sat, aware of Miss Hudson's eyes on me.

"Mr. Corden is a friend from Datchet," said William, apparently aware of my discomfort. "He's interested in our work."

"An astronomer?" asked Miss Hudson.

"No, he's a butcher," I said.

"And a well-educated, deep-thinking man," added William.

If only I'd been brave enough to say those words. Instead, as I heard Mr. Corden's footsteps approaching, I grew warm. He appeared in the doorway with Comet at his heels. If we'd been alone, I would've asked the butcher if he'd found the dog in the fields or stealing meat in the village. We would've laughed. I watched Miss Hudson scrutinize him from across the table. She squinted as if to sharpen her vision. Did she see him as I did? A dark-haired man with kind eyes and a frank, hopeful expression. Or did she notice that, despite how clean and neatly pressed his shirt, trousers, and waistcoat were, they weren't London-bought? Did she see that his shoes were dusty and that his curls had the disheveled look of someone who favored the sun on his head rather than a hat? These things, which I liked about Mr. Corden, were probably not in his favor as far as Miss Hudson was concerned. I wished I didn't care.

Mr. Corden said he hoped he wasn't intruding. William assured him he was welcome, introduced him to Miss Hudson, and invited him to sit. Mr. Corden smiled at me. I looked down, begging my veins not to bloom. I poured and distributed more tea while William and Miss Hudson peppered Mr. Corden with questions.

"How are things in Datchet?"

"Does the hot weather make things difficult for a butcher?"

"Where are you on your way to?"

"How does a butcher become interested in the night sky?"

Eventually, the questions dwindled, and the teapot was empty. Mr. Corden looked at me, but before he could speak, I addressed William, "Perhaps you should show Mr. Corden the works? I'm sure he doesn't have long to dally. I'll keep Miss Hudson company."

As they left, closing the door behind them, I turned to Miss Hudson. I planned to take the opportunity to reiterate William's assertion that we'd take good care of her cousin's house. It was also another chance for me to clear the air. It had been a tense morning, but something positive might still come out of it.

"I hope you'll visit regularly," I began. "You'll see we're serious about making sure the house isn't damaged, and you can tell me all about life in London."

She might not have heard a word. "I've just remembered where I know the butcher from," she said, her eyes glittering. "You were in his arms in the hedge the day the coach I was traveling in took a detour near Datchet. I knew I recognized those curls!"

That Miss Hudson was in the coach that nearly trampled us was astonishing, but what shocked me most was her glee.

"You were in the coach?" I asked.

She smiled.

"Did you realize it almost flattened us?" I continued. "The driver wasn't paying attention, and the horses came around the corner at an uncontrollable pace. It was terrifying."

She brought her hand to her mouth and began laughing. I stared at her, incredulous. Did she truly dislike me so much that the idea of me being pulverized by hooves and wheels amused her? I wanted to shake her. Eventually, she stopped giggling, but still, she was unsympathetic.

"I knew it was you immediately. I recognized your cloak and diminutive form. Of course, I've been wondering about your lover ever since. A butcher!" She tittered. "I thought for a while I might ask your brother if he knew about your passionate escapades in the countryside."

"What? No! It was nothing like that," I said, battling to stay calm. "We had to dive into the hedge to avoid the horses. You must've noticed how narrow the road was."

She leaned back and folded her arms across her chest. "That doesn't explain why you were alone with him in the first place. Did you simply happen to pass one another as the coach approached?"

I should've said Mr. Corden and I were friends, that he was my only friend in Datchet. After all, we weren't in Bath anymore. No one watched their neighbors or gossiped about them in the country, did they? My lessons with Miss Fleming had been helpful, but I was years older, and if I chose to befriend a butcher, that was my business. William liked Mr. Corden. He never questioned our friendship. Why should I care about what Miss Hudson thought? I should've told the truth, but I didn't.

"He was on his way to visit his mother, and I was walking the dog. Mr. Corden drew me out of the way of your coach. He saved my life," I said.

"And since then he's become a family friend, has he?" she asked.

I pretended not to notice her disdain. "I suppose so," I replied.

She got to her feet. "I won't stay. I need to get back to my cousin and tell him what I've seen."

"I hope you'll reassure him all is well," I said, standing too.

"I don't believe all *is* well, Miss Herschel. It doesn't matter what you and your brother say. The place was built for people to live in. It cannot withstand these conditions. I'll be back next month, and if I see any signs of damage either to the buildings or the garden, I shall have to reconsider our agreement. Tell Mr. Herschel so there's no room for misunderstanding."

We were waiting for her carriage at the front door when William and Mr. Corden appeared. Miss Hudson told my brother she was in a hurry and repeated what she'd said to me about coming back the following month. Then she turned to Mr. Corden.

"I believe Miss Herschel owes you her life," she said.

He frowned and glanced at me. I swallowed and looked down.

Miss Hudson peered at him. "You've forgotten how you *happened* to be at the right place at the right time in a remote, narrow lane near Datchet when a coach sped toward you?" she asked.

"Miss Hudson was a passenger," I murmured, daring to glance at him. "She recognized us."

Mr. Corden narrowed his eyes and nodded. "Oh? Yes, I see. Yes, it was very fortunate that I happened to be there."

William watched me, his brow furrowed. I hadn't mentioned the occasions I'd met Mr. Corden while out with Comet. Neither had I told him about the near mishap with the coach. I'm not sure why. Maybe I was afraid of what I might give away about myself in telling him about Mr.

Corden. Whatever the reasons I'd *not* told my brother, at that moment, I wished I had.

"Oh!" said Miss Hudson, her eyebrows raised as she looked at William. "You didn't know you had the butcher to thank for saving your sister's life?" She chuckled. "We're all discovering new things about one another today, it seems."

We watched in silence as she climbed into her carriage.

"I'll see you in four weeks!" she called, waving through the window as she was driven away.

I wanted to flee but also to explain to Mr. Corden why I'd pretended we weren't together when Miss Hudson had seen us. On the other hand, I felt he should understand the perceived impropriety of the situation. Miss Fleming had insisted it was scandalous for an unmarried woman to be seen alone with an unmarried man who wasn't related to her. Didn't men know that? Was the burden of shame to be carried by women alone?

William and Mr. Corden looked at me. Both expected an explanation. I shook my head, mute.

Mr. Corden broke the silence. "I've kept you long enough, Miss Herschel, Mr. Herschel," he said, his smile self-conscious. "Thank you for the tea and for showing me your work."

William stared at me. I was relieved at Mr. Corden's leaving.

My brother stepped forward and shook the other man's hand. "I hope you'll come again, Mr. Corden. Your interest and understanding of the heavens continue to grow. It's a pleasure to discuss them with you."

"Travel safely," I managed.

William found me at my desk a short while later. His day had been disrupted by Miss Hudson and Mr. Corden. Typically, he'd be eager to get back to work. However, he pulled up a chair and sat opposite me.

"His visit wasn't unexpected, was it?" he asked.

I didn't look up from my notes. "No, he said he would come in June or July."

"You exchange letters regularly?"

"He said you thought I might help him understand the heavens better,"

I replied.

"I did," said William.

He shifted his weight. I didn't look up.

"Why didn't you talk to him today?" he asked.

"I did."

"Barely. He would've stayed if you'd asked," he said.

Now I looked at him. "Why didn't *you* tell me our landlord is Miss Hudson's cousin?"

He ran a hand over his head. "I didn't think it mattered. Also, I hoped you'd never find out."

"Why?" I asked.

He took a deep breath. "She began writing to me after that awful visit. I replied. It seemed I owed her the courtesy. As the letters continued, her tone became increasingly, erm, intimate. I stopped responding regularly and kept my correspondence as impersonal as possible." He exhaled. "There's nothing wrong with Miss Hudson. She's lively and interesting. But I..."

"I know," I said, feeling closer to him than I had all day.

"It was only after we'd moved here—I'd long since signed the lease—that I discovered the man who owns the house was the very cousin with whom Miss Hudson lives in Kensington. It wasn't ideal, but it didn't concern me unduly. Why should it? It's his house, not hers. I didn't imagine she'd have anything to do with it. I didn't mention it to you because it seemed inconsequential." He slapped his thigh. "And I didn't want to talk to you about Miss Hudson."

"You didn't expect her today?" I asked.

"No. Mr. Kent told me Lord Sutton might visit at some point. Said he was interested in what we're doing here. However, I knew Miss Hudson was aware that we'd moved here. She'd mentioned it."

That surprised me. "Your correspondence is ongoing?"

William nodded. "She writes often. I reply occasionally, briefly. Today, before I brought her to you here, she... Well, I was shocked by her arrival and her, erm, familiar tone." He cleared his throat. "I felt compelled to tell her plainly that our friendship would never evolve into anything else. She was upset. Accused me of being dishonorable, leading her on. That's when she began condemning our use of the house," he said.

"I *knew* there was something more amiss," I said.

"I wish it weren't so. But if you'd been there when I told her, saw how her mood changed in an instant and how vindictive she became, you'd understand," he said, his voice weary.

"What did you say? I mean, how did you explain you don't reciprocate her affection?" I asked.

William got to his feet. "It doesn't matter. The damage is done."

He was right. I stood, went to him, and placed a hand on his arm. "No, it doesn't matter. But what were you to do? Pretend otherwise to placate her?"

"I didn't imagine she'd be irrational. It surprised me she hadn't perceived how I felt from the tone of my notes. Though she says otherwise, I gave her no reason to hope." He groaned. "I'm sorry I upset her and hope that, with time, she'll see reason and her resentment will wane."

For a while after William had gone, I stood at the window, watching Thomas and two other men lifting sheets of metal from a wagon in the yard. *Will Miss Hudson see reason?* I wondered. I thought about how she'd laughed when she recognized Mr. Corden and how she'd enjoyed describing seeing us together. She'd reveled in my embarrassment. Perhaps it was a reprisal for how I'd made her feel that snowy night in Datchet. Perhaps she was smarting from William's rejection. I hoped she had friends in London who might distract her and that she'd forget about William, me, and Mr. Corden.

Mr. Corden.

I'd treated him poorly. I'd encouraged him to visit but, as William pointed out, had barely spoken to him. It was unlikely I'd hear from him again. Would it have been different if Miss Hudson hadn't been present? I wanted to believe so but couldn't be sure. I didn't know how to interact with Mr. Corden when William was with us. William and I were like a two-wheeled curricle. We traveled quickly and smoothly together. He didn't want Miss Hudson, and I didn't need Mr. Corden. There was nowhere to put the third wheel. It would topple us.

CHAPTER 21

October 1785
Clay Hall, England

ALTHOUGH MISS HUDSON NEVER FOREWARNED US PRECISELY WHEN SHE'D come, she inspected Clay Hall once a month. At every visit, she was untiringly critical of our activities, marching from room to room and building to building, pointing out alleged damage the workmen were doing or might do to the ceilings, doors, floors, walls, and windows.

"Look at the floor! The wood is worn. It isn't meant to be trampled by men in boots carrying heavy items."

"These walls will need repainting soon. They're grimy from the abnormal dust and dirt. This was a parlor meant for needlepoint and music. Not metalwork and carpentry."

"These windows shouldn't be opened so frequently. They're sure to fail soon."

William and I followed her, him nodding meekly and me making notes as she spoke. He was determined to take everything she said seriously and instructed me to record all her comments and orders. After each visit, we'd clean and make repairs, and William would write to Mr. Kent. In every letter, he'd detail what she'd said and what we'd done to mitigate the perceived harm.

He also asked Mr. Kent to send monthly updates to Lord Sutton. The agent, a businesslike, whiskered man with the bowlegs of a veteran horseman, visited infrequently. On these occasions, he reassured us the only thing concerning our landlord was that he was still too unwell to visit and see how William's giant telescope was progressing at Clay Hall.

"Truly, Mr. Herschel, Lord Sutton is flattered by the idea of the famous machine taking shape at one of his homes," said Mr. Kent.

"You see," said my brother when the agent left. "We have nothing to worry about."

"Then why do we waste our time showing Miss Hudson around, making notes, and writing to Mr. Kent?" I asked. "Why should we humor her?"

"Because she'll grow bored and her visits will stop. We mustn't give her reasons to become more vengeful," he replied.

But she didn't stop coming. Although she rarely lingered to take tea with us, Miss Hudson continued sweeping into Clay Hall every month without fail. When, as was often the case, William wasn't home, I followed her around, scribbling notes and gritting my teeth to prevent saying anything that might upset her. As much as I resented it, I was determined to play along as my brother desired.

After one of her tours on a particularly warm morning, she accepted my offer of apple cider. As we waited in the dining room for Hannah to serve it, Miss Hudson turned to me from where she stood at the window and asked, "Have you met the woman who has your brother's heart?"

"Yes," I replied. "Though they didn't stay long."

"*They?* She brought someone from her family with her?"

"No. It was only her and Alex. They visited shortly before we left Datchet," I said.

She scowled and shook her head. "I wasn't referring to Mr. Alex Herschel. I meant William."

What did she mean? What woman had William's heart? My brother had been as busy as ever and had no time to socialize. Then it dawned on me. William must've told Miss Hudson he was romantically interested in another woman so she'd understand why he'd rejected her. I needed to go along with the ruse.

"Oh, no, I haven't met her…yet," I said, grateful to see Hannah appear with our drinks.

"And what about the butcher?" asked Miss Hudson, ignoring the maid. "Do you see much of him?"

"No, we don't," I replied, clenching my jaw. Mr. Corden had neither written nor visited again. I'd accepted our friendship was over. "We get our meat from the butcher in Old Windsor."

She narrowed her eyes, lifted her glass, and drank.

When William returned the next day, I told him about Miss Hudson's visit and, watching his face carefully, recounted her question about "the woman who has your brother's heart."

"I have *no* idea what she's talking about," he said, his eyes steady.

"You didn't say anything that might've suggested you were courting someone else when you rejected her?" I asked, not without a twinge of disappointment. I wanted to understand how she'd arrived at the idea.

"No, I didn't. If that's what she believes, she conjured the idea herself." He tugged at his cravat, unwound it, and looped it over a chair. "If you give me your notes, I'll write to Mr. Kent, and then we need to get back to work."

We didn't speak of Miss Hudson again until, several weeks later, William handed me a letter from Mr. Kent. He stood, breathing like an agitated bull, while I read it. The agent wrote that Lord Sutton had succumbed to his illness. That our landlord was dead was unfortunate, but we'd never met him. As such, our sympathies were practical rather than emotional. What *was* calamitous was what Mr. Kent wrote about Miss Hudson: She was to administer Lord Sutton's estate until his successor was in place.

"Lord Sutton's heir is in India and will only return in the new year. Miss Hudson insists she will not wait and, I regret to inform you, demands you leave Clay Hall by Christmas," wrote the agent.

"Christmas? What will we do?" I asked, holding out the letter to William.

He pushed it away, his face unusually ruddy. After being well—rested even—for months when we first arrived at Clay Hall, and everything was going smoothly, William now looked haggard.

"We will *not* leave," he said. "She has no right to insist upon it. We have not reneged on the agreement. Mr. Kent has records of everything that's gone on. We've done more than any other tenant would do to keep her happy. If she wants to evict us, she'll have to engage the law to prove she has the right to do so."

His fighting talk was unexpected. If there was anything William disliked more than idleness, it was conflict. His usual, immediate response to any dispute was to mediate peace and find a solution that suited both sides. In many cases, as he'd done in response to Miss Hudson's concerns about the house until now, he'd take on additional work and responsibility to appease the other party. I'd never seen him go into battle. He'd fled Hanover to avoid conscription.

"But, you have so much to do and think about. Do you really want to add a duel with the embittered Lydia Hudson to your concerns?" I asked.

He glared at me. "What's the alternative? Move again? That'll set us back even more than defying her will. Clay Hall is ideal. We haven't even been here for a year. I don't have time to find another place. I need to focus on the forty-footer. We're getting behind. I received a letter from Sir Banks yesterday asking how work was proceeding and asking when he might visit to take a look. I can't put him off much longer. I can't show him anything more than the eyepiece, and it's proving more difficult than I imagined to find someone with the expertise we need to cast the reflectors."

William pressed the palms of his hands against his forehead. My stomach lurched, warning me of impending doom. I'd anticipated troubles in creating the enormous reflectors, but I wasn't prepared for its confirmation.

"Perhaps we need to look farther afield for a qualified foundry. Beyond England even," I suggested.

My brother raised his head. "What? No. We don't want to risk having to move the disks far. I'll keep looking in London."

"But if the expertise doesn't exist nearby, we could—"

"Please, Lina. I'll take care of it." He exhaled, his thoughts plagued by Miss Hudson. "Why should we make the effort and incur the expense of moving because of her unsubstantiated, vindictive claims? Bitterness isn't a legitimate reason to breach a contract. What kind of woman is she? I won't allow her to continue to persecute us," he said before stomping from the room.

A while later, I called Comet for a walk. I hadn't ventured out much since we'd left Datchet. It wasn't just that I was too busy. Walking the dog reminded me of Mr. Corden. Thoughts of him were laden with shame, regret, and hopelessness. Now, however, I was preoccupied by Miss Hudson.

I wondered if I should write to her again. Would it help if I apologized once more? Or was she so preoccupied by William it wouldn't make any difference? There must be something I could do.

By the time I got home, I'd resolved to go to London. Visiting Miss Hudson would be more compelling than writing to her. I'd do it without telling William, because he would surely object. However, that evening, my brother told me he'd changed his mind.

"I've given it some thought. I'm going to make one more attempt to get Miss Hudson to see reason," he said. "I'm going to write to Mr. Kent and ask him to propose another meeting with her, preferably here. I think I know what I must do to make her change her mind."

"What?" I asked, aware of my heart speeding up. "What must you do?"

"Hmm? No. I don't want to discuss it. Let's not let it distract us from our work. It's a beautiful night. There won't be many like it before the season changes," he replied.

My calm, self-assured brother was back. My nerves, on the other hand, were on high alert, jingling like the bells on a carriage at Christmas. What was he planning? How far would he go to get Miss Hudson to drop her relentless crusade?

"*I'm* going to see her," I blurted. "I'll go to London tomorrow."

He scowled at me. "No, Lina."

"Yes. This is all my fault. I have to do something," I said.

William glared at me, his eyes flashing. "I will take care of this. You will not visit her. Or write to her. *You* will only make matters worse! Remember what happened in Datchet. Let's not have to revisit that incident!"

I sat back as if he'd slapped me. For the first time, I recognized Jacob's threatening snarl in William's voice. It reminded me who held the reins. If I was to stay in England, I must obey William.

Of course, I didn't contact Miss Hudson. Instead, I tried not to think about her. It wasn't easy, especially since she'd driven me and William apart once more. We worked with little conversation and no laughter. He hadn't said it in so many words, but I understood I'd be banished to Hanover if I angered him again. I also realized how ridiculous it was I'd imagined I might one day be my brother's equal, an astronomer like him. I was powerless and must live by William's rules. It didn't stop me worrying about the proposed compromise he'd make Miss Hudson.

When she arrived at Clay Hall with Mr. Kent weeks later, she was wearing a black gown with reams of delicate black lace coiled about her head, and I offered my condolences. However, I felt nothing but contempt for her. The agent and I followed as William escorted her from room to room. As usual, I made notes, but finally, at the library door, William turned to me.

"I'd like to talk to Miss Hudson for a moment. Ask Hannah to bring tea to the dining room, and we'll meet you and Mr. Kent there shortly," he said.

Mr. Kent and I stood at the dining room window for several minutes after I'd spoken to Hannah. Outside, brown and yellow leaves fluttered beneath the twenty-footer like stranded fish. I thought about how we'd have to dismantle the frame again and make several trips to transport it elsewhere.

"It isn't going to make any difference to her, is it?" I asked.

Mr. Kent scratched his beard and pursed his lips. "I don't think so. As I've told your brother, Miss Hudson wouldn't want the pair of you here if you lived the quiet lives of a clergyman and a nun who did nothing but pray all day. She did, however, propose to raise the rent because Mr. Herschel's new telescope could be considered an improvement to the house."

I stared at him. "What? But that's absurd."

He chortled. "I told her as much."

"Do you know anywhere else that might be suitable for us? You understand what we need and that it needs to be hereabouts, close to Windsor Castle," I said.

"I don't. I'll let you know if I come across anything," he replied.

I turned to him. "Don't say anything to my brother about my request. At least, not for the moment. I, well, I don't want him to think that I've given up hope of staying on."

He nodded and gave me a tiny smile. Mr. Kent was a good man.

I heard the library door open and expected Miss Hudson and William to come into the dining room. However, she paused at the door. Her eyes swept over me. There was something triumphant in the look as she said, "Mr. Kent, we'll be going now."

The carriage had barely left the property when I turned to William and asked, "What's going on?"

"I don't know," he said, his tone impassive. "She said she'd think about it."

I felt sick. "Think about what? What did you propose? She looked so, erm, so self-satisfied."

He shrugged and walked away.

CHAPTER 22

December 1785
Clay Hall, England

THE DAYS AFTER WILLIAM'S CRYPTIC PROPOSAL WERE INTERMINABLE. I AWOKE every morning hoping and dreading in equal measure it would be the day Miss Hudson made her decision—whatever that meant. However, days became weeks, and weeks turned to months. Winter settled in with gloomy skies and red-nosed chill, but Clay Hall was troubled with no further visits from our former friend.

A month without her appearance was unnerving. As the second approached, I dared to dream she might've lost interest in us. Still, I remained vigilant. On high alert for letters in her or Mr. Kent's hand, I examined every note delivered to our door and found none. Hannah or one of the workmen might have handed letters directly to William, but he didn't raise the subject of our tenancy, and I didn't ask. I also tiptoed around the issue of his search for a suitable foundry for the reflectors. However, William did surprise me with other news: Alex and his wife would visit for two weeks over Christmas.

"I hope you'll open your heart to Margaret," he said. "Alex says her health has improved. She's eager to be with us. It won't be like last time. And we haven't celebrated Christmas properly since we left Bath. Let's be cheerful."

"Oh! Does that mean we'll not work during the holidays?" I joked, buoyed by my brother's chirpiness.

He chuckled. "We'll take time off on St. Nicholas Day and Christmas Eve, go to church, and have a leisurely midday meal."

His tone was playful, but we both knew, season notwithstanding, there'd be more working at Clay Hall than celebrating. It was the true purpose of Alex's visit. Although William had hoped we could focus on the forty-footer, as ever, we'd been obliged to take on other commissions. Among them was the construction of a ten-foot telescope His Majesty wished to present to the observatory at Göttingen. The Brass Man hadn't completed the eyepiece. This was to be Alex's Christmas project. I also planned to quietly consult Alex about the reflectors for the forty-footer. He might be able to convince William to look beyond London for a foundry.

Work aside, I realized I *was* open to celebrating Christmas. Lulled by Miss Hudson's continued absence, I opened the door to hope. It would be nice to decorate the house, enjoy some special meals, give and receive gifts, and sing Christmas carols. I'd rally what I remembered of Miss Fleming's lessons on English tradition and hospitality and be as gracious a hostess as I could. I'd also rearrange the rooms so that William wouldn't have to give up his bedchamber again.

The day before Alex and his wife arrived, Hannah carried armfuls of ivy, hawthorn, holly, and rosemary into the house. I joined her in the drawing room, where we wove the leafy boughs together, adding shiny ribbons and clusters of red berries to create festive wreaths. We balanced on chairs and tabletops as we looped and draped our handiwork over the mantelpiece, window ledges, light fittings, and door frames. With the last of the garlands hung, Hannah and I stood side by side, breathing in the heady fragrance of the foliage and admiring the effect.

"Now it *truly* feels like Christmas," she said, patting her cap from which some wayward strands of hair had sprung free.

"Do you decorate your home?" I asked.

"Yes. I did so a few days ago."

Although I'd never seen Hannah's home, I pictured her adorning a room, something like the tiny, dark parlor I'd known in Hanover. Perhaps she hadn't used as much ribbon as we had at Clay Hall, but I imagined her wreaths as pretty and sweet-scented. *Does her family appreciate her creations?* I wondered. Who were her family? Hannah had mentioned her husband, but I didn't know if she had children.

I glanced at her, taking in her familiar stance. She stood, hands on hips and legs slightly apart, as solid as a pony and just as strong. Obviously, Hannah was taller than me, but she was shorter than most. Even so, I'd never heard her ask for help. She was robust, capable, and reliable. I knew little else about her. Despite having seen her almost every day for about three years, I didn't know about Hannah's childhood, family, hopes, dreams, partialities, dislikes, or customs. On the other hand, she knew my every routine, from dawn to dusk. Hannah knew what I did all day. She overheard many of my conversations, witnessed my interactions, and understood my preferences and habits. I barely knew her, but Hannah saw everything I was. *Does she also know that, just thirteen years ago, I was also a servant?* I wondered.

"How will you celebrate Christmas?" I asked.

"We'll have dinner on St. Stephen's Day. When I'm off work," she said.

Of course, Hannah would spend Christmas Day preparing our meal. As was customary, servants had the following day off. It had slipped my mind.

"We're having some guests this year," she said, smiling. "Mr. Corden and his wife will join us."

His name—rolling off Hannah's tongue rather than floating about in my thoughts—startled me.

"Mr. Corden? From Datchet?" I asked, aware of my voice rising.

"Yes. Gabriel. As you know, he was married a few weeks ago. We thought Christmas dinner would be a fine way of welcoming his bride to the village," she replied.

Married a few weeks ago.

I didn't know. I wasn't sure why she thought I did. Perhaps, since Mr. Corden had visited, she assumed we were friends, and I would've been informed. But we weren't friends. I might've once believed it so, but I'd ruined that when I snubbed him during Miss Hudson's visit.

I avoided Hannah's gaze by straightening some foliage above the fireplace. All I could think of was how foolish I was to have once again imagined I might ever sustain a friendship. Hadn't I learned from what happened with Miss Hudson? Moreover, to fancy it conceivable to befriend someone like Mr. Corden—a single man, a tradesman—was laughable. It didn't matter that William liked him or that he was educated and curious about astronomy. It didn't matter that I liked him. Just as I knew nothing about Hannah's life, I was ignorant about Mr. Corden's life. No wonder news of his marriage shocked me.

Then, something else dawned upon me, and oh, the shame of it!

It was likely that, as I'd desperately timed my walks in Datchet to coincide with his routine, Mr. Corden was already courting the woman who'd become his wife. It was a dizzying thought. Had he told her about the King's Astronomer's diminutive sister with her big, ugly blemishes? I leaned a hand on the mantelpiece to steady myself.

"You've done a wonderful job here," I finally said, still not daring to look at Hannah. "Let's get on with the day."

My mood was greatly altered by the news of Mr. Corden's matrimony. I shooed away hope and bolted the door, telling myself that even if Mr. Corden and I *had* been friends, his marriage would've put an end to that.

It's better this way, I thought.

But I couldn't shake my misery or the contradictory deliberations about what he meant to me, what I'd hoped for, and what might've been possible had I been braver. Just as the last leaves of autumn were swept away by the December winds, all happy expectations of Christmas were scrubbed from my thoughts.

I'd looked forward to seeing Alex, but now my old resentments resurfaced and spoiled the anticipation. Marriage was harmful. I'd seen how little joy our parents took from it, the misery it had brought our sister and, more recently, how it had prevented Alex from being more involved in our lives. It had also destroyed any tiny chance I might've had of reestablishing a friendship with Mr. Corden.

With every day, William's excitement about Alex's arrival grew. I did my best to mask my misgivings and pretend I was looking forward to the festivities. However, the couple had barely set foot in the house when my guise slipped.

"Oh, Miss Herschel! How splendid!" said Alex's wife when we led them into the dining room. "I've never seen a place so gay."

"It's Hannah's handiwork," I replied.

"We're going to do Christmas the right way this year," said William, his eyes on me. "Lina has great plans for Christmas Eve and dinner after church."

"I've left the meal in Hannah's hands entirely," I said.

Alex's wife gave me a shaky smile. "I've heard it said a good servant is only as good as his master."

I stared at her, confused. Had Alex told her I'd been a servant in our mother's home? Or was she just making conversation?

"I don't understand. Are you—" I began.

William stepped forward. "We're fortunate to have in our employ several excellent people," he said. "And we're looking forward to a most enjoyable family Christmas. Will you pour, Lina?"

He held my gaze, his eyes steady. I looked away and went to the table.

"The dog is in the kitchen," I said, pouring a cup of tea and handing it to Mrs. Herschel. "But I assume, since you're healthy now, I can release him?"

She swallowed and gave Alex a beseeching look.

"It'll be easier if he stays there," he said.

"Oh. I understood Mrs. Herschel had recovered," I replied.

Alex took a seat alongside his wife. "Margaret *is* better." He laid a hand on her arm. She looked away. "But when there are animals in the same room, her eyes swell, she coughs, and generally feels unwell."

"The dog will stay in the kitchen," said William. "It's a small price to pay to have you enjoy your visit, Margaret. Isn't it, Lina?"

"Of course," I replied, regretting my surliness but at a loss as to how to set things right. After what had happened with Miss Hudson and then Mr. Corden, I had no confidence in my ability to befriend anyone.

I didn't participate in the conversation that ensued. Mrs. Herschel was also quiet. William and Alex discussed the eyepiece for the telescope for Göttingen. There were so many hours of work on it ahead for Alex, I wondered if he'd have time to consider the matter of the reflectors.

When Hannah arrived to clear the table, she handed William a letter. As was his way, he immediately opened and read it.

"Well," he said, the paper still in his hand. "I suspected it was too much to hope that she'd come to her senses." He sighed. "It's from Miss Hudson's lawyer. She wants us out of Clay Hall by the end of January."

The news didn't shock me. It was almost a relief to finally receive word from her.

"I thought you'd reached an agreement," said Alex.

William was surprisingly calm. "I proposed and hoped."

"What did you propose?" I asked.

"That I'd secure her an invitation to the handover of the forty-footer to His Majesty. I hoped it would appeal to Miss Hudson's ambitions and satisfy her vanity," he said.

"She refused it?" I asked.

"Not completely," said William. "She agreed, but only if she could attend on my arm."

Alex frowned and shook his head.

"On your arm?" I echoed.

"Yes. As my betrothed," he replied.

"Ha! She'll stop at nothing," I said. "What a cruel joke. She knows you'd never agree to it. She simply wants us out of the house."

"It doesn't matter," said William. "I will not back down. She's unreasonable and set on sabotaging us."

"What about involving someone at court?" asked Alex.

"No," said William. "This is our battle. I'll reply to the lawyer immediately, refute her demands again, and once more provide minute details about how we've not violated the terms of the rental agreement. I don't care how long the letter is, we'll itemize every tree we've touched and describe each room and how we use it. We'll also explain again what we'd done to avoid damaging the property."

As William walked to the door, Mrs. Herschel got to her feet and followed him. "Will you point me to our chamber?" she asked.

They left together. I turned to Alex. "The only thing he'll do by continuing to fight her is exhaust himself. It's pointless. Lydia Hudson is determined to get rid of us. We should be concentrating on building telescopes and watching the heavens, not waging war with a scorned woman."

"You might be right," he replied. "But William says the alternative is worse. Moving will disrupt operations again. And where will you go? There's nowhere else suitable."

"He won't entertain the idea of moving, so he hasn't considered any other places," I said.

"Do you have any suggestions?"

"No." I'd heard nothing from Mr. Kent. "Perhaps you could help me make some inquiries while you're here."

Alex was quiet.

"I could put the word out to land agents," I suggested.

"No, don't do that, Caroline. It'll infuriate William. Let him follow his process. You know what he's like when he feels forced into something. He needs to decide on his own. Let's give it some time."

I wanted to protest and say that William's ways weren't always the best. I'd worked alongside him long enough to understand that. I'd wanted to start looking for another place for months. I also believed William was being short-sighted about where we might find someone with the expertise to make the reflectors. He insisted they should be manufactured in London because of the ease of transporting them on the Thames, but he still hadn't located a suitable foundry in the city. I felt we needed to look elsewhere. However, I realized Alex wouldn't side with me. I couldn't risk upsetting one brother, let alone two.

"All right," I said, taking a deep breath as I watched him head to the door. "And Alex." He stopped and looked at me. "I'm sorry I was impolite to Mrs. Herschel earlier."

"If you bother to get to know her, you'll realize how silly it is to feel threatened by her," he said.

CHAPTER 23

December 1785
Clay Hall, England

IF I HADN'T KNOWN ABOUT MISS HUDSON'S LITIGIOUS BEHAVIOR, IT WOULDN'T have occurred to me William was fretful about anything during the weeks that followed. Once he'd written and mailed his response to the lawyer's letter, we didn't mention it. Our pleasure at working with Alex again spilled over into everything else at Clay Hall. We celebrated Christmas Eve with songs and games and presented one another with gifts the next morning. My present from Mrs. Herschel—a blue tapestry travel bag with a golden oak-leaf motif— outshone all others.

"Thank you! It's splendid," I said, holding up the case to admire. "Though I'm not sure when I'll use it."

"You could visit us in Bath," she said shyly.

We went to church in high spirits and lingered long over the feast of goose, roast potatoes, and three different vegetables Hannah prepared and served us. She even doused a Christmas pudding with brandy and set it aflame.

"This is a first!" exclaimed William. "I do believe we are now truly immersed in English tradition."

Despite my initial resentment about having to confine Comet to the kitchen, I saw he was happy. Hannah's cheerful company, the constant warmth of the room, and greater access to tidbits apparently made up for the indignity of not having free rein of the house.

One morning, as I tucked my shawl around my shoulders in preparation to take the dog for a short stroll, Mrs. Herschel appeared.

"Can I join you?" she asked.

"I was going to take the dog out before the weather closes in again," I replied.

"I know," she said.

"But I thought your eyes—"

"Only when I'm indoors. Please. I'd like to."

So it was that Mrs. Herschel and I came to regularly walk Comet together. We didn't go far. The icy wind and the fact that I needed to get back to work weren't the only reasons. Alex's wife might've been healthier, but she was quickly short of breath and prone to coughing spells. We didn't talk much either. Our conversation was limited to trivial comments about the weather, landscape, vegetation, and Comet. We didn't chat about ourselves or my brothers. We spoke about nothing of consequence. It didn't matter. The peaceful outings somehow brought us to an undefined understanding, which prevailed throughout the visit.

It was while Comet and I were waiting in the garden for Mrs. Herschel the day before she and Alex were due to return to Bath that I saw the outline of a man beyond the high hedge between the property and the road. As he entered the driveway, I recognized his agile gait and the dark curls escaping his cap. My heart skipped. It was Mr. Corden.

The distractions of Christmas and Alex and Mrs. Herschel's visit hadn't been enough to eliminate thoughts of him. I'd barely restrained myself from asking Hannah about their dinner.

"Good day to you too, Comet," he said as the dog trotted to greet him.

They came to me together.

"Good morning, Miss Herschel," he said, removing his cap.

"Mr. Corden, good day," I managed.

"I hope you've had a good Christmas?"

"Yes. Thank you," I replied.

"Forgive me for stopping by unannounced, but I wanted to talk to you and, well, I should've written but wasn't sure it was the right thing to do. I'd rather speak to you about it," he said.

"I know you're married," I blurted. "Hannah told me."

His eyes widened. "Yes, I, erm, I am. Recently."

"Well," I shrugged, "congratulations."

He frowned. "Thank you, Miss Herschel."

"Is there anything else?" I asked.

"What? Oh, no, I didn't come here to tell you that." He looked at his hands as if surprised to find his cap there. "I didn't think that would interest you. I came because of the house."

"The house?" I asked.

"Yes, the house. Well, you see, it's awkward because I suspect you and Mr. Herschel don't realize the men know about your trouble at Clay Hall. It's not their business. Or mine. Of course, it's not my business," he said.

He was twisting his cap now.

"Go on," I said.

"There's a house in Slough that I believe will be ideal for your work. Of course, I don't know everything about what you do, but I think it might suit you, and, well, it'll be available soon."

I stared at him, speechless.

He exhaled. "You see, Miss Herschel, Thomas, Hannah, Mr. Harris—everyone, really—know that Miss Hudson wants you out of Clay Hall. Her coachman told them months ago. She's determined to evict you, he said. You'll need another place close by. A place with a large yard and outbuildings, and it needs to be near the castle." He took a breath. "My aunt worked for Mr. Baldwin, who owns a country house called Grove House on the edge of Slough. It's about three miles north of Windsor Castle. My aunt knows it well and told me that it'll be up for rent soon. I suggested Thomas or Hannah mention it to you, but they're afraid of meddling. I don't have anything to lose, so here I am."

My mind whirred. Of course the servants knew about our troubles. During one of my earliest lessons with Miss Fleming, she'd explained that although discretion was the mark of a good servant, it was unrealistic to expect them not to talk about the affairs of the house.

"They're people, after all, and people love to talk," she'd said.

No, it wasn't surprising our servants knew, but what was unexpected was that Mr. Corden had come to me with the idea of an alternative property. If the house and grounds were as he described, they might be exactly what we required.

"Why is it important to you that we find another house?" I asked, thinking, *Particularly after I was so rude to you.*

He swallowed, twisting his cap once more. "Your work is important. You're discovering things we'd not know otherwise. My friends work for you. They like it. I like you and Mr. Herschel. You've treated me like I might understand things that other men like me—butchers—don't. It's important because I thought it might help you."

For a moment, the only sound was the melodic warble of a robin on the other side of the hedge.

"Where is the house? Whom should I write to about it?" I asked eventually.

He reached into his jacket pocket and handed me a folded piece of paper. "I've written all the details here."

I took it from him. "Thank you, Mr. Corden."

He gave me the same tiny smile I'd first seen when Comet raided his shop.

"Would you like to come in?" I asked. "See my brother? He's busy with our brother from Bath, but—"

"No, thank you," he said. "I hope it's going well. Thomas says you're busier than ever. But I should go. My wife and I came to Old Windsor to visit her sister. I said I'd only be gone briefly. I must go."

I wasn't ready to say goodbye. "I'm sorry, Mr. Corden," I said.

He stared at me, his mouth ajar. "What do you mean?"

"I should've made the time to teach you about the heavens when I had the chance like you asked," I replied.

He shook his head. "No, Miss Herschel, no. I shouldn't have asked. We're worlds apart, you and me. There aren't enough hours or words in a lifetime to hitch me to your star."

I could offer no response. I understood why he felt that way. I'd behaved as if I was superior to him by snubbing him during Miss Hudson's visit. I'd never apologized. However, I was aware of a sharp sting deep in my chest.

Mr. Corden was wrong. Something *had* hitched us together. Only now, we were unhitched. His eyes held mine. Did he feel it too? I heard the door open behind me.

"Goodbye, Miss Herschel," he said.

"Goodbye, Mr. Corden."

I watched him walk away.

"Sorry to keep you waiting, Miss Herschel," said Alex's wife.

"Caroline," I replied.

"I beg your pardon?"

"You should call me Caroline," I said.

"And I'm Margaret."

CHAPTER 24

January 1786
Clay Hall, England

I^F^ IT HAD BEEN ENTIRELY UP TO ME, I WOULD'VE INVESTIGATED THE HOUSE IN Slough immediately. However, I was cautious about how William might respond. It wasn't only Alex's warning against pressing our brother to do things that held me back. I was also uncertain how to broach the subject without making him feel uneasy about the fact Thomas, Mr. Harris, and the other men had discussed our difficulties with Mr. Corden. So, for a while, I said and did nothing.

One uncommonly clear January night after Alex and Margaret had returned to Bath, William and I bundled up against the cold and went out to continue work on the catalog of double stars. This involved finding, measuring, and recording occurrences of two stars that appeared close to one another given our line of sight but that prolonged observation proved were, in fact, far removed from one another. We'd even discovered that some double stars orbited one another. These findings allowed us to more accurately calculate distances between celestial objects, and we were determined to record every incident of double stars to complete our records of the heavens.

As usual, William went onto the platform of the twenty-footer while I waited below, ready to move the winch if required and to note his observations and the time so we could determine the exact location of each object later. If we'd been in Datchet, I would've tucked myself inside the open library doors from where I could hear William's calls. However, the layout of Clay Hall didn't allow it, which explained the added layers of clothing. As I rubbed my arms against the chill, it occurred to me that extra woolen petticoats and outer coats seemed more effective when I was busy with my telescope. Observing alone absorbed and distracted me in ways waiting upon William and note-taking did not.

"Is everything in order? Do you require adjustments?" I asked, wondering why William was taking longer than usual to begin calling out his observations.

"No. I mean, yes, everything is in order, but don't move it," he replied, his tone pensive.

I waited, pulling down my hat and wriggling my toes in my boots. It was no surprise Comet hadn't left the warmth of the fire to come out with us. There was movement above. I looked to see William descending the ladder.

"What's going on?" I asked.

He stepped onto the ground. "Go up. Take a look. It looks like another planet."

"What? Really? But why didn't you give me notes?"

"Look at it. Go quickly. I want your eyes on it first," he said.

It was unprecedented for William to see anything and not call his observations to me, but I didn't linger to ask more. I climbed the ladder as fast as I dared, went to the eyepiece and looked.

The aperture was pointed toward the Draco constellation, with its winding pattern of stars headed up by the brightest, Eltanin. There I saw what had excited my brother and immediately understood why he'd imagined it could be a planet. The small blue-green blob was a similar size and color as those of the Georgium Sidus. I'd never noticed it before.

"Do you see it? What do you think?" shouted William.

I held up my hand, signaling for quiet, a gesture typical of him when he was above and I below. It gave me a warm jolt of pleasure.

Holding still, I examined the object. On closer inspection, it wasn't solid like the planet. It had a hazy quality with a bright center surrounded by a glowing, weirdly shaped halo made up of multiple shells and lobes. Its outer layer was a striking blue, and the rings gave off a ghostly glow.

"It could be a cat's eye," I called to William.

"Cat's eye? Yes, yes, I see what you mean. But what do you think it is?"

"A nebula, I believe. The haziness is the clue. I'd say it's an extremely distant nebula," I replied.

William sighed. "I was afraid you'd say that. I thought the same, but there was a tiny glimmer of doubt. Come down. I'll go back and call my notes to you."

"Or I could call mine down to you," I said, not taking my eye from the instrument.

There was no reply. Was he considering it? Or had I gone too far? I held my breath. The distant howl of a fox, high-pitched and eerie, cut through the quiet.

"Come down," repeated William eventually.

As I descended, I thought about the house in Slough. Perhaps there would be room for me to shelter there while on note-taking duty.

"It might not be another planet, but it's another of your island universes and no less fascinating. Congratulations," I said as we swapped places once more.

"Exactly! And that's why I do not want to move again. Imagine all the nights of observing we'd miss if we had to go through another relocation," he said.

I didn't respond but was pleased I hadn't dared to mention the other house. William's denial was firm. However, there was no harm investigating the place myself.

Days later, after we'd observed it again, cross-checked its position against our celestial maps, and added the cat's eye–like nebula to our records, William went to London for a series of meetings with Dr. Maskelyne. I took the opportunity to write to Mr. Baldwin, the owner of Grove House in Slough, inquiring if I might inspect it. To my surprise, I received a response from Mr. Kent the next day. In a stroke of good luck, he had just been appointed agent for Grove House and, he wrote, would be delighted to show it to me at my convenience.

The following afternoon, as I waited for Mr. Kent in the street outside the imposing, three-story house, I wondered if I was at the right address. With its steep roof, five chimney stacks, and ivy-covered walls, Grove House seemed too large to be a family home. The house bordered the road, and there was no evidence of the garden Mr. Corden had spoken of. However, Mr. Kent arrived brandishing a large key and a broad smile.

"I wish I'd been the one to tell you about this place, Miss Herschel, but you beat me to it," he said. "I suspect, since he's not here, your brother is still hopeful Miss Hudson will change her mind?"

"I'm afraid so. My visit might be premature, but I like to be prepared," I replied as I followed him into the hallway, up the stairs, and down the passage.

As we went from room to room, I noted the generous space and light and peered through the windows onto the expansive backyard. It was much larger than I'd anticipated when I'd stood on the street. I inspected the floors, doors, windows, roof tiles, and brickwork. Grove House showed none of the decay that had bedeviled us in Datchet. My inspection included the stables and a washhouse, which ran along the far boundary of the property.

"What do you think, Miss Herschel?" asked Mr. Kent when the tour was over.

"It would most certainly do," I said.

"Will you tell Mr. Herschel about it? Suggest he have a look at least?" he asked.

"Yes, I will," I replied, deciding in that moment that I'd no longer protect William from his own folly. It eased matters to have Mr. Kent involved. We liked and trusted him. I'd tell my brother about Grove House as soon as he returned from London.

What I hadn't counted upon was Miss Hudson's lawyer's response to William's letter arriving while I was in Slough. William tore it open as he sat down moments after walking through the door. As I watched him read, I knew my brother was defeated. He leaned back in his chair as if the letter had wrestled him into submission.

"We're to be gone by the end of March," he said. "She now claims her cousin's heir plans to occupy the house, but only after renovating it." He sighed and dropped the paper on the table. "Two months. As if we can simply pack up and relocate anywhere. What are we to do?"

Relief flooded through me. At last, we could plan the next step. I understood William's concerns about how disruptive another move would be, but I had also believed it was inevitable. Finally, he had to accept it.

"I visited a place on the outskirts of Slough yesterday. It's ideal," I said evenly. It felt good not to have to tiptoe around the issue.

William sat bolt upright. "Slough? You did? But—"

"Yes, I know. You were adamant we *not* move, but when I heard about it, I thought I'd look at it," I said.

He leaned toward me. "And you found it suitable? Ideal, you say?"

I nodded. "It's called Grove House. Mr. Kent is the agent. We'll have to cut down some trees, but otherwise, I believe it'll be perfect. And it's available next month."

"Why didn't you tell me about it before?" he asked.

"Because you continued to hope Miss Hudson would see reason."

He eased back against the chair. "And yet you knew otherwise. Tell me more."

I explained where it was and described the rooms and yard. I said how I'd measured the garden and worked out where we might reassemble the twenty-footer and build the forty-footer when the parts were ready. I told him about the stables and washhouse.

"The rental is higher than what we're paying here, but I believe the additional space and other advantages will more than make up for it," I concluded.

The next day, William and I went to Slough to see the house. I watched his face as Mr. Kent repeated the tour. In every new room, I felt an overwhelming sense of satisfaction. My brother was pleased. I'd done well. I left him talking to the agent as I strolled around the garden, silently apologizing to the trees we'd fell to make room for our telescopes. My brother was still smiling as we walked to the carriage. When Thomas called to the horses to move, William raised his eyes.

"It's perfect," he said. "The right size, location, and condition. That it's available just when we need it is very fortunate. However, this time, I will meet the owner, Mr. Baldwin, and tell him exactly what we plan to do on the property before we pack a single thing."

CHAPTER 25

March 1786
Grove House, Slough, England

It was less than a year since we'd packed and carted our worldly goods and heavenly machines from Datchet to Clay Hall. We knew what was required. But practice didn't make our relocation to Slough any less arduous. Once William had secured Mr. Baldwin's agreement about how we'd use Grove House, we began the process. But for the reflectors, we'd undertaken a great deal of work on the forty-footer in recent months, which meant there were significantly larger components and more tools to convey. Once again, we were grateful that Hannah, Thomas, Mr. Campion, Mr. Harris, the Brass Man, and several other valued men agreed to move with us.

"Oh, aye," said Mr. Harris when I told him how pleased I was he'd come to Slough with us. "I don't mind the change of scenery. Of course, it's a good thing it's still within three miles of Datchet, or Mrs. Harris might suspect I was running away from her."

Not only did the move demand the concerted efforts of everyone in our employ, but we were also obliged to engage several additional people. Still more were required when we arrived at Slough. Here, for a time, more than thirty workers toiled in the yard, felling and uprooting trees and preparing the soil for bricklayers to build foundations for the twenty- and forty-foot telescopes. Finally, with Mr. Baldwin's consent, we could construct permanent bases for the apparatuses.

I chose a bedchamber in the far corner of the house. With windows in two walls, the room looked toward the stables at the back and, on the side, into the trees that bordered a neighbor's field. I positioned a writing desk so that I could look out through the branches and into the countryside. As much as I enjoyed working alongside William in the library and helping as he observed in the garden, it pleased me to occasionally get away from the hubbub. I particularly liked waking up to the birdsong and gentle snorting and stamping of Juno and the two carriage horses William had recently purchased.

While Mr. Campion converted the washhouse into a forge and was, within a week of the move, able to commence working on the tube for the forty-footer, Thomas and Mr. Harris oversaw the establishment of the other workrooms in the house and reassembled the twenty-footer.

One day, as I walked through the yard looking for William, I overheard Thomas talking to one of the carpenters who was adjusting the frame for the twenty-footer.

"Tell your man we must have the planks delivered to us at Observatory House within the week," he said. "My master observes the heavens every night, and I will not risk his safety with this unsound wood."

It wasn't just Thomas's firmness and concern about my brother's safety that caught my attention but also that Grove House had been renamed. I mentioned it to William when I found him.

"'Observatory House.' Hmm, it's perfect," he said. "From here on, Observatory House it shall be."

Once we'd sorted and arranged our notes, manuscripts, catalogs, and atlases in the new library, William and I resumed our routine. The warmth of spring sweetened my sense of being home after years of impermanence at Datchet and Clay Hall. We were determined to submit a catalog of one thousand new nebulae and clusters of stars to the Royal Society within the year. Once again, our nights were spent observing and our days calculating, checking, and recording.

My work didn't slow when William was away. On those nights, I used my telescope to observe, silently greeting the beautifully familiar objects and keenly searching for hidden mysteries. While my instrument wasn't capable of the deep-sky searches conducted by the twenty-footer, it was perfect for my needs. The long, quiet nights alone rekindled my desire to know as much as William and his colleagues and discover more. I also began paying more attention to work on the forty-footer. If I was to be an astronomer, I should know everything, and after having found Observatory House, I felt emboldened. I must've advanced my worth in William's eyes by now, surely? I'd be more forthright with him from now on, I thought, and ensure I knew what was going on with all projects at all times. It was the natural next step, wasn't it?

I'd helped William and Alex design and construct so many telescopes over the years, I understood the instruments better than most astronomers, whose handling of the machines was limited to observing. I couldn't help believing that that, coupled with the knowledge I'd amassed by working alongside my brother and scanning the skies when I was alone, meant that I was more experienced than several of William's colleagues. But if it was so, what was I to do? I didn't want to work anywhere else or with anyone but William, even more so since I'd found the perfect place for our undertakings. However, I fantasized about hearing my brother say, "You write and submit this paper under your name, Lina. You've done the work," and "I'm going to commend you to the Royal Society. You belong with us."

With my dreams to sustain me and plenty to do, we settled quickly into life in Observatory House. Indeed, the only one who seemed unhappy in our new home was Comet, who disappeared regularly during the day, reappearing only when the workers left in the evenings.

"He'll adjust once things calm down," said William. "Perhaps you should ask Hannah to keep him with her? The kitchen is the quietest place at present."

It wasn't a bad suggestion, but I liked having Comet around. I was accustomed to seeing him at my feet when I was at my desk, hearing the tip-tap of his paws behind me when I walked through the house, and waking up to him sleeping on the carpet alongside my bed. Did he feel neglected because I'd been busier than usual leading up to and during the move? I resolved to take him into the field nearby whenever I could. But even then, he continued to disappear.

One night, the dog was nowhere to be found. I wandered from room to room and across the yard, calling him until William, who was observing and wanted me to record his findings, grew impatient and demanded I return to my desk. We continued working until the early hours of the next day, but still, Comet didn't appear. It was only when Hannah served breakfast that his whereabouts were revealed.

"I'm sorry, Miss Herschel," she said as she placed the teapot on the table. "I'm sure you were worried last night, but when I arrived home, I found Comet had followed the coach. I kept him with me."

"He was with you in Datchet?" I was shocked.

"Yes. I brought him back this morning," she replied.

"Where is he now?"

"In the scullery."

I hurried to the kitchen to find Comet stretched out in front of the hearth. He glanced at me, wagging his tail slowly. I went to him.

"Is that all you have to say?" I asked. "You're out all night, didn't bother to let me know you're home, and now you lie there as if nothing is wrong?"

He gave his tail three more desultory flaps.

"Come," I demanded.

The dog got to his feet slowly and followed me to the dining room, where he lay near my chair while I finished breakfast. I heaped attention upon him for the rest of the day, patting him, feeding him tidbits, and taking him for a stroll in the early afternoon. My endeavors to win his favor appeared to succeed. He stayed home the whole day and was still there when Hannah left that evening. I continued the strategy for several days.

"You can't go on treating him like an insecure child," said William.

"I'm trying to reassure him this is his home," I replied.

"He adjusted to Datchet and Clay Hall without any special treatment. I'm sure he'll settle here once the place is quieter," he reiterated.

"I don't want him following Hannah again," I muttered.

My brother laughed. "You feel betrayed by him."

I didn't respond, but it was true. I was deeply unsettled by the prospect that Comet preferred Hannah to me. I'd relied on the dog's loyalty but was now unsure. Surely, I wouldn't also lose his affection the way I'd lost my sister's and Mr. Corden's? Or had I misjudged him the way I had Miss Hudson?

For a few more days, I ignored William's raised brows and brazenly continued my campaign to earn Comet's absolute devotion. While he didn't remain with me all the time, he stopped disappearing, and I stopped worrying. My brother was right. The animal had simply needed time to adjust to his new surroundings.

However, it emerged I'd let my guard down too soon. One night, he was once more nowhere to be found. This time, rather than being worried, I was angry. He'd no doubt followed Hannah again. What was I to do to keep him at Observatory House? Hannah and Comet had always been fond of each other, but I couldn't think of what might've happened to compel him to swap his allegiance. Had I missed something? I resolved to interrogate Hannah, but she arrived without Comet the next day.

"No, Miss Herschel, he isn't with me. I haven't seen him since yesterday afternoon," she said.

No one else had seen Comet either. I'd imagined he'd gone for the night, but this time he didn't return.

Over the days that followed, I thought of nothing else as I searched the neighborhood and nearby countryside for the dog. Hannah and Thomas helped. We knocked on doors, stopped coachmen in the road, and spoke to farmers in the fields. No one had seen him. We marched along the banks of rivers and ditches, peered into crevices and holes in trees and between boulders. Could he have chased something and found himself trapped? Hannah searched the roadside between her home near Datchet and Observatory House every morning and evening, but the dog had vanished.

"I'm sorry," said William when Comet had been gone for almost a week. "But he grew up alone on the streets. He survived without us for who knows how long. He may have chosen to live like that again."

"That doesn't make sense," I replied, annoyed by the idea. "Why would he give up a place at which he was assured of food, safety, warmth, comfort, and attention? What else could he want? It's been years. Why now?"

My brother shrugged. "I don't know, but I think you must accept the dog has gone. You've looked for long enough."

"There's one place I haven't searched."

"Where?"

"Clay Hall. He might've gone exploring, become confused, and headed back there. If you don't need the carriage tomorrow, I'll go to Old Windsor. If he's not there, I'll let it go," I said, certain that I'd *never* stop looking for the dog.

"Thomas can drive you," said William.

We left early the next morning, Thomas up front and me, with my head through the window, searching the roadside for signs of Comet as the carriage trundled along the familiar roads to Clay Hall. As Thomas reined in the horses, I saw the gate to the property was closed.

"It's not locked," he said after hopping down and peering through the bars. "And the house appears unoccupied."

"Open up. We'll go in," I replied.

With the doors bolted and the windows barred, Clay Hall looked more like a fortress than a home. How different it had seemed when we lived there, and how unlike Observatory House it was. When we'd moved from Datchet, William and I had celebrated Clay Hall's smaller rooms, glad they'd be easier to heat than the large, drafty spaces we'd known. Now, though, the place seemed tiny, with too many bricks and too few windows and doors. At Observatory House, an abundance of openings gave way to light and fresh air. Several of the back rooms opened onto the garden, offering views of the telescopes and countryside in the distance. We might've been forced to move out of Clay Hall, but it had been to our advantage.

Thomas stopped at the front door. We left the carriage, and I sent him around the house in one direction while I went the other, calling for Comet as I walked. I waited for a moment, listening for the dog, but the only sound was the distant *crunch, crunch, crunch* of Thomas's footsteps on the gravel. There were no other signs of life. I called again. At the back of the house, I saw that the stables were also barred. Thomas appeared around the corner.

"No sign of him, Miss Herschel," he said. "I'll look around here." He gestured to the stables. "Perhaps there's a gap in the woodwork and he's gone in."

It was unlikely, but I didn't stop him. However, as I followed the path around the house, my calls diminished. Comet wasn't there to hear them. A series of sandy indents and lines marked the spot where the twenty-footer had stood. I pictured it at Observatory House. If only it had been as straightforward to relocate Comet as it had been to move the machine.

As I approached the front of the house, I heard the jangling of harnesses and clip-clopping of hooves. Assuming it was a carriage passing by, I thought little of it until I realized the sounds were drawing closer. The vehicle had passed through the gate we'd left open. I backtracked, slipping out of sight behind the corner of the house. The carriage went by and stopped alongside ours. I gritted my teeth. I couldn't remain hidden. As I left my hiding place, a stocky young man wearing a maroon, fur-trimmed jacket stepped out of the carriage. He turned to help someone else exit. I immediately recognized the tall frame and mound of hair. It was Miss Hudson. She stalled on the step, her hand in his and her eyes on me. Thomas appeared behind her from the other side of the house.

"Good day, Miss Hudson," I said, bobbing the tiniest of curtsies.

Still frozen halfway out of the carriage, she opened her mouth to speak, but I took charge.

"My dog is missing, and I thought he might've come back here." I glanced at Thomas. "We've looked, but there's no sign of him. Is there, Thomas?"

He shook his head.

"We'll be on our way," I concluded.

Thomas hastened to our carriage, opening the door for me. I had to walk past Miss Hudson to get there, which broke the spell that had immobilized her.

"Just a minute, Miss Herschel," she said. "I do believe an apology is called for."

I should've ignored her, climbed into the carriage, and told Thomas to leave, but her words contained an invitation too good to pass by.

"Oh, by all means," I said, turning to face her. "Go ahead and apologize."

It took her a moment to understand. By then, her cheeks were inflamed. "How dare you," she said. "You're trespassing!"

She looked at the man. He'd moved away to examine the front door.

"Cousin!" said Miss Hudson, her voice shrill. "This is the woman who, with her brother, was set on destroying Clay Hall."

He looked at me. His expression was passive as if he was bored. "Ah, the reason the place is now empty," he said quietly before glancing at her. "Shall we go in?"

Miss Hudson handed him a key. I climbed into the carriage and sat down. Before Thomas could call for the horses to move, she came to the window.

"I believe your brother is finally courting in earnest," she said.

I didn't respond. She grinned, and I wondered how I'd ever imagined we were friends.

"Oh, of course. You know nothing about it," she said. "Well, prepare yourself, Miss Herschel. One day, you'll *have* to accept that even the saintly Mr. William Herschel is human and that a sister is no substitute for a wife."

I rapped my knuckles on the side of the carriage, and we set off.

Later, when we arrived at Observatory House, I thought about how fleeting joy could be. A few weeks earlier, I'd never been happier. We'd moved to a wonderful place, and although the matter of the reflectors for the forty-footer was still unresolved, our other work was going well. The catalog was progressing and the ten-foot telescope was on track for delivery to Göttingen in a few months, with Alex agreeing to accompany William to deliver it while Margaret stayed with me.

However, everything had changed when Comet disappeared. He'd taken my peace of mind with him, and now, despite knowing how devious she was, Miss Hudson had further unsettled me. She was a troublemaker. I was certain William wasn't courting. He'd *never* courted. He had no time. Neither did I have the time to search for Comet, I thought. Perhaps William was right. I should give up looking. The dog was gone. For whatever reason, he'd abandoned me.

As I made my way across the yard, William approached, his arms bent at the elbow, powering him forward as they did in times of urgency. He stopped a few yards away from me, turned, and called to someone. I looked beyond him. To my amazement, Comet appeared in the doorway of the library. He looked at me, his tail wagging.

"Comet!" I shouted, running past William to the dog, crouching, and wrapping my arms around his neck.

"Where have you been?" I asked, aware that my voice hadn't been as croaky since I'd stopped singing. "Where on *earth* have you been?"

Comet placed his cold nose against my ear.

"Well, you wondered what else he might want in life," said William, standing alongside me now. "Now we know."

I looked at him. "What do you mean? Where has he been?"

"Visiting a hunting pack somewhere between here and Datchet," he said.

"A hunting pack?"

"Yes. It seems he's grown attached to one of the breeding bitches who is in season. The houndsman tried to chase him away, but he was persistent, kept returning, and was eventually caught fighting his way into the bitch's kennel. The man locked him up to keep him from her," said William.

I got to my feet. "Locked him up? How did he get out? How do you know all this?"

"Mr. Corden," he said, smiling and shrugging as if *that* explained everything.

"Mr. Corden?"

"Hannah told him about the dog's disappearance. He put out the word among his customers. Yesterday, the houndsman's wife happened to come to the butchery. After listening to her husband's complaints about the persistent stray dog, she recognized he might be Comet. This morning, Mr. Corden went there, and, well, here he is!"

"Mr. Corden brought him back?" I asked.

"Yes. He left minutes ago."

Of course he did, I thought.

"He was given some advice by the houndsman," continued William. "Comet will probably want to go back to the bitch. You'll need to confine him for a while. He also suggests you get another dog."

"Another dog?" I echoed.

"Yes. Apparently, dogs get lonely and bored. It's why they start wandering."

"But I'm with him all day. That's how it has always been. He's been fine until recently. Why now?" I asked.

"I'm telling you what I was told. You're here, but you're busy. Perhaps Comet needs something else. Someone else. We all need someone," said my brother.

William was smiling, but his tone was serious. Was he still talking about the dog?

"This is a wonderful surprise," I said, crouching to pat Comet again. "Pity the timing wasn't better." I looked up at William. "I had the misfortune of being at Clay Hall when Miss Hudson arrived."

He groaned. "It was always a risk."

"She tried to insist I apologize for trespassing. I declined," I said.

"Were you trespassing?" he asked.

"Well, there was no one there when we arrived," I replied.

"Ah, Lina, why goad her? Wouldn't it have been easier to simply say you were sorry?"

I took a deep breath and exhaled. William was right. It would've been. If I'd groveled like she wanted me to, Miss Hudson probably wouldn't have uttered her lies about William. I said nothing.

"Mr. Corden said he knows of someone with a litter of puppies—if you decide you want to get Comet a companion. Said to tell Hannah to let him know," said William before walking into the house.

I ran my hands over Comet. His coat was shiny, and his ribs were covered. The houndsman might not have appreciated my dog's eagerness to visit the bitch, but he hadn't mistreated him.

"Are you lonely, Comet?" I asked. "Is that the problem? If I get you a canine friend, will you stay at home? Will that make you happy?"

I already knew the answer. I'd immediately ask Hannah to tell Mr. Corden that I'd like a puppy. I wanted Comet to be happy. I wanted to be happy. But a tiny voice told me I shouldn't be too happy. After all, I wasn't enough, not even for Comet. Even he needed more than I alone could offer.

CHAPTER 26

July 1786
Observatory House, England

IF MARGARET WAS EVER PLEASED BY THE IDEA OF STAYING WITH ME WHILE William and Alex went to Germany to deliver the ten-footer, she possibly reconsidered soon after arriving at Observatory House.

"Oh! Another dog," she said, peering into the garden through the open doors of the library shortly after we'd said goodbye to my brothers. "Is he also yours, Caroline?"

Comet and Star, the lanky, brown puppy Mr. Corden had sent with Hannah several weeks earlier, were engaged in a frenzied game of pursuit, charging about and diving over, under, and around the frame of the twenty-footer.

"She is," I replied, although, in truth, if the puppy belonged to anyone, it was Comet. "I'll do my best to keep them outside and away from you. As you can see, the youngster is full of energy, and Comet is determined to keep up."

"He seems happy with the company," said Margaret as the older dog wrestled the pup to the ground in a dusty tangle of fangs, tails, and paws.

That was an understatement. By all accounts, Star satisfied Comet's every wish. He hadn't left her side from the moment Hannah placed her on the scullery floor. All it took were a few sniffs and a little licking, and the bond was sealed. There were no disputes about territory, belonging, or hierarchy. Comet and Star were on the same path, moving at the same pace. They explored the yard shoulder to shoulder, played for hours, ate from the same bowl, and slept curled together like a pair of unfurled fern fronds. I was relieved Comet had stopped straying. However, I missed his companionship. He no longer waited alongside my desk, pit-patted at my heels, or fixed his bright, eager eyes upon me when an outing seemed imminent. Even when I took the pair into the field nearby, Comet paid me little heed. Star had all his attention.

"It must please you too," said Margaret, her eyes following the dogs.

I frowned. "Hmm?"

"Seeing them so happy together."

"Well, the puppy has stopped Comet from wandering. I'm pleased about that." I turned away from the door. "I have things to attend to. I'm making curtains for the shelves where we store the smaller instruments. The dust from the yard can be troublesome. Then I'll clean and rearrange the polishing room."

"Alex said you were working on another catalog," she said.

"Two. We're updating Flamsteed's catalog. When it was published, it was only taken up at forty-five degrees from the Pole because the available apparatus couldn't sweep in the zenith. We're also creating our own, listing around a thousand new nebulae and star clusters," I explained, thinking how I'd summoned the courage to ask William to acknowledge me as "assistant" in the opening credits of the catalogs and how thrilled I was that he'd agreed to do so.

Margaret blinked and fiddled with her hair. I'd forgotten how little she understood about astronomy.

"It means I'll be observing, checking, and note-taking every clear night. Do you want to join me?" I asked.

"Observing? I wouldn't know what to look for," she said.

"No, of course not. I meant making curtains and cleaning the polishing room."

"If you don't mind, I think I'll go to my bedchamber for a while," she replied. "The journey was tiring."

Alex wanted to believe Margaret's health had improved, but she was far from robust. The most lively I'd seen her was over Christmas at Clay Hall. Even then, after our short walks, she'd rested for several hours. Now, she was as pale as ever.

Her lips were blue, and despite it being a warm day, she clasped her shawl tightly across her shoulders and chest. She was, it seemed, perpetually poorly. It was why she couldn't be alone. Exactly what ailed her, no one had told me. I wondered if Alex had confided in William and, if so, why neither had enlightened me. How could I take care of her without knowing what was wrong?

"Are you unwell, Margaret?" I asked.

"Fatigued," she replied, trying to smile but unable to meet my eyes. "Rest will help. I don't want to be any trouble. You have so much work to do."

It was true. I was determined to achieve a great deal in William's absence. When he returned, he should be reassured he'd left Observatory House in hands as capable as his.

In addition to updating Flamsteed's catalog and having our own printed and ready for editing, finishing the curtains, and reorganizing the polishing room, I also planned to steadfastly sweep the skies every night and investigate options for the large reflectors for the forty-footer. William had had several discussions with metalworkers, none of which had useful outcomes. I hoped to find one or two experts who might be suitable for the job to whom I could introduce to William when he returned.

Welcoming visitors was another of my duties. Days before his departure, William had repeatedly reminded me how I *must* pin up my hair and dress up to receive guests every morning—even if I wasn't expecting anyone. In his absence, it would be my place to welcome the visitors who came to see his instruments and hear about his work. Many were important. Some arrived unannounced. Their number and diversity had grown. While in Datchet and at Clay Hall, our visitors had comprised primarily other astronomers, Observatory House drew interest from various fields. In addition to welcoming scientists, we received noblemen, clergymen, court officials, foreign dignitaries, and others from countries and walks of life I'd never heard of. News of the forty-footer had spread, and people were eager to see evidence of it and learn what William hoped to discover using its powers.

Margaret didn't leave her room again for the first four days of her stay. Hannah and I served her meals in bed. She didn't consume much. Neither did she complain. Even when I pulled up a chair and sat for a while, she wouldn't concede she was ill.

"I'll be fine tomorrow. A little rest is all I need. I'm sorry to be such an inconvenience," she said.

"It's no trouble," I replied, struggling to mask my frustration. "But if you explain what's ailing you, I'll be more helpful. Perhaps a physician is necessary." She shuddered and shook her head. "No! Please, no physician," she said, more animated than usual. "I'm sure I'll be stronger soon."

I thought about explaining that I understood how it was to be ill. I hadn't forgotten how, when I had smallpox, my mother had confined me to a tiny, windowless room. Fearing I'd infect them, she'd forbidden anyone to see me. Even when I wished death would rescue me from the feverish itching, endless nausea, and blinding headaches, I longed for the comfort of a familiar voice. I'd prayed to die, but I didn't want to be alone. *Where is my father?* I'd wondered. Why didn't he come, if only to the door, to reassure me he remembered I existed? Weeks, it seemed, went by until one day, I heard a shuffle outside, followed by a whisper.

"Caroline, you must be strong."

It was Sophia Elizabeth, but she wasn't alone.

"Lina, Lina, be like the stars. Shine on. Shine on," said William.

They hadn't stayed long or returned, but their visit was enough to reassure me that they cared. It's possible I was already recovering by then, but I believed the sounds of my sister's and brother's voices at the door had rescued me.

"All right," I told Margaret. "No physician. But I know how lonely illness can be."

She gave a small smile. "I'm not ill. Or lonely," she said.

Margaret was right. She wasn't lonely. Alex would return. He was devoted to her. She wouldn't understand my woeful childhood story. I had been alone. She was not. I left her to rest, resolving not to worry about her anymore. Just like Comet, she didn't need me.

A few hours later, as I stood alongside the twenty-footer with Dr. and Mrs. Maskelyne, who'd brought Dr. Anthony Shepherd of the University of Cambridge to see William's telescopes, I saw Margaret standing in the doorway. Her hair and face were buffed as if for an evening of entertainment in

Bath. She wore a pale green gown, which gave her a cool elegance despite the midday heat. I gestured that she should join us and, when she arrived, made the introductions.

We weren't outside for much longer before returning to the library, where Dr. Maskelyne led the conversation about William's work.

"When we last spoke, Mr. Herschel mentioned he hadn't found anyone capable of casting and polishing the big reflectors," said Dr. Maskelyne. He turned to Dr. Shepherd. "Working with speculum is difficult at all times. It's even trickier when such large volumes are cast."

"Once it's set, there's the challenge of grinding and polishing it accurately without breaking it," I added.

"Have you found the experts you need?" asked Dr. Maskelyne.

"Not yet," I said.

He pressed his lips together. Concern about the forty-footer being complete on time and within budget had extended beyond Observatory House, I saw. I caught Margaret's eye and she smiled.

"Can I show you how things are progressing on the new catalog?" I asked the men, eager to distract them from the reflectors.

Dr. Shepherd questioned me about my work on the catalog. I explained what William required and described my progress.

"This is important work, Miss Herschel," said Dr. Shepherd, as he and Dr. Maskelyne scrutinized the pages of notes and illustrations I'd toiled over for months. "A more extensive register will help direct future discoveries. Your dedication and meticulousness are to be commended."

There was something familiar about his words. Or was it the way they made me feel? Then it came to me. I was experiencing the same warm and unexpected satisfaction of recognition that had surprised me when I received my first applause by an audience in Bath. It had made me feel taller and proud and accomplished then. It did the same now. My work on the catalogs was important. My observations and the discoveries I hoped to make would indeed direct the future, and yet, unless I stepped out of my brother's shadow and boldly pursued my ambition independently, my work would never come to light. Everyone believed astronomy was William's passion, not mine. My work might've been commendable to Dr. Shepherd, but to most I would always be the sister of the genius. If I wanted to realize my dream, I had to stop dreaming and take action.

"Thank you, sir," I replied. "I've learned a great deal and plan to do more."

The visitors left shortly thereafter, and when I returned from seeing them off, I was surprised to find Margaret still in the library.

"I thought you'd have retired for the afternoon," I said.

"Indeed, that's my intention," she replied. "Thank you for including me today. I enjoyed it."

"It's good to see you up and engaged with life," I replied.

Margaret smiled. "You're a remarkable woman, Caroline."

"What do you mean?" I asked.

"Your knowledge of astronomy, the instruments, and all of this is extraordinary." She waved her hands toward the bookshelves. "It seems to me you're as knowledgeable as William."

"I'm not," I said, wishing I could add "Not yet."

"Really? But it doesn't seem to matter whether others talk to you or him; the conversation is equally comprehensive and well received. I've seen you both in action. I think it's a pity you don't accept what an expert you are," she said.

"I'm William's assistant," I said.

"Yes, but you work independently. William is not here. He's gone for several weeks, and you continue to work as ambitiously and calmly as ever." She clapped her hands together lightly and spoke with uncommon energy. "If I understood correctly, Dr. Maskelyne is the Astronomer Royal, and Dr. Shepherd is a professor of astronomy at a university. William is hundreds of miles away. Yet you stand here, confidently discussing iron tubes, eyepieces, speculum mirrors, and screw bolts. You observe the heavens so you can correct one catalog and create a new one, both of which few others understand. How is all that possible for a mere assistant? Can you imagine anyone else aside from William being able to do any of that? Not even Alex is capable."

It was my turn to laugh. "Alex builds telescopes," I said.

She giggled. "Yes, he does. And so do you. You instruct workmen building the world's largest telescope."

We were quiet for a moment.

She eased herself out of her chair. "I must rest," she said.

"Do you think it's possible for a woman to be more than an assistant?" I asked, reluctant to end the conversation.

Margaret raised her shoulders. "It's unlikely, isn't it? We're not expected to be more. But I don't think that's your greatest challenge."

"What do you mean?"

She fixed her eyes upon mine, her expression serious. I'd never seen this side of Margaret. She was resolute and unflinching. I had a glimpse of who she could be when she wasn't ill.

"Assistant is just a word," she said. "You're already more than that. I think your challenge is to step away from William. You work so closely, it's hard to separate the two of you. What will happen to you if something changes and he no longer needs you?"

"Ah, you and your husband think alike! Did Alex tell you to have this conversation with me?" I asked.

"No, he didn't, but perhaps that we think alike might give our opinions more weight," she replied quietly before leaving the room.

I sat for a while with my thoughts. What was I to do? On one hand, Dr. Shepherd's and Margaret's words buoyed me. I wanted to do important work, be as proficient an astronomer as William, and lay claim to how much I was capable of independently. That was my dream. On the other hand, even though I'd thought it myself moments before, what Margaret proposed made my stomach flutter. If I didn't work alongside William and do as he required, what would happen? If I tried to be more than my brother wanted, would he and Jacob insist I return to Hanover? How was it possible to do what I wanted without letting William down?

CHAPTER 27

August 1786
Observatory House, England

ALTHOUGH MARGARET LEFT HER ROOM FOR A FEW HOURS EVERY DAY OVER THE next week and even helped me hem the curtains, we returned to the impasse that characterized our initial interactions. It was as if we were embarrassed by having been frank. Our exchanges were once again perfunctory and stilted.

"There's more cotton on the desk."

"Hannah has some errands to run this afternoon. We'll eat an hour earlier."

"A letter was delivered for you this morning."

I didn't urge her to confide in me about her illness, and she didn't reopen the discussion about how I might emerge from William's shadow. I diligently tackled the tasks I'd set myself and was pleased with my progress. There was even a glimmer of hope regarding the mirror for the forty-footer.

Everyone at Observatory House understood the urgency of finding a speculum specialist, so when Mr. Campion heard that such a man was briefly in London from Edinburgh, he told me and I quickly investigated. My inquiries indicated that the man, Mr. Glashan, might indeed be the expert we needed. I wrote to him and was pleased when he replied saying he'd stop by for a quick visit when he passed through Slough in a few days.

The morning Mr. Glashan was due, Margaret surprised me by being up early.

"Could I join you and the dogs on your outing today?" she asked.

"Well, yes, but—"

She cut me short. "It's cooler. I'll manage. Please, Caroline."

I'd wanted to suggest we wait until the afternoon or following day. Mr. Glashan had emphasized he wouldn't be able to stay long. However, Margaret never asked for anything, and her gesture touched me. Had she been thinking about our Christmastime walks at Clay Hall? I had. Then, we'd spoken about nothing more than how it might snow, that the countryside looked barren, and how energetic Comet was. Walking together had triggered the tentative start of our friendship. It was the best of times for us. *We should go*, I thought. We'd have about an hour, which was surely enough.

"We'll leave when you've eaten," I said.

She was soon ready, and we headed out. Comet and Star bolted through the front gate, sped up the road, turned right, and disappeared.

"They know the way," said Margaret.

"It's almost unnecessary to follow. By the time we get to the top of the hill, they'll have circled the meadow several times, sniffed out all the interesting spots, and be rolling about in the shade," I replied.

She walked slowly but steadily, her eyes on her feet as if appraising every step. We didn't talk, but it felt easier being together outdoors. A short storm the previous afternoon had moderated the summer heat. The air seemed crisper and grass perkier than it had for weeks. It was good to be out.

Eventually, we stopped at the gate leading into the empty paddock and, with Margaret leaning heavily on the wooden rail, watched the dogs romping through the grass. It had taken much longer than I'd anticipated to climb the hill, but clearly she needed to rest before we went back. The descent would surely be quicker, I thought.

"We should go back," I said when Comet and Star trotted toward us minutes later.

Margaret tried to smile, but it didn't reach her eyes. "Just a little longer." She sounded breathless, which surprised me, since she'd walked so quietly and we'd rested for a while.

"Are you all right?" I asked.

She looked down. "I'll be fine in a few minutes."

I wished I hadn't agreed to go out until after Mr. Glashan had been to see us. I wouldn't have another chance to talk to him before he returned to Edinburgh if I missed him today. Perhaps I could leave Margaret to walk home alone.

"You're in a hurry to get back," she said.

I hadn't mentioned Mr. Glashan, but neither could I disguise my impatience.

"It's just—"

She stepped away from the gate and turned toward home. "I'm sorry. Let's go," she said.

Within a few steps, she stopped. She was breathing hard and held her hand to her chest. Our eyes met. I recognized her fear. She looked down. I was accustomed to her pale complexion, but now her face was gray.

"Will you rest?" I asked, looking at the grassy verge.

She blinked. I took her hands and supported her as she slowly sank onto the bank. I thought she'd sit, but she closed her eyes and lay back, panting now. I sat alongside her. I couldn't leave.

"Margaret," I said, placing a hand lightly on her arm. "What can I do for you? How can I help?"

She didn't respond, but her breathing slowed.

I gently shook her arm. "Margaret?"

She didn't stir. Was she sleeping? Unconscious? Her chest rose and fell in stutters. I'd wait a while, I thought.

I'm not sure how long we were there, but I realized I'd probably miss Mr. Glashan. There was nothing I could do, and I'd resigned myself to the fact I'd lost the opportunity when I heard footsteps crunching up the hill. It was Hannah.

"I should have known something was amiss when the gentleman arrived and you weren't back," she said. "It was only when the dogs returned that I realized I must look for you."

"Stay with her," I said. "I'll get Thomas to bring the gig."

As I ran to the house, I prayed Mr. Glashan would wait, but he'd gone, leaving no word about where I might find him.

Margaret was strong enough to be helped into the gig and, once at the house, into her bed. However, she didn't leave her bedchamber for the next two days and only for an hour or two every day thereafter.

On the third day, I asked Hannah to discreetly inquire if we might call the physician.

"She begged me not to and asked me to tell you so," said the maid when she found me in the library.

"Perhaps I should write to my brothers, urging them to hurry back," I said.

"She writes to Mr. Alex," said Hannah. "Gives me a letter to mail every second day."

"Of course," I replied. "He knows more about what's happening under this roof than we do."

She left, and setting aside my concerns about Margaret, I worked on for another few hours before I laid down my pencil with some satisfaction. I'd finished checking the pages of our catalog and would ask Thomas to deliver them to the printer. Although William would edit them on his return, I felt deeply satisfied for having systematically located and identified so many new nebulae and star clusters. I pictured my name beneath my brother's in the credits, "Assistant: C. L. Herschel." It wasn't only that no other woman's name had appeared in a catalog of stars but also that we'd done something no one had done before. Just as explorers discovered new lands on the other side of oceans and mountains, we'd used instruments we'd built to find celestial objects no one else had ever seen. Our records provided information others hadn't thought to ask for. I didn't need the applause of an audience to tell me how extraordinary our work was.

I was roused from my thoughts by a rap on the frame of the outside door, which stood open. It was Mr. Campion.

"You'll be pleased, Miss Herschel," he said. "The plates for the forty-footer have arrived."

The delivery of the material meant Mr. Campion could make good progress on the inner tube for the forty-footer before William's return. The news and completion of the catalog allayed my disappointment about not meeting Mr. Glashan. It was a good day and about to get better.

CHAPTER 28

August 1786
Observatory House, England

THE AIR WAS STILL AND THE SKY CLEAR WHEN, AT TEN O'CLOCK THAT NIGHT, I observed an unfamiliar object through my telescope. I leaned back, blinked a few times, and looked again. It was curious. I hurried inside, opened Charles Messier's astronomical catalog, and bent over it, holding a candle close to examine the pages.

In color and brightness, the object resembled the twenty-seventh of Mr. Messier's one hundred and ten nebulae star clusters. However, the object I'd seen was round. Tucking my notebook under my arm, I went out again, peered through the instrument, and observed the spot. I also saw a bright red but small star above it and another faint white star following. There was a third, even fainter star preceding and perhaps others that might've appeared on a finer evening but were not distinct enough to take account of. Indeed, it could be a comet, but there was a haziness to the sky that prevented me from being sure it moved. It didn't help that I was breathing fast.

"Slowly, Lina," I whispered, imagining what William might say if he were there. "Don't let your thoughts run away with your good sense and practical assessment."

I continued observing, measuring, sketching, and making notes about the object and everything around it, afraid to waste a second lest it disappear. Accuracy was crucial if I was to make effective comparisons over forthcoming nights. My shoulders ached and my eyes stung. My focus was unflagging, but my heart raced and my hands were damp. I couldn't remember being as excited.

For a moment, I pictured my father when he'd ignored our mother's protests and taken me outside to see the comet. He didn't name it but knew enough to be exhilarated. He urged me and my siblings to imagine it up close and to ask what it was made of, where it was going, and why. *Would Father have been proud of me tonight?* I wondered. Would he have celebrated the fact that, despite being denied an education in childhood, I now knew as much about the heavens as William? Would my father have regretted not standing up to my mother and insisting I received the same opportunities as my brothers despite my sex, size, and scars? I thought about how, shortly before he'd died, I'd begged him to overrule my mother and allow me to go to school.

"It'll do us no good to go against her wishes," he'd said, looking away. "Your mother knows what is best for you. She says you'll thank her one day."

I'd run from the room, crying. How could he have imagined her sentiments to be true?

"If this is what I believe it is, Father," I whispered now, "I've discovered a comet. It's not only *my* discovery but also proof that I deserve more than what Mother and Jacob believe and more than what you were willing to fight for."

Even when clouds hid the sky, I didn't go to bed. Instead, I sat at my desk, finalizing my notes and sketches and checking several times what I'd seen against Mr. Messier's catalog. Finally, I wrote to William, explaining what I'd seen. I was about to compose the closing paragraph and sign off when I stopped. Was writing to my brother the right thing to do? The best course of action? Shouldn't I be certain about what it was before I did so? I set the note aside and stared at the candle flame. Eventually, too blurry-eyed to focus and yawning incessantly, I plodded upstairs and fell into bed.

The sound of water spilling off the roof woke me hours later. I groaned. If it wasn't clear by evening, I'd be unable to verify what I'd seen. How long would I have to wait? Would the comet still be visible?

"Is everything all right, Miss Herschel?" asked Hannah when she brought me tea in the library later.

"Yes. Why do you ask?"

"It's just that you've been sighing like a weary cow all morning," she replied.

I glared at her.

She hung her head. "Oh, I'm sorry, miss. I meant no offense. Sincerely. I was worried."

"My bovine groaning is on account of the weather. It's important I see the sky tonight," I said.

Hannah glanced at the window. "Oh, it'll clear up. Mr. Harris is sure of it."

That night, I was able to see the comet and its rays. I examined it in relation to several other stars, comparing distance and angles. I observed it through the telescope and without the instrument so I could estimate its distance from visible stars. Even when I thought I was sure I'd found a comet and suspected it hadn't previously been recorded, I was too excited to sleep. I read the letter I'd drafted to William the previous night, set it aside, took another leaf of paper, and began writing a second missive.

Late to breakfast the next morning, I was startled to find Margaret at the table. She smiled as I hesitated in the doorway.

"I can't let summer pass without spending a little more time outside in the sunshine," she said.

"Outside?"

"No walking," she replied. "I thought I'd read in the garden for a bit."

I sat quietly while Hannah poured my tea, but as she left the room, I was unable to contain my excitement. "I think I've found a comet," I said.

Margaret stared at me. "I don't know much about astronomy, but I know enough to understand that's extraordinary," she said.

"It is," I replied, delighted by her response. "Of course, it must first be ratified, but, well, I cannot express the thrill it gives me."

She placed her cup in its saucer. "What must you do to have it ratified?"

"I've written to William and two of his colleagues. I'm not certain which, if any, of the letters to send," I replied.

"What are you uncertain about? Whom have you written to?" she asked.

"Dr. Charles Blagden is the secretary of the Royal Society. He and Mr.

Alex Aubert are both astronomers and William's friends. They could observe immediately and confirm whether I have discovered a comet."

"Then you should send the letters immediately," she said.

"Perhaps, but what about William? Shouldn't I send his letter first? Will Dr. Blagden and Mr. Aubert even pause to consider the seriousness of my words without my brother's endorsement?" I asked.

Margaret scowled. "By the time William receives your letter and replies, you may have found *another* comet," she said. "This is your discovery, Caroline."

I didn't respond. Although my brother's colleagues—including Dr. Blagden and Mr. Aubert—were generally polite and sometimes even expressed interest in my work on the occasions we communed, they knew me as William's sister and assistant and nothing more. As far as they and other men were concerned, women were not scientists. How could we be? We weren't worthy of the kind of education men received. Women's brains, said men, were smaller. We were, they said, also intellectually inferior because we were governed by our emotions. How could such creatures be scientists, they asked? But I was definitely not governed by my emotions, particularly when I worked. I scanned the skies, watched the time, measured and calculated distances, and consulted the records with clear-headed objectivity. I asked questions and double-checked everything I saw. I was a scientist. However, I hadn't wanted to risk embarrassing or otherwise upsetting William, so I'd kept my thoughts to myself. Now, although I'd written the letters, I worried I might overstep the mark by sending them.

"Do you know what William would do if he were here?" asked Margaret.

"Yes, he'd tell Dr. Blagden and Mr. Aubert immediately," I said.

She smiled. "There's your solution."

I ate quickly, went to the library, and read what I'd written to William's friends.

Sir,

In consequence of the friendship which I know to exist between you and my brother, I venture to trouble you, in his absence, with the following imperfect account of a comet:

The employment of writing down the observations when my brother uses the twenty-foot reflector does not often allow me time to look at the heavens, but as he is now on a visit to Germany, I have taken the opportunity to sweep in the neighborhood of the sun in search of comets; and last night, the first of August, about ten o'clock, I found an object very much resembling, in color and brightness, the twenty-seventh nebula of Mr. Messier's record in the Connaissance des Temps, with the difference, however, of being round. I suspected it to be a comet. However, with a haziness coming on, it was not possible to satisfy myself as to its motion till this evening. I made several drawings of the stars in the field of view with it and have enclosed a copy of them, with my observations annexed, so that you may compare them together.

These observations were made with a Newtonian sweeper of twenty-seven-inch focal length and a power of about twenty. The field of view is about two degrees and twelve minutes. I cannot find the stars detailed in my drawings as 'a' and 'c' in any catalog, but suppose they may easily be traced in the heavens, whence the situation of the comet, as it was last night shortly after ten thirty, may be pretty nearly ascertained.

I hope, sir, you will excuse the trouble I give you with my vague description, which is owing to my being a bad or (what is better) no observer at all. For these last three years, I have not had an opportunity to look as many hours in the telescope.

You will do me the favor of communicating these observations to my brother's astronomical friends.

I have the honor to be, Sir, your most obedient, humble servant,

Caroline Herschel.

I folded the letters with my drawings and sealed and addressed them. I wanted them gone from the house immediately. It wasn't only that it was important to get them to Dr. Blagden and Mr. Aubert quickly but also that my resolve might waiver, and I'd keep them and send the letter I'd written to William to him instead.

CHAPTER 29

August 1786
Observatory House, England

D\R. B\LAGDEN'S REPLY ARRIVED JUST THREE DAYS AFTER I SENT THE LETTERS. He wrote that while he'd not yet had the opportunity to make the necessary astronomical observations, he *had* told several other principal astronomers about my discovery when he visited the Royal Observatory. He'd also reported it to astronomers in Paris and Munich, adding that I might expect a visit from Sir Joseph Banks, who would like "to beg the favor of viewing this phenomenon through your telescope."

"And to think you imagined he wouldn't take a report from you seriously without William's commendation," said Margaret when I read her the letter.

"Well, I did remind the good doctor of William's absence. I had to explain why I was writing and not my brother," I replied.

She didn't respond, and I went on with my day. However, despite my attempt at nonchalance, I was unable to snuff the flame of pride Dr. Blagden's reaction had ignited. The little fire was rekindled and, in truth, flared fiercely when I read Mr. Aubert's response two days later.

Dear Miss Herschel,

I am sure you have a better opinion of me than to think I have been ungrateful for your very, very kind letter of the second of August. You will have judged I wished to give you some account of your comet before I answered it. I wish you joy, most sincerely, on the discovery. I am more pleased than you can well conceive that you have made it, and I think I see your wonderfully clever and wonderfully amiable brother, upon the news of it, shed a tear of joy. You have immortalized your name, and you deserve such a reward from the Being who has ordered all these things to move as we find them, for your assiduity in the business of astronomy, and for your love for so celebrated and so deserving a brother. I received your very kind letter about the comet on the third but have not been able to observe it till Saturday, the fifth, owing to cloudy weather. I found it immediately by your directions; it is very curious, and in every respect as you describe it. I have compared it to a fixed star on Saturday night and Sunday night.

You see, it travels very fast—at the rate of two degrees and ten minutes per day—and moves but little in North Pole Distance. These observations were made with an equatorial micrometer of Mr. Smeaton's construction, which your brother must recollect to have seen at Loam Pit Hill. I need not tell you that meridian observations with my transit instrument and mural quadrant must have been much more accurate. I give you a little figure of its appearance last night and the preceding night upon the scale of Flamsteed's Atlas Coelestis.

By the above, you will see it will be very near nineteen of Coma Berenices tonight, and it will be a curious observation if it should prove an occultation of one of the stars of the Coma. Notice has been given to astronomers at home and abroad of the discovery. I shall continue to observe it and will give you by-and-by a further account of it. In the meanwhile, believe me to be, with much gratitude and regard, dear Miss Herschel.

Your most obedient and obliged humble servant,

Alex Aubert.

Shamelessly, I took Mr. Aubert's letter, ran upstairs, and tapped on Margaret's bedchamber door. As expected, she was on her bed. She might even have been sleeping, though she was fully clothed, and it was mid-morning. Blinking and smiling, she pushed herself up to receive me. Her pallor matched the white of the pillows.

I hesitated. "I've disturbed you; I'm sorry. I'll—"

"No, please. Do *not* say it. You have news. Tell me," she said, looking at the letter in my hand.

I read it to her, trying to keep my voice steady. At Mr. Aubert's sign-off, Margaret took my hand in hers and gave it a quick, gentle squeeze. The cool pressure of her fingers lingered.

"You see," she said. "'You have immortalized your name.' And what else? You deserve a reward 'for your assiduity in the business of astronomy.' Oh, Caroline, this is wonderful!"

I lifted the letter and reread a line to her. "'And for your love for so celebrated and so deserving a brother.'"

"Hmm," said Margaret. "But read it again. Mr. Aubert writes first about 'your comet' and only then about 'your wonderfully clever and wonderfully amiable brother.' This is your moment. There is change."

I smiled, shook my head and said nothing, but couldn't help wondering if there might be a chance one day that people think of me as Caroline Herschel first and William Herschel's sister second.

That evening, Dr. Blagden accompanied Sir Banks and Lord Palmerston to Observatory House, and, though my heart beat so loudly I feared they might hear it, the men were able to observe the comet. Afterward, when our conversation about the object was exhausted and they sipped glasses of port in the library, Sir Banks gravitated toward my desk, where several piles of my notes were stacked in rows. He lifted a page and examined it.

"This is your hand, is it, Miss Herschel?" he asked, peering at me from beneath his heavy brows.

"It is," I said.

He put down the paper and took a step toward me. "So, the comet is not your first discovery then?"

"It's my first comet. I found a nebula observing in Datchet in December 1783. My brother recorded it with my initials," I replied.

"Of course. I recall the nebula," said Sir Banks. "But I recognize your hand from other reports, perhaps going back almost three years. Am I correct?"

"Yes. As you know, I've worked alongside William ever since he became a Royal Astronomer. I've lost count of the number of reports I've written at his instruction," I replied.

Dr. Blagden smiled as if satisfied with my response. However, Sir Banks wasn't finished.

"And you observe using your own telescope. Even when Mr. Herschel is away." His tone was musing, rather than inquiring.

I wasn't sure whether he required a response but nodded anyway.

"That's extraordinary," he said.

"Why so?" I asked.

There was a moment of silence as the three men stared at me. Then Sir Banks chuckled and said. "Her Majesty will enjoy my account of our visit."

I wanted to ask what he meant. However, Dr. Blagden interrupted. "What are your thoughts on your brother's giant telescope, Miss Herschel? Does it excite you? Will you operate it?"

No one had asked my opinion about the forty-footer before. If they had, I wouldn't have disclosed my worries about the reflectors. Neither did I now. "It'll be extraordinary and allow him to see deeper into the heavens than ever. I'd be thrilled to operate it," I said.

"That reminds me," said Sir Banks. "His Majesty wants to celebrate progress on the machine with a feast at Observatory House at some point. He wishes to invite special guests from abroad to see it. I must speak to your brother about it."

My pulse quickened. "He wants to see it? But—"

"In time, Miss Herschel, in time. I know it's far from being ready for demonstration. However, we must agree on an approximate date when His Majesty will be able to show off the mighty structure and its powerful reflectors. You can understand his impatience. He wants reassurance his money is being well spent, and, of course, he'd like to prove the preeminence of his personal astronomer. But don't worry. I'll give your brother reasonable warning," he said.

I might've pretended otherwise, nodding and smiling, but I was worried. Even if the move from Datchet to Clay Hall to Observatory House and commissions for other telescopes hadn't disrupted work on the giant instrument, there would still be much to do to have it ready. Above all, I was concerned about the unresolved issue of finding someone to construct the reflectors. I pictured His Majesty and his entourage traipsing into the yard at Observatory House to find the bare bones of the tall gantry looming against the sky and the tube lying uselessly nearby, like a disemboweled, wormy monster. My neck and shoulders ached and I was grateful when Sir Banks declared, given the hour and because they'd leave at dawn the next morning, he'd like to retire. The three men drained their glasses in quick succession, wished me a good night, and left the library for the bedchambers I'd assigned them.

The next morning, after I'd seen Dr. Blagden and his friends off, I called Comet and Star. With the dogs galloping ahead, I set off across the yard to visit Mr. Campion at the forge. He showed me the metal plates and explained how he'd shape them into the giant tube. He also complained about how incompetent his young assistant was.

"He's been gone an hour on an errand that would take me half the time," he muttered.

"But Mr. Campion," I joked. "Is incompetence in someone so young not just inexperience? Perhaps part of the frustration is because when one is older and experienced, one forgets what it was like to still have to learn."

He grunted. "Hmm, maybe, Miss Herschel, but I don't recall ever being *that* inexperienced."

I laughed and left the forge for the stables. Juno was looking into the yard over the half door. Was she bored and missing William?

"He'll be home soon," I said, rubbing her prickly muzzle. "And I know he'll take you out at the first opportunity."

When I turned to make my way back to the house, I saw Hannah running toward me.

"It's Mrs. Herschel," she said as she drew nearer. "She's barely conscious."

"What? Again? Is she still—"

"Yes. In her bed. Her pillow is a pool of blood."

I gasped. "Blood? Where's Thomas?"

"He's out front with Mr. Harris. They're—"

"Tell him to take Juno and call the physician," I said.

I was halfway up the stairs when I realized Comet and Star were still following me. I turned, raced back down, and closed them in the kitchen, arriving at Margaret's door just before Hannah. We went in together.

Despite Hannah's warning, I shuddered at the blood-stained pillow, which lay on the floor like a scarlet-and-white corpse. Margaret's breathing was labored, and while her eyes were half open, she didn't acknowledge us. I leaned over her. The corners of her mouth were caked with blood.

"Margaret," I said.

There was no response.

I tried again. "Margaret, can you hear me?"

"She didn't hear me earlier either," said Hannah.

"Thomas has gone to call Dr. Perry. He'll be here soon, Margaret," I said, louder now.

Her eyelids flickered, she struggled to swallow, and her mouth moved. "No," she whispered. "No physician."

My eyes met Hannah's. She grimaced. "Get a cloth and some warm water," I said. "And take that away." I looked at the pillow.

When she returned, we settled Margaret in a half-sitting position, and I gently wiped her mouth. "You've been coughing again?" I asked.

She bobbed her head and took a small sip of water from a cup Hannah offered.

"Please, don't call the physician. I beg of you," said Margaret, her eyes flicking from me to Hannah and back again.

"But you're ill. You need help. I don't know what to do. He'll help you," I replied.

"No. He *can't* help me," she said, her voice ragged. "We've seen so many. They've tried everything. The bloodletting, purging, dark rooms, clean air, exercise, vegetable broth. Please, no physician."

How was it possible, I wondered, that I knew none of this about my brother's wife? That she was delicate and sickly, I'd seen the moment we met, but *so* ill that she'd undergone all that she mentioned? Why hadn't Alex told me? Did William know? Was she dying?

I heard a door open downstairs and voices. Dr. Perry had arrived.

"Go down," I told Hannah. "Tell him to wait there. I'll come shortly."

She nodded and left.

"Are you sure you don't want to see the physician, Margaret?" I asked. "Perhaps there's something he can do to still the coughing? Ease your discomfort? Give you a little more energy?"

"I'm sure," she said, closing her eyes. "I can't bear the hopelessness of it all. Please don't make me go through it again. Last night was bad. I'm sorry. It'll be better today."

CHAPTER 30

August 1786
Observatory House, England

DR. PERRY DIDN'T HIDE HIS DISPLEASURE AT BEING URGENTLY SUMMONED TO Observatory House only to be told the patient wouldn't see him. However, the physician was appeased when I offered to show him William's instruments. After he'd admired the twenty-footer, I took advantage of his improved mood to describe Margaret's symptoms and ask how I might make her more comfortable.

"Consumption," he said. "Of course, since she won't see me, I cannot confirm it, but if it's as you describe, I'm almost certain. She needs clean, mountain air and gentle exercise. And she should eat clear vegetable broth."

Well done, Margaret. You recalled the treatment precisely, I thought.

By the time William and Alex returned a few days later, Margaret had rallied and was even strong enough to join us for dinner that night. Despite my relief at having them home and the joy I felt when William praised me for finding the comet and the way I'd communicated its discovery, I remained peeved that Alex hadn't warned me about how ill Margaret was.

"So, your wife has consumption, has she?" I asked him after she'd retired for the night.

Alex looked at me blankly. "She told you?"

I clenched my jaw. "No. The physician did."

"Physician?" he echoed, his eyes wide now.

"Yes. I sent for him when we discovered her on a pillow of blood and struggling to breathe," I replied.

He glared at me. "You called a physician? She didn't say. Did she—"

"No. She refused to see him. Said he couldn't do anything for her. She seems terrified by the idea of even being examined," I said, glancing at William, who showed no sign of being surprised.

"She is," said Alex. "The last man cut her. Insisted bleeding would help. All it did was create more pain and suffering, including wounds that festered."

"Why didn't you tell me?" I demanded.

"She asked me not to. Doesn't want to be thought of as 'the sick woman,'" he said.

I couldn't help but snort. She *was* a sick woman.

Alex went on, "She admires you, Caroline. Says you're so strong, intelligent, and capable. She didn't want to burden you. It was hard to convince her to come here."

We didn't speak for a moment.

"If I'd known, I—"

"You'd do what?" he asked.

I shrugged.

Margaret's eyes glistened when, as she and Alex prepared to return to Bath two days later, we gathered in the hallway to say goodbye.

"Thank you, Caroline," she said. "You have been so kind."

I felt a hollowness beneath my breastbone. How gracious she was. I'd done so little, and despite her illness and my impatience, she'd been thoughtful and encouraging. I'd never forget how she'd admired my abilities and firmly urged me to take charge independently of William. I wished I'd known her before she was ill.

"Farewell, Margaret, Alex. Travel safely," I said, aware of my brothers' shared glance as I backed away. "I won't linger and keep you. You have a long way to go."

William found me at my desk a short while later. "Are you all right?"

"Yes. Of course," I replied without looking up.

He waited. I pretended not to notice.

Eventually, he sighed and said, "I'm going to court to tell His Majesty about our trip. I believe he wants to know more about your comet too. Would you like to join me?"

I stared at him. He'd never proposed I go to Windsor Castle with him before. William knew how self-conscious I was about my diminutive form and deformed face. It had taken months of coaxing and coaching to prepare me to stand in front of an audience and sing for the first time years ago. It was only when I was certain my voice would detract from my appearance, but mostly because I feared being sent back to Hanover, that I finally managed it. More recently, even though I was intrigued by the place that demanded so much of my brother's time and despite having grown accustomed to meeting dignitaries at Observatory House, I hadn't pictured myself visiting the castle. Did I want to go with him? Perhaps, but not yet. I needed time to prepare for such an event.

"No," I said. "I'm sure you and His Majesty have much to discuss after your trip."

"Your comet is big news. 'First lady comet hunter.' I think your presence at court would create great excitement," he said.

I imagined eyes on me and heard the whispers.

"The pox."

"Size of a child."

"And her brother is so handsome a man."

No, I wasn't ready.

"Another time. Go. Enjoy the ride. Juno will be overjoyed to be out," I said, looking down at my notes.

"Thomas could drive you in the carriage," he said.

"No. Not today." I raised my head. "Did Sir Banks write to you while you were away?"

"No. Should he have?" asked William.

"He wants to talk to you about His Majesty's visit…here. To see progress on the forty-footer," I said.

He pursed his lips. "To be expected, but premature. I'll discuss it with him."

"Good," I replied.

There was a pause. I guessed he was also wishing for His Majesty's protracted patience.

"I may be gone overnight. I have some other business to attend to too," said William eventually.

"Other business?" I asked.

"I'll see you tomorrow," he said as he left the room.

I wanted to call out to him and ask what the "other business" was. I knew everything that went on at Observatory House. What business could William have that I didn't know about? I went after him and found him standing alongside Juno, talking to Thomas outside the stables.

When Thomas left, I spoke. "I didn't hear what you said as you left the library."

My brother ran a hand down Juno's shiny flank. "I'll be gone overnight," he said.

"You'll be at Windsor?" I asked.

He looked at me, his eyes steady. "Thereabouts."

As I watched him ride away, I felt a trickle of perspiration run down the back of my neck. It was a warm day, but not the hottest. A low voice came to me from inside the stable. Thomas was talking to the other horses. I went to him.

"Did Mr. Herschel tell you where he'd be this evening? I didn't catch what he said as he left," I said, grateful that the poor light in the stables disguised my shame.

"He's going to Upton to pay his respects to Widow Pitt," he said.

Although I hadn't met Mrs. Pitt, I knew who she was. She was the wealthy youngest daughter of our landlord, Mr. Baldwin. She and her much older husband, Mr. John Pitt, lived in Upton House in the nearby village of Upton-cum-Chalvey. Mr. Pitt and William had been friends, and his death had saddened my brother. He'd attended the funeral. Why he felt he couldn't tell me he was going to visit to pay his respects to his friend's widow, I didn't understand.

CHAPTER 31

February 1787
Observatory House, England

IF WILLIAM WAS AWARE I KNEW ABOUT HIS VISIT TO THE WIDOW PITT, HE didn't mention it. He returned the following day with tales about what had been said about my comet at court. I'd never heard him as animated about the conversations of courtiers.

"Miss Frances Burney declared it 'small and neither grand nor striking in appearance' but significant because it is 'the first lady's comet,'" he said.

"Who is Miss Frances Burney?" I asked.

"She's one of Her Majesty's ladies, well known for her penmanship and quick wit, I believe," he said. "But apparently it was Sir Banks who first told Her Majesty about how 'clever Caroline Herschel, the lady comet hunter, is.' He was allegedly enraptured by how you'd discovered it while you were alone and accurately recognized and recorded it as a previously unknown comet. Sir Banks said no man could've done better."

I wished there was a way I could've heard the conversations without being seen. "What did you say?"

He smiled. "I said nothing because I know how clever you are."

His praise warmed me. *Can lady comet hunters one day become astronomers?* I wondered.

"His Majesty said he'd like to meet you. Perhaps when he visits to see how matters are progressing on the forty-footer," said William, his tone serious now.

I groaned. "He's eager to see what we've done then?"

"Yes, and Sir Banks has proposed we hold a Royal Telescope Garden Party to show off the instrument," he said.

"But—"

William ran his fingers through his hair. "I know. I said it will be difficult. There is much to do. His Majesty, says Sir Banks, won't wait beyond two springs."

"We could do it," I said, relieved that it wasn't sooner.

He rose to leave. "If all goes well."

"The reflectors…" I ventured.

"Yes. I'm aware and engaged in the matter," he replied.

William was frequently absent from home during the weeks that followed. If he wasn't at court, he was at Greenwich. He also made regular visits to artisans working on the instruments and continued his search for someone to make the reflectors. In addition, when Dr. Watson ordered the royal sculptor, John Charles Lochée, to make a bust of William, he was called upon to undertake several sittings.

Again, work on the forty-footer intensified at Observatory House, requiring more hands. The workrooms and garden once more swarmed with laborers, workmen, blacksmiths, and carpenters. I managed to secure the assistance of a few men to install a new reflecting comet sweeper on a flat section of the roof above my room. By fitting a small ladder alongside a window, I was able to climb onto the roof and observe the skies in comfort when William was away.

Despite the extent of his workforce and the demands on his time, William kept a close eye on everything. In fact, according to Mr. Harris, he missed nothing.

"Nay, it's not just that he *watches* everything we do," I overheard the gardener telling a carpenter one afternoon. "There's not one screw bolt about any of the apparatus that is not fixed under the eye of Mr. Herschel."

Is that why William brushes me off whenever I mention the reflectors? Is he determined to control everything? I wondered.

William and I looked forward to adding Alex's expertise and quiet diligence to our efforts. He was to return to Slough when the Bath season ended. We created a list of the tasks we hoped he'd undertake and added to it daily. I'd told William about Mr. Glashan and how I'd come to miss the meeting I'd hoped to have with him.

"Perhaps we can find his address in Edinburgh, write to him, and tell him we're still looking for speculum expert to make the reflectors," I said.

"It won't be necessary. I've more names of foundries in London. When Alex is here, we'll inquire together. Don't worry about the mirrors, Lina. Alex and I have enough experience to find the right men for the job," he replied.

William's apparent confidence in the matter didn't satisfy me. I hoped having our brother around would see results. However, a week before Alex was due, we received a letter from him saying Margaret was too ill to travel or be left alone. A week later, he wrote again. His wife was dead.

I stared at the page without seeing the words long after they'd registered. Kind, encouraging Margaret was gone. She'd recognized my ambition even if I hadn't admitted to it. She'd urged me to be brave and go after what I wanted. I hadn't thanked her or even said a proper goodbye.

"Do you think Alex will come now? I don't think we should delay finding someone to cast the reflectors. They're going to hold up the entire project. Will you ask him?" I asked, handing the letter back to William.

He rubbed his forehead. "No, I won't. Have you forgotten what our brother is like? Did you not see how devoted he was to Margaret? He'll grieve, as he should."

"But must he grieve alone?" I asked. "Won't it help him to be with us? To be busy?"

"If he decides to come, he'll let us know. I'll not suggest it," he replied.

"Surely we should invite him," I said.

"He knows he's always welcome. Please, Lina—give Alex time to mourn Margaret in peace. It's the least we can do."

I didn't respond but wondered what William would think if I suggested that Alex should come to Slough so we could mourn Margaret's death with him. Perhaps, if Alex came, I could help him. It might be a way for me to make amends for not having shown her my appreciation.

Willian folded the letter, placed it on his desk, and walked to the door as if to leave the library. However, he changed his mind, stopped, and turned to face me. "Lina, there's something else I must tell you."

His earnest expression made my skin tingle. "Go on," I said, holding my breath.

"I've appointed someone to show the telescopes to visitors. He'll start next week," he said.

"Oh! That was quick. Excellent," I replied, relieved.

William and I had discussed how inconvenient and time-consuming it was to be regularly interrupted by other astronomers and members of the Royal Society, along with foreign visitors who wanted to see the telescopes and discuss our work. Although Sir Banks had given us time to prepare for the Royal Telescope Garden Party, we understood that if we were to sustain His Majesty's interest and investment in astronomy, we'd have to continually entertain the curiosity of others. However, hosting such visits took us away from our work. We'd agreed we needed to appoint and train someone else to show-and-tell those visitors who didn't require our attention about the telescopes.

"Yes, it was quick because when I mentioned it to Thomas, he said he knew someone who might be interested." He hesitated and took a step toward my desk. "Asked if I minded if he mentioned the position to Mr. Corden."

I stared at him. "What? Mr. Corden? The—"

"The same Mr. Corden. Gabriel. Yes," he replied.

"But—"

"I went to see him on the way to Windsor yesterday. As you know, he's educated, agreeable, interested, and well informed about our work. He's read a great deal about it. The timing is good too. His cousin has been working in the butchery with him for more than a year. Mr. Corden will leave the business in his hands," he said.

It occurred to me that I should feel something else—doubt, disquietude, perhaps even indignation that William had gone ahead and appointed him without consulting me—but I didn't. Mr. Corden was perfect for the position. William was correct. He had the right disposition, was sincerely interested in astronomy, and would be a quick study. Despite his having found Comet with the hunting pack and sending Star to Observatory House with Hannah,

I hadn't seen him since he'd arrived unannounced at Clay Hall to tell me about the house at Slough.

"What are you thinking?" asked William.

"That Mr. Corden is the ideal person," I replied.

And I look forward to seeing him again, I thought.

The following Monday, I looked through the open library doors and saw Mr. Corden standing alongside the twenty-footer with William. Moving closer to the exit, I squinted to get a better view. He was *just* as I recalled. It had only been a year or so, but I'd imagined being a husband would alter him. However, his hair was as dark, curly, and unruly, his form as lean and agile, and his expression as open and eager as ever. He laughed at something William said, and I recognized the warmth and energy I'd admired in Datchet. Single or married, Mr. Corden, it seemed, was the same man. I watched, unseen, until Mr. Campion appeared, spoke to William, and they walked away together, leaving Mr. Corden at the telescope. I walked out, calling Comet and Star, who lay near the stairs, to accompany me.

Mr. Corden grinned when he saw us. I almost broke into a trot.

"Miss Herschel, Comet and, um, Pup, good day!" he said.

"Star," I said. "Her name is Star."

Comet shoved past me, and Mr. Corden crouched to pat him. Star was uncharacteristically shy and, while she wagged her tail, remained with me. Mr. Corden straightened and approached her slowly, his hand outstretched.

"Hello, Star. You've forgotten, but I fetched and gave you to Hannah to bring here," he said.

"Of course," I said. "And I've not thanked you." Our eyes met, and I felt myself color. "I know you were paid, and I asked Hannah to give you my thanks, but I should've…"

I was going to say, "I should've written," but was suddenly aware that Mr. Corden wouldn't expect my thanks. He'd purchased the puppy as a service, not because he was a friend.

"I'm pleased she's settled well and that Comet has given up his dreams of joining the hunt," he said.

There was a pause, and then we spoke at once.

"My brother—"

"I'm sorry—"

Mr. Corden motioned for me to continue.

"My brother asked me to make notes for you. We thought it would be helpful to have a guide to refer to, at least initially. I've written down the information we typically give visitors and some of the questions we're asked and our responses," I said, aware that I was talking fast but powerless to slow down. "Of course, it'll all soon become familiar to you, and you'll be able to show them around without the notes. Will you come into the library, and we can discuss them?"

He followed me inside, where we sat side by side at the table with my notes in front of us. As we leaned forward to read, I felt the warmth of his arm near mine, and there, in an instant, unbidden and as clear as if it had happened yesterday, the image of us pinned together in the hawthorn hedge in Datchet appeared. Too late, I put a hand to my mouth to stifle the giggle that accompanied the image. The sound emerged like the confused snort of a dog who wasn't sure whether to bark or sneeze.

Mr. Corden turned to me. "Are you all right, Miss Herschel?"

I swallowed and tried to speak. "I'm sorry," I said between chortles and gasps. "I just…it was…" However, I couldn't form full sentences, so I leaned forward, put my head in my hands, and gave in to laughter.

Eventually, I pulled myself up, took a deep breath, and was able to explain. "I apologize, Mr. Corden. It's just that, out of the blue, I pictured us in the hedge that day," I said, exhaling loudly.

He peered at me from beneath his brows. "Oh?"

"Silly, I know, but for the first time, it seems funny," I said.

His mouth twitched.

I babbled on, "Of course, the incident was anything but amusing. We could've been killed. But if you imagine it as a caricature or from the point of view of Miss Hudson as she happened to look through the coach window, you might see the humor."

He chuckled. "Well, I doubt poor Comet would agree," he said, his shoulders shaking now. "He had to dive beneath the hedge and was almost impaled by thorns. He might've still been trapped there if he weren't such a scrawny beast."

"I thought I might have to go under the hedge to get him out. You wouldn't fit," I added.

Even *that* seemed funny. We laughed freely until spent, and a little sheepish, we quietened, rearranged our chairs, and reapplied ourselves to my notes. There was nothing complicated about them. Mr. Corden asked a few questions, and we were soon done. We briefly talked about how he should make regular rounds of the workrooms to keep up with what the workmen were doing, which might add to his descriptions of our work. He mentioned that William had told him that when he was not busy with visitors, we'd assign him other ad hoc tasks.

"If you'd like me to copy catalogs or do any note-taking, I'd be pleased to do so," he said.

"You're confident of your penmanship, are you?" I asked.

"I am, but I'll gladly demonstrate it, should you require." He smiled, looking pointedly at the quill and ink pot on my desk.

Having gathered my notes, I handed them to him and stood up. "I'm sure there'll be an opportunity soon."

Mr. Corden rose, placed his chair neatly beneath the table, and turned to me, serious once more. "I meant to offer you my condolences earlier."

I stared at him.

"Hannah told me about Mrs. Herschel," he explained.

"Oh. Thank you." I didn't know what the appropriate response was. "She was a kind woman. My brother will miss her dearly."

He lifted his chin, his eyes on mine. Even then, I knew I shouldn't say any more. Miss Fleming would've condemned me for revealing too much of myself, for embarrassing myself and Mr. Corden. However, it didn't stop me talking.

"I wasn't aware how ill she was initially. No one told me," I said. "She didn't want to burden me with it, particularly when my brothers went to Germany. If I'd known, I might've taken better care of her. Been more patient."

"I'm sure you were good to her," he said quietly.

"No, I wasn't. I didn't like her when she arrived. It upset me that she kept

Alex from us. But it wasn't her fault. That's what marriage does, doesn't it? Makes rules, takes people away from their families, from their friends."

Mr. Corden took a deep breath and looked down. For a moment, I imagined I saw Miss Fleming and Miss Hudson standing behind him. The former shook her head. The latter sniggered.

"Well," I said, turning my back on them all. "I have work to do."

CHAPTER 32

March 1787
Observatory House, England

MORE WORK ON THE GIANT TELESCOPE AND THE INCREASE IN THE NUMBER OF employees at Observatory House meant another upsurge in costs. An unexpected visit from Sir Banks early one spring morning proved opportune. After examining the carpenters' work on the gantry, the foundations for its turntable, and the recently assembled zone clocks and micrometers, he declared himself pleased by how much we'd achieved. Crucially, he also acknowledged the extent of the work still to be done and the costs involved. He would, he said, request another grant from His Majesty.

William turned me as Sir Banks's carriage carried him away. "I want to be excited, but I'm afraid I might wish for too much."

"We'll work on in hope, but without expectation," I said, noting how even my ever optimistic brother had his doubts.

However, as William exclaimed when he returned from court a fortnight later and found me at my desk, Sir Banks exceeded our hopes and once again proved himself a consummate diplomat and our most valuable patron. He would not only replenish William's purse with another two-thousand-pound grant but had also succeeded in persuading His Majesty to add two hundred pounds to my brother's annual salary.

I clapped my hands together. "Oh, how excellent. Congratulations! That'll make a great difference to everything."

He took off his coat and hung it on the stand. "Yes, but I have something even more astonishing to tell you."

I waited, expecting him to continue, but first, he walked across the room and looked out into the yard, checking on the men. Presumably finding nothing untoward, he turned to me again.

"You might've imagined that the excitement caused by your comet had died down," he said.

I nodded.

He went on. "Well, apparently not. His Majesty has settled upon giving you a salary of fifty pounds a year."

"What? Me?" I placed my hands on my head as if to contain my thoughts. The day was full of surprises.

"Yes. You!" William's eyes danced.

"But a salary? Because I discovered a comet?"

It was inconceivable and yet, I'd dreamed about being an astronomer. Did receiving a salary mean I'd become one? I placed a hand on my chest. My heart was pounding.

"Partly, but also because you're my assistant. You're at my side constantly. You always know and understand what's going on here. You've checked, calculated, corrected, and updated papers and catalogs. You discovered a nebula and a comet. I am His Majesty's astronomer, and you are my assistant," said William.

"Fifty pounds?" I said, allowing the news to sink in.

"Yes, isn't it extraordinary? No lady has ever been paid to practice astronomy or indeed to study anything scientific until now," he said.

"I'll be a salaried astronomer," I said, trying to calm my thoughts and understand what it meant.

"A salaried *assistant* astronomer," said William. "But yes, you will have your own money. You are in the employ of His Majesty. You will be at liberty to spend your salary as you wish."

"As I wish," I echoed as I realized what it meant. "I know how I'll spend it."

He raised his brows.

"I'll use it to find someone to make the reflectors. Someone beyond London if necessary," I said.

William scowled. "We've discussed this. I don't want—"

I interrupted him. "I know. But you have so much else to do and you've had no luck in this regard. Let me try. With my own money, I'll be able to explore other options."

He sighed. "I can't see how you might succeed when I haven't."

"Let me try," I repeated.

The room was still for a moment.

"All right," he muttered.

I took a deep breath. My heart skipped. I wasn't sure where I'd begin but was eager to get started. "Do you think—"

William raised his hand. "Not yet. Only when you receive your salary, Lina. Slow down." He glanced out of the window. "I see Mr. Campion. I must talk to him."

As I watched him open the door and leave, I wished I could call my brother back and describe how encouraged I was by the news of my salary and by his agreeing that I might investigate the reflectors. Above all, I wanted to tell him how I wished to be more than his assistant. I could be more! The money would afford me greater independence. It wasn't a fortune, but it proved I was worthy, not only to my brother but to the world in a time of curiosity, discovery, and exploration. What would William say if I revealed my ambition? Was it time? Could I finally let go of the fear of being sent back to Hanover? Surely, Jacob couldn't argue I wasn't useful in England when he heard I'd been added to His Majesty's payroll?

I slumped against the back of my chair, staring at the notes in front of me. Before William's arrival, I'd been checking the record of his observations from the previous night. Now, I was unable to concentrate. The door opened, and I looked up, expecting to see William. It was Mr. Corden.

"Mr. Campion asked me to give you this," he said, handing me a page containing drawings and notes of materials that required ordering.

"Thank you," I said, my eyes on the paper. I sensed his hesitation and looked up. "What is it?"

He rubbed his hands together, smiling. "I, um, heard about His Majesty's proclamation."

"Proclamation?"

"About your salary as Mr. Herschel's assistant," he said. "Congratulations."

I pushed my chair away from my desk and stood. "His Majesty made a proclamation?"

Mr. Corden blinked. "As I understood it. One of the men told us about it less than an hour ago."

"An hour ago? I've only just heard about it myself. It still seems incredible," I said.

It occurred to me that this was another conversation I shouldn't be having with Mr. Corden. It was uncouth to talk about money. What would Miss Fleming and Miss Hudson have said? This time, however, the ghosts of the women weren't present. Was I finally free of them?

"Well, Miss Herschel, perhaps it's proof I'm not the only one who believes you know as much about the heavens as your brother," he said.

I sighed. "And yet, I'm only his assistant."

He frowned and tilted his head, expecting me to continue.

I smiled and held up my hands. I shouldn't say more.

"Is it true Her Majesty petitioned on your behalf?" he asked.

"Is that what is being said? I wasn't aware," I replied.

"As you know, Her Majesty is a naturalist, a botanist. Her interests are one of the reasons Sir Joseph Banks spends so much time in court. He has her ear, and she was among the first to hear of your discovery," said Mr. Corden.

I recalled Sir Banks's comment about Her Majesty's interest when I'd shown him the comet and what William had told me about the chatter at court.

"Rumor has it she's argued that if women were given the same advantages as men in their education, they'd do as well. Your discovery shows it could be so. Perhaps that's why the queen urged His Majesty to pay you a salary," he said.

"How do you know all of this?" I asked.

He chuckled. "Ah, I could ask you how you don't know any of it. Are we not all in awe of our king and queen? We follow them as holy figures of authority, hoping that they will help us understand and improve our own lives. We know we're not the same. They are chosen by God. We look to them to guide us on the right path. We watch their every move and listen to every utterance. We want, if not to participate, to belong to their world."

His eyes flashed, telling me that he was teasing me—at least, in part.

"So, I should welcome His Majesty's proclamation as an opportunity to belong to his world, should I?" I asked.

"No. You should welcome *Her* Majesty's awareness and celebrate your wisdom and hard work," he said, his tone serious now.

"Thank you," I replied, looking at the note he'd brought and wondering what Mr. Corden would think if he knew how much more the salary meant to me, regardless of who petitioned for it.

CHAPTER 33

October 1787
Observatory House, England

WHEN THE FIRST QUARTERLY PAYMENT OF MY SALARY WAS DELIVERED IN October, I crept upstairs, clutching the little purse of twelve gold crowns as if I'd stolen them. In my bedchamber, I removed them one by one, laying them in a neat row on my nightstand before standing back and gazing at them. The coins gleamed against the dark wood as if lit by tiny, internal lanterns. I stared on, entranced.

It wasn't that I hadn't seen or handled money before. I'd been the keeper of my brother's purse since we'd left Bath. However, I'd never looked upon coins that, as inconceivable as it seemed, were mine. Compensation for my singing in Bath was always paid to William. At the time, it had seemed right. William had taught me to sing, and I performed with his musicians. He'd trained, fed, and lodged me. He'd once given me money with instructions to buy a new gown. He'd probably have given me more had I asked, but it hadn't occurred to me. However, the money on the nightstand was mine. It came from His Majesty, not William.

As I gathered the coins and slipped them back into the purse, I realized the churning I'd felt in my stomach for months had ceased. I could finally begin trying to track down a metalworker to get started on the reflectors. We were running out of time. I'd already drafted specifications. Up until to now, William had relied largely on verbal exchanges, but I wanted to be exact about our requirements and would ask him to check the stipulations. I'd attach these to letters of inquiry addressed to prospective foundries claiming expertise with speculum that my brother hadn't already spoken to.

I placed the purse in the top drawer of the nightstand. As I closed it, I recalled Mr. Corden's words, and walking toward the window, I addressed my faint reflection in the glass, "Caroline, I commend you for your wisdom and hard work and for the doors your salary will open."

With William in Greenwich for the night, I was alone. I sang quietly as I went downstairs, ate supper, and returned to the library. It was cold and overcast. There'd be no observing tonight. Instead, I'd work on a paper we hoped to submit to the society before Christmas.

Stepping over the dogs stretched out in front of the hearth, I added wood to the fire. As I turned, I spotted a folded newspaper lying on William's desk. I read the headlines and turned the page. It was impossible to miss the large sketch on the right-hand page, but it took me a while to understand the caricature.

The picture featured a telescope, alongside which knelt a woman. She was looking through the eyepiece. The illustration was captioned, "The Female Philosopher smelling out the Comet." Even *that* didn't expound its full meaning. It was only when I examined the woman's face and saw that the cartoonist had drawn a large, red carbuncle below her left eye that I recognized myself.

I lifted my hand quickly, placing my fingers on the scar on my face. It wasn't as bulbous as the artist—was a cartoonist an artist?—had portrayed. However, as I traced the raised edges and distinct crevice, I was reminded that it was the deepest, ugliest of my disfigurements. My stomach churned.

Keeping my fingers over the blemish, I examined other elements of the cartoon. The cartoonist had depicted the comet as an angry-looking, naked cherub sitting on clouds encircled by an object that might've been the sun. The chubby, wingless child blasted rays from between his buttocks, which streamed directly at the telescope. The word "catch" had been written in the rays, while, as inscribed in the bubble above her head, the woman—me—said,

"What a strong sulfurous scent proceeds from this meteor." An astronomical quadrant lay useless on the ground. It was a reference to William's rejection of old instruments, I guessed.

Whatever the intention of its creator, the cartoon was nonsensical. That was the point of such material, wasn't it? I wanted to fold the newspaper, push it away, and think no more about it, but I couldn't. I couldn't stop staring at the pictorial lump. It not only bulged but also contained a dark spot as if infected. Had the artist seen me? Had we met? If so, where? I didn't socialize away from Observatory House much. Had he visited, examined me, and then rushed home to publicize and immortalize my unsightly face? Did it bring him joy? Worse still, had he never seen me but learned about my deformities from others? Did the workmen talk about it? William's friends? Mr. Corden? Of course they did. They all did. I couldn't hide the scars. I couldn't pretend my skin was smooth and that I was of average height. I was a freak. I always had been, but until His Majesty drew attention to me by deciding to pay me a salary, no one cared. While I worked quietly in the shadows, I wasn't worthy of caricature. An hour before, I'd celebrated my salary and what it meant. I'd even imagined it might be a step toward me becoming an independent astronomer. What a fool I was to imagine that might be possible for a woman!

"No, Caroline," I said, snatching the paper from the desk and taking it to the fire. "Not just a woman. A tiny, blemished woman."

I tossed it onto the logs and watched it smolder briefly before it burst into flames so ferocious that Comet raised his head in mild alarm.

My mood hadn't improved much by the time William returned the next afternoon. He was later than anticipated, but I was surprised to see he didn't appear unhappy to have been kept from his work.

"I made a final visit to Mr. Lochée," he said when I asked what had delayed him.

"The sculpture is complete?" I inquired.

William's smile was almost smug. "Yes, it's done, and despite my doubts, I like it. He's a very skilled man. Of course, he flatters me."

I looked at my brother with his high forehead, strong nose, and smooth skin. Any artist would flatter him. He was a fine-looking man.

"How gratifying it must be to be immortalized by the royal sculptor," I said, unable to keep the sneer from my voice. "I only understand how demoralizing it is to be the subject of a vulgar cartoonist."

"Ah," he said, his expression serious now. "You saw it."

"Would you have hidden it from me?" I asked.

"I don't know. Perhaps. It's a silly cartoon. A caricature. It's not meant to be taken seriously. Nobody takes such things seriously. It's already forgotten," he said.

"Not by me," I replied.

William didn't respond.

"Do you remember how terrified I was to perform in front of an audience for the first time?" I asked.

"Of course," he said.

"I thought the stares, the whispering, and the pity would paralyze me, petrify my vocal chords. But you began playing, I heard the overture and somehow I managed. And once I was singing, I didn't care how they looked at me, only that they listened. And when they listened, there was no repugnance in their eyes. In Bath, I discovered it wasn't necessary to hide myself. I could perform in public. Now, here, where I rarely go out, where I study the stars, seldom go into the village, and haven't even been to court, I discover I should've concealed myself better. If I'd kept to the night, stayed in the shadows, I wouldn't have been ridiculed in a newspaper," I argued.

"You're making too much of this," said William.

My body tensed. "Too much?"

How dare he? He had no idea what it was like to yearn to do something, to toil toward it and to want to be included, only to find—behind the door you hoped would admit you—a room full of detractors and jesters.

He sighed. "You found a comet. Your work is applauded the way your singing was. It's earned you a salary."

"And ridicule," I muttered.

"A silly cartoon," he repeated. "It means nothing."

I swallowed deeply. "Did you see my face? My deformity in the 'silly cartoon'?"

His eyes held mine. He'd seen it. Of course he had. How could he miss it? How could *anyone* miss it?

"It was cruel," he conceded. "I'm sorry. But it's meaningless to anyone but those who know you. Strangers would make no sense of it. They wouldn't even notice it. And those who know you don't see or care about your scars."

"If no one cares, why is my scarring a feature in a newspaper?" I asked.

William shook his head and, in an uncharacteristic physical demonstration of support, gently laid his hand on my forearm. "I'm sorry you feel like this. It doesn't matter that I am certain others don't care about how the cartoonist depicted you; it upsets you, and I'm sorry for that. As I said to Mrs. Pitt this morning, I wish I could protect you from how you feel, but I cannot."

I took a step back. "Mrs. Pitt? You discussed me with Mrs. Pitt? This morning?"

"Yes. Mrs. Mary Pitt. The widow of my friend from Upton, James Pitt. You surely remember him?" he asked.

"Of course," I replied.

"She met me at Mr. Lochée's rooms to see the bust," he explained.

"Why?" I asked. My mouth was dry.

"Because she was curious," he said, smiling again.

I stared at him, silently demanding an explanation.

"I've been courting her," he said.

My legs threatened to give way. I sat down. "I don't understand, William. Why—"

"She's a fine woman, Lina. I've never met anyone like her."

"Courting. Does that mean you plan to marry her?" I asked.

He took a deep breath and rubbed his hands together. "I do," he said. "Of course, she'd have to agree."

My head spun. "Do you have any reason to believe she won't?"

William laughed. "No."

"Then why haven't you asked her yet? Could it be that you know it's an absurd idea? You're almost fifty years old. You're so busy, you barely have time to dine, let alone get married. We're already behind on the forty-footer. Have you forgotten we've committed to have it ready for the garden party Sir Joseph has promised His Majesty? The months are passing and we still have so much to do. There's no time to, to, to get married. It makes no sense!" I was breathless.

"Perhaps not to you. As I said, I've never known anyone like her. I've never felt like this before. I'm not a young man, and yet it doesn't matter. I'm going to ask Mary Pitt to marry me, and I believe she'll accept," he said.

I put my head in my hands and closed my eyes. William hadn't previously expressed an interest in matrimony. Or had I simply never perceived it?

"I believe your brother is courting once more." I recalled Miss Hudson's goading when she'd found me searching for Comet at Clay Hall.

Certain she was motivated by spite and bitterness, I'd assured myself she was lying. Now, however, I wondered if Miss Hudson had known about Mrs. Pitt. Or was I so ignorant about my brother's life that he'd courted several women? Was that why Miss Hudson had imagined he might be interested in her? Perhaps he *had* courted her?

My stomach churned. Was it really only yesterday that I'd looked at the gold crowns and imagined how they might be the key to my becoming an independent astronomer? The cartoon had reminded me how I would never be accepted in the circles in which William moved so freely. It wasn't just that I was a woman but also an unsightly one. I'd never amount to anything more than an assistant. Now, even that was under threat. If Mrs. Pitt agreed to marry William, she was unlikely to want me to continue managing the household. That was the duty of a wife. She might even want me gone. Where would I go? What would I do? Would William grant Jacob's wish and send me back to Hanover?

CHAPTER 34

October 1787
Observatory House, England

"I've invited Mrs. Pitt to Sunday lunch," said William a few days after his disquieting announcement.

"Sunday lunch? But we agreed we'd finalize detailed specifications for the reflectors for my letters after church. I'm eager to send them," I said.

"Ah, I meant to tell you. I don't think it'll be necessary to look further afield after all. I have the name of another man in London who is perfect for the job."

"Another man in London? But you've spoken to several and found them all incapable. What makes you think this one is different?" I asked.

"He comes highly recommended," he replied.

"He's worked with speculum before?"

"I'll meet him soon and get all the information we need. Tell Hannah we'd like a roast with all the trimmings," he said.

William's stubbornness about the reflectors baffled me. Despite having agreed I could help when we received news of my salary, he was once more determined to keep me out of it. Had he forgotten how I'd helped him and Alex make mirrors ever since he began constructing telescopes?

"I still believe we should investigate other artisans," I said. "Let's not leave it until you've seen the man from London. I could write—"

My brother held up his hands and shook his head. He wouldn't listen to me.

"I wrote to Alex, asking him to come," he said.

"To help with the forty-footer? But you argued that we should wait for him to come in his own time, to let him grieve at his own pace. What's changed?" I asked, though I knew the answer.

"I'd like to introduce him to Mrs. Pitt," he said.

"And? Is he coming?"

"Yes. Unfortunately, he won't be here in time for Sunday lunch, but he'll arrive on Monday and stay for a few weeks," he replied.

I wanted to be excited about seeing Alex again. However, his reason for coming placed a damper on the news.

The days until Sunday were never-ending. For the first time, my work seemed meaningless, and although I took notes for William while he observed, it was hard to care about heavenly objects while, on Earth, I felt untethered, adrift. It wasn't just that I was worried about how William's marriage might disrupt my life; I was also still smarting from the humiliation of the cartoon. I couldn't help wondering what the others at Observatory House thought. Had they laughed when they saw it? Were they still sniggering? The matter of the reflectors troubled me too, particularly when I saw no signs of William meeting with the man he'd spoken of.

When Sunday finally arrived, I was awoken by throbbing pain that began at the top of my spine and ran hot up and over my forehead. After asking Hannah to tell William I wouldn't go to church, I returned to bed, placed a wet cloth over my eyes, and hovered in an uncomfortable blur between sleep and despair.

Hours later, I heard William's voice and the murmured responses of a woman. I groaned, got up, and dressed. The ache hadn't gone, but as much as I rued Mrs. Pitt's very existence, curiosity propelled me downstairs.

By the time I got there, William was showing her the telescope outside. It gave me a chance to examine her from the library. Almost as tall as my brother, Mrs. Pitt had the vigorous, upright posture of someone who'd never known illness or uncertainty. They stood close, and for a moment, I thought she was about to step into my brother's arms, but it was an illusion created by the wind teasing the hemline of her pale blue skirt from beneath her coat. Her dark hair had been swept into a mass of curls on top of her head and was held there by invisible means. Although her dress and coat—tight against her arms and torso and full-skirted below—were fashionable and more extravagant than anything I owned, Mrs. Pitt sported no hat, feathers, or elaborate jewelry. Such self-assurance required no fancy adornments.

As if sensing my gaze, she turned, and her strikingly large eyes met mine. Instinctively, I drew back, but she raised her hand and waved. I forced myself forward and responded likewise. How young she was.

They came to the library, where I was struck by how different meeting Mrs. Pitt was from my introduction to Alex's wife. There was nothing meek about Mrs. Pitt. She was as robust as Margaret had been delicate. And, whereas Margaret had demonstrated the apprehension typical of a stranger when she arrived at Clay Hall, Mrs. Pitt's easy manner reminded me that her father owned Observatory House. Of course she felt at home here. It had been her home.

"At last! I've been so eager to meet you and learn more about your work, Miss Herschel," she said, bobbing a small, excited curtsy, which made her seem even younger than I'd thought.

"I'm sure my brother has told you everything. He's the astronomer, after all," I replied.

She and William shared a glance. Already, I was the outsider.

"Ah, William warned me about your famous modesty," she said. "I hope you'll indulge my interest in time."

What did she mean? I wondered. Had William already proposed? If not, why was she confident we'd have time to discuss my work? My head throbbed. Now, though, the pain was accompanied by nausea. It intensified as I breathed in the rich, smoky aroma of roast beef and potatoes as Hannah opened and closed the kitchen door. My stomach flipped at the thought of eating, sending a bitter bubble into my throat. I put my hand over my mouth.

"Are you all right?" asked Mrs. Pitt.

I shook my head and turned to address William. "I'm unwell. I won't join you for lunch. Please excuse me."

He tilted his head, but it was Mrs. Pitt who came to me. "Let me help you," she said, reaching for my arm.

I stepped away. "No. Please don't," I said, heading for the stairs.

By the following morning, my head and stomach had recovered. I suffered only from resignation when my brother found me at my desk and cheerfully told me how, after Sunday lunch, he'd proposed to Mrs. Mary Pitt, and she'd accepted.

"We'll get married in St. Laurence's Church in Upton in May," he said.

"Why wait so long?" I asked.

William attempted a consolatory smile. "There's a great deal I want to get done beforehand. Mary needs to settle various matters, too," he said.

"What will she do with her house?"

"We're thinking of living there, in Upton House," he replied.

I hadn't expected that. "What? Why?"

"It's a spacious, comfortable home with stables for Juno. I could easily ride between here and there."

It was on the tip of my tongue to point out how impractical that would be, given the hours he kept. However, I saw it could work in my favor. If Mrs. Pitt remained in Upton, life at Observatory House might go on largely as before. William would work here and, as usual, through the night whenever possible. We'd keep his bedchamber as it was so he could sleep when it suited him. I'd manage the household just as I'd always done while Mrs. Pitt took care of Upton House and accommodated William whenever he might stop by.

"Mary hopes you'll become friends but insists it's too much to ask of you to allow her to become the mistress of Observatory House," he said.

I realized then what my brother truly wanted. He hoped I'd step aside for Mrs. Pitt. Saying that they'd live in Upton was a ruse to shame me into inviting her to move into Observatory House. I pretended ignorance.

"That's perceptive of her," I said.

William huffed. "I know this is difficult for you, but please try to understand. Mary makes me happy. I've never been happier. Can't you see that?"

I put my hand over my eyes. I didn't want to look at him. Neither did I want him to recognize my pain. I'd believed William to be happy and thought I knew and understood him. What had I missed?

"It's just that it's happened so fast," I said eventually, meeting his eye once more. "Everything has changed in a matter of a week."

"I've known how I feel about Mary for a long time. We've known and discussed what we want," he replied calmly.

"But William, what if it's infatuation? Just as it was for Miss Hudson? She was so smitten by you, she behaved irrationally. Perhaps you are now. Is it possible you're rushing into things?" I asked.

William smoothed his hair. "No. I'm sorry you're unsettled, but it doesn't change anything. I'm going to marry Mary."

"Is it the money?" I asked.

"What?"

I swallowed. "Hannah told me Mrs. Pitt is wealthy."

He squeezed his eyes shut, opened them, and glared at me. "You truly don't know me, do you?"

"I know you better than anyone," I said quietly.

William nodded. "Then hopefully you'll forgive yourself for thinking and saying such a thing. I'll do my best to pardon you too," he said.

Alex arrived later that afternoon. While his misery was obvious—his clothes hung loose, as did the flesh on either side of the downturn of his mouth, and his hair was lank—he brushed me off when I offered my sympathies.

"Thank you," he said. "But it's easier if I don't talk about Margaret. I think about her all the time. Talking to others about other matters is a good distraction. We could talk about William's imminent marriage, for example. He says you're unhappy about it."

"Are you not shocked by it?" I asked.

"No."

"He's almost fifty years old. He's never indicated he wanted a wife before. You must be surprised," I insisted.

"Just because he never spoke about being married doesn't mean he didn't want it. I was looking for a wife for as long as I can remember," he said.

"Hmm," I said, mildly amused that, by explaining it, Alex implied we might not have known how desperate he was to be married.

He continued. "I don't think William ever *looked* for a wife, but I'm not surprised he'll marry. You are. I'm certain he is too."

"He's surprised? Did he say as much?" I asked.

"No, but it makes sense. William is in love. We've not known him to be in love before. It must've taken him by surprise, and I think it is wonderful," he said without emotion.

"In love? But that's my point. Love is for young men and women. Not for thinkers and scientists. He's the King's Astronomer. He's, he's so…busy," I said.

Alex leaned forward in this chair and rested his elbows on his knees. "Perhaps you don't understand because you've never experienced it. There are no rules in love."

I looked away. What would my brothers think if they knew how I'd felt about Mr. Corden? Alex might understand, given he believed there were "no rules in love." I wasn't brave enough to say I might understand, even if my affection wasn't reciprocated.

"Anyway, it doesn't matter how we feel. William is getting married, and I hope he will be as happy a husband as I was, and I hope you will become fond of his wife the way you grew to like Margaret," he said.

"I thought you didn't want to talk about her," I said.

He sighed. "It's impossible. As I said, I think about her all the time."

CHAPTER 35

April 1788
Observatory House, England

ALEX WASN'T WITH US LONG BEFORE I UNDERSTOOD HE'D MOURN MARGARET for the rest of his life. He'd always been melancholic, so his grief had a home. Despite his gloom, our brother's presence eased the tension between me and William. We instinctively slipped into our old roles of gentle joker and task-master (William) and long-suffering caregiver (me), distracting Alex with an unending series of jobs, asking Hannah to prepare his favorite dishes, and cajoling him into a conversation when the darkness threatened to shut him from us.

Our brother had planned to be with us only for a few weeks, but neither William nor I mentioned it when the weeks turned to months. When the green fuzz on the trees unfurled and became leaves, daffodils aimed their star-shaped faces to the sun, and the birds began chorusing earlier each morning, Alex made his revised plans known.

"It's only weeks away, so I'll stay for the wedding and go home immediately afterward," he said one morning, as if we'd asked.

As ever, I wanted him with us. *He should move to Slough permanently*, I thought. Without Margaret, the only reason he'd return to Bath would be to resume his work as a musician, and it seemed he no longer found joy in it. His skills and efforts were invaluable at Observatory House. I glanced at William, hoping he'd urge our brother to stay indefinitely. Sir Banks had set a date for the Royal Telescope Garden Party, and we'd begun counting down the months to when we'd welcome His and Her Majesty and a large party of dignitaries to Observatory House to see the forty-footer in action. However, the matter of the reflectors was still unresolved.

"Excellent. Mary and I will be pleased to have you here for the celebrations," he said instead.

I winced. William's conversations were increasingly infused with the words "Mary and I." She'd only had to say "yes" for him to fasten her name to his thoughts, decisions, and opinions.

"Why leave after the celebrations?" I said, looking at Alex. "You've seen how much is going on here. Stay and help us prepare for the royal visit. Return to Bath, pack all your belongings, and move here for good."

His reply came quickly. "No, I must go back and stay. I assured the band I'd return. And anyway, there'll be enough disruptions here. I'll come again later in the year for a bit."

"Disruptions? What do you mean?" I asked.

My brothers shared a look, but neither replied.

The following Sunday was clear and windless, and, as was my inclination when the weather allowed, I walked to church for morning service.

Less than a mile separated Observatory House from the church, but the short walk brought me great pleasure. As I followed the footpath through a dewy field, I watched a small raft of white ducks gliding across a mirror-still pond. Their intermittent quacks peppered the quiet. A little farther on, I squeezed through a stile and paused to enjoy the sweet lemon scent of a tangle of pale pink roses on the fence. A dapple-gray mare and her much darker foal lifted their heads to watch me as I walked alongside their paddock. The foal emitted a cheeky snort and trotted beside me, the wooden rails between us. His legs were gangly, his knees knobby and oversize, and his foal coat soft and fuzzy. He turned his head, keeping his dark eyes on me until, as if he'd been counting the strides since leaving his mother, he gave a short squeal, raised his tail, spun around, and galloped back to her. I laughed and lifted my head to the sky. The air was morning cool, but the sun was bright enough to promise warmer hours.

Later, with the vicar preaching the importance of prayer, his voice low and indistinct but persistent, I shifted on the cold, hard pew. As impious as it was, I'd been more comforted by the sights, smells, and sounds outside than I was by his sermon. I consoled myself with thoughts of walking home. I'd pay penance for being distracted from the sermon by silently thanking the Lord for all things bright and beautiful, all creatures great and small. I might even pray.

I didn't dally when the vicar finally dismissed us. As others slowly filed out of the church and lingered at the door, I pulled down my bonnet to hide my scars and marched down the stairs and onto the stone pathway. However, as I neared the small gate leading onto the road, I heard a voice behind me calling, "Miss Herschel! Miss Herschel!"

It took me a moment to recognize Mrs. Pitt. A few locks of hair curled around her face from beneath a bonnet trimmed with ribbon in the same dark blue as her dress. Her cheerful confidence was unmistakable, but her presence at our church was unexpected.

Ignoring the stares of others, she bounded toward me with energy that rivaled that of the foal. *Did she also snort when she set off after me?* I wondered.

"Oh, good! I caught you," she said, skidding to a halt. "I thought I'd walk home with you."

I took a step back. "What are you doing here?"

"I woke up and felt like a change this morning. Isn't it a perfect day?" She glanced around before leaning closer and whispering, "Indeed, I hoped for something new, but when I shut my eyes in there, it seemed your vicar and mine could be the same man. Certainly, they look different, but their voices are identical. Do you think they're taught to preach in only one tone?"

I shrugged, determined not to be amused.

"Anyway, it's such a lovely day, I told my driver not to wait. He's taken the carriage directly to Observatory House. So, I can walk home with you," she said.

"Directly? Home?" I was puzzled.

"For luncheon with you and your brothers," she explained.

"Of course," I replied, though William hadn't mentioned she'd be there. "But, um, are your shoes suitable? I don't stick to the road."

She slightly lifted her skirt and raised a foot to reveal a neat, leather half boot with front lacing. Mrs. Pitt might've arrived in her carriage, but clearly, she'd left home planning a walk. *What is it she wants to achieve between church and Observatory House?* I wondered. I imagined it had something to do with the wedding. Perhaps that was why she'd come to our church. Or maybe she and William wanted to get married there rather than at St. Laurence's as originally planned. Or did she want to propose I play some kind of role in the ceremony? I set off, and she fell into step alongside me.

"We share a love of walking, you and I," she said. "William told me how much you enjoy taking the dogs into the countryside."

I could've told her how, since Star had arrived, I'd stopped walking as regularly. The dogs had each other and didn't rely on me for company and entertainment. Also, I was busy. However, it had occurred to me on the way to church that I should make time to take them out more often. Walking brought me joy, and I'd missed it. If I'd cared to make conversation with her, I might've told Mrs. Pitt this, but I said nothing.

"Do you ever wonder why you enjoy walking?" she asked.

"For the silence it offers," I replied, not looking at her.

She chuckled. "Yes, there's a quiet rhythm to putting one foot ahead of the other. Even when one is walking away from home, away from everything and everyone one knows and feels comfortable with, there's something safe and reassuring about the sound of one's footsteps. It's as if you're walking away but, at the same time, getting closer to yourself." She turned to me. "Does that make sense?"

"Not really," I lied.

"When my husband died, I didn't venture outdoors for weeks," she said. "It wasn't that I didn't want to but rather that I was afraid of what I might find on a solitary stroll. What if I enjoyed it just as I had when he was alive? It didn't seem right to experience the pleasure of a long walk. If I was to grieve properly, I should be confined and punished. It was William who persuaded me I was wrong."

"William? But—"

She laughed again. "I know. You'd expect him to propose a ride. But he didn't. He invited me to walk with him. He said John, my husband, would want me to keep living, doing things that brought me joy. I didn't agree to walk with William the first time he asked me, but a few days later, I went alone. My repetitive steps along paths I'd walked many, many times seemed to lead to a wider world. The countryside I'd seen for years and years seemed new. I saw that life might indeed hold more for me despite John's absence. It wasn't that I didn't mourn his passing. Even as I walked, I cried. I may have cried harder than ever before. But I also realized that I was alive and that William was right; I should keep living."

"When did you go?" I asked.

"What do you mean?"

"You said you didn't walk with William the first time he asked," I said. "When did you go with him?"

"Many months later," she replied. "I reminded him of his invitation, and eventually, we walked near Upton House. After that, when the weather was good and he could spare the time, we did it more regularly. It was during those walks, as we matched strides and spoke without looking at each other, that we reached a mutual understanding—even before we spoke of it."

"Of course," I said, speeding up as we approached the paddock where I'd seen the horses. "You don't need to explain any further. Say no more."

It wasn't just that I didn't want an exhaustive account of how William and Mrs. Pitt's relationship had developed. It unsettled me to hear how my brother, who'd never taken a walk with me, had frequently strolled around the countryside with her. Their courtship, it seemed, had been a walking affair. As long as I'd been in England, William had always been too busy for leisurely rambles. He loved being in the countryside. That was one of the reasons he enjoyed riding Juno. He also knew how much joy I got from walking. He'd told his betrothed as much. Yet, my brother had never conceded to walk beyond the garden gate with me. Was it possible William was oblivious to who I was and what I enjoyed beyond being his devoted sister and assistant?

The mare and foal were grazing on the other side of the paddock. When I'd thought about them while in church, I'd hoped the foal might trot alongside me again. Now I was pleased they didn't notice us. I resented the idea of sharing them with Mrs. Pitt. However, she spotted the pair.

"What a pretty picture they make," she said, pointing at them. "Such a young foal. I know you don't ride, but do you like horses?"

I nodded without looking at her or the animals.

A few yards later, Mrs. Pitt stopped, dipped her nose into one of the roses I'd appreciated earlier, took a deep breath, and sighed. I pretended not to notice. We walked silently until, after having navigated the stile and we set across the field, she exhaled loudly and said, "Do you think, since we're going to be family, we could call each other by our first names, Caroline?"

"Let's wait until after the wedding," I replied.

"All right." She paused. "There's something else I want to ask you."

"Of course. That's why we're walking, isn't it?" I said, looking at her.

She closed her eyes briefly but smiled. "Miss Herschel, would you mind if William and I turn the room Alex is using at the moment into our bedchamber?"

I gasped. "What?"

"It's lighter and warmer than William's, and I like the view onto the twenty-footer. I've told Alex we'll wait until he returns to Bath. There's no rush. And we'll ensure that William's old room is ready for his future visits," she said.

"But I don't understand," I said, breathing hard. "Why do you and William need a room in Observatory House? You'll be in Upton."

She looked down. "No, we're moving into Observatory House immediately after the wedding."

"But William said you didn't want to move. That you felt that, erm, that you and I wouldn't…" I couldn't go on.

"Yes, that was what I proposed initially. But William has been against it all along. He said it wasn't realistic. Now, having seen the long hours William works, I accept it's impractical and agree. I'd never see my husband if we made Upton House our home," she said.

I looked away and saw the pond I'd admired earlier. A few of the ducks were perched alongside the water while the others continued to drift about. They were just ducks doing duck-like things. The peace and beauty I'd seen earlier were gone.

"Why didn't William tell me?" I asked at last.

"Because *I* wanted to, Caroline." She came toward me and tried to take my hands in hers. I stepped away. "I want us to be sisters, friends, allies," she continued. "We can share a house. It's large, and we're reasonable women. I won't interfere with your work. There's plenty for us to do without treading on each other's toes. We both love William."

For a moment, I couldn't breathe. *We both love William.* What did this woman know of William? What made her think she could step in, take over my home, and turn my life upside down? I'd spent sixteen years creating a life and home with William. I couldn't imagine sharing that with another woman. What about what I wanted? Mrs. Pitt was like my mother, selfish and manipulative. Even Alex was under her spell.

"When did you talk to Alex? Why did you tell him about the room before you'd spoken to me?" I asked.

"He visited me in Upton last week. We spoke about the wedding and our plans, and I mentioned what I hoped to do," she said.

"*Hoped to do*? What do you mean? You've already decided. That's why you told Alex." I stepped toward her, my fists clenched. "What would you say if I said I didn't want you to move into that room?"

"Caroline—"

"Don't call me that! I don't want you to *ever* call me Caroline. We are not friends, family, or sisters. We will never be sisters. I had…I *have* a sister in Hanover. I do not want you rearranging rooms and moving furniture about. I do not want you living in Observatory House. I do not want to walk with you!"

I turned toward home and ran.

I arrived at Observatory House to be greeted in the hallway by Comet and Star. They slowed their wagging as I pushed past them and went upstairs. William and Alex were assembling an eyepiece in a chamber close to mine. I heard their murmured conversation as I went into my room and shut the door. I couldn't face anyone. However, as I discovered when I got there, neither did I want to be in my bedchamber. Even as the sunlight lit and warmed the space, the walls seemed too close. I should've continued walking or called the dogs and headed out the back to avoid meeting Mrs. Pitt. It was too late now. I was trapped. I turned the key in the door, pulled off my shoes, and flung myself onto my bed.

Just as I'd used sleep to evade anxiety in the past, I slept that afternoon. Whereas, without Mrs. Pitt's revelation, I might've spent more time in the sunshine, eaten lunch, and worked alongside my brothers, I escaped into slumber. On the occasions I awoke and thought of her, I immediately closed my eyes, shut her out, and slept again.

By the time I was roused by several loud knocks on my door, the subdued orange-pink colors outside indicated it was evening. I sat up but didn't respond. There were three more knocks.

"Lina! Lina!"

It was William. I remembered how reassured I'd been to hear his and Sophia Elizabeth's voices after the terrible, lonely days when I'd been ill and alone in Hanover. How I wished he'd comfort me now.

"Open the door," he said, his voice firm. "I must talk to you."

I unlocked it, walked to the window, and looked out, not wanting to face him.

"Is she here?" I asked.

"No. Mary left after lunch. She was very upset and wanted to talk to you, set things right," he said.

I turned. "Did she? What did she want to say? The only way to 'set things right' would be for her to stay away," I said.

William scowled, narrowing his eyes. "I'd hoped you'd calm down and understand, but I see it's too much to ask. You're being unreasonable. I am going to marry Mary, and she is going to move in here. We will turn the room Alex is in into our bedchamber, and Mary will be mistress of the household. If you cannot accept that—"

"Then what?" I said, dreading his response.

"Then you must go."

I collapsed against the windowsill. I wasn't sure what I'd expected or feared, but it was unimaginable that William would banish me.

"Why are you punishing me?" I asked, my cheeks wet with tears.

His hair stuck up and out in several directions. He'd been dragging his fingers through it. His face was drawn, and his eyes were weary. "I don't mean to punish you. But I will marry Mary, and we want to live here peacefully and happily. After today, I cannot see how that will be possible if you stay."

"So you'll send me back to Hanover?" I cried.

His chin dropped. "What? No, of course not! Why would I do that? Anyway, you wouldn't go." He shook his head as if confirming to himself how preposterous the notion was. "You should find lodgings nearby. Continue to work with me. We work well together. But you cannot live here with me and Mary."

I remained on the windowsill for several minutes after William left. That was it then. I'd find somewhere else to live. My head spun. The idea of moving out and living alone was crushing. But that wasn't all that shocked me. William had said he wouldn't send me to Hanover. I was surprised and relieved, but what struck me above all else were his words, "Anyway, you wouldn't go."

Ever since I'd arrived in England, I'd been imprisoned by the fear of being sent back to Hanover. It had ruled my thoughts and decisions. Never once had I imagined I might refuse to go. When had that become an option? What other choices did I have in life that I hadn't seen?

CHAPTER 36

May 1788
Observatory House, England

As one thing ends, another begins. My role of mistress of Observatory House ended on the eighth of May, the day William and Mrs. Pitt were married in St. Laurence's Church in Upton.

Although it wasn't discussed again after the teary conversation in my room, I'd accepted I'd leave as soon as Mrs. Pitt arrived. Until then, William, Alex, and I had gone about our business as if nothing had changed. We'd limited our talk to work matters, including William's declaration he'd finally found "the right man for the reflectors" when he visited a forge master named Mr. Gibbs at his foundry in London. Alex and I expressed our relief, and I was reminded again how adept we Herschels were at compartmentalizing and containing our troubles until we arrived at a point of no return. The only thing I'd arranged for my new life were temporary quarters. I'd told the innkeeper at The Swan in the center of Slough to expect me on the day of the wedding.

The evening before, as I packed a few essentials in the blue travel bag Margaret had given me, I contemplated not attending the ceremony. I'd already decided I'd leave Observatory House before the wedding feast. Going to church was one thing, but pretending to celebrate with the couple's friends and family was another. I couldn't do it.

I was closing the bag when there was a light tap on the door, followed by a familiar voice. "Miss Herschel, it's Dr. Watson. I've just arrived and wanted to say hello."

Typically, I was pleased to see William's old friend. Wasn't he also my friend? However, the circumstances—he'd be groomsman the next day—dulled my pleasure. I took a deep breath, opened the door, and greeted him with all the warmth I could summon.

"I won't keep you," he said after we'd exchanged a little small talk. "I wanted to confirm you'll accompany me to the church tomorrow. My carriage will be ready at eight."

"Well, I wasn't sure whether I…"

Dr. Watson frowned. For a moment, the only sounds were the murmured voices of William and Alex from somewhere downstairs.

When he realized I couldn't or wouldn't go on, Dr. Watson continued. "This is difficult for you, unsettling. So many changes. But Miss Herschel, you and I care for William. For years, we've deliberated how we might persuade him to rest more. Mrs. Pitt, their marriage, is going to be good for him. She'll distract him, perhaps even teach him to relax." He smiled, encouraging me to agree. "This is to be celebrated."

I forced a smile. "I'll be ready by eight."

So it was the next morning I accompanied Dr. Watson and witnessed the marriage of William and Mrs. Pitt. Although I kept my eyes down for most of the ceremony, I heard everything. There was no doubt my brother was married.

I didn't wait for the couple to leave the church. Instead, I asked Thomas to hurry me back to Observatory House. There, I found Hannah in the kitchen, where she was up to her elbows in flour, preparing the bridal pie.

"The dogs are to stay here," I said.

She stared at me. "Of course, Miss Herschel. They're in the yard. I'll ensure they don't go into the dining room."

"I mean, they must stay at the house for the time being while I'm gone. I've packed a small bag. I'll sort out my other things once the hubbub has died down and I've found permanent lodgings," I said.

"Lodgings? I don't understand," she said.

It hadn't occurred to me the servants didn't know I was to move out when Mrs. Pitt moved in. Even if William hadn't told them, I expected them to have discerned the news somehow.

"Mrs. Pitt—I mean, Mrs. Herschel—is now mistress of the house," I said. "I'll be at The Swan until I find something more suitable."

Hannah stared at me, her floury hands hanging at her sides like a pair of lifeless, white doves. "I see. Yes, Miss Herschel, but will you—"

"I'll be here every day to work with Mr. Herschel. That won't change. But she'll keep house. As I understand it, Mr. Alex will leave tomorrow. I'm going now," I said.

"You won't stay for the wedding feast?" she asked.

"No."

I fetched my bag and, leaving it in the hallway, went to the garden to say goodbye to Comet and Star. It was unnecessary, of course. They'd barely notice my absence. However, I felt compelled to do *something* to mark my departure.

The dogs lay stretched out, tail to tail, in a patch of sun. I stood and looked at them, wondering—not for the first time—if it would be fair to move them from Observatory House. It was their home. They were accustomed to the large grounds and permanent presence of people. Even if I eventually found myself lodgings with a garden, it would be small, and they'd be alone when I came to work. However, they were my dogs and I disliked the idea of leaving them with Mrs. Pitt. On the other hand, why should they be uprooted?

Comet lifted his head and lazily wagged his tail as I approached. Star stood and came to me, her head angled for an ear scratch. I crouched to pat her with one hand and Comet with the other. Their fur was soft and warm, their salutations happy and pure.

"Look after each other," I said, aware of how silly my sentiment was. The dogs were as inseparable as ever. Still, it seemed I was deserting them.

As I straightened, I heard footsteps. It was Mr. Corden, who looked at me with an uncertain, lopsided smile. I'd grown accustomed to his calm, cheerful presence. He was eager to learn and rarely without questions, and his interest and knowledge of astronomy had grown immensely. Our conversations were once again happy and easy.

"You're not working today, are you?" I asked, aware William had given the men the day off.

"My cousin asked me to deliver meat to Hannah," he said.

That he'd just spoken to Hannah explained the tentative smile. "Ah, so she told you she has a new mistress," I said.

He drew in a long breath. "It'll be strange, you not being here. For Hannah, I mean."

"But I will be here. Working. I just won't live here," I said.

"I understand." He paused. "Hannah said you're on your way to The Swan this morning."

"Yes."

"I drove the gig from Datchet. I'd be happy to take you and help you with your bags," he said.

The inn was within a mile of Observatory House, and my bag was light. However, the thought of not immediately being alone pleased me. Only Mr. Corden and Hannah had given any indication anyone cared about how unsettled I was. For all the misery that had seeped between the roof slats and gusted through the rickety woodwork at Datchet, the village had introduced me to Hannah and Gabriel Corden. For that, I was grateful.

The pale chestnut flicked her ears toward us as I followed Mr. Corden to where he'd left her and the gig at the stables. He hoisted my bag into the small luggage holder behind the seat and, when I placed a foot on the iron step, he took my hand to help me up.

"So, you're still working at the butchery, are you?" I asked as he sat alongside me and took up the reins.

"Aye. Whenever I can. My cousin's doing well. He's very capable but appreciates a hand. You know how it is. There's nothing like working with your kin," he said.

"Nothing like it," I said so quietly he might not have heard me.

As the gig bounced across the track that ran alongside Observatory House and led onto the road, I looked away. I didn't want to think about Hannah and her helpers bustling between the kitchen and the dining room. *Did William notice I left the church early?* I wondered. Would he ask Hannah where I was when he and his bride returned to the house?

Mr. Corden glanced at me. "Will you move back once Mrs. Herschel has had an opportunity to settle?" he asked.

"No. Why? What will have changed?" I replied.

"Well, she might've adjusted the household to her preference by then, made her mark, taught Hannah her ways," he said.

"It won't matter. She'll be the same person. She'll still be here, managing my brother's life."

He laughed quietly. "Is that why you're leaving? Because Mrs. Herschel will take over the role of managing Mr. Herschel's life?"

His amusement stung. I stared ahead.

"I'm sorry," he said. "I don't mean to make light of matters. This is difficult for you, I understand. You've taken care of Mr. Herschel, looked after his house, and worked with him for many years." He hesitated and cleared his throat. "It's just that, from what I've seen and heard, Mrs. Herschel is a fair woman. She's, erm, thoughtful and generous."

I turned to him. "Really? Fair, thoughtful, *and* generous? In that case, turn around immediately. Take me back!"

He glanced at me, blinked, and looked away.

"Whose expert opinion is that?" I asked.

"I know several people in her service in Upton and a man who worked for Mr. Pitt for many years," he said, eyes ahead.

"Of course you do," I replied.

"And you might remember, she was there when we showed Sir Banks and Dr. Maskelyne the platform for the forty-footer," he added.

"Sir Banks and Dr. Maskelyne endorsed Mrs. Herschel's attributes, did they?" I asked.

He swallowed. "No. But I saw how she was."

"Oh, how was she?" I asked, despite myself.

"Curious. Happy to listen and eager to learn. Gracious," he said, speaking slowly and quietly.

I closed my eyes. "Why are you telling me this?"

"Because perhaps if you got to know her, you wouldn't be so unhappy," he said.

I looked at my hands where they lay on my lap, willing myself not to cry.

"I'm sorry, Miss Herschel. It's just that Hannah and I thought if you knew that we—"

"Hannah?" I gasped.

"Yes, she—"

"No! Stop. I don't want to hear how you and Hannah—others too, I assume—believe it's unreasonable for me to be unhappy about having to leave my home and the life I made for myself, the life I enjoyed," I said.

"That's not what—"

I ignored him. "Did you know they initially planned to live at Upton House? That's what my brother told me. I could've stayed. Nothing would've changed. But, no, she decided against it. So now I must endure the hardship of walking between my lodgings and my place of work in all weather and at all times of the day and night. Does that seem fair and generous?"

He tried again. "I didn't—"

"Please don't say any more. You've said enough," I muttered.

For several minutes, we traveled without speaking, the rhythmic clip-clop of hooves on the cobblestones and the gentle jiggle of the carriage prising me from the life I knew. It was only when the white, two-story walls of The Swan appeared at the end of the road that Mr. Corden spoke again.

"If you need any help finding more permanent lodgings, I'll be happy to oblige," he said.

"Yes, I know. Thank you," I said, thinking about how often he'd come to my rescue.

We pulled up in front of the inn. With its neatly paved front yard and red flowers tumbling earthward from a double row of window boxes, The Swan was probably a welcoming sight to the average traveler. However, with my home less than a mile away, it held no appeal to me.

"Should I come by on my way tomorrow and accompany you to work?" asked Mr. Corden as I took my bag from him.

A wave of shame washed over me. How could I have doubted his friendship? I tried to smile. "Of course not. It's out of your way, and I'm quite capable of getting there alone."

"I know." He paused. "Well then, I'll wish you a good day."

He turned to climb onto the gig.

"Mr. Corden," I called.

He looked back.

"I am much obliged to you," I said.

CHAPTER 37

May 1788
The Swan, Slough, England

ACCORDING TO THE INNKEEPER, MY ROOM WAS THE BEST IN THE HOUSE. I WENT in, looked around, and tried to evoke something more than indifference. The space was small and crowded, with a large wardrobe wedged between the bed and a wall, and a washstand holding a basin on the other side of the room. As I peered out of the window and into the flower box with its dense foliage and vivid blossoms, I wondered if the plants had earned the room its superior status.

I sat on the bed and looked at my bag on the floor. What would Margaret have thought had she known the first time I'd used it was because I'd been banished? It contained only a few essentials, but I was struck by how diminished my life had become.

The telescope William gave me in Datchet had quickly become my most precious possession. Just as he'd prophesized, the more I'd learned, the hungrier for discovery I'd grown. Once I'd installed the reflecting sweeper on the roof at Observatory House, I'd spent even more time observing on my own.

Now, in this impersonal place with neither my instruments nor my dogs with me, I felt bereft. A conductor without an orchestra. A cook without her fire. A farmer without his sickle. I lay back, wondering if William might think about me when he saw my telescopes. Would his wife? It hadn't occurred to me she might be intrigued by our work. I'd spent too little time with her to perceive her interest might go beyond perfunctory inquisitiveness. But Mrs. Herschel was "curious, happy to listen, and eager to learn," Mr. Corden had said. With me out of the way, she'd have William's full attention. He'd teach her everything she wanted to know. Perhaps she would get involved in preparations for the royal visit in the spring?

I turned onto my side and drew my knees to my chest. *Will William also give his wife a telescope and encourage her to sweep the heavens?* I wondered. I closed my eyes, aware of warm tears tickling the side of my nose.

It took me a while to remember where I was when I awoke the following morning. Once I'd gathered my thoughts, I got up, made the bed, washed, dressed, and went downstairs for breakfast. I ate quickly and returned to the room to fetch a shawl before leaving for Observatory House.

As I stepped through the door, my eyes fell upon the bag, which sat empty alongside the wardrobe. The image triggered a rush of emotions. Fear and panic clutched at my chest, squeezing the air from my lungs and setting my nerves a-jangling. I wrapped my arms around my torso and leaned against a wall. My chest burned, and my stomach heaved. For a moment, I thought I'd regurgitate my breakfast. The room was airless, and my head spun. I stumbled to the window, pushed it wide open, and leaned out, taking deep, desperate breaths. Gradually, my heart stopped racing and my head cleared, but I wasn't strong enough to return to Observatory House. I wasn't ready. Perhaps I never would be. I locked the door, removed my shoes, and fell onto the bed.

Once my breathing calmed, I shut my eyes and willed myself to sleep. No easy drifting into slumber or quietly slipping into darkness. What I once more craved was oblivion, an escape into unconsciousness.

At some point, I heard harnesses jingling, horses snorting, and men talking. The musky, ammonia-laced smell of horse sweat and the earthy scent of leather wafted into the room. I imagined walking to the library door and looking out for William and Juno. When I opened my eyes and recognized where I was, I closed them again.

An hour or so later, I awoke to rapping at the door. I sat up, startled and then angry. If the maid wanted to clean the room, she might've been less strident. I dragged myself off the bed, marched, barefooted, to the door, and pulled it open.

"Is there any reason to—"

It wasn't a maid. It was Alex. I stepped back and opened the door wide. He stared at my feet.

"What are you doing here?" I asked, my voice breaking.

He came in, slowly looking around as if for something or someone. "I waited for you this morning. Wanted to say goodbye. William said you'd come, but I couldn't dally any longer," he said.

"I'm sorry, I was…" I glanced at the bed, at a loss for words.

"Are you ill?" he asked.

I shrugged and shook my head simultaneously and took a long, shuddering breath. "I don't think I can do it. I can't be there with her."

Alex ran his hand across his forehead. "Do you remember when we spoke about the risk of entangling your life so closely with our brother's? Before you left Bath?"

I hung my head.

He walked to the window and glanced out. "There's a whole world out there," he said before turning to me. "You know that. You see it. Why don't you find your own pathway to the stars? Why must you follow William's?"

"So you think I should stay away? What, build my own telescopes?" I asked.

"Not necessarily, though I believe you could. Work with him. Use his instruments. Your own. Make your own observations. You've already found one comet. Find more. Live your own life. Focus on what you enjoy. Our brother no longer needs you to keep house. Do what you want," he said.

Do what you want.

Four such simple words, but Alex didn't know it was impossible for me to do what I wanted. I wanted to be an astronomer. However, even if it was possible for a woman to do so, as long as I worked with William, I'd forever be his assistant. And, if I somehow dared to work independently, I risked being ridiculed the way I had in the cartoon when news of my comet and salary came to light. How easy it was for men to say, "Do what you want." How little they understood. I didn't have the energy to try to explain it.

"I guess you're going to tell me how wonderful William's wife is," I said instead.

"She's a fine woman," said Alex in his detached way.

I sat on the bed and placed my head in my hands.

"When will you go back?" he asked.

"I don't know," I said, looking at him.

He was silent as he stared at the floor near the wardrobe. He'd recognized Margaret's gift.

"You can't stay here, Caroline," he said, eventually dragging his eyes away from the bag.

"Why not?" I asked.

"You need space. You need more than a bed. You need the sky. Your stars."

I smiled. It was impossible not to. I'd left Observatory House without saying goodbye to Alex. I'd barely thought about him as I'd pined for William, the dogs, my telescopes, my home. Yet, Alex was the one who'd tracked me down and told me what I needed to hear.

"When will you come back?" I asked.

"You know the answer to that," he said, with no hint of humor.

"Of course, 'As soon as it is possible,'" I replied.

"Will you write to me? Tell me all is well?" he asked.

"Yes. I'll send you my new address. Goodbye, Brother."

"Ah, that reminds me," he said, reaching into his jacket pocket and handing me a note. "It's from Mr. Corden. Said you might be interested in this place."

I unfolded it and read in Mr. Corden's hand, "*Elizabeth Cottage, Slough.*"

The roses on the front wall of Elizabeth Cottage won me over immediately. The parent vine scaled the ridge of the kitchen chimney and spread across the brickwork with prickly determination. Bunches of yellow blossoms burst from above and beneath the windows. The plant was particularly verdant over the peaked arch of the front door. Although the house was built from red-brown bricks and had a dark slate roof, Elizabeth Cottage looked like the home of a hundred suns.

The innkeeper had given me directions and sent his son to tell the man responsible for the cottage's rental to meet me there. I made my way around the garden while I waited. Although the place was uninhabited, the grass was neatly trimmed, and the flower beds were flourishing and free of weeds. I counted nine different colors of roses, and when I peered through the windows, I saw, while the rooms were small, they'd suit me, Comet, and Star. There was also space for Alex, should he, as I hoped, stay with me rather than with Mr. and Mrs. Herschel when he returned to Slough.

From all accounts, Elizabeth Cottage would be suitable. However, it was the large area of lawn that signaled the turning point for me. Just a few yards from the door leading from the parlor and unshaded by trees, the spot was ideal for observing. Unbidden, I saw myself sitting at my telescope in the dark, the stars alive above me. It dawned on me. If I lived here, I could observe whenever it suited. I wouldn't be limited to the times when William was away. Even if I helped at Observatory House during the day, my nights would be free to gaze at the stars—*my stars*—hunt for comets, and admire the moon, planets, and nebulae. I could be an assistant during the day and an astronomer at night. It didn't matter what William or anyone else thought I was. I'd know I was an astronomer.

I recalled William's shock when I'd asked if I'd have to return to Hanover. "No, of course not!" he'd said. "Why would I do that? Anyway, you wouldn't go."

It had surprised me, because I didn't know I had a choice. Now, standing in the garden at Elizabeth Cottage, I realized I could choose to do other things. I could choose to live here, watch the skies independently of my brother, and decide what to do with the rest of my life. I had the freedom to choose, and even if I didn't know exactly what I'd do in all instances, I knew what I'd do immediately.

Although I'd made up my mind before the agent arrived, I followed him through the cottage and around the grounds before asking him when I could move in.

"Monday would suit me," I said.

So, it was agreed that I would rent Elizabeth Cottage from the following week. For the first time, I'd live alone. I'd have to find furniture to fill the rooms, and I'd need a maid. If Mr. Corden hadn't mentioned Hannah's admiration of Mrs. Herschel, I might've asked her to move with me. Now, I wouldn't risk it. My spirits weren't up to further rejection.

The next day, I rose with resolve and left The Swan for Observatory House. It seemed like years since I'd traveled the reverse route in the gig with Mr. Corden. Had the sky been blue that day, too? I couldn't recall. Today, the grass alongside the roadside seemed greener and thicker, the trees taller and the town prettier. A farmer leading a brown cow with soft, dark eyes smiled and tipped his hat at me. Two boys, laughing with the liberty of youth, ran by with a black-and-white dog gamboling at their heels. I thought about the home I'd make for Comet and Star at Elizabeth Cottage. The house had a sizable fireplace. I'd make it cozy. The garden was large enough for their games. We'd explore the countryside nearby and establish a new routine. We'd make our own paths.

I slowed as I approached Observatory House, thinking about how I'd greet William and his wife. Despite my change of heart about living alone, I still doubted the wisdom of the marriage. It was too quick and unexpected. It might be better to say nothing at all, let them initiate conversation, and gauge how they felt about my absence from the wedding feast. If there was no conversation, I'd simply get on with my work. I didn't have to speak to Mrs. Herschel at all. I couldn't think of anything I might say to her that would smooth the passing of time.

My thoughts were interrupted by the rustling of some tall grass on the roadside several yards ahead of me. To my surprise, Star leaped out of the undergrowth, followed closely by Comet. The pair bolted toward me. What on earth were they doing here? Then I saw her. William's wife followed the dogs onto the road.

Once again, I was struck by how young she seemed as she glided purposefully toward me, the hem of her ruby-red skirt dancing ahead of her feet with every step. She was bareheaded but for a matching red ribbon, which she'd draped over her head and plaited through her curls. Mrs. Herschel could've stepped out of a portrait by Thomas Gainsborough. I stared until the dogs skidded to a halt before me, torsos gyrating with excitement, tongues dripping, and chests heaving.

"Morning, you two," I said, reaching out to pat them as they shoved their muddy muzzles at me.

"They've missed you," said Mrs. Herschel, smiling as if she, too, might be pleased to see me.

I glanced at her but didn't respond. I hadn't practiced for this scenario.

"They were waiting at the door when I came downstairs this morning. I wasn't sure if they suspected you were on your way and wanted to welcome you or if they hoped for a walk. I thought I'd bring them out, and now they've found you. Perhaps they were hoping for both things, a walk and to find you, and here we are," she said, running a hand down Star's back.

"I don't usually bring them this way," I said, unable to quash a throb of resentment that not only had she walked my dogs but also that they'd enjoyed the outing. "I take them to the field on the other side. There's more space to run there."

"Of course, but I knew you'd approach from this direction," she said.

With their greetings over, Comet and Star resumed their exploring. I set off once more, Mrs. Herschel at my side.

"I'm sorry you didn't stay for the wedding feast," she said. "But I understand. This isn't what I wanted either."

I took the obtuse option. "Oh, you didn't want to move in?"

"What I wanted was to get to know you, Caroline. See if it was possible to live together. It didn't have to come to this," she said.

"But it has," I replied.

"William and I looked at the lofts above the stable and agreed we could convert the area into a sizable apartment. We could add a staircase to the roof to allow you to carry out your comet sweeps from there," she said.

"A place for me in the stables? How lovely. But I have found somewhere of my own. So, no, thank you. And I'll take the dogs with me."

CHAPTER 38

May 1788
Observatory House, England

ON THE FACE OF IT, NOTHING HAD CHANGED AT OBSERVATORY HOUSE. Hannah greeted me with a wave as she made her way upstairs. William was outside at the frame for the forty-footer with the carpenter and several other men. A loud clanging of metal beating metal came from the forge. Thomas was grooming Juno in the sun near the stables. My writing desk was just as I'd left it.

However, the table at which William worked had been transformed. Rather than displaying the usual hodgepodge of papers, notebooks, catalogs, sketches, and instruments and parts thereof, the tabletop was so orderly it could've been the workspace of a physician or chemist. The papers were arranged in neat piles held down by shiny, black river pebbles. Queued from largest to smallest, the notebooks stood upright between two larger stones. The catalogs had been similarly arranged on the other side of the table, and the instruments and parts were contained in a row of open wooden boxes of various sizes. I'd never seen a tidier space and was still staring at it when Mr. Corden appeared.

"Good morning, Miss Herschel," he said, carefully placing a sheet of writing paper in the center of the tabletop.

"What is this?" I asked.

"They're plans for an additional—"

"No, I mean the table."

"Ah," he said, smiling. "Mrs. Herschel decided he'd be less harried if it was tidied."

"What? But my brother loathes anyone moving anything he's busy with. He'll be furious," I said.

"That's what I thought, but he laughed when he saw it. Said she was right and that he'd do his best to keep it neat. I saw him straightening it himself this very morning," he said.

It wouldn't last, I thought. William wouldn't have time to tidy up, and he'd grow tired of his wife's interfering. He'd resort to his ways, and we'd work as we always had. The sketch Mr. Corden had placed on the table drew my eye. I picked it up and examined it.

"Are these the stables?" I asked, seeing no suggestion in the drawing of the apartment Mrs. Herschel had mentioned.

"Aye. Mrs. Herschel will be bringing three horses here. We're going to enlarge it."

"For her carriage?"

"Two are, yes. The other is a young hack she bought as a wedding gift for Mr. Herschel," he said.

"But he has Juno. Or does Dr. Watson want her back?" I asked.

"No, to the contrary. Mrs. Herschel purchased Juno. She'll ride the mare, and Mr. Herschel will ride the youngster," said Mr. Corden.

"I didn't know she was a horsewoman," I said, as much to myself as to him.

"Yes, an excellent horsewoman," he replied.

Of course she is, I thought.

I sat at my desk and stared across the room for several minutes after Mr. Corden left. Someone had arranged some wildflowers in a jug and placed them on a shelf. We'd never brought flowers into the house before. I might've imagined that nothing had changed when I stepped through the front door, but now I saw how everything was different, and I'd only been gone a day.

The irony of Mrs. Herschel's giving William a horse was not lost on me. Miss Hudson had sought to enmesh herself in his life by offering the same without the preamble of marriage. Mrs. Herschel's horse sealed the covenant. And how clever she was to have bought Juno for herself. William loved the mare and would've been sad to see her go. He had a young horse, an old horse, and a young wife to gallop across the countryside alongside him.

The door opened behind me. Ashamed of my idling, I bent my head over my notes. The red of Mrs. Herschel's dress appeared in front of me. "Can I ask Hannah to make you tea or bring you something else to drink or eat?" she asked.

"Can I not ask her myself?" I replied, not looking up.

"Of course you can," she said, moving as if to leave.

"I understand you've bought William a young horse," I said.

She stopped. "I have."

"Young horses are inexperienced. They can be unpredictable. I hope you've chosen carefully," I said, staring at her now.

"My brother helped find him. He's a splendid animal, well schooled. And, as you know, Caroline, William is a fine horseman," she said, holding my gaze with her large eyes.

"He's a fine horseman, but my brother is not a young man."

"Neither is he an old man. He deserves more in his life than endless hours building telescopes, observing the skies, entertaining His Majesty, and toiling over his notes and papers. We're going to ride for enjoyment, keep sensible hours, and even take holidays," she said, her eyes dancing.

"Pfft! There's too much to do, particularly with the royal visit in a few months. Do you know whom you've married?" I asked.

She smiled. I'd never met a more self-assured woman. "I do," she said. "And I'm eager to enjoy life with him. Now, I'm going to ask Hannah to make tea. You are welcome to enjoy a cup with me. Or you can ask her to brew you a pot of your own."

William and his wife were not home much over the days that followed. He was at court, and she, said Hannah, was arranging her belongings at Upton House, many of which would be relocated to Observatory House. Every day, I noticed adjustments to the rooms as her furniture was moved in and William's was shifted around. Although I did not comment, the house was better for it. Mrs. Herschel had an eye for opening spaces, allowing more light in the rooms, and arranging items attractively. It helped that most of the items from Upton House were more elegant than the furniture William and I had purchased bit by bit whenever money had allowed over the years. The only room left untouched was my old bedchamber.

At the end of the week, I gathered my telescopes and a few pieces of furniture, packed two chests with more books than clothes, and arranged a wagon to fetch them on Monday. I was on the roof dismantling the stand for my telescope when Mr. Corden's head appeared as he climbed the ladder and approached. He set about helping me remove screws and nails and strap planks together.

"So, you've taken Elizabeth Cottage, I believe," he said as he bound a nest of nails in cloth.

"We move in next week," I replied. "Thank you for once again coming to my aid. It's the ideal place."

"I was lucky to hear about it," he said. "You say 'we.' You'll take the dogs then?"

"Of course," I said.

"Will you bring them here with you while you work?" he asked.

"Probably. They're not used to being alone all day."

Mr. Corden nodded. I sensed he was restraining himself.

"What is it?" I demanded.

"Do you know who has been feeding them since you left?" he asked.

I stared at him. "Hannah. I asked her to."

He shook his head. "No. Mrs. Herschel has done it herself."

"Why would she do that?"

He shrugged. "I think she likes them. She and Mr. Herschel take them out too."

It was unbelievable. I'd been taken aback to learn that William had gone walking when they were courting, but that he and his wife were now going out with Comet and Star stunned me.

"When?" I asked.

"In the evenings, after they've eaten and before he starts observing. She insists it's good for his constitution," he said.

I snatched up a small pile of planks and made my way to the window. "Well, she'll have to take care of his constitution without my dogs."

On Monday evening, I called Comet and Star. They bounded after me as we left Observatory House for Elizabeth Cottage, where my effects had been delivered earlier. Beyond the yard, the dogs trotted ahead. As the distance between us and the house grew, they shot me dubious looks to confirm they were on the right track. Their excitement about reconnoitering the new route was unmistakable, but they were also increasingly on edge.

Comet bristled as we passed by unfamiliar yards and growled at a small congregation of bullocks who eyed us through the slats of a gate. Star was also on high alert and was especially uneasy about a deep ditch running along the roadside. The dogs' appetite for exploration was checked by caution. It reminded me of one of my mother's countless warnings.

Responding to my repeated hankering for the schooling, adventure, and freedom my brothers enjoyed, she'd snapped, "Be careful of what you wish for, lest it come true."

The sight of Elizabeth Cottage—red-orange in the evening light with bright flashes of yellow roses—ousted the memory.

"What do you think?" I asked the dogs as they stood on either side of me, panting quietly, ears pricked. "Don't worry. There's no one else here. It's ours."

They followed me into the garden, where I inspected the frame Thomas had reassembled for my telescope. There was something desolate about the structure. It'd been a while since I'd seen a solitary telescope stand in a yard. However, when I pictured myself there, looking into it, I felt a ping of excitement. It was as if the stars, like my life, might invite a different perspective viewed from Elizabeth Cottage.

The dogs entered the house hesitantly, stretching their necks as they peered into each room and sniffed every corner. Unfamiliar scents, spaces, and sounds and the darkening sky offered them no comfort. I closed the door, and although it wasn't a cold night, I lit the fire in the parlor, hoping they'd stretch out in front of it and sleep after I'd fed them. But the pair remained restless, taking turns to pace between the furniture and standing at the door, whining and watching me expectantly.

"Come, Comet," I called. "Lie down. This is our home now. Isn't it lovely? No, Star. Don't get up again! Go to sleep."

Eventually, accepting that the in-and-out, up-and-down nature of observing would add to the dogs' anxiety, I went upstairs. They followed and, when I climbed into bed, lay on the carpet. However, they didn't settle completely, and it was an uneasy night. I woke up several times to the sounds of their agitation. They wandered around, whimpered, and scratched at the door and, when I opened it to let them into the garden at dawn, disappeared. I half-heartedly called after them, but I knew they'd not listen. They were on their way back to Observatory House.

I was relieved the following afternoon when they heeded my calls and came with me when I left Observatory House.

It might take a little time, but they'll adjust to the new arrangement, I told myself.

They were considerably more relaxed than they had been the day before during our walk to Elizabeth Cottage and casually entered the house. However, when I went into the garden to observe the skies later, they snuck away and returned to Observatory House.

After repeating the process three more times, during which time I only once more managed to confine them at Elizabeth Cottage overnight, I conceded that Comet and Star did not want to move with me. Perhaps if we hadn't all trooped back to Observatory House during the day, they'd have eventually yielded and stayed at the cottage. Even then, I might've had to accept that the dogs were happier in the place they knew—with William and Mrs. Herschel.

Consoling myself that they continued to welcome me to Observatory House with eagerness every morning, I finally admitted defeat and stopped cajoling Comet and Star to leave with me in the evenings. No one mentioned my failure to relocate the animals.

CHAPTER 39

December 1788
Elizabeth Cottage, England

FOR A WHILE, MRS. HERSCHEL—WHO'D INSTALLED HER WRITING DESK IN THE library and continued to keep William's table shipshape—greeted me every morning and engaged in some small talk, hoping to incite conversation.

"Did Mr. Corden tell you that Sir Joseph was here last night? He commended your work on the new catalog and sent you his best wishes."

"Did you observe last night? William said the heavens were magnificent. Of course you'll compare notes."

"Hannah says the cook has made a delicious pot of white soup. I do hope you'll have some today."

In truth, many of her comments intrigued me, and I was often eager to accept her proposals. However, I remained churlish and offered no more than perfunctory responses. It had become a habit. I'd decided William's wife was my adversary the moment he said he intended to marry her, and I was determined to hold on to the idea. My pride was at stake. Also, if I admitted I was wrong, I'd have to accept the blame for my eviction from Observatory House, and despite having recognized the advantages of living on my own, I wasn't ready for that. However, Mrs. Herschel was unrelentingly polite and steadfast in her attempts to befriend me. But just as I thought she'd *never* give up, she did. One day, she said, "Good morning, Caroline," and no more. From then on, Mrs. Herschel spoke to me only when absolutely necessary. She too, I saw, had her pride.

It wasn't that different with William. Although he inquired if all was well at the cottage a few days after I moved, he said no more about the arrangement and never mentioned my absence from the wedding feast. We were civil colleagues who exchanged essential information about work and only that which involved me directly. My brother no longer shared his joys and frustrations with progress on the forty-footer. However, I understood from the frequency of his visits to London and snippets of conversation I overheard that work on the reflectors remained a challenge. He didn't mention events or developments at court or among his friends in the Royal Society either. We didn't discuss Alex. We spoke about my transcripts of his observations, papers I was writing or checking for him, and catalogs I was updating on his behalf. He didn't volunteer anything more, and I didn't ask for it. After a while, despite my mourning the easy, cheerful relationship we'd had, our aloofness became the norm. Moreover, I sensed that as long as I was cold toward Mrs. Herschel, William wouldn't make the effort to mend things. We were stuck in an impasse.

It was from Mr. Corden I learned William's young horse, the "grand and high-spirited" Apollo, had arrived.

"Mr. Herschel is eager to ride him, but Thomas will first take the horse out for a few runs to settle him," he explained, reviving my concerns about William overextending his horsemanship.

Hannah chattered about other household occurrences, including how Mrs. Herschel had redecorated William's old bedchamber for Alex.

"You should inspect it, Miss Herschel. It's so striking and comfortable, I'm quite certain that, when he comes, Mr. Alex will never leave Slough," she said.

I didn't inspect the room, but I suspected the chamber I'd created for Alex at Elizabeth Cottage wouldn't compare.

Once I'd accepted Comet and Star wouldn't live at Elizabeth Cottage with me, I settled quickly. Before long, I'd transferred the evening routine William and I had followed for years to my new home.

On clear evenings, I'd move a chair and small table outside, place them alongside my telescope, and, with a notebook at the ready, scan the skies. For a while, I felt silly about how I continued to talk as if William were there. I'd tell him what I saw and ask questions. It was a habit as sure as the phases of the moon. Eventually, I accepted the talking would continue. What should I stop? There was no one around to ridicule me. Whether I was talking to myself or my brother's specter didn't matter. Speaking out loud helped clear my thoughts, kept me focused, and allowed me to evaluate my observations. There was something comforting about hearing my voice in the quiet of the night. What surprised me most, though, was the satisfying sense of awakening I experienced as I realized how quickly I could answer my own questions and how easy it was to reach conclusions alone.

So it was on the twenty-first of December 1788 that I pulled my shawl over my head and around my shoulders, rubbed my hands together against the icy night air, and put my eye to my sweeper. It amused me to think about how, when William had encouraged me to observe in Datchet, I'd silently vowed I'd never voluntarily subject myself to the bitter cold of the outdoors in winter.

"And yet here you are, Caroline, risking the loss of fingers and toes in the name of astronomy," I said.

I'd been sweeping for about an hour when I spotted a bright head and broad, glowing tail of what looked like a comet not far from Beta Lyrae. It was unfamiliar. My heart lurched. I lifted my face from the telescope, took a deep breath to steady myself, and leaned forward to look again. There it was, bold and magnificent. I met its singularity with audaciousness. It was a comet, and I'd discovered it.

After examining, making notes, and checking it against the atlas for another hour or so, I went inside and stood at the hearth, warming my hands before I left. It didn't matter how unhappy William and I were with each other; I had to tell him. It wasn't just that it should be reported to a member of the society as soon as possible for verification, but it was also inconceivable to me not to show it to him before anyone else saw it. In that moment, nothing else mattered. I had to go to William. I found my mittens and, with the notebook tucked under my arm and a lantern in my hand, headed into the night for Observatory House.

When I arrived, Mrs. Herschel was where I'd stood many a time, at the base of the twenty-footer, looking up at William, who was on the platform observing. For months, I'd shuddered when I'd pictured her there. Now I saw how I'd tormented myself. She was just a woman helping my brother. She turned at the sound of my footsteps.

"Oh! Caroline! Is something wrong? Are you all right" she asked, approaching me.

I was ashamed by her concern. "I believe I've found a comet," I said, holding up my notebook as if it explained everything.

William descended the ladder. "A comet? And you came to show it to me?" he asked.

"Of course." My voice was croaky, not because of the cold air but rather from emotion.

We stood in an awkward, silent triangle alongside the twenty-footer. An owl hooted from somewhere in the distance. "Hoo-hoo-hoooo," he called. Or was it "I'm very sorreeee"? I wondered what Mrs. Herschel was thinking. Did she hope I'd say something to clear the air? Or did she feel like I did, the way I suspected my brother did, that emotional expression often made difficult situations worse and should be avoided, particularly when there was something else so important to attend to?

"Come. Let's go in, see your notes, and then take a look," said William eventually, confirming I was right about how he felt.

After we'd discussed my notes, we spent several hours examining the comet through William's ten-foot reflector, which revealed more of its irregular round form and showed how it gradually grew brighter in the middle. Mrs. Herschel's excitement reminded me how new she was to our lives. However, her questions and observations confirmed what Mr. Corden had said, that she was curious and astute. Eventually, though, the hours overtook her.

"I'm going to sleep for a bit," she said. "If you'd like to do the same, Caroline, the bed is made up in Alex's room."

She went inside before I could respond, but an hour later, when I yawned, William said, "Sleep for a few hours. I'll wake you up at about five so we can see whether it has moved."

I saw his teeth glimmer as he smiled and, despite the cold, felt myself glow with pleasure.

"Well done, Lina. Now there are two comets with your name to them," he called as I went indoors.

Too tired to inspect the room, I climbed into Alex's bed and fell asleep instantly. William shook me awake a few hours later, and after taking turns to observe the comet, we agreed that it had moved toward Beta Lyrae.

Later that morning, I wrote to Dr. Maskelyne, detailing my discovery and asking the Astronomer Royal to observe and, hopefully, verify it. I'd just signed my note when Mrs. Herschel burst through the door, smiling widely and brandishing a letter.

"I have good news," she said. "More good news, I mean."

I stared at her, waiting.

She held the paper toward me. "It's from Alex. He says he'll come in spring before the royal visit to help. Isn't that wonderful?"

"He wrote to *you*?" I asked.

"We exchange letters every week. Sometimes, I even get William to add a paragraph or two. It's important to keep in touch. I can only imagine how lonely he is in Bath without Margaret," she said.

The elation I'd experienced over the preceding hours when I'd found the comet and observed it with William waned. It was one thing that Mrs. Herschel wrote to Alex. That he replied every week was another. We'd exchanged letters only once since he'd left.

"But you didn't even know Margaret," I said.

Her smile vanished. "No. I mean, yes, you're right, I didn't. But I understand the pain of losing a loved one."

I stood. "Yes, you do." I said, my eyes welling. "And you're teaching me how it feels too."

"No, Caroline, please," she said, her arms dropping to her sides. "That's not how it is. I love William, and I care for Alex. And you. I want us to be a family. Don't force us apart. There's no need for it. I know how much you love your brothers. I admire you for it. Just because I care about them, too, doesn't change that! Don't you see? Affection doesn't come in limited quantities. It's not like a bag of flour from the miller that gets used up. It's, it's…" She waved

Alex's letter around again. "It's like the night sky. There's no obvious end to it, no matter how powerful your instrument is. There's no limit to love."

She'd been well instructed by William, but her metaphor didn't convince me. It was easy for her to talk about the limitlessness of love. She lived at Observatory House with William and held a letter from Alex. Mrs. Herschel had even won the affection of my dogs. I lived alone. *That* I'd accepted. I even appreciated the advantages. What I struggled with was the feeling that Mrs. Herschel had replaced me in everyone's affections.

CHAPTER 40

December 1788
Elizabeth Cottage, England

ALTHOUGH DR. MASKELYNE'S RESPONSE TO MY LETTER CAME SLOWER THAN I'D hoped—he cited sluggish postal services and bad weather as the culprits for his delay—my discovery was well received by him and other esteemed astronomers. Sir Henry Englefield, to whom William had written, replied saying that I would "soon be the great comet finder and bear away the prize from Messier and Mechain." *Is he serious?* I wondered. *Does he believe it possible for a woman to achieve such a thing?* If so, would it mean I would be an astronomer rather than an assistant and that, as such, a woman might finally be accepted as a member of the Royal Society?

However, Alex Aubert's response to the news reminded me how enmeshed my name and achievements were with William's.

"You cannot, my dear Miss Herschel, judge the pleasure I feel when your reputation and fame increase; everyone must admire your and your brother's knowledge, industry, and behavior," he wrote.

Would anyone ever cite me without mentioning William? It seemed doubtful. Crucially, discovering a second comet proved I was more than lucky. I knew what to look for and how to do it. I should be taken seriously and not lampooned by cartoonists. My second comet also showed that Her Majesty hadn't been misguided if, indeed, she had urged her husband to give me a salary. These were the things I resolved to focus on.

I'd planned to write to Alex immediately after I learned of his letters to and from Mrs. Herschel, but I recognized everything I wanted to tell him was unreasonable. If I complained about him not writing to me more frequently, he'd say he'd replied to the only letter I'd written and was awaiting my response. If I scolded him for agreeing to stay at Observatory House and not with me, he'd remind me I hadn't invited him. If I grumbled about being cast off, he'd be embarrassed on my behalf.

So, instead of writing to Alex, I resolved to dedicate myself to observing on my own, working on another catalog, and hunting for comets. During the day at Observatory House, I'd returned to my bubble of sullen silence, where William and Mrs. Herschel left me.

Christmas brought days as dark as night and a series of blizzards that swept over the cottage in frosty, white waves. I kept the fire in my parlor burning fiercely as I huddled over the catalog. The weather imprisoned me for several days, and it was only by doggedly concentrating on the work that I kept from constantly obsessing about how the others were spending the season. Whenever my focus wavered, the questions came. Had Mrs. Herschel lured William from work with hearty meals and playful games? Were Alex and his band cheering Bath's Christmas crowds? Was Mr. Corden working in the butchery with his cousin, or was he home with his wife? Had they visited Hannah and her husband the day after Christmas again?

On the thirty-first of December, I followed a tradition Miss Fleming had taught me. I opened the door just before midnight to shoo out the old year and allow in the new one. But, alas! The old took with it the warmth, and the new arrived with a bone-chilling blast—and I was gloomy *and* cold. However, two days later, the skies had cleared long enough to render the road passable, and I pulled on my walking boots, gathered my notebooks, and set out for Observatory House.

When I arrived, the men were in their workrooms and the yard. William and Mrs. Herschel, on the other hand, were nowhere to be seen. I asked Hannah about their whereabouts.

"Mrs. Herschel insisted they take advantage of the weather to go for a ride," she said.

Dr. Watson had been right about William's wife reforming him. As much as he enjoyed riding, my brother had never gone out for pleasure alone before. His rides had always been purposeful, work-related travels. That he'd go after the holidays with the royal visit just three months away was even more remarkable. The William I'd known would've been impatient to get back to work.

I decided to make use of their absence and, with Comet and Star at my heels, went into the yard to examine work on the forty-footer. I'd lost touch with day-to-day progress on all the components of the giant machine since Mrs. Herschel's arrival, but I'd tried to keep an eye on what was happening around me.

Work on the seventy-foot-high gantry, which had been installed on its revolving platform, was nearing completion, and as I looked up, several men perched high upon the beams raised their hammers to greet me. The structure looked like a latticed pyramid. Even though it was only partially built, its proportions were awe-inspiring and a little disconcerting. Unlike the twenty-footer, which William and I had often managed alone, the giant telescope would require several men to operate.

Mr. Campion, who'd been talking to a carpenter on the far side of the platform, saw me and approached. "Is the tube on track?" I asked after we'd exchanged greetings.

"We're a little behind after the holidays, but I'm confident we'll make up time in the next few weeks," he replied. "Of course, the problems with the reflectors might mean it won't matter if my work is complete anyway."

"Problems with the reflectors? I thought the forge master in London—Mr. Gibbs, is it?—had everything in hand," I said.

He blinked, and I understood he was surprised I wasn't aware of what was going on. "His first attempts failed. His men ground the disks too thin and they cracked. It's possible they didn't anticipate the cold spell."

My flesh prickled. If the reflectors weren't ready in time, it would be impossible to show the instrument to His Majesty. Sir Banks had made it clear we couldn't delay the demonstration beyond spring.

"What are they going to do? Do you know?" I asked.

"I believe Mr. Herschel has paid them to make more," said Mr. Campion.

It was even worse than I imagined. William was already once again over budget before he'd found the foundry for the reflectors. Where he'd find money to pay for the construction of additional mirrors I didn't know. It wasn't something I'd discuss with Mr. Campion, but I realized I must immediately set aside my resentment and offer to help prepare the forty-footer once again. We had to get it ready. In addition to the royal visit, the instrument was the focus of attention in astronomical circles far and wide. It wasn't just that I wanted to support my brother. I also wanted to be part of its success.

As I turned to go back to the house, a shout came from the stables. Thomas ran out as Mrs. Herschel sped toward him on Juno. She pulled up as Thomas grabbed her reins, looking up at her. She was agitated, waving her arms and shaking her head. I couldn't make out her words. Thomas ran into the stables. What was going on? Where was William? I snatched my skirt, lifted it, and ran.

"What's happened?" I shouted.

William's wife turned to me, her eyes larger than ever and her pale face streaked with dirt. "Oh, Caroline, thank God! William fell. He's hurt. Thomas will follow me with the carriage. He can't move."

I gasped. "No! Is he conscious?"

"Barely," she said, her eyes brimming now. "It was a bad fall."

"That horse! I told you—"

"Please don't," she cried. "Send for Dr. Perry. Thomas and I will bring him here. Go now, Caroline."

"I must go to him," I said. "I'll come in the carriage."

"No," she replied, her voice firm. "Call the physician. Get him here immediately."

"Ready," called Thomas from the other side of the stable.

"Go," said Mrs. Herschel, rocking forward to urge Juno to move. "Go now, please, Caroline!"

Although Mrs. Herschel and Thomas had barely left when I'd sent Mr. Campion's assistant to call the physician, they were back before Dr. Perry arrived. I stared at Mrs. Herschel's face, looking for clues about William's state as she rode Juno and led Apollo alongside the carriage. She was drawn, and the front of her riding habit was smeared with dirt.

"Is he all right?" I asked, taking Apollo's reins from her.

"Yes. No. I don't know." Her voice quivered.

"Take him to the front door," I told Thomas.

Mrs. Herschel nodded, and as they continued down the track to the main road, I left Apollo in a stable and ran to the house. I'd already told Hannah to have hot water and clean towels ready in the drawing room, where I hoped Mrs. Herschel's large Chesterfield sofa would provide a suitable resting place for William.

"Come," I called to Hannah as I headed through the house. "We must help him in."

Mrs. Herschel had dismounted and opened the carriage door when we approached. I heard William groan as she murmured to him. I wanted to shove her out of the way and get to my brother but held back. She turned to where Hannah, Thomas, and I stood.

"Is Mr. Corden here?" she asked, looking at Hannah.

"No," replied the maid.

"Why?" I inquired.

"We need another strong man to carry him," said Mrs. Herschel.

"But I—"

She ignored me. "Hannah, get Mr. Campion. He's here, surely?"

Hannah hurried up the garden path.

"I don't want to risk hurting him anymore," said Mrs. Herschel, her eyes back on me. "Thomas and Mr. Campion will be able to move him with greater ease than we will."

"Let me see him," I said.

She stepped aside to allow me to climb onto the step of the carriage and look inside. William was lying flat on the seat with his head propped up against the far wall. His face was drained of color, and his arms rested limply across his chest on his white shirt. The garment was emblazoned with blood. His breathing was ragged, and his eyes were almost closed, their lids juddering as if he was struggling to stay awake.

"Hello, Lina," he said quietly. "I took a bit of a fall."

I shook my head. My mouth was dry, and my throat constricted. "Don't talk. Save your breath."

Hannah returned with Mr. Campion as Dr. Perry arrived. Mrs. Herschel hurried to the physician, but he held up a hand, smiled, removed a handkerchief from his pocket, and wiped the perspiration from his brow.

"Right," he said, nodding at her. "Where is the patient?"

Mrs. Herschel took my elbow and drew me aside so that the physician could get into the carriage. I stood beside her, numb with shock and helplessness, as the man disappeared into the carriage. After several minutes, Dr. Perry reemerged.

"What happened?" he asked. "Give me the details."

Speaking fast, Mrs. Herschel described how she and William had galloped the horses homeward, following a track bordering the beech woods about a mile from the house. William, she said, leaned forward, his cheek on Apollo's neck, and urged him on.

"We were pretending to race, laughing at the joy of it, but neither of the horses was at full tilt, and we were in total control," she said.

However, the control didn't last. She described how William and his horse were several yards ahead of Juno when Apollo took fright at something. The young horse spun sideways, unseating my brother before skidding to a halt, facing the woods. William flew over the horse's shoulder and crashed to the ground.

"It happened fast but didn't look like a bad fall from a distance. However, when I got there, dismounted, and ran to him, I saw William had landed, chest first, on a partially sawn tree stump. Oh heavens, it was awful! He groaned, managed to roll over, and tried to sit up, but he blanched, closed his eyes, and fell back. For several moments, he didn't respond to me." She seemed oblivious to her tears. "Then he opened his eyes, moaned, and I saw the blood on his chest."

"Has he been conscious all the time since then?" asked the physician.

"I can't be sure. I had to ride home for the carriage. He cried in pain when we lifted him into it. It was difficult. There were just two of us. Thomas and I. William was in agony. He might've fainted afterward as we brought him home," she said.

Dr. Perry put a hand on her forearm. "That'll do," he said.

"Will he be all right?" she cried.

"I don't know. He's almost certainly broken ribs, which is why his breathing is labored. His sternum may be cracked too. That adds to the pain and risk," he explained.

"What's the risk?" I asked.

Dr. Perry looked at me and wiped his brow again. "His lungs. They might be damaged. But we're getting ahead of ourselves. I want him somewhere I can examine him properly."

Mrs. Herschel, Hannah, and I watched as the physician, Thomas, and Mr. Campion gently maneuvered William out of the carriage and carried him into the house. My brother's eyes were closed. He was as still and silent as death. We followed into the drawing room and watched as they settled him on the couch. When Dr. Perry dismissed the men, Hannah and I turned to leave too, but Mrs. Herschel stopped me.

"Please stay, Caroline," she said.

CHAPTER 41

January 1789
Observatory House, England

THAT NIGHT, AS MRS. HERSCHEL GAVE WAY TO EXHAUSTION AND DOZED IN A chair alongside William, who remained on the Chesterfield, I sat at the card table and wrote to Alex. Concentrating on practical matters eased some of the panic coursing through me. I'd wrestled with myself about what to say to Alex after I'd learned about his and Mrs. Herschel's correspondence, but I knew exactly what to write now. He must come to Slough immediately.

My quill glided quickly across the paper. It wasn't just the urgency of the news that propelled me but also the prospect of William's accident bringing the three of us back together. Moreover, it was comforting to share my fears.

I paused between paragraphs to look at William. He'd whimpered and cried out in pain when Dr. Perry examined him but hadn't said anything coherent since his brief words to me in the carriage. Now he lay on his back motionless, quiet but for the irregular gasping that sounded like he was snatching at fleeting pockets of air. It was disturbing but also reassuring. As long as he was inhaling and exhaling, William was alive.

In my letter, I explained what had happened during the ride. I wrote about how Mrs. Herschel had raced home to fetch the carriage and described the physician's examination, findings, and prognosis.

Once he'd removed William's shirt and cleaned the area, Dr. Perry saw the bleeding had stemmed. Thankfully, it appeared worse than it was because of how it had soaked into the white garment. He cleaned it and found that no suturing was required. However, the physician thinks William's sternum is cracked and has no doubt our brother has broken several ribs. As you might know, Alex, this could be fatal. The damaged bones are impinging upon the lungs. It's possible they're perforated, which is why William's breathing is so tortured. Dr. Perry administered laudanum, and our brother slept almost immediately. It's a relief, but even as he sleeps, William pants like Comet after a strenuous run. It is most disconcerting.

Dr. Perry can't hide his worry, but, because of William's place at court, he's hopeful he will be granted an audience with one of His Majesty's physicians and perhaps a surgeon, who can advise him on how to treat our brother. One of them might even attend to William himself. I am holding on to every hope that William will be granted the attention of the most learned men available.

As you can imagine, everyone at Observatory House is deeply shocked. Mrs. Herschel has only this minute found enough peace to fall asleep. I understand her worry and regret. I warned her against encouraging William to ride a young, inexperienced horse.

I urge you to waste no time getting here. I want to believe that all will be well, but I would be lying if I said I am not full of dread. Please come quickly, Alex. Be with me in this time of distress. Be with our brother for whatever comes.

As I signed the letter, I realized my heart had sped up again. My thoughts reeled. What would we do without William? No, I shouldn't even imagine it. The room seemed too hot, and my head swam. Had I eaten since breakfast? I couldn't recall. I placed my hands on the table and laid my head on them for a moment, taking the kind of deep breaths William couldn't.

I straightened to the sound of Mrs. Herschel shifting on her chair. Her eyes shot open, and she looked around, confused and disorientated. When she saw me, she blinked, staggered to her feet, and bent over William. For several seconds, she held her mouth close to his. Was she breathing for him? She gently touched her lips to his forehead before sighing and pulling the blanket over his shoulders. I looked away. It was a tender moment.

"I thought it was a dream," she said as she added a log to the fire.

"It's a nightmare," I replied.

She nodded, looking into the flames. Her hair was undone, and I was surprised by its bulk and length. She'd barely left the room, and yet she'd somehow found the time to wash, change, and brush her hair.

"Don't you want to get some rest?" she said. "You could take the guest room, erm, your old chamber, or use Alex's."

"I'd rather stay here. Keep an eye on him. Anyway, Alex will come soon. I've written to him," I said, holding up the letter.

"Thank you. I might write to Sir Joseph," she said, holding her palms toward the flames.

"Why?" I asked.

"Perhaps if I petition him, he'll expedite matters. Urge His Majesty's physicians to take William's case. I must do something," she said, rubbing her hands together.

"It's only been hours. Dr. Perry understands the urgency," I said.

"Of course, but William's health isn't as important to him as it is to me, to us," she replied.

"If his health is so important to you, why didn't you listen to me?" I asked.

She froze, staring at me.

"I warned you about the danger of giving him an untrained, young horse. You wouldn't listen, and here we are," I said.

"No, Caroline. The horse took fright, as horses do. Apollo is not untrained. He's as reliable as Juno," she replied.

"And yet Juno didn't throw William," I seethed.

"It was an accident. An awful accident, but it wasn't Apollo's fault," she said.

"I didn't say it was his fault," I replied, thinking, *I said it was yours.*

She swallowed deeply.

"I don't think it's necessary to write to Sir Joseph," I said. "Word will get around court quicker than a letter. Dr. Perry will see to it. William's friends will rally the king."

Mrs. Herschel rubbed her temples and went back to the chair alongside my brother.

Dr. Perry returned with more laudanum the following morning. I watched as he urged William to take a few sips of water and a spoon of the broth he'd instructed Hannah to prepare. Mrs. Herschel observed too, giving me a tiny smile when our eyes met.

"Hurts," said William, giving his head a little shake.

I wanted to applaud. He'd finally spoken again.

"I know," said the physician. "You've done well. I'll give you something for the pain now, but you should try to drink more in a few hours." He looked at Mrs. Herschel. "He must drink, and the broth will give him strength."

"Of course," she said.

He set down the bowl and reached into his bag for the small brown bottle. "I spoke to one of His Majesty's physicians. He believes Mr. Herschel's condition requires the attention of a surgeon. He's referred me to a man. He's not someone who has attended to His Majesty himself, but if he's trusted by a royal physician, we're in good hands," he said.

"A surgeon? That implies an operation, doesn't it?" I asked.

Dr. Perry didn't look up as he opened the bottle, drew some liquid into the dropper, and fed several drops to William, whose eyes were narrowly open. "Yes. There are techniques. Ways of supporting the bones, mending them."

William's Adam's apple rose and fell with a shudder. He took a few short breaths and whispered, "Watson. Ask him."

Dr. Perry looked at Mrs. Herschel, frowning. She leaned toward William. "What did you say, William? Try again."

William looked at me.

"All right," I said. "I will. I'll ask Dr. Watson what he suggests. I'll write to him immediately."

"Who is Dr. Watson?" asked Dr. Perry.

"He's a physician in Bath," said Mrs. Herschel.

"And my brother's dearest friend," I added.

Mrs. Herschel gave a faint smile.

"Hmm," murmured Dr. Perry as he gathered his things. "I'm not affronted by your wishing to consult another physician. However, you won't receive more learned advice and treatment than from the men who attend His Majesty. You did agree that I should speak to them. You wouldn't want to offend them by dismissing their counsel in favor of your brother's old friend from Bath."

"Of course not," said Mrs. Herschel. "But he'll be a comfort to William."

The physician left, saying he'd return in the afternoon. As the door closed behind him, Mrs. Herschel said, "Will you write to Dr. Watson, or shall I?"

"I'll do it," I said.

She gently brushed William's forehead with the tips of her fingers. His eyes were once again closed. "Why do you think he wants us to speak to Dr. Watson?"

"Because he trusts him," I said. "We don't know Dr. Perry or any of His Majesty's men or those they recommend. William knows and trusts Dr. Watson."

Although we were encouraged when William drank the day after his accident, he refused to do so again. For the most part, he slept, stirring only when the pain was too much to ignore. Mrs. Herschel and I pleaded with him, but he wouldn't or couldn't swallow anything other than the laudanum. He clamped his jaws and slowly rocked his head side to side, tears sliding from beneath his eyelids.

"No," he murmured.

Eventually, Mrs. Herschel resorted to gently wiping his lips with a wet cloth, hoping he'd unintentionally swallow some water. Dr. Perry returned that evening, but he too failed to get William to take anything more than the potion.

The following day, the physician was accompanied to the house by the surgeon. Although Dr. Perry introduced us, Mr. Wills—a disgruntled-looking man with a stoop and bushy, gray eyebrows—scarcely acknowledged us before telling Mrs. Herschel and me to leave the drawing room.

"Why?" asked Mrs. Herschel. "He's my husband and Caroline's brother. We're here with him all the time, taking care of his every need. There's no need to send us away."

The surgeon glared at Dr. Perry from beneath his brows. "Please, Mrs. Herschel, he's a busy man. Do as you're asked," said the physician.

We waited outside the door, and within a few minutes, the men reappeared. Mr. Wills walked by without a word.

"I'll let you know what he advocates when I visit tomorrow," said Dr. Perry, running after the surgeon like a chastened schoolboy.

Exhausted from worry and sleeplessness, Mrs. Herschel and I agreed on a schedule that allowed us to rest. I'd taken occupancy of my old room while she made a bed of pillows alongside William. We took turns to sleep. Even so, we were spent. William was rarely conscious, roused only by unbearable pain. His pleas for relief were agonizing. We fed him laudanum and watched him shrink with every hour that passed. An additional concern was the rattle now accompanying his breathing.

When Dr. Perry arrived to inform us of the surgeon's recommendation, we asked Hannah to sit with William while we convened in the hallway. Mrs. Herschel rested her back against a wall, and I leaned on a cabinet while the physician spoke.

"Mr. Wills insists an operation is essential. To relieve the pressure on Mr. Herschel's lungs, he proposes making incisions, splinting the broken ribs, and attaching hooks to the splints," said Dr. Perry, scratching his ear.

"Hooks?" asked Mrs. Herschel.

He continued. "The hooks would be attached to cables, which would be suspended to a structure created around the bed. The idea is that lifting the broken bones would ease the pressure and allow the lungs to expand so that Mr. Herschel can breathe as the bones heal. This should happen in a matter of about two months."

I was appalled. "What about the bleeding? Will his flesh be open all this time?" I asked.

"No, no, of course not. The surgeon will suture as much of it as possible once the hooks are in place. When the bones are healed, he'll open Mr. Herschel up again and remove the hooks," said Dr. Perry.

Mrs. Herschel's mouth hung open like a small, dark cave on a white cliff. She heaved herself upright, slowly came to me, and reached for my hand. Her eyes had a faraway look about them. She may not have been aware that she'd moved, let alone grasped my fingers. I didn't pull away.

"This is the only way?" she said, her voice unusually high.

"Well, yes," said the physician. "I don't know any other. He's declining fast."

The hallway was silent but for the ticktock of the longcase clock against the far wall.

"Has it been done successfully before?" I asked eventually.

Dr. Perry looked at his feet. "I don't know."

Mrs. Herschel released my hand and walked toward the front door. Was she leaving? I almost followed. She stopped and turned back to me. "What do you think, Caroline?"

I looked at the drawing-room door, thinking of my brother wasting away on the other side. We had to do something, but the surgeon's suggestion sounded extreme, brutal.

"There must be another way," I said, addressing Dr. Perry.

"As I said, I don't know of one. And again, you won't find more knowledgeable men than the royal physicians," he said.

"But Mr. Wills is not one of His Majesty's men," I reminded him.

"He was recommended by them," he replied before turning to William's wife. "You cannot dismiss the surgeon's advice, Mrs. Herschel."

She walked toward him, her eyes flashing. "Oh yes, I can, Dr. Perry. My husband's life is at stake, and if the surgeon's suggestion doesn't best serve him, I will dismiss his recommendation. I will not simply accept it because one of the king's men thinks highly of Mr. Wills," she said.

"But Mrs. Herschel—"

"There's nothing more to say on the matter, doctor. Miss Herschel and I will give the matter our consideration. We might consult other physicians. Even other surgeons. I will let you know when we have decided. Thank you. I must go to my husband," she said, marching toward the drawing room.

I was speechless. What an extraordinary woman my brother had married. I watched as she closed the door behind her.

"I hope you'll talk some sense into her, Miss Herschel," said the doctor.

"She has ample sense," I said, as much to myself as him.

There was a loud rap at the front door. Before I could get there, it opened. I felt my heart lift at the sight of Alex and, alongside him, Dr. Watson.

CHAPTER 42

January 1789
Observatory House, England

ONCE AGAIN, I'D UNDERESTIMATED ALEX. ON RECEIVING MY LETTER, HE'D gone to Dr. Watson and they'd immediately left Bath for Slough, arriving at Observatory House before my note even reached William's friend.

Alex went directly into the drawing room while Dr. Perry gave Dr. Watson a full account of William's condition and treatment. It was clear Dr. Perry understood that the other physician would take care of my brother now. Dr. Watson listened impassively as Dr. Perry described the proposed procedure.

"I'm unfamiliar with the technique," he said. "I'll examine the patient and let you know what I think."

"As I explained to the ladies, Mr. Wills comes highly recommended," said Dr. Perry.

"Of course," said Dr. Watson. "We'll be in touch."

With Dr. Perry gone, I asked Dr. Watson what he thought of the surgeon's idea.

"Radical," he said. "Let's hope it's not necessary. I'll go to him now."

"It's a relief to have you here," I said to Alex moments later as he and

I stood at the fire while Dr. Watson knelt at our brother's side with Mrs. Herschel.

Alex's face was drawn. "Despite your letter, I hadn't expected this."

He wrung his hands, and I cupped mine over them.

"We can't lose him. He's my, I mean, our anchor," he said.

We stood quietly, Dr. Watson and Mrs. Herschel's muted conversation washing over us and William oblivious to all.

"Mary says the problems with the reflectors for the forty-footer have mounted," said Alex eventually.

"I believe so," I replied.

Mrs. Herschel and I hadn't discussed work since the accident. That she'd thought of anything other than William's suffering surprised me.

"What did she tell you?" I asked.

"The project has already greatly exceeded moneys allocated to it, and Mr. Gibbs needs more to complete them," he said.

"And it's the second set he's cast. The first failed. I understood William had already given him more money," I said.

"Yes, but Mary says he's *still* having difficulties and needs more," he replied.

"Even if it were possible, would it be wise to give him more? What if he's simply incapable?" I asked. "Anyway, it doesn't seem to matter now, does it?"

Alex rubbed his neck. "I suggested the same to Mary," he whispered. "She was upset, furious with me. Told me that it mattered greatly because for William to recover quickly and fully, we need to get the forty-footer ready for the royal visit. Did you know His Majesty and his family will be accompanied by the archbishop of Canterbury?"

I shook my head.

"Visitors from abroad as well and, of course, Fellows of the Royal Society."

"It'll be a grand event," I said. "But perhaps we should ask Sir Joseph if we can postpone it. Surely, he'll agree given the circumstances."

"Mary insists William wouldn't want that. He's afraid His Majesty will withdraw all grants and refuse any further funding if he feels let down at this stage," said Alex.

"So, work must go on," I said.

"Yes," he said. "Mary says as soon as William begins recuperating, he'll want to know what's going on. If matters are still amiss, it'll distress him, which will hinder his recovery. Mary is firm on that, and she has a point, Caroline. She understands our brother well."

She did. I'd imagined that, like mine, Mrs. Herschel's thoughts would be entirely consumed by worry about William's survival. However, she was also thinking about what he needed to recover. I glanced where she crouched alongside my brother and it came to me. I took a breath.

"Are you all right?" asked Alex.

"Yes."

But I wasn't. I was ashamed it had taken such misfortune for me to see that William's wife and I wanted the same things. She'd tried to tell me, but I wouldn't listen. Mary cared about my brother and our work, just as I did. But I'd shut her out, which is why she'd confided in Alex about the troubles with the reflectors and not me. If I was to be of any use to anyone, I had to make amends.

Finally, Dr. Watson stood and came to Alex and me. Mary rearranged William's bedding and followed.

"Dr. Perry was right about his broken ribs and sternum," said Dr. Watson, looking into the fire. "And I'm sorry to say that I also concur with him about how critical things are. The rattling indicates his condition is worsening."

"What about the operation?" I asked.

"I've never heard of such a procedure. That doesn't mean it hasn't been done or it wouldn't work. But it doesn't matter. I don't think William would survive it. He's too weak," he said.

Mary sniffed. Alex placed his hand on her shoulder. "So there's nothing to be done?" he asked.

Dr. Watson didn't respond immediately and, when he did, was pensive. "A few years ago, a colleague told me about his groom who was kicked in the chest by a draft horse. A huge, powerful animal. It resulted in several broken ribs. My colleague couldn't do anything for the man and sent him home, expecting him to die. To his utter amazement, the man returned to work a little over two months later, fully recovered."

"How? Go on, for goodness' sake," urged Alex.

"The groom's wife was crippled. He went home but needed to care for her and couldn't lie in bed waiting to die. There was no one else around to attend to the couple. Although, for a few days, he was in too much pain to do much, he propped himself up so that it wasn't impossible to stand when he had to help his wife. He forced himself to keep breathing evenly despite the pain, which remarkably eased after a week. Every day, he forced himself up for a little longer and did more. Gradually, he recovered fully," said Dr. Watson, glancing at each of us in turn. "My colleague speculated it was the man's decision not to lie flat and to force his lungs to keep working that kept him alive. He didn't have a choice. He had to keep going and essentially strengthened and retrained his lungs to breathe properly again."

"But how will that be possible for William?" asked Mary. "He's not conscious. He doesn't respond to us. How will we help him retrain his lungs if we can't wake him up?"

"I'll have to reduce the laudanum drastically," he said.

"You can't," said Mary and I in unison.

Dr. Watson raised his brows, looking at her and then me.

"Go on," I said.

"He's in such pain without it. It's the only thing he wants," she said.

I nodded.

"He also wants to live," said Alex.

"It won't be easy. Not for any of us, but mostly not for him," said Dr. Watson. "But if he's going to have a chance, we must prop him up and get and keep him conscious for a few hours every day. He must breathe as strongly as possible, eat, drink, and eventually even move around. It's our only hope."

I looked at Mary. Her brow wrinkled. I knew what she was thinking. Dr. Watson and Alex had no idea how much pain William was in when the drug wore off and how difficult it would be to ignore his suffering.

Propping up William was easy. We stacked pillows behind his head and gently maneuvered him against them so he reclined at a forty-five-degree angle. He didn't wake up while we moved him but did so about two hours later, twisting his head from side to side as he murmured Mary's name.

"I'm here," she said, taking his hand.

William opened his eyes and blinked several times. Dr. Watson crouched alongside Mary, smiling.

"Hello, my friend," he said. "I believe you called for me."

My brother's lips moved, but there was no sound.

"It's all right. We're all here, and we have a plan. Where are you, Alex?" asked Dr. Watson.

Alex stepped forward and hunkered alongside the Chesterfield. "I'm here, Brother," he said. "To help you get well."

William tried to smile, but it was more of a grimace.

I looked at Dr. Watson. It was just beginning. He scowled, his eyes on William.

"We've adjusted your pillows," said Mary. "It's more comfortable, isn't it?"

William glanced left and right and gave a tiny shrug.

"I want you to drink this water," said Dr. Watson, holding up a small, half-full glass. "And your sister is going to get some broth."

I left for the kitchen immediately. When I returned with the broth, Mary and Alex had moved away and were standing at the fire, their backs to the Chesterfield.

"It's the only way, William," said Dr. Watson. "The laudanum kills the pain, but it also induces a drugged sleep, prevents you from eating and drinking and staying alert enough to allow me to help strengthen your lungs. I'm sorry, my friend. I cannot give you as much relief as you were getting. It will be the death of you."

"Hurts," whispered William. "Such pain."

My eyes welled at the sight of his tears.

Dr. Watson sighed. "First, some broth. Then, a little gentle blowing out and breathing in. And then, I'll give you the potion."

I handed him the bowl and joined Alex and Mary at the fire. "It'll be all right," I said. "He'll listen to Dr. Watson. We must believe it will be all right."

Mary took my hand. Alex blinked.

"Why didn't you tell me about the trouble with Mr. Gibbs and the reflectors?" I asked quietly, though I knew the answer.

She glanced at Alex. "I didn't want to add to your worries."

"My worries are our worries," I said, giving her hand a squeeze.

She and Alex looked at me.

Blood rushed to my face, but I held steady, my eyes on Mary's. "I'm sorry I've been difficult. Stubborn. Unreasonable. Bitter. I see it now and I'm determined to change and make amends."

She closed her eyes. My stomach fell away. Was I beyond redemption? Did she want me to beg for forgiveness?

"Please, Mary," I said.

It was the first time I'd addressed her thus. Perhaps that's what persuaded her to open her eyes.

"You don't have to make amends," she said. "Just help me with William and do what you can to get the forty-footer ready for the king's visit" She smiled. "That's all I ask."

Alex shuffled his feet.

"Thank you," I said, taking my hand from hers. "What was William going to do about the reflectors?"

"He planned to visit Mr. Gibbs this week. Insist he explain why he's taking so long and spending so much. He wanted to see the progress on the new set himself," she said.

"Then that's what we'll do," I said, looking at Alex. "Alex and I will go to London."

Alex blinked again. "Well—"

I ignored him. "We'll go through the drawings and agreements tonight. Make sure we understand exactly what was expected of Mr. Gibbs and pay him a visit. At minimum we'll have an explanation for William when he asks," I said.

Mary looked from me to Alex. "I'd like that," she said.

That evening, Alex and I spent an hour in the library. Mary's organizing of his papers made gathering William's notes and sketches easy, and I added the notes I'd made when I'd proposed searching for an expert. We'd talk to Mr. Campion the following morning in case he had any other useful information.

When we returned to the drawing room, Dr. Watson insisted we leave him to care for William for the night. We finally agreed on condition he'd awaken us should he tire or if our brother's health worsened.

"I'm not sure I'll sleep," said Mary as she and I made our way up the stairs.

"Me neither," I conceded. "The idea is compelling, though."

She stopped, clutching the banister with both hands. "Do you think it'll work? Reducing the potion? Keeping William conscious? It seems so cruel, making him endure the pain. And what if it's for naught?"

"Dr. Watson believes it's our only hope," I reminded her.

She gave a long, shuddering sigh. "I know."

"Come. Go to bed. Get some rest even if you don't sleep."

She shook her head. "No, I can't leave him. I'm going back."

I watched as she descended the stairs and disappeared toward the drawing room.

CHAPTER 43

January 1789
Observatory House, England

THE HOUSE WAS UNUSUALLY QUIET WHEN I WENT DOWNSTAIRS THE FOLLOWING morning. As I passed the library, I looked out into the yard. For the first time in days, sunshine fought its way through the clouds. Several workers gathered near the gantry of the forty-footer, their faces turned to Mr. Campion, who was addressing them with an unusually solemn expression. I hesitated. Should I investigate? Yes, but only after I'd seen William.

The first thing I noticed as I entered the drawing room was the cold. Lumps of coal lay lifeless on a gray blanket of ash in the fireplace. The curtains were drawn, and the air was damp and musty. Alex sat alongside William, his head in his hands. Neither moved. They were alone. My heart sank at the lifelessness in the room.

"What happened?" I asked, my voice catching.

Alex raised his head slowly, sliding his hands down his face as if he couldn't bear to look at me. His eyes brimmed.

"No!" I gasped, hurrying across the room and falling to my knees at William's side.

I felt Alex's hand on my shoulder. It was cold and heavy. "He's slipping away," he said.

"No," I whispered.

William's chest was still. His eyelashes lay inert on his pale, sunken cheeks. Everything about him was diminished, old, deathly. I held my breath, meeting his silence with my own, and placed my hand lightly on his upper torso. That's when I felt his chest rise and fall by the tiniest measure. I sat upright, examining his face closely. It was true that William had stopped panting. However, his mouth was slightly ajar, and I saw, on a trickle of saliva glistening in the corner of his lips, the hint of breath.

"Wait," I said.

I found his hand beneath the blankets and took it in mine. His fingers were cold, but when I applied a little pressure, they curled in my hand.

"Shine on, William, shine on. Be like the stars. Shine on," I whispered, bending to place my forehead against our hands. "There are heavens to observe. So much to do and see. You must shine on."

After a few moments, I settled his hand back beneath the blanket, stood, and looked at Alex. "Get the fire burning," I said.

He stared at me as if I'd told him to fly to the moon. I went to the hearth and began stacking kindling. I had to warm the room. Alex came to help.

"What happened last night?" I asked. "Where are Mary and Dr. Watson?"

"They didn't sleep. William was restless, in agony. Kept them up all night. When I got up, Dr. Watson was struggling to keep his eyes open. Mary was sobbing at William's side. They'd just capitulated and given him the potion. They couldn't let him suffer," he said.

"Dr. Watson fed him laudanum?" I asked.

"Yes. But less than half of what the other physician gave him."

"That's why he's sleeping," I said, feeling weak with relief. "It doesn't mean he's slipping away."

Alex hesitated, his eyes searching mine. "Look at him, Caroline. There's nothing left. He's hardly breathing. He can't hang on."

"Is that what Dr. Watson believes?" I asked.

"He didn't say. He wouldn't. But—"

"Don't give up, Alex," I said. "Go to the kitchen. Ask Hannah to bring some hot coals. We must warm the room. Mary and Dr. Watson will be shocked to find it so cold."

When he left, I returned to William's side. "Our doleful brother hasn't changed," I said. "You must get better so you can cheer him up. No one else can do it."

By the time Dr. Watson appeared, we'd had the fire burning for more than an hour. I watched as he examined William, trying to read his thoughts. He saved me the trouble.

"I've never had a more difficult night," he said. "It wasn't just that he was in pain. He was agitated and nervous. I began to wonder if Dr. Perry's potion wasn't contaminated."

"But Alex said you eventually gave him more," I said.

"Not from Dr. Perry's supply. I used my own."

"What does that mean?" asked Alex. "It doesn't look like he's recovering."

The doctor sighed. "I don't know what it means. Not yet. His breathing is worryingly shallow, but his chest is no longer rattling, and his pulse is stronger. I'd like to believe he might be improving because we propped him up and encouraged him to breathe more deeply last night. Perhaps changing the laudanum has made a difference. I can't say. I wish I could tell you he'll recover, but I don't know."

"What do we do?" I asked.

"I'm going to continue as planned. Water, broth, breathing exercises, and as little laudanum as possible. Of course I'll let him rest, but I don't want him sleeping continuously," he said.

"Will you wake him now?" asked Mary, who'd slipped into the room without our noticing.

"We'll let him sleep a little longer. It's one of nature's finest remedies: sleep. But, if the groom's experience is anything to go by, we also need to have him conscious and fighting to survive for several hours at a time," said Dr. Watson.

Alex and I left Mary and Dr. Watson with William, went to the library, and summoned Mr. Campion. The blacksmith perched on the edge of a chair as I explained how we planned to go to London to clarify what was causing the delay and the increased costs of the reflectors.

"It's a good idea, and I'm sure it'll be useful. The problem is, it's not just the mirrors that are creating problems," he said.

"Go on," I said, recalling the serious scene I'd observed in the yard earlier.

He took a deep breath. "It seems the measurements of the tube are incorrect. I met with the carpenter and his men this morning, and we agreed a lower section of the gantry doesn't match the requirements of the tube," he said.

"How's that possible, particularly at this advanced stage?" asked Alex. "Someone must've misread Mr. Herschel's drawings."

"I don't know where the problem originated. All I know is something doesn't line up," said the blacksmith.

"But surely the carpenters can simply adjust the gantry?" I asked.

Alex made a sound that might've been a growl. "Yes, but if the error is with the tube, it'll mean the reflectors—if they've been cast—won't fit either," he said.

We sat quietly for a while.

"One thing is certain: We must establish where the error is before we go to London," I said.

My brother nodded. "Yes. We need the correct information before we confront Mr. Gibbs, or we risk incurring further mistakes and greater costs."

I looked at Mr. Campion. "Mr. Herschel and I will gather our brother's papers. We'll compare them to what you and the carpenters have and remeasure where necessary," I said. "Do you agree, Alex?"

"That's exactly what we'll do," he said.

Once we'd gathered the plans for the tube and gantry from the library, Alex went to the forge while I took the carpentry papers into the yard to compare what William had noted and how the carpenters had interpreted it. I wasn't there long when Alex arrived.

"I found it," he said. "There's an anomaly with the tube. It's narrower than it should be."

I groaned.

"I know," he said. "I also hoped it was the gantry. It would be easier to correct."

"What went wrong? Whose mistake is it?"

He shrugged. "It doesn't matter. I'm going to work with Mr. Campion to fix it. It'll take a few days, but I've worked out how to make the adjustments without having to start the job all over again."

"A few days? But what about the reflectors?" I asked.

"You could go to London," he said.

I didn't reply. It was true, I *could* go. I understood William's work and his plans for the forty-footer better than most. I knew the importance of getting everything right and the implications of delaying the project. We had to have something ready to show His Majesty. Would my knowledge be enough? Would Mr. Gibbs take Mr. Herschel's tiny, scarred spinster sister seriously? I'd never met the foundry master and had no idea what kind of man he was. What would I have to do to induce him to get back on track and deliver the reflectors as required?

"You could ask Mr. Corden to accompany you," said Alex.

"Really? Does he know enough about casting speculum? The reflectors?" I said, a little stung by Alex's apparent lack of confidence in me.

"Possibly. Mr. Campion says Mr. Corden has been working closely with William recently. But you know a great deal more. I wasn't suggesting he accompany you because you're not capable of checking the foundry's work and hastening their progress. It's just that it might be reassuring to have his support and company. If you weren't available but I was, I'd ask him to go with me," he said. "He's perceptive and diplomatic. He understands people but won't interfere unless you ask for his advice."

I wanted to tell him I knew Mr. Corden's attributes better than he did, but I said nothing.

"It was just an idea," said my brother, turning and walking back to the forge.

As I returned to the library from outside, Mary came through the other door.

"He's awake," she said.

"And?"

"Well, he's more coherent, alert, but, oh, Caroline!" She leaned against the table as if her legs wouldn't hold her. "He's so frail. Weak. In agony. He's aged by twenty years. And the way he struggles to breathe breaks my heart!"

"But if he's lucid, that's an improvement. It says Dr. Watson's method is working. Is he making William do his exercises?" I asked.

"Yes. That's why I left. It's too painful to watch. I want to beg Dr. Watson to give him the drug," she said.

"I know," I replied. "It seems so cruel, but there's nothing else to do."

She closed her eyes. "I won't imagine life without him," she said. "William saved me. He brought me back to life after John died. He made everything seem possible."

That William had helped Mary after her husband died wasn't news to me. She'd told me how he'd encouraged her to go walking. However, it hadn't occurred to me that she believed he'd saved her. She hadn't seemed like someone who'd ever required rescuing.

How little we understand those we hastily judge, I thought.

I wanted to tell Mary everything would be fine. I wished I believed it would be, but William's deterioration had been shocking and swift. My brother's energy and ambition were unprecedented. I'd imagined he was invincible. Yet, within days, he'd withered away. William had become a frail, helpless man, dwarfed by the Chesterfield, a man whose mortality now spoke louder than any other part of him. Despite Dr. Watson's experience and resolve, he was uncertain of William's treatment. He remained troubled by his condition, perhaps even afraid. Mary was afraid, as was I. I couldn't think of what to say to comfort her, so I tried to distract her instead.

"We discovered another problem with the forty-footer, this time with the tube," I said.

She squeezed her eyes shut.

"No! Don't worry, Mary. It's all right. Alex is working with Mr. Campion to sort it out, but it means he can't come to London with me," I said.

Mary frowned. "You'll go alone?"

"I thought I'd ask Mr. Corden to accompany me," I replied.

"That's a good idea," she said. "If William were stronger, I'd come too."

"Oh. Why?" I asked.

"I've heard so much about what a skilled astronomer you are, but the only time I've seen you wield your expertise was the night you came to tell us about the comet," she said. "I want to see more."

"A skilled astronomer? Who said such a thing?" I asked, unable to curb my curiosity.

Mary raised her brows. "It is widely understood, as you surely know?"

I shook my head.

"Really? Why, the last time Dr. Maskelyne visited, William joked about how, when you and he—William, I mean—practice astronomy together, it's not always self-evident who of the two of you is the planet and who the moon," she said.

"What?" I asked.

"I believe he meant it isn't always clear who orbits who. A moon orbits Earth, but—" she said.

"Yes, I understood that. I couldn't imagine William saying such a thing," I replied.

"But he did, and your brother is not alone in believing you are as much an expert as he is," she said.

For a moment, I saw myself standing alongside the Thames in Datchet as I had the day Comet stole the meat. I remembered how I'd visualized the river bearing part of me away, the tiny, invisible bit that had imagined, as a soprano, I might've one day become more than William Herschel's sister. It had seemed all was lost. Although I'd dreamed of being my brother's equal in astronomy since then, I hadn't thought about the moment at the river. Was it possible William truly believed I was his equal? Why would he say such a thing to the Astronomer Royal if he didn't mean it?

I looked into the yard where two workmen carried a pile of planks toward the gantry and smoke rose from the forge, and I remembered how I'd brought my brother here and how we'd turned the place into a hub of astronomy. I wasn't just William Herschel's sister; I was Caroline Herschel, salaried astronomer to the king and entirely capable of keeping work going at Observatory House, regardless of the circumstances. The river hadn't carried anything away. Until now, I'd so effectively hidden what I was capable of from the world that it had been lost to me too.

I smiled at Mary. "Well, until the planet—or is he the moon?—has recovered, I'll orbit for both of us," I said.

CHAPTER 44

January 1789
Observatory House, England

MARY, DR. WATSON, AND I SAT UP WITH WILLIAM THE ENTIRE NIGHT BEFORE I went to London. Alex nodded off for a couple of hours. After having been relatively alert during the day—when he'd done some breathing exercises and accepted a few spoons of broth—William was spent. Although his chest sounded more like a watery purr than the rickety cart it had resembled, and his moaning had diminished, he was weaker than ever. He slept as if unconscious, but while I understood he needed to rest, his slumber brought me little comfort. I wanted to see my brother's eyes shine again, have him demand an update on work, and ask if I'd scanned the skies since he'd been indisposed. Nothing about the inert form beneath the blanket resembled the vigorous man we'd known. Dr. Watson repeatedly warned us his convalescence was far from certain. He couldn't say how badly damaged William's lungs were, whether other organs had been impaired, or if my brother was bleeding internally.

Although we'd agreed I must go to London urgently, a tiny voice urged me to remain at William's side.

Stay with him until you're sure he'll recover, it whispered.

"You'll only be gone a day," said Alex when I voiced my doubts.

"We are not going to let him go," said Mary. "Not while you're gone and not when you're home. You must go. When he asks about the reflectors, we must have positive news. It'll be all he needs to recover."

Dr. Watson and Alex shared a glance. I tried to interpret it. Did they approve of Mary's optimism, or were they worried she was delusional?

"You're right. I must go. I will go," I said.

So, at twilight, after I'd leaned over William and whispered, "See you soon," I pulled on my cloak and gloves and went to the stables where Mr. Corden and Thomas were readying the carriage. Neither had hesitated when I'd told them my plans the previous day.

"The weather looks good for a trip," Thomas had said. "I've driven Mr. Herschel to Mr. Gibbs's workshop before. It's a journey of about three hours."

Mr. Corden had said, "It'll be my honor."

Now, with dawn hours away, he helped me into the carriage, climbed in, and sat opposite. We didn't talk as Thomas urged the horses on, and the vehicle bumped along the track to the road. As I looked into the darkness toward the field where I'd brought Comet and Star to run, I silently promised to bring them again as soon as William was better. We'd celebrate life, all of us.

When I'd ached to sleep while I was with William, I'd comforted myself with thoughts of doing so as soon as I was in the carriage. Now, though, my mind was too busy to rest. Alex and I had agreed on the objectives of meeting with Mr. Gibbs. We'd added our notes to William's. However, I needed to think about the best approach. It was important to see what had been done and understand what needed doing as well as why it wasn't happening. Only then would I press Mr. Gibbs to work with greater diligence, prudence, and speed. I couldn't risk his becoming defensive before I had all the facts. I looked at Mr. Corden.

"Do you know Mr. Gibbs?" I asked.

"Yes, I was with Mr. Herschel a few times when he came to Observatory House," he replied.

"What kind of man is he? Can you say?"

It was just enough light for me to see him flick a dark curl from his forehead, which reminded me how his hair had bounced as he'd hounded Comet from his butchery.

"I ask because I'm trying to establish the most effective way of getting him to urgently complete the reflectors," I explained.

"I understand." He nodded, and the wayward curl fell forward again. "Mr. Gibbs is a man of many words. He talked a great deal, loudly and quickly. Didn't give Mr. Herschel many opportunities to question what he said. It made me wonder if he was trying to conceal something."

"Like what?" I asked.

"If he knew as much as he implied," he said.

"You think he's a charlatan?" I asked.

He hesitated. "Not necessarily. Rather a proud, ambitious man. He seemed exceedingly self-satisfied about working with Mr. Herschel, as if that might be more important than the job itself."

"You don't think he's capable of constructing the reflectors? He's been at it long enough," I said.

"I don't know, Miss. Herschel. I'm sorry. I'm guessing, and I shouldn't because it only adds to your worries. We'll know the truth soon," he replied.

"Don't apologize. It helps, having your perspective," I said.

He was right to caution me not to judge matters prematurely, but I'd keep what he'd observed in mind. Something had prevented Mr. Gibbs from completing the job. Until we understood the problem, we couldn't solve it. He wouldn't be the first person to allow pride to get in the way of success. If I was to help, the key would be to encourage, not shame him into being accountable. We couldn't afford the time or expense of scrapping the second set of reflectors.

"Usually, when I'm in a bind, I ask myself what my brother would do," I said, resting my head against the side of the carriage.

"But not now?" asked Mr. Corden.

"Now I think he might've been as uncertain as I am. It's possible he'd tell me to trust my intuition and use common sense. Or perhaps that's what I would've recommended he do," I replied, thinking about Mary's story about the moon and the planet.

"It's a good idea, whoever came up with it," he said.

We sat quietly for a while.

Mr. Corden shifted. "How is Mr. Herschel?"

I folded my arms over my chest, wishing he hadn't asked. I didn't want to evoke the uneasy quiet of the drawing room. It had been excruciating to watch Mary cling desperately to hope as if for all of us and to see Dr. Watson's mask of optimism wearing thin. Neither did I want to amplify the fear hanging over me like the blade of a guillotine.

"He's struggling," I said eventually. "Night before last was bad. Unbearable for him and us. Yesterday, we thought he was rallying, but it was momentary. I worry he's giving up."

I repeated the story of the groom and explained Dr. Watson's theory about how he'd cheated death, and I told him about the laudanum and the breathing exercises.

Despite my reluctance, talking made me feel strangely lighter, as if a heavy cloak had been lifted from me. Contrary to being dragged back into William's infirmary, I was liberated and calmer than I'd been for days. Was it because I'd left the house and wasn't burdened by the need to protect Mr. Corden from my fear? With Mary, Alex, and Dr. Watson, I had to be brave. They must believe that *I* believed William would survive. Now I could be honest, stop pretending, and admit I was terrified he might die.

"I can't imagine the world without him," I said.

Mr. Corden leaned toward me. For a moment, I thought he was going to take my hand. Instead, he said, "I hope you won't have to experience it. But if you do, Miss Herschel, you will continue to make him proud."

I nodded, turned sideways, tucked my head into the corner of the carriage, and closed my eyes. I fell asleep knowing if William had overheard Mr. Corden, he'd have agreed with him. My life didn't depend on my brother. I was knowledgeable and skilled. William knew it. So did I. Most importantly, I finally understood I had choices.

CHAPTER 45

January 1789
East London, England

I was awoken by a rush of cool, smoke-infused air when Thomas opened the carriage door. Mr. Corden looked away while I wiped my eyes, ran my fingers through my hair, and pulled on my bonnet. Gathering my skirts as I stepped onto the cobblestone street, I saw we'd drawn up in front of a large, windowless building with wooden doors as wide as two carriages and twice as tall. A pair of immense chimneys rose from the roof, black and lifeless. I looked left and right. The street was empty as if it were Sunday rather than the middle of the week.

"Are you certain this is the place?" I asked Thomas.

"Yes, Miss Herschel. I brought Mr. Herschel here several times," he replied.

Mr. Corden rapped his knuckles against one of the doors. We waited. He tilted an ear toward the entrance and held still, listening.

"Not a peep," he said.

He knocked again, louder and longer. We waited again. I was about to suggest Thomas look for another entrance, perhaps at the back, when we heard the clunking and sliding of bolts and latches. At last, one of the doors was opened by a young man. His narrow, boyish face bore the blemishes of youth, and his eyes darted from Mr. Corden to me and back again. He didn't speak.

"Good morning," I said. "I'm here to see Mr. Gibbs."

He blinked. "Aye, that's me."

"Oh? Pleased to meet you, Mr. Gibbs." I held out my hand. He raised a grubby palm, coloring. I smiled. "Of course. Well, I'm Miss Herschel. This is Mr. Corden. We're from Observatory House."

He swallowed deeply but didn't say anything or move aside to admit us.

"I've come to see how you're progressing with the reflectors. Can we see them?" I asked, stepping forward.

Mr. Gibbs scowled and looked at his feet as if seeking a reason to deny us. Finally, he stepped back and opened the door, and I followed him into the dimly lit, cavernous room. Several rows of workbenches lined one of the walls. Tools were neatly laid upon some of the worktops while various materials were stacked on the floor. Two furnaces stood dark and empty, gaping as if yawning from boredom. On the far side of the room, a man leaned over a worktop, his eyes on us. The workshop was more desolate than the street.

Mr. Corden caught my eye and gave his head a small shake. I hesitated, wanting him to explain, but the young man stopped and turned to us.

"There's nothing here to show you," he said, speaking fast. "We've sent the disks elsewhere to be polished. If you'd let me know you were coming, I would've told you."

I froze. "Why did you send them away?"

"Because they, the other men, are better equipped. They'll do the, erm, job quicker, better than we can," he said.

"Where have you sent them?" I asked.

Mr. Gibbs scratched his head as if I'd asked him to work out a difficult formula. I looked at Mr. Corden. He mouthed something. I couldn't make it out and went to him.

"It's not him," he whispered. "This is not Mr. Gibbs. Not the man who visited Mr. Herschel."

"What? Are you sure?" I asked.

He nodded.

"Mr. Gibbs," I said, turning to the young man and enunciating the name.

"It seems we've come to the wrong place. Mr. Corden tells me you are not the man Mr. Herschel commissioned to make the reflectors. Can you explain why you're pretending to be? Where is Mr. Gibbs, and where are the parts? What's going on?"

He wiped a hand across his forehead, leaving a dark smear from one side to the other. "I *am* Mr. Gibbs," he said, exhaling loudly. Then he added quietly, "I am Toby Gibbs. My father met with Mr. Herschel."

"Your father?" I said, glancing at Mr. Corden.

He shrugged as if to say it was possible. Behind him, the man I'd noticed earlier left the room, shoulders hunched and head down.

I turned to Toby, who was wiping his hands on his grimy leather apron. "Where is he?" I asked.

"At home. He's ill," he replied, meeting my eyes squarely for the first time since we'd arrived.

"And where are the reflectors? The disks?" asked Mr. Corden.

He sighed again. "Over there," he said, tilting his head to behind one of the workbenches.

Mr. Corden and I went to where he'd motioned. I caught my breath. Partly covered by a dull red blanket, two large, round metal disks lay side by side on the floor. It didn't require close inspection to see they had barely been ground and were nowhere near ready to be polished. Their solid, gray surfaces were rough and dull and showed no promise of reflecting anything. While Mr. Gibbs and his men might've cast the disks, they'd done little more before abandoning them.

A strange tingling ascended my spine. My head throbbed, and the room rocked, making me sway. I felt a hand on my elbow, steadying me.

"Sit here," said Mr. Corden, leading me to a low bench.

"I'm all right," I said, but I sat anyway, taking several deep breaths before staring at the disks. I'd come to find out what was happening. The evidence lay in front of me. Now, I needed the facts. I turned to the young man.

"Tell us what's going on, Toby. Or rather, why it is *not* going on. Leave nothing out," I said.

He groaned quietly and moved to stand directly in front of me, leaning lightly against the edge of the workbench, his chin on his chest. "My father is in awe of your brother, Miss Herschel. He was so excited to have an opportunity to make the reflectors and then, when we failed the first time, another," he said. "He told us he knew exactly how to get it right the second time. What he didn't know was that he was ill."

"How long has he been ill? What's wrong with him?" I asked.

I watched as the young man ran his hand across his temple again. He looked wretched, and I wondered if he felt as I had when Mr. Corden had asked me how William was. Perhaps he also couldn't stomach the idea of articulating his misery. Maybe he too would be surprised to find how restorative it was.

"He started feeling bad just before we cast the metal, but he dragged himself here every morning and told me and the men what to do," he said, the pitch of his voice rising and falling as if grappling to find its footing between that of a boy or man. "It was complicated. Speculum is hard to work with, and once more, it kept going wrong. My father was feeling worse by the day. He couldn't walk or stand. Things got more and more difficult for him, and we couldn't keep up. Or get it right."

Mr. Corden glanced at me as he sat on the bench a short distance away. He'd witnessed more emotional outpourings in one day than was surely usual.

Toby continued, explaining how the foundry had had to turn away other work and had eventually laid off several workers. Finally, his father had collapsed, was bedridden, and work on the reflectors had stopped altogether.

"I pleaded with him to give the disks to someone else to complete, someone who understood what was needed, but he said we couldn't afford to pay anyone else. We'd run out of money and time," he said, his eyes still on mine.

"Why didn't you tell us? My brother is a fair, understanding man," I said.

The young man hung his head once more. "I hoped my father would recover and we'd be able to continue work. Make up the time we'd lost and somehow afford to complete the parts. If I'd written to Mr. Herschel and told him we couldn't finish the reflectors, it would be like handing over my father to death."

I sighed, slumping as if it were my last breath.

Toby looked up. His eyes glistened. "He's not dead, Miss Herschel. I don't want to give up on him. I can't. Look at all this," he said, waving his arms at the room. "It's all my father's doing. He started with nothing. He built this. When he's well, the room is full of men. There's work at every bench. It's a good business. Some accuse my father of talking too big, but he also thinks big and works really hard. He's ill, but I can't give up on him."

CHAPTER 46

January 1789
East London, England

I stared silently at the disks long after Toby Gibbs stopped talking. There was a heaviness in the pit of my stomach as if I'd overeaten or swallowed a stone. Did Mr. Corden share my despair at the sight of the lifeless, dull circles of metal? Did he also lament the brilliant components they should've been? Where were the magical mirrors capable of drawing distant universes closer to us for inspection? It seemed hopeless. On the other hand, I couldn't ignore what Toby had said. His words had moved me in a manner they might not have a week earlier.

Eventually, I stood and went to where the disks lay. I felt Mr. Corden's eyes on me. "Taking a closer look," I explained.

He followed, and we crouched alongside them. Toby shuffled nearer, watching as we ran our hands over one of the disk's cold, rough surfaces. The edges were sharp, and the imperfections created during the casting were evident. I took the ribbon Alex and I had marked the day before from my reticule and, handing one end to Mr. Corden, measured the diameter and width of both disks at various points. Mr. Gibbs and his men might've failed to finish them, but the disks had been cast precisely. The stone in my stomach shrunk a little.

"Good, that's good," I said, standing up. "But they'll require many hours of grinding before they're ready to polish. Do you have a turning machine and an emery, Toby?"

"Yes. Over there. But, well, it doesn't help. It's the application we can't master. My father gave me instructions, but we couldn't get it right. That's where things went wrong with our first attempt, and we ruined them," he replied.

"You said you suggested your father give the reflectors to someone else to complete. Did you have a man in mind? Someone who might be capable?" I asked.

"One of my father's men said he'd heard about a master manufacturer of looking glasses who is currently in London," said Toby.

"He works with speculum?"

"Yes. Casting, grinding, and polishing. His name is Mr. Glashan," he replied.

"Glashan?" I echoed. "Does he come from up north? Edinburgh?"

Toby nodded. "I believe so."

I clasped my hands together. Could fortune be smiling upon us at last? It seemed unbelievable, but I knew I had to be bold. "Where can we find him? Do you know?"

He tugged at his collar. "We'd have to ask the man who told me about him."

"Then we should do that." I turned to Mr. Corden. "Mr. Campion told me about Mr. Glashan and I planned to meet him. But things went awry, and I missed the opportunity and didn't have the chance to track him down until now."

Toby cleared his throat. We looked at him. "He doesn't have a foundry in London."

"Perhaps he could work here?" said Mr. Corden.

"Yes. We might reach an agreement that works for all of us." I turned to the young man. "What do you think, Toby?"

He rubbed his hands on his apron again and said quietly, "But I have no means of paying him."

"If he agrees to work here, using your tools and machinery, we could come to an arrangement," I said.

"I could assist him, contribute that way," he added, his eyes brightening.

I glanced at Mr. Corden. He gave a small nod.

"Let's find Mr. Glashan," I said.

Minutes later, having removed his apron and washed his face and hands, Toby sat alongside Thomas while Mr. Corden followed me into the carriage, and we set off to track down Mr. Glashan. We hadn't gone far before the streets grew thick with vehicles, horses, and people traveling in all directions. Pedestrians wore expressions of grim purpose as they scurried by, and I'd never seen such a variety of carriages, carts, and gigs. On both sides of the road, the buildings huddled close as if bracing for a storm. Houses, shops, factories, people, animals, and vehicles crowded together. There was no unfettered earth for plants to take root. No horse was unharnessed. No dogs frolicked. Not even the children seemed playful. It was a gloomy, gray, and brown world under a cloud-encrusted sky. How different these streets were from those I'd known in colorful Bath. How unlike Slough, where trees flanked fields, the night sky flaunted its boundlessness, and rose vines scaled bricks and bloomed brilliantly. How fortunate I was to live there.

"You were shocked when you saw the disks. Did you believe they would be closer to completion?" asked Mr. Corden, drawing my attention from the streets.

"I had hoped Mr. Gibbs and his men would be working on them," I replied. "It upset me to see nothing happening."

"Young Toby was at a loss as to what to do. He's afraid and helpless without his father's guidance," he said.

It was true. Toby Gibbs was young, inexperienced, and fearful. Misfortune had rendered him powerless. What would happen to him if his father didn't recover?

I looked at Mr. Corden. "How old were you when your father died?"

"Thirteen," he replied.

"You took over the butchery when you were thirteen?" I asked.

"Yes."

"It must've been hard," I said, remembering how little I'd known and understood at that age.

He shrugged. "To lose a father, to accept he was gone, that was hard. I'm sure you felt the same when your father died. And yes, I was sorry to leave school. I liked learning. But it wasn't hard to work in the butchery. There wasn't an option. What I didn't know, I learned one way or another. My mother and sisters relied on me. I didn't think about it being hard. It had to be done."

"They must be grateful, your mother and sisters," I said.

His eyes met mine. "It's what families do," he said. "Take care of each other."

"Not everyone in every family," I said.

Thomas stopped the horses on the corner of a street that looked much like every other we'd traversed. Toby hopped down, ran to a nearby building, and knocked on the door. It was partially opened, and the young man had a conversation with someone inside before hurrying to the window of the carriage.

"He's working in a building not far from the foundry. We'll find him back there," said Toby.

My hopes wavered. "Working? Do you know what he's doing? Is it something he won't mind giving up?" I asked.

"I don't know," he replied.

"Let's talk to him," said Mr. Corden. "It's the only way to find out."

Toby climbed back alongside Thomas, and we set off again. The view was as dismal in the other direction as it had been on the outward journey. My energy waned alongside my optimism.

"London doesn't please you," said Mr. Corden when I sighed for the third or fourth time.

"Not this part of London. William has spoken of beautiful parks, buildings, and shops. Clearly, we're not in a fashionable area," I replied. "What will we do if Mr. Glashan doesn't want to work on the disks or we can't reach an agreement? Or if we discover he's incapable of the job?"

"We'll look for another solution. What else is there to do?" he said.

I leaned back against the seat without replying and closed my eyes. He was right. If Mr. Glashan couldn't or wouldn't help, we'd have to think of something else. I hoped it wouldn't come to that, but it didn't scare me, which surprised me. I'd lived in fear for so long. In fact, I couldn't remember when I hadn't been afraid. When I was locked away with my illnesses, I was afraid of dying alone. After that, I feared a life as my mother and Jacob's servant. Once I was in England, I was terrified of being sent back to them. I'd been terrified to show my face and sing for audiences, and of losing Alex and William to marriage the way I'd lost Sophia Elizabeth. I'd been afraid to admit to my dream of being an astronomer because it might upstage William and attract attention to my scarred face. When the cartoon was published, my fear seemed justified. However, somehow I'd overcome it. I was fearless. Or was I? What if William died? Surely, I had reason to fear that? What would I do? It didn't matter how much I loved and knew about the stars. The world thought of me as William Herschel's sister and assistant. I'd never been to Greenwich. Nor was I a member of the Royal Society. Without my brother, who would I be?

"Some believe the stars control our destiny, but it's often in the hands of other people," I said without opening my eyes. "What do you believe, Mr. Corden?"

He shifted on his seat and I opened my eyes. He leaned toward me as he spoke. "We've been friends for long enough for me to speak plainly to you, haven't we, Miss Herschel?" He paused, I nodded, and he went on. "There's nothing wrong with the affection and admiration you have for others. But your destiny—in so much that any of us have power over our destiny—is yours. Neither Mr. Herschel's will nor his life are your destiny. He's too great a man to want it. More importantly, you're too great a woman to have it thus."

I was overcome by an unfamiliar, warm sensation. My throat was thick, and I knew if I tried to speak, the tears would come. It was all right. I wanted to savor the moment so I might recall the feeling forever. I was joyful, not because Gabriel said I was "too great a woman" but because he'd pronounced me a friend.

CHAPTER 47

January 1789
Observatory House, Slough, England

It was well after midnight when we returned to Observatory House. I'd slept for much of the journey and suspected Gabriel had done the same. I said good night to him and Thomas at the stables and instinctively looked at the sky as I made my way across the yard.

Finally, after persisting for weeks, the curtain of clouds was gone, revealing a familiar, black canvas. I stopped and found the Georgium Sidus, faint without my telescope. Saturn had already set, but an expansive sprinkling of stars remained, gently blinking their welcome. My stars. How I loved them. I was home. Not necessarily at Observatory House, but anywhere beneath the heavens.

The house was dark but for a lantern burning low in the hallway. Comet and Star wandered out of the kitchen, greeting me sleepily as I untied my cloak and tugged off my gloves. I looked at the dogs for clues. Would they recognize death if it had come to the house in my absence?

"Is all well, my friends?" I whispered. "What can you tell me? I'll only listen if it's good news."

I stared at the drawing-room door. It was closed, of course. That didn't mean anything. I approach slowly, tipping my ear toward the entrance the way Gabriel had outside the foundry. Was that only yesterday? It seemed long ago. I heard the crackle of the fire and the gentle clunk of a piece of wood as it fell. Someone was in there, keeping the fire burning. I took a deep breath, reached out, and opened the door.

Mary sat alongside the Chesterfield. She turned to me. Her eyes were red-rimmed and her face drawn. I froze in the doorway. Where was Dr. Watson? Why wasn't he there?

"At last," she said. "We were beginning to get worried."

I stared, afraid to approach. Then I saw her hand move and realized that she was holding William's. No! *He* was holding her hand. His fingers were wrapped around hers.

"William?" I asked, my voice croaky.

Mary smiled and leaned forward so I could see my brother propped against the pillows, awake and looking at me. I flew across the room.

"You're awake," I said. "How are—"

"Better, much better," he replied with a tiny smile.

"Thank God!" I didn't bother to contain my tears. "It doesn't seem possible. You were so frail last night, yesterday. I've only been gone a day. How is it possible?"

He gave a tiny shrug. "You told me to shine on, so I did," he said.

Mary's brow crinkled as she glanced at me.

"What happened? How did this happen? Where's Dr. Watson?" I asked.

"He finally agreed to rest," she replied.

"He's confident that all is well?" I asked.

"We were as surprised as you are," she said. "After you left, William awoke at about nine. His eyes were clearer, and his breathing calmer. He even tried to pull himself up. But what shocked us most was that he volunteered to do his lung exercises—but only once he'd had breakfast! Can you imagine our astonishment?"

"I was ravenous," said William. He paused for a breath and added, "For anything other than broth."

Mary giggled. "Dr. Watson calls it the 'Groom's Miracle.' Because William didn't lie flat and did the exercises, his lungs improved enough to expel any liquid collected there. He'll have to rest for some time yet, but look—he's on his way to recovery."

"We owe the groom enormous gratitude," I said.

William smiled, took his hand from Mary's, and reached for mine. "Tell us about London. What did you discover?"

I glanced at Mary. "Alex and I told him everything. He insisted," she said.

"Go on. We must see the brambles if we're to remove them from our path," said William.

I pulled up a chair, sat, and began my account of the visit. Neither interrupted until I explained how ill Mr. Gibbs was.

"But he was such a robust man. I don't think I've ever met anyone as lively," said William.

Mary caught my eye. I guessed what she was thinking. *How quickly life can change.*

He closed his eyes and shook his head slowly as I described how far from complete the disks were. I moved on quickly.

"One of Mr. Gibbs's men heard that Mr. Glashan was once again in London," I said.

William frowned. "Glashan? Is that the man you spoke of? From Edinburgh?"

I nodded and went on to explain how we'd found Mr. Glashan and asked him to accompany us to Mr. Gibbs's foundry to see the disks.

"Mr. Glashan is a man of few words. The absolute opposite of Mr. Gibbs senior, according to Mr. Corden. He examined the disks for ages before asking anything. His questions were few. He knows what is required and how to do it. He also inspected Mr. Gibbs's tools and equipment. He's quiet and thorough. I was beginning to think we'd be there all night, so I made him an offer," I said.

"Go on," said William.

"I proposed Mr. Glashan complete the reflectors in Mr. Gibbs's foundry. If necessary, he should employ men who'd worked for Mr. Gibbs. Toby will also assist. I said we'd need to come to an agreement about payment. You've already paid Mr. Gibbs. We could offset the expense against the use of the Gibbs workshop and tools," I explained.

"But we'd have to pay Mr. Glashan," said William.

"Yes. And the other men," I said.

"And? What did he say?" he asked.

"We agreed to meet at the foundry next week. I said I'd have a detailed proposal and a breakdown of how everyone will be paid by then," I said.

William nodded. "Next week? I'll come with you."

Mary narrowed her eyes, but I smiled. "No. You must recover. I will attend to it," I said, getting to my feet. "Remember how you agreed I could use my salary for the reflectors?"

"I did," he replied.

"Good. Then you'll leave it to me. The stars will still be there when you're healthy, and the forty-footer will be ready for His Majesty's inspection. I'll see to it."

My brother sighed. "I'm in your hands. But one more thing before you go to bed."

"Yes?"

"You know we want to build an apartment for you above the stables. We could begin immediately. Will you return to Observatory House? Please," he said.

I patted his hand. "I don't know. I shall think about it, but only after I've slept," I replied.

It wasn't the first time I'd faced the prospect of change, but what was novel was knowing I had the power to oppose or escape it. My will would shape my destiny.

AUTHOR'S NOTE

One of the things that struck me as I read the early sections of the *Memoir and Correspondence of Caroline Herschel* was how self-deprecating Caroline was and how she diligently credited her brother William for everything she achieved.

Caroline and William studied the heavens during the era British academic and author Richard Holmes described as "the revolution of Romantic Science." At the time, women were considered unequivocally inferior to men. They had few rights and were excluded from all areas of influence, including intellectual circles occupied by thinkers, philosophers, and scientists. Even if she recognized her genius, Caroline understood others would not. So, for the most part, society determined it necessary for her to downplay her interests and intellect. It didn't help that, scarred and stunted by illnesses as a child, she was self-conscious about her appearance.

However, as I got to know her better and learned how William rescued her from a life of servitude in their mother's home, taught her, provoked her curiosity, and gave her purpose, I realized Caroline's reasons were much more complex. Dismissed as unworthy of an education and unmarriable by her mother and oldest brother, Jacob, Caroline believed she was saved by William. As such, she felt beholden to him. Even when she became an accomplished soprano and, later, a salaried astronomer, Caroline inferred her self-worth in relation to William.

Matters were further complicated by their mother's extracting a promise from William that he'd send Caroline back to her in Hanover if she wasn't useful to him in England. How the threat must have plagued her!

For years, William and Caroline's codependency was practical. He was a Georgian workaholic, driven by curiosity and passionate about his work.

Caroline took care of everything for him. She not only managed all their household affairs but also increasingly assisted him with his work as the King's Astronomer and the world's foremost manufacturer of telescopes. First at William's side and then also alone with her own telescopes, she learned the heavens and grew confident as an independent astronomer. In fact, Caroline became so competent an astronomer that, as William noted to Astronomer Royal Nevil Maskelyne, it was not always clear which, brother or sister, was the planet and which was the moon. Even so, they worked well together.

Everything changed when, at almost fifty years old, William fell in love with wealthy widow Mary Pitt. Caroline's life was upended. Her identity was so interlocked with William's that she was unmoored. If she wasn't his keeper, who was she?

That's where Caroline's memoir became mysterious.

The actual circumstances of Caroline's leaving Observatory House and how she and Mary eventually grew close are unknown. For undeclared reasons, Caroline destroyed all correspondence and other records that might've shed light on what took place during this period. There is nothing aside from the gleaming absence of information to hint at what happened. We know Caroline was distressed by the marriage and having to leave her home. Whatever took place afterward to bring the women together is a mystery that begged speculation. As such, my version of Caroline and Mary's conciliation and the role it played in empowering Caroline and releasing her from her self-imposed obligation to William is imagined.

What is fact is that Caroline Lucretia Herschel was a dedicated astronomer in her own right. Using the telescopes made for her by William, she discovered several new nebulae and, in 1786, became the first woman to discover a comet, which is now known as Comet C/1786 P1 (Herschel). She went on to discover eight comets in total. Today, several other astronomical objects bear her name. They include an asteroid called Lucretia, a lunar crater known as C. Herschel, and a star cluster that is named Caroline's Cluster.

When she was added to King George III's salary roll, Caroline became not only the first woman to earn a living from astronomy but also the first female in Britain to earn a salary for any scientific work.

In addition to observing and recording what she saw, Caroline calculated, amended, checked, and updated the *Historia Coelestis Britannica*, a catalog of nearly three thousand stars compiled by John Flamsteed more than sixty years previously. She later improved the catalog by adding five hundred more stars and making additional corrections.

In 1799, Caroline worked alongside Dr. Nevil Maskelyne in Greenwich. Ironically, it was Nevil, not William, who declared Caroline "my worthy sister in astronomy."

Caroline never married, and although she briefly stayed in an apartment above the stables at Observatory House, she never lived in Observatory House again after William's marriage. Although the forty-foot telescope was only partially assembled in time for the Royal Telescope Garden Party, it was eventually finished. However, despite being heralded an extraordinary machine and a triumph of King George III's reign, it didn't achieve everything William had hoped it would. The twenty-foot telescope remained the most effective instrument at Observatory House.

After William died in 1822, Caroline returned to Hanover, where she continued working in astronomy. She also helped William and Mary's son, John Herschel, with his astronomical endeavors. Among John's projects was the observation and recording of the southern skies. For this purpose, he and his family moved to Cape Town, where they resided not far from where I live from 1834 to 1838. As such, there's a unique connection between the family and my hometown. "Herschel" is a familiar name hereabouts, where it's used for streets, schools, buildings, products, and companies. I am often reminded of William's, Caroline's, and John Herschel's contributions.

Caroline received a gold medal from the Royal Astronomical Society in 1828. Seven years later, she and Mary Somerville became the first two women to be accepted as honorary members of the society.

In 1848, at the age of ninety-seven, Caroline died. The inscription on her tombstone, which she wrote herself, reads, "The eyes of her who is glorified here below turned to the starry heavens."

Caroline's legacy is that of an extraordinary woman whose curiosity, intelligence, and diligence placed her among the great scientists of history. I hope, like me, you will turn your eyes to the starry heavens and think of her with wonder and admiration for the role she played in helping us understand our world better.

READING GROUP
GUIDE

1. Caroline is troubled by having to leave Bath and give up her singing career when William is appointed King's Astronomer. However, she resolves to go to Datchet with him. Have you ever been obliged to leave a place and the life you love because it suits someone else? How did you feel? Did it work out for you?

2. William doesn't demand that Caroline go to Datchet with him, but neither does he urge her to stay in Bath. It suits him to have her with him. Do you think he is selfish by not encouraging her to pursue her singing career? Have you ever sacrificed your career for the benefit of someone else? How did it effect you?

3. The more Caroline learned about astronomy, the greater her fascination grew. She soon realized she got as much pleasure from sweeping the night sky and recording her findings as she did from singing. Have you experienced similar? What have you been surprised to discover how intriguing something is as you have learned more about it?

4. William told others—including Mr. Corden and Dr. Maskelyne—how much he admired his Caroline's understanding and skills in astronomy. Yet, he didn't tell her directly. Why do you think William withheld his admiration for Caroline's abilities from her?

5. After having been a servant in Hanover, Caroline was uncertain about her status in England. As William's sister, she had a reputation and influence.

She and William employed servants and workers. Yet, Caroline was conscious of the fact that she was recently in service like Hannah and Mr. Corden. How do you think that affected her relationships with Hannah and Mr. Corden? How?

6. Although Caroline was attracted to Gabriel Corden, she wasn't certain what it meant. When she snubbed him during Miss Hudson's visit, Caroline accepted that she'd spoiled any connection she had with Gabriel. When he got married, she was certain it was the end of their relationship. However, Caroline and Gabriel overcame their awkwardness and resumed their friendship. Do you think there was ever a chance of any romance between them? Or was their connection always destined to be a platonic one?

7. While Caroline admired William as a charismatic, hard-working visionary and was beholden to him because he rescued her from servitude in Hanover, she came to recognize many valuable characteristics in her quieter, less ambitious brother, Alex. Do you have introverted family members or friends who have surprised you with their inner strength and steadfastness?

8. Mary extols the virtues of walking when she accompanies Caroline home from church. She says, "…there's a quiet rhythm to putting one foot ahead of the other. Even when one is walking away from home, away from everything and everyone one knows and feels comfortable with, there's something safe and reassuring about the sound of one's footsteps. It's as if you're walking away but, at the same time, getting closer to yourself." Do you agree? What are the benefits of going for a walk? When do you enjoy walking and where do you go?

9. Caroline kept her dreams about becoming a full-fledged astronomer secret for many years. It hadn't occurred to her she could actually pursue her dream. What was the reception like from other astronomers when Caroline started making discoveries of her own? Do you think William

and his colleagues would have welcomed her into their circle had they known all along that she wanted to be an astronomer and not William's assistant?

10. It took William to be incapacitated for Caroline to step in and, using her own money, take control of the problems with the reflectors for the forty-footer. She finally got the chance to demonstrate that she was not only an exceptional astronomer but also that she understood the mechanics of the instruments. Do you think she would've found a way to do so had William not been injured?

11. Women were considered intellectually, physically and emotionally inferior to men during Caroline's lifetime. She understood the unlikelihood of being admitted to scientific circles. Yet, her fascination and ambition didn't wane. What do you think drove Caroline to continue working in astronomy? Do you think she possessed characteristics that are still essential among females determined to succeed today? What are those characteristics?

A CONVERSATION WITH THE AUTHOR

Caroline Herschel was an extraordinary woman who has had profound impact on the field of astronomy. What inspired you to write her story? Are you a lover of astronomy yourself?

Yes! Caroline Herschel was involved in astronomy during the Age of Enlightenment when ideas concerning religion, reason, nature, and humanity came together, revolutionizing the way some people viewed the world. It was an exciting time, particularly for emerging scientists who, given the patriarchal nature of society, were almost exclusively men. But then there was Caroline. It was while I was studying the life of Bertha Benz for my novel, *The Woman at the Wheel* that I discovered her. Caroline's name popped up in my research when I was investigating women who might've inspired Bertha. Albeit a century earlier, like Bertha, Caroline was born in Germany. Indeed, it's possible Bertha admired Caroline and, given Bertha's fascination with technology, she would've been intrigued by the astronomer's involvement in building telescopes. As such, in *The Woman at the Wheel,* I have Bertha discussing Caroline with her friend, Ava. The reference to Caroline sparked a conversation with my editor. "What about a novel about Caroline?" she asked. I did some more research and was hooked!

Am I lover of astronomy? Yes. Like Caroline, the more I've learned about it, the greater my interest has become. I'm particularly fascinated by how, despite how much more we know about celestial bodies since Caroline studied them, the same sense of wonder and mystery prevails. So much has changed in the world, but the night sky remains mesmerizingly indefinite. Whenever I gaze at the stars, I imagine I share Caroline's amazement and appreciation.

You write historical fiction novels about women who have been forgotten or overshadowed by history. Why do you think this kind of revisioning is important?

Throughout history and in all fields and spheres of life, women's contributions have been ignored. In some cases, women's achievements are acknowledged in relation to what their husbands, fathers, or brothers achieved. Caroline Herschel's accomplishments were largely recognized because she was William's sister. She might've disappeared into oblivion if not for her famous brother. I believe it is essential to celebrate women from history, including trailblazers like Caroline, Mary Leakey (*Follow Me to Africa*), Bertha Benz (*The Woman at the Wheel*), and Aleen Cust (*The Invincible Miss Cust*). Not only does it shine a light upon women who helped shape the world, but it also inspires others to follow their passions and pursue paths in traditionally male dominated fields. Gender inequality still exists. By recognizing women's contributions through the ages, we can challenge stereotypes and champion women who have always been at the forefront of society, but whose contributions were ignored or minimalized. Although my novels feature women who have achieved extraordinary things in their fields, I'm conscious of the millions of women from history who have done amazing things that we'll never know about. I hope that, as we celebrate known pioneers, we also honor the many other exceptional unidentified women from history whose stories we'll possibly never know.

Caroline is a complex character who struggles to find her place in the world and often makes decisions for others rather than herself. Did you find anything about writing her story particularly challenging? If so, why?

Caroline is the most complicated character I've written about, and it took me a while to get to know her. I understood what motivated Aleen Cust, Bertha Benz, and Mary Leakey and related to most of their ambitions and decisions. Caroline's difficult childhood and her mother's and brother, Jacob's cruelty and contempt for her wishes instilled fear and loathing in her. When William rescued her, Caroline felt indebted to him. She was guarded and governed by fear on one hand and gratitude on the other. This was further complicated by her aversion to marriage, which created mistrust and misconception. It didn't help that she felt betrayed by her parents, sister, Miss Hudson, Comet, and—when he fell in love with Mary—William. All of this made it difficult for me to understand what Caroline wanted for herself. She was afraid to reveal her dreams and terrified of change. When she and William left Bath, she worried about giving up singing in case she never succeeded at anything else. Then, when she fell in love with scanning the heavens, she was afraid of revealing her ambitions in case William sent her back to Hanover. Caroline was an enigma to me until my editor, Liv Turner helped me recognize key characteristics that showed up in Caroline's actions. That was when I saw how Caroline could break free from her fear and indebtedness to appreciate how smart and capable she was. Thank you, Liv! So yes, it was challenging to write about Caroline, but ultimately, I loved getting to know and understand her.

What do you hope readers will take away from Caroline's story?

I hope they'll be inspired by how much Caroline overcame to lead the kind of life she dreamed of. Although she had William to thank for taking her from her mother's home and teaching her music and then astronomy, Caroline succeeded because she was driven and dedicated. I hope readers will be moved by her curiosity and determination. Although she was aware of the disadvantages of being a woman and understood how unlikely it was that she'd be welcomed as a scientist, she took up the telescope and applied herself to learning everything she could. Even when she kept her ambition secret, she didn't stop doing what she loved. I'm excited by people who recognize what it is in life they hope for and then do everything they can to work toward that hope.

The Woman and Her Stars is a rich portrayal of England's Georgian era. What did your research and writing process look like for this novel?

My primary research was Caroline's memoirs and letters. It was when I discovered she'd destroyed everything she'd written around the time William married Mary until months later that I became intrigued by what might've happened then, why Caroline left Observatory House, what happened to change the way she felt about Mary, and how she realized her autonomy as an astronomer. My research also included books and articles about Caroline and William. The Herschel Museum of Astronomy at 19 New King Street in Bath was helpful, and I reread many historical novels, particularly those by Jane Austen, which are set around the same era. Once I'd decided what period of Caroline's life I wanted to focus on, I created a rough outline of my story and began writing. Of course, the research continues throughout. There are always new things to explore and confirm. One of the joys of writing historical fiction is that you never stop learning.

What are you reading these days?

As I mentioned, I've been rereading many of the classics and recently finished *North and South* by Elizabeth Gaskell. It was first published in 1854 and reminded me how, despite all the changes in the world, many things remain the same. Hope, fear, ambition, love, joy, doubt, and every other human emotion exist just as they always did. I loved the journeys of self-discovery undertaken by the main characters, Margaret Hale and John Thornton. Another novel I read and enjoyed recently was Ariel Lawhon's *The Frozen River*, which is an immersive work of historical fiction about Martha Ballard, midwife and all-round wise woman who lived in Maine in 1789. *The Frozen River* is set at the same time as *The Woman and Her Stars* and I loved the idea of Caroline and Martha living very different lives in other parts of the world at the same time, but both doing extraordinary things. Next on my reading list are *Confessions of a Grammar Queen* by Eliza Night and *The Ghostwriter* by Julie Clark. Although I love reading historical fiction, I enjoy mixing up my reading with other genres too.

BIBLIOGRAPHY

Bryant, Greg. *Universe: The Comets of Caroline Herschel.* May 1997.

Herschel, Caroline Lucretia. *Memoir and Correspondence of Caroline Herschel.* London: John Murray, 1876.

Holden, Edward S. *Sir William Herschel—His Life and Works.* New York: Charles Scribner's Sons, 1881.

Holmes, Richard. *The Age of Wonder.* London: Harper Press, 2008.

Hosken, M. *Alexander Herschel: The Forgotten Partner.* Journal for the History of Astronomy, Vol. 35.

Roberts, Jacob. *Distillations Magazine: A Giant of Astronomy.* November 16, 2017.

Royal Museums Greenwich. *Caroline Herschel: the first paid female astronomer.* https://www.rmg.co.uk/stories/topics/caroline-herschel-first-paid-female-astronomer.

Steavenson, W. H. *Herschel's First 40-Foot Speculum.* The Observatory, Vol. 50.

Tillman, Nola Taylor. *William Herschel Biography.* Space, September 4, 2012.

West, Doug. *Owlcation: William Herschel and the Giant 40-foot Telescope.* December 7, 2023.

ACKNOWLEDGMENTS

As you might imagine, siblings were much on my mind as I researched and wrote *The Woman and Her Stars*. Caroline Herschel's relationships with William, her other brothers, and her sister dictated many of the things she did, places she went, and choices she made. It sparked thoughts about my own brothers' effect on my life and work.

Laurence and Glen are older than me, but not by much. As such, we were raised as a trio, with me forever trailing them and determined to be included in all their activities. I resisted the notion girls couldn't do what boys did and tried to keep up with them. They didn't dissuade me, encouraging me to be determined and resourceful, which are helpful characteristics for most pursuits in life, including those of an author. Caroline's siblings weren't all wonderful. Mine are, for which I am grateful. Thank you, Laurence and Glen, for a lifetime of encouragement and support and for being such generous, caring, and fun brothers.

Brothers are one thing; editors are another. I learned the value of working with good editors at the onset of my journalism career decades ago and greatly appreciate how their objective feedback lifts my writing and stories. It's an enormous advantage and joy to work with someone who can point to the gaps and present ideas to bridge them. Sometimes, as a writer, one senses something is off-kilter in a manuscript, but it's only when an editor underlines it that you see it. Indeed, the significance of a good editor cannot be overstated. I was reminded of this afresh as I worked with my editor, Liv Turner, on Caroline's story. Thank you, Liv, for your energy, passion, and thorough, detailed, and all-round excellent expertise. Thank you for showing me the peaks and valleys and helping me build the bridges. It has been a wonderful journey. My gratitude, too, to Sara Walker for your good humored, eagle-eyed copy editing and my apologies for not paying enough attention to possessive gerunds during grammar classes.

It's always exciting to see a book in production, but my heart did a delighted somersault when I saw the cover for *The Woman and Her Stars*. It was as if James Iacobelli had looked inside my head as I wrote. Thank you, James, and to all the designers, production editors, and proofreaders at Sourcebooks Landmark who pored over my words, cleaned them up, and presented them so beautifully.

The work doesn't end with production. Books don't succeed if retailers and readers don't know about them. I'm lucky to work with a team of astute, energetic, hard-working, and creative marketers and salespeople. Thank you to Cristina Arreola, Kate Riley, and your team at Sourcebooks Landmark and Frieda le Roux, Ellen van Schalkwyk, Vis Chetty, Jethro Vlag, Gabi Blight, and your dynamite colleagues at Penguin Random House South Africa. Your drive, ingenuity, proficiency, warmth, and all the things I don't know about that go into the business of promoting books are greatly appreciated.

The Woman and Her Stars is my sixth book. With each one, my appreciation of the people in the trade beyond those at my publishers has grown. As ever, I'm grateful to have the finest literary agent in Jill Marsal at Marsal Lyon Literary Agency. Thank you, Jill. I'll never take for granted the privilege of having someone as experienced, calm, and competent as you at my side.

Thank you, too, to the amazing support I've received and friendships I've formed with booksellers, particularly Christy and Tellie at Liberty Books; Linda and Natasha at Exclusive Books; Veronica, Anna, Jessie-Lee, and Calvin at Wordsworth; Janine at Books & Books; and Lorraine at Nuts About Books & Toys.

Although I've acknowledged how much I value the support and interest I receive from my friends and family in every book I've written, it seems wrong not to thank them here again. Thank you, Annette, Claudia, Gail, Inga, Jan-Lucas, Joelle, Justin, Karen, Karina, Katie, Lee, Marianne, Nancy, Paul, Pippa, Peter, Rina, Sue, Sebastiaan, and Ulf. It wouldn't be half as much fun without you!

ABOUT THE AUTHOR

Photo credit: J-L de Vos

Penny Haw worked as a journalist and columnist for more than three decades, writing for many leading South African newspapers and magazines before yielding to a lifelong yearning to create fiction. Her novels, including *The Invincible Miss Cust*, *The Woman at the Wheel*, and *Follow Me to Africa*, feature remarkable women, illustrate her love for nature, and explore the interconnectedness of all living things. She is the recipient of the 2024 Philida Literary Award and lives near Cape Town with her husband and three dogs, all of whom are well walked.